Outlaw Complex.
The Spirit Callers Saga

OJ Lowe

Dedicated to my dad for buying the first huge unwieldy tome.

·

Contents

Chapter One. Second Round Fixtures.

"We're not discussing changing it again. It's not happening. Never. Not while I'm in office. I like it, it stays. If the competitors don't like it, nobody's forcing them to enter. End of discussion. Anyone who wants to carry on, there's the door right there. It opens, they can walk through it. Just don't expect to come back. We won't miss them."

Ronald Ritellia's trademark diplomacy in reaction to calls to change the 'Worst Winner' rule in the Quin-C second round at an ICCC meeting pre-tournament.

The fifth day of Summerpeak.

Terrence Arnholt was uncharacteristically moody during the meeting the next morning, an uncomfortable void permeating through the room from his seat at the table Nobody could especially blame him, just as nobody wanted to set him off. Nobody wanted to take the brunt of his anger. It would be far too easy for him to suddenly decide to blame someone in the room, most of whom had been at the dance, for not spotting the psychopath with the grudge against his daughter. It would have been unreasonable, but nobody wanted to chance it being directed at them.

The tables had been laid out in a U shape in the middle of the room, Arnholt, Brendan King, Derenko and Noorland sat together along the base of the shape. Wade himself stood in the middle, Nick Roper, David Wilsin, Lysa Montgomery, Fank Aldiss, Anne Sullivan, all to one side, Chris Fagan, Pree Khan, Tod Brumley, Will Okocha, Mel Harper and Jacques Leclerc towards the other.

"I suppose I'd do well to thank Agent Okocha," Wade said, glancing over to him. "He got in touch and warned me to look out for this guy. You all have the report in front of you, island authorities put out an issue on him because of the body in his hotel room. One Maxwell Mikel Brudel, plenty of prior criminal records mainly for theft, some narcotic distribution, some unlicensed possession of a blaster. Never been in jail for long though for one reason or another. Was bailed out just a few weeks ago on this very island in fact."

A holoimage flashed up of Brudel on the wall across from them, followed by images of his corpse and the crime scene. The hotel bathroom looked like it had seen better days, the volume of the water damage on the floor had worn all the way through, leaving a massive hole in the ground. "People in the room below complained when the ceiling came through, management forced their way in, found Mr

Brudel in the bath. Looked like suicide although why he'd do it in a room that was registered to someone else is open to…"

"Hey, I know this guy," Wilsin piped up. "I think… Yeah, I'm sure it's him. I handed him over to the authorities on the boat over here. He was robbing some people on the boat, I apprehended him. Not sure how he got out of jail so fast, I figured he'd still be in processing."

"Small world, eh?" Nick said. "So how did he get out of there?"

The images of Brudel were replaced by those of Harvey Rocastle, three in a row, one of him on the spirit dancing circuit wearing his flamboyant green tuxedo, one an image that looked like it had come from a security recorder, the third of him with a broken nose and arm in a healing cast, a bruise matching the one already blossoming across Wade's forehead. "Meet Harvey Rocastle," Okocha said. "He was the one who the hotel room was registered to. Hence why I put an Eyes Open out on him. If he was seen, we could take it from there."

"It's a bit below our remit," Fank Aldiss said. "Suspected suicides of petty criminals."

"And yet, it was a good thing he did," Anne retorted. "I'd say that was good thinking on Will's part. Otherwise we'd be on full alert looking for Mia Arnholt." She bit her lip, looked over at the director as if wondering what reaction her words might have brought, yet he remained impassive in his silence.

"Regarding Harvey Rocastle, you may or may not know his reputation," Okocha said. "He is a kingdom class spirit dancer, yet the more you dig down into his history, it's littered with unsavoury outbursts, mainly against women. He's been warned about his verbal conduct several times on the spirit dancing circuit. Not a pleasant individual. And yet, it is the first time anything like this has truly transpired involving him."

"Director," Wilsin said. "Has your daughter ever mentioned him before in passing? Any sort of connection between them?"

Arnholt shook his head. "Other than a professional rivalry, I don't think so. They know each other, that's about it. I don't know why he'd want to kidnap her."

"Who knows why anyone does anything," Fagan said. "Short of asking him. I assume we've tried. Or is he out of our jurisdiction?"

Wade smiled. "Oh no. See as he attempted to escape, he was caught up by two competitors in the tournament." The holoimages disappeared to be replaced by ones of Scott Taylor and Peter Jacobs. "He attacked them with his spirit. Aggravated assault atop a kidnap of a spirit dancer. That makes it one of ours. It's tenuous but we can get him for it. There're agents waiting to talk to him at first available opportunity. This is a dangerous individual. He managed to defeat these two men at the same time. Neither are shabby fighters."

"I think we're missing the most important question here," Tod Brumley said. "Why is a spirit dancer with no known connection to any competitor here out on this island when there's no reason for him to be here?"

"Could be for the battling," Pree offered. "As unlikely as that might be.""

"We do have some intelligence in regards of that," Will said. "I managed to loop into the interview process, got the local authorities to ask Ms Arnholt it when they were getting her side of the story for their records. Just in case. Rocastle told her himself, and I quote 'he was here on a scouting mission for callers who looked like they need a fresh start'."

"Excuse me?" Melanie Harper asked. "That sounds like a lie."

"Not necessarily," Derenko said. "It's not an uncommon practice at smaller levels. Why he'd be scouting around here is suspicious, I'd say. To get here, you need to be at least uncannily talented."

"Not the sort of people who'd look for a fresh start anyway," Fank added. "That makes it a cover then. It feels like a cover."

"Don't suppose she happened to say who he was working for, did she?" Jacques Leclerc inquired. Okocha shook his head. "Ah that'd be too easy, would it not?"

"Was anyone here approached by this individual?" Brendan asked, to an immediate sea of shaking heads. "Damn, that'd have been even easier."

"Do we know anyone who was?" Nick asked. "That'd be the next step, surely. See if you can trace his presence around the island, see if you can see him talking to anyone..."

"It's a long process, Agent Roper," Okocha said. "I'm still finishing up doing the Jeremiah Blut work that you left me needing to. I already had to outsource the triplet work back to the mainland headquarters. That said, it's about our best chance."

"I wouldn't say it is urgent," Noorland say. "We have Rocastle in custody. However, I think it prudent to see if we can find out what his intentions truly were in regards of this so-called scouting mission. If only for our own peace of mind nothing sinister is involved."

Aldiss spoke next. "I do have one opinion to voice. The young woman, Director Arnholt's daughter. Are we quite sure this wasn't a plot against him?"

"That thought has occurred to me, Agent Aldiss," Arnholt said. "And it's one that kept me awake last night. Will?"

"We have no evidence suggesting. it was anything beyond coincidence. However, we're unwilling to rule it out yet," Okocha said. "It's something we have to keep in mind."

"Because there's no such thing as random coincidence," Brendan remarked. "It's too risky to ignore that link."

"Regardless, I'll be speaking to my daughter and warning her to be more careful," Arnholt said. "And my son. Any hint of a threat and measures will be taken."

It was the unspoken feeling all of them there had held at one point or another. The fear that someone they loved would fall into the hands of someone who wished them ill. All the protocols and plans were in place to protect that and yet the fear remained a factor deep in the recesses of the mind.

"Anyway," Brendan said. "With that out of the way, we can get down to the allotted purpose of this meeting, I believe. Since we arrived here, it has become clear something is going on."

"Understatement," Wilsin said dryly. It brought a few laughs out of the other agents, Brendan's face kept impassive, though his lips tightened against each other.

"Thank you for that input, Agent Wilsin," he said. "As you know, there was an unexpected phenomenon earlier in the week, freak weather patterns believed to be linked to the actions and subsequent deaths of several unknown parties at the hands of Agents Wilsin and Roper. These men have not been identified."

Several images of the three triplets appeared on the wall behind him. "Although the others found dead at the scene of the crime were known memories of the Vazaran Suns Group," he added, naming the most famous mercenary company in the five kingdoms. "The only one we have an identification on would be Doctor Jeremiah Blut..."

A fresh image of Blut appeared to replace the others. "Expert in religious theory and radical academic troublemaker. Unfortunately, we haven't been able to discover much about what he was doing here. We've sent agents to his home to no avail. No immediate family, his home had been cleaned out of anything that might hint as to his motives. Either way..."

"Although we're currently following a financial trail," Okocha offered. "Sorry for interrupting, Chief. Just pointing that out. We've checked the payments into his personal accounts and he was slowly becoming a very rich man. Frequent monthly payments of fifty thousand credits a time."

"Nice work if you can get it," Nick said dryly. "Who was paying him."

"The company that paid him only exists as a shell corporation. We're trying to find a way to the top, although I have a theory if anyone would like to hear it?"

"Please, voice it," Arnholt said. "We're all ears."

"I think the Chief was right about there being something suspicious about this whole thing. I can't help but think there's a few isolated incidents too many here, rather there's got to be a bigger picture. Harvey Rocastle, Maxwell Brudel, Jeremiah Blut, the triplets and their cohorts, hells even Carcaradis Island itself being used to hold the tournament. What's the connection here?"

For a moment the room went silent and then Lysa spoke up. "Credits?"

"It's always about credits," Okocha continued. "Just hear me out. Okay, someone unknown paid Harvey Rocastle to do his little scouting mission here. Just as someone paid Max Brudel's bail. Just as someone's been paying Jeremiah Blut a small fortune for the last several years and even hired a gang of mercenaries who are notoriously not cheap. You hire the Suns in Vazara if you want it done right."

"I don't know," Nick said. "Agent Wilsin and I went up against those guys in the sewers, I don't think they were the Suns' best. We took them down too easily. I know we got the drop on them but still!"

"That's irrelevant. Maybe you're just that good," Okocha said dryly. Nick smirked at that and rested both hands on the table as if to say he wasn't disagreeing. "My point is, to do this, you need an absolute fortune in credits. You need credits to burn. None of us could do it, just as an example. So, we're looking at who might be able to afford it all."

"Well that narrows the list of suspects down from billions to thousands," Wade said thoughtfully, furrowing his brow for a moment as he mulled it over. "Unless…"

"Reims," Leclerc said.

"Reims," Okocha repeated. "If you've sunk a small fortune into this island to not only hold a prestigious tournament here but also build an exclusive resort, you can probably stretch a bit more."

"And Reims do occasionally do sponsorships of callers," Mel Harper offered. "So, maybe they did hire Rocastle."

"I'm certain they didn't hire him to run off with Mia Arnholt though," Fagan said. "It's possible they brought him in to do the job and didn't realise he was nuts. It's not the first time that's happened."

"Agent Okocha, it's a neat theory," Arnholt said. "Unfortunately, you have a lot of conjecture and not much proof."

"I said it was a theory," Okocha said defensively. "I think it'd make a lot of sense. But I fully agree you're right. Until we have more to go on…"

"Can you point out the flaws in your argument?" Brendan asked.

It wasn't a criticism, nobody thought as such. Unisco agents were often encouraged to consider all points of view regarding a theory, not to fixate on one outcome. Doing so was dangerous, it led to possible evidence being passed over because it didn't fit.

Okocha nodded. "I can. I mean, as the director said, it's a neat theory. But I just can't see it being likely. I mean Reims are a big company and there's always that hint of shadiness about their business practices like any other massive corporation but it's a bit of a step up going from competitive rivalry to outright murder. They have the resources but no motive. And what resources they are. Do they really need to do this? I don't know, I'm not privy to the way their CEO's mind works. Or maybe she doesn't know anything about it. That weather statue or whatever the hells it is of Kalqus isn't exactly practical."

"Unless you know how to use it," Harper offered. "Which we almost certainly don't. I'd suggest smashing the whole thing up if y'know, it wasn't sacrilegious."

"Can't do that," Aldiss said. "It's evidence."

"Any other theories about what's going on?" Arnholt asked. "Or are we going to move past the speculation stage."

"Like I said," Okocha said. "It was just a thought."

"I liked it," Anne smiled at him. "I mean, saying they went through the process of moving the natives off the island and then them being found dead instead, there's definitely something suspicious there. If Reims weren't directly responsible for it, I think they had to have at least being complicit. I can see the Suns being hired for something like that."

"It's a pretty big target," Derenko said. "You don't go after something like Reims unless you have a rock-solid case. You don't aim unless you're sure you can kill them. If we're wrong, the fallout could be catastrophic."

"That is true," Noorland said. "I think we should wait. Maybe it'll all blow over. Maybe Agent Okocha is wrong and these are just isolated incidents. Wouldn't that be nice? It'd make our job so much easier."

"We don't do easy," Pree said as the polite laughter died down. "But I agree with Agent Derenko. We can't do anything until we know more."

"Exactly!" Arnholt replied. "Hence I made the choice not to inform the press of our discovery of the natives until after the tournament has concluded."

"Yeah, I wondered why I'd not seen anything about it in the media," Nick said. "Half expected Kate Kinsella to start blaming Ritellia." That brought a few chuckles.

"If they should start their own investigation at this point, it might cause untold disruption to the tournament," Arnholt continued. "And Reims made an unholy amount of effort to ensure that it took place here. I for one would like to know why. I'll do it first thing the moment the tournament concludes."

He didn't sound like he was justifying it. Just stating the facts. "And speaking of the tournament." He rose to his feet. "Congratulations Agents Roper, Wallerington, Wilsin and Montgomery for getting to the knockout rounds. I speak for all of us here when I say, do us proud in the next matches."

Nick had his own plans, yet he found himself thinking back to the previous night as he wandered back into the plaza, hands in the pockets of his jeans. Targeting the daughter of a city champion like Arnholt was a stupid thing to do, it'd bring a massive amount of heat down on you. And that was even before you brought the whole director of Unisco variable into the equation. Combine the two and you'd have to be suicidal.

Arnholt likely wouldn't even have to ask. He was liked well enough by those who worked under him, a rare attribute to one so high, there would be volunteers to take his revenge by proxy if the need arose. He wouldn't abuse his power by openly asking, but justice would be done. Just as it had been by Wade.

That Rocastle fellow wasn't going to be seeing the light of day any time soon. Probably for the best, Nick had seen him being carted away, just as he'd seen the daughter in the arms of that kid, Scott Taylor before it all kicked off, looking cosy with each other. Interesting. Idly he wondered how many guys Arnholt had made the attempt to run off his daughter in the past. Probably a few. He was an intimidating man, even before you knew he carried a blaster.

Nick glanced at the time, cursed silently. The draw for the second round of the tournament was today and he needed to be there. Scratch that. He wanted to be there.

He hadn't missed much as he jogged into the stadium, uncomfortable memories of that first ever draw to take place at this competition coming back to him. They'd all been cramped down onto the battlefield, two hundred of them. How had they been whittled down to fifty so quickly, even with still a fair few more rounds to go yet? That was the key to winning though, surviving the attrition getting through the competition bore down on you. Unlike the draw for the group stage which had held scant attention to the competitors and observers alike, the atmosphere was buzzing here. Everyone, it seemed, was interested in what would come next.

Because after all, it wasn't just about winning here, it was about winning well. Scrape through, perform badly in your victory and you risked being eliminated. It was the time for the controversial 'worst winner walks' round, something participants in the competition absolutely despised. Because after all, every bout was a gamble your strategies might not come off on the day. Where Sharon was, he didn't know, but she had to be in here somewhere. He'd not told her where he'd been, Unisco had come first once again, and that was something he found himself regretting. He'd meet up with her afterwards. Maybe slip out when his name came up and see if he could procure some flowers for her. Pre-empt her in case she got snippy.

Still, he settled in his seat and wondered what awaited. After all, he'd won his group, so in theory should be entitled to an easier draw than if he'd finished second. All the winners of the groups would be put in one pot, all the runners up would be put in another and they'd be drawn to be pitted against each other. Strange the competitors and the fans had shown up for it but most of the dignitaries who had been there for the opening ceremony weren't.

Ronald Ritellia hadn't even shown up, sending his aide Thomas 'Falcon' Jerome. Nick had to concede that where nicknames went, it wasn't a bad one. He'd gotten it from being the fastest to the political kill, a dangerous man to have fixated upon you but ultimately one who you wouldn't trust to be in the top job. Jerome often gave off the impression he'd sell his entire family into slavery if there were a few more credits on the line for him.

He'd been assured by Sharon that the man was dangerously good looking, he exuded a sense of danger that made him exotic and mysterious. Idly he found himself wondering once more what she'd say if she found out his history with Unisco, proving he was even more dangerous. He had a higher body count for one thing, even before that business with Jeremiah Blut and the Suns in the sewers. Even so, Nick had to concede he'd seen killers who looked less like killers than Jerome did.

Picking up a microphone when everyone was settled, Jerome cleared his throat and began to speak. "Well hello there everyone. Lovely, lovely turnout. All to see me? You know how to touch my heart. Just as how this tournament is touching our imaginations. So far, we've seen some impressive stuff, and you know what? We're not stopping there! Hells no, we're taking what you've seen so far and we're pushing it some more. It's all down to our fifty combatants left to make this the best damn tournament we've ever seen. And as fifty becomes twenty-four, just remember. You're just four matches from the final. You're half way there. So, ladies and gentlemen honouring Carcaradis Island today, let me be the first to say, let's get this show on the road!"

Whatever the rumours about his personal life, he had a gift for whipping a crowd into a frenzy, Nick found himself applauding with the rest of them as Jerome reached over and thumped the button in front of him, the names appearing up on the screen above him to reveal the draw, the names matching up in a matter of seconds.

Theobald Jameson vs Wim Antonio Caine.
Katherine Sommer vs Matthew Arnholt.
Sharon Arventino vs Darren Maddley.
Wade Wallerington vs Mark Meadow.
Elaine Harper vs Peter Jacobs.
Steven Silver vs Scott Taylor.
Nicholas Roper vs Glenn Wright.
Harry Devine vs Meadow Laine.
David Wilsin vs Iain Monks-Cooper
Vincent Fratelli vs Reginald Tendolini.
Jack Hawley vs Lysa Montgomery.
Crystal Clear vs Mary Dale.
Carlo Tyson vs Blake Reinhardt.
Tengo Teevar vs John Sunday.
Kelly Burgess vs Adebalo Drogba.
Connor Caldwell vs Nwando Eliki
Lucy Tait vs Gareth Smith.
Orion Lamb vs Richard Bream.
Caan Wickard vs Yvette Martial.
Uri Stavale vs Carly Symonds.
Timothy Jean vs Stefan Smiles.
Rei Renderson vs Jane Ryan.
Weronika Saarth vs Daniel Roberts.
Kayleigh Chambers vs Willa Carpenter.
Simon Shaw vs Edyta Bryckov.

His first reaction was one of interest as he tried to think if he'd ever heard or fought Glenn Wright before. If he had, it wasn't coming to him. Far more interesting was Sharon's bout with Darren Maddley.

Not for the first time in his life, Nick found himself struck by how often life felt the urge to have a laugh at someone else's expense.

"Happy with that?"

"I think so," Nick said as he looked at her. Sharon looked decidedly calm about what had just happened on screen, like she didn't have a care in the kingdoms. "I mean, I don't know too much about him, so I guess that means he's punching above his weight. If he was that good, I think I'd have probably registered him before now. You?"

"No, I never heard of Glenn Wright before this tournament. Or my guy, really. Have you?"

"Maddening Maddley? Yeah, I know of him. And you should too, if I'm honest." Nick's expression said nothing else.

Sharon shrugged at that. "Should I? I mean, I've met a lot of people in my life. That name sounds familiar, I mean a lot do after a while. Help me out here, will you?"

"Darren Maddley. Son of Luke."

She knew then. "Luke Maddley? Wow." Sharon didn't quite know what to say. There was a name for the past, not one that offered up some pleasant memories. "I haven't thought about him for a while."

"I hadn't either. Not until… Well until I heard about Maddley the younger. He has some talent."

"And you already gave him a cute nickname?"

"Well, he left an impression. You probably knew his father better than I did."

"You could say." She didn't have anything more to add. Although the memories hadn't involved her personally, it didn't make them any less painful. Sometimes stuff was just tragic and there was no getting away from it. He wasn't going to let it go though.

"I mean I remember he had that spell in the Serran Knights, he was strong. The videos are still in the system."

"Doesn't matter how strong you are, there's still the chance that you can crack. If you crack…"

"You can break," Nick finished. "And if you break, you can't always be put back together again."

The tale of Luke Maddley had been one used as a cautionary for aspiring spirit callers over the years. The story of how such a steep rise can lead to a fall, the principle of what goes up will inevitably come down. The faster the rise, the faster the fall. He'd risen in Serran, gotten his summoner at the age of fifteen, having read everything he could on the subject theory, gathered every shred of knowledge he could accumulate and sought to use it. He'd studied the mechanics, he'd analysed the best way to tailor each spirit to its maximum based on the efforts of previous account he'd read, because he believed knowledge was power.

The story went that as soon as he got out into the real world, he fell flat on his face. His approach, fine in theory, either hadn't worked or needed tuning but something hadn't been right. Maybe he'd been too caught up on the theories and the strategy to be able to focus on what was happening on the battlefield, more likely he was suffering from the lack of practice all fresh callers find themselves afflicted with. Either way, the young Maddley had found himself struggling to score victories not just in tournaments but in practice bouts on the road. Whatever he was going through with his spirits, whatever his strategies were, however he was building himself for the future, it just wasn't happening. It was all a matter of public record, according to his posthumously produced biography and tournament records.

The actual truth behind what happened next had long been disputed and debated, but what wasn't up for discussion was he'd gotten that first win. He hadn't just defeated the favourite in the tournament in Peruz, he'd absolutely destroyed him. The crowd had been silenced, shocked this stranger who hadn't made it past the early rounds in any of his previous tournaments had suddenly stormed it. And although it might have only been the start, Luke Maddley had no intention of it being a fluke. Suddenly he was flush with success.

He'd rose like a phoenix in the peak of life, seemingly unbeatable to all but the very best and even then, victories were often never decisive against him. He'd gone from a nobody to a major player in a matter of months. He'd married a former Ms Premesoir and fathered a child with her, young Darren. He'd amassed a fortune, become a champion and a pundit, he'd even set up several academies to see that underprivileged callers could get the best advice and help available to start them on their journey without being beholden to sponsors. In just a few short years, he'd reached the top and he looked like he'd enjoyed every minute of it.

He'd stayed there until that fateful day when Sharon Arventino had entered his life in a fight to decide the grand champion of Serran. Maddley had been the holder, Sharon had been the challenger, not quite a novice but neither the spirit caller she would become years later. Nobody in the stadium that night would ever forget what had happened, many who hadn't been there made a habit of viewing the match footage once every few months. Some enjoyed seeing the spectacle of it for their amusement. Others just used it as a reminder of how quickly things could change if they weren't careful.

Maddley had gone out, done exactly as he had done in many of his previous bouts, same tactics that had served him so well over the past decade...

And he'd bombed spectacularly. Sharon had outmanoeuvred him at every turn, hadn't just beaten him, she'd annihilated him in crushing fashion, he'd barely managed to land a hit on her. Maddley had been so shocked he hadn't been able to speak in full coherent sentences when talking to the press afterwards. Still, he'd had ten years of prime experience behind him and everyone had conceded that nobody was perfect forever. He'd get over it, put it behind him and move on.

Except he hadn't. In his next bout, he'd been smashed again. And again. And again. Many experts had theorised as to why this had been the case. Some had stated their opinion he'd gone stale, everyone had figured him out, he was too set in his ways to change, to adapt. Others said his nerve had gone with the first beating, his confidence shattered beyond repair. A third train of opinion had said that surely, he'd get it right again sooner or later and once again the five kingdoms would see the manic genius of Luke Maddley.

In the end, nobody had been proven right. With depression overtaking him at his sudden failures, divorce looming over the failure of his marriage, the failure of his school and the shrinking of his fortune, Maddley had taken the easy way out. They'd found him in his office at the school, a blaster in his mouth and a new coat of paint needed for the ceiling.

Now, Nick noted, it appeared history was giving a second chance to someone by the name of Maddley to defeat Sharon Arventino. Privately, he was interested in this far more than in his own bout, as strange as it sounded. Very interested indeed.

She'd returned to the office when the special summoner rang, the one she kept in her desk solely for communication with her contact. If it should fall out of her hands, she dreaded to think what might happen. It had been supplied by her own personal agent inside Unisco, to lose it would be a major step back, with that being the best-case scenario. The worst, she didn't want to think about. It was a simple device, hard to track and even harder to monitor despite the common make. You could walk into any store across the five kingdoms and buy any such device for a few credits. Rookie callers usually did.

Somehow, she suspected that there was more to it than met the eye. She didn't even know if it could function as an actual spirit projector, despite the space for a capture crystal. A useful tool. She suspected that it would be able to project. Her contact prized accuracy, he knew how out of place a fake device would look amidst her collections

She ran her thumb over the activation pad and placed it on the desk in front of her, it flashed into life with a beep.

"Speak to me," she said.

"Something you might be interested in," her contact said, the voice electronically muffled. There was no way to tell if it was even male or female let alone nail down an identity. "Harvey Rocastle was just arrested on Carcaradis Island for attempted kidnap."

If her attention had threatened to wander before, it was sharply and painfully brought back to reality. She repeated the words to herself, pondering their full meaning before letting out a series of sharp curses bringing into doubt Rocastle's lineage, masculinity and sexual preferences.

"Yeah, I thought that might be your reaction," the contact said without a hint of amusement in the electronic voice. "He actually tried to drag her off in the middle of a dance, if you can believe it."

"And he got caught?" She tried to keep the disbelief out of her voice. Of course, the idiot had gotten caught. What was wrong with him?! She gripped the sides of her chair keep her hands from shaking. How could Rocastle have been so stupid? "Where is he now?"

"Locked up in the jail cells. They're transporting him to Vazara in the morning. By hoverjet, special prisoner transport series, some agents from the mainland are coming to get him. I'll send you the transponder ID and specs if you want to do something about it. They know he was scouting, they don't know why but they're sceptical about the logic behind it."

"We can't let Rocastle get into the system," she said. "What sort of guard detail is he likely to have?"

"Standard. One hoverjet for transport, minimal armaments but heavy shielding, six assault HAX class ships for escort duty. Be at least four agents on the transport, not including the pilot and co-pilot."

This time she cursed silently, before asking the question, "Can you delay his transportation? Allow us the chance to get the preparations in place for his retrieval or his termination."

"I'm not entirely sure I can. This has pissed off someone high up. Anyone else, I might be able to fudge it. I'll see what I can do but no promises I'd want to make"

That was aggravating but she held her tongue. Her contact wasn't a miracle worker, she knew that. Throwing a fit wouldn't help the situation, she needed to keep a cool head. If the worst came to the worst, Rocastle would have to die.

"Thank you," she said. "Do everything you can. What you have given me may be enough. If you can't do anything more, it'll have to be." She couldn't keep the snippiness out of her voice, as petulant as it might have sounded. "Usual payment will be on its way to you."

"Oh no, thank you Mistress," the voice said, still electronically devoid of emotion. It might have sounded sarcastic in human tones. She couldn't tell, that alone annoyed her as much as anything. "I'll be in touch if I have anything else.

The line went silent as quickly as it had burst into life and she leaned back in her chair, attention momentarily catching on the holoimage Sinkins had forwarded to her earlier in the day. Hovering in three dimensional images high above the projector were words she had never heard before with meaning that still escaped her. And yet, her interest had been piqued.

First came the Source, the well of everything past, present and future.

Second came the Statue, the sign of a riddle yet to be solved, a door to be opened.

Third came the Stone, the key to all you seek.

Together awaits infinity and all its treats.

Cryptic enough. Sinkins hadn't forwarded any information as to what it meant, meaning either he wished to surprise her or, more likely, didn't know himself. Either way, it could wait. She sought out another number, cursed Rocastle again. Who knew what this was going to end up costing her.

"I need to talk to Phillipe Mazoud," she said as the connection was made. "I have some more urgent work for the Vazaran Suns."

Chapter Two. The Vos Lak.

"The vos lak can grow up to thirty feet long, and under the right circumstances, it will. It's a shame they're extinct in the wild now because they were beautiful creatures in a savagely graceful way."
Professor David Fleck on the vos lak.

The sixth day of Summerpeak.

"Status report, Wing One?"

In the cockpit of his HAX, a stubby high-speed aircraft with twin sets of wings protruding from its guts and six powerful thruster jets, as well as enough armament to lay siege to a small city, Unisco combat pilot Commander Richard Wolfmeyer considered the voice for a moment before diverting his attention back onto the task at hand. "Everything looks good up here, Box. Got nothing on my sensors, everything's running fine."

"He's gone and jinxed it now," Wing Three said, her voice crisp and throatily feminine. Wolfmeyer found it incredibly sexy amidst the roar of engines. Strange really given behind her flight handle, Ellen Thwaite wasn't really anything to write home to mother and father about. "Watch."

"Thanks for the optimism there, Wing Three," Wing Two said, his voice bearing a Burykian accent. Jiro Hasigawa, Wolfmeyer's second in command, was a jolly man in life but over the comms he always sounded so serious. "How would we ever cope without your little bit of sunshine in our lives?"

"Badly, I think," Wing Six offered. "That's when we used to know to head to the hills. When everyone starts to think the best is going to happen, it's when you run." Wolfmeyer hadn't really gotten the chance to know Beck McCaffrey yet, he'd only been in the unit for a few months but so far, he'd proved himself to be a good pilot. He'd replaced Alara Coselli as Wing Six when she'd been KIA, Something Wolfmeyer still regretted.

It wasn't your fault. Nothing you could do. Twin sets of four words he'd grown so used to hearing, they'd lost all meaning.

"Personally, I think heading for the hills is best," Wing Four said. Alexandra Nkolou, a pretty Vazaran had been in the squad nearly the same length of time as Wolfmeyer and Hasigawa and he liked having her around. She made things interesting, she had an uncanny ability to perform perfect manoeuvres bordering on suicidal. "Been too long since we did some good old-fashioned hill flying."

"What is hill flying?" Wing Five sounded interested. Ross Navarro had been in the squadron only slightly longer than Six, a pleasant mixed race Premesoiran/Serranian with an interest in mechanics, a broad accent and broader love of women. "Most I ever hear of flying over hills is when folks go crashing because they ain't got a clue what they're doing."

"Hill flying, Five, you dip," Wing Three said. "Up and down, up and down. You getting motion sick yet? You probably did it in training. If you didn't, why the hells are you flying with us?"

"You need someone to fill that charming rogue quota, I think Three. Don't say you don't. I know it, you know it, hells Box knows it down there."

"Ah this is the famous Wolf Squadron banter then," the pilot of Box One said. The transport had been designated Box due to its design, something Hasigawa had accurately pointed out resembled an overweight boxbug, an oval shaped craft with twin wings painted silver. Wolfmeyer knew that its armour and shields were top of the line, all but impenetrable in full force. Only the nose of the craft broke up the otherwise smooth shape, a triangle point concealing a pair of powerful laser cannons. "Not all you hear it's cracked up to be."

Wolf Squadron. He'd been given the authorisation to form the unit years ago, he'd named it for himself, a touch of ego but it had stuck, and slowly they'd become as much a part of Unisco Air Division as he'd dared to believe. It might have surprised some to find the organisation had its own entourage of pilots, but at the same time, it usually dawned on them there was no reason why they shouldn't. After all, it was a big world and although Unisco could co-opt aid from the armed forces of individual nations, sometimes they liked to keep their activities in house.

In the time that he and Jiro had been running the group, they'd gotten a reputation and although the mission might be an easy one, escort the transport of some sick scumbag from Carcaradis Island to mainland Vazara, it didn't mean he wasn't intending to see it went through without a minimum of fuss. They were as close to the best as they were ever going to be, he wanted to keep it up. Wolfmeyer had immense pride in his squad, flying with them was one of them best feelings he'd ever have, and nothing would take that away. Even in the few events where death had taken some of those around him, the hurt had eventually faded replaced by the sense of peace in motion.

They'd met up with Box just a few miles off the island, flying for half an hour so far amidst smooth conditions. He'd chosen not to relax though, still on edge in his cockpit as if something might come out of nowhere at any moment. His sensors weren't picking anything up. Neither were Box's. If anything, their sensors would be far more sensitive than those on the Hensley Assault eXecutioner that Wolf Squad had come to favour. Yes, Wolfmeyer conceded, the HAX was likely the most dangerous thing in the sky. It was unlikely they'd face any sort of need to exert that dangerous side on this trip.

Unlikely but not impossible. Jacques Leclerc, a former Wolf himself and rumoured to be the pilot who'd flown the director to Carcaradis Island for the tournament and since transferred to the main investigative arm of Unisco, had told Wolfmeyer in private the priority regarding this prisoner. He'd attempted to kidnap a spirit dancer, tried to run off with her only to be stopped violently by Wade Wallerington from accomplishing his goals.

Wolfmeyer knew Wallerington by reputation but what a reputation. He'd liked to have stopped by the Quin-C himself, but duty had permitted it. He hadn't been one of the employees detailed to go, much to his dismay but he hadn't let it get in the way of what he'd had to do. He'd managed to keep track of it as much as possible, most of the pilots on his squad had. A barracks sweepstake had been running since the start, Wolfmeyer had some broad named Katherine Sommer and he was hoping she did the business.

Around him, the banter continued across his wings, he didn't discourage it as a rule where others likely would. He'd always believed it built morale, helped his team function as a unit rather than a group of individuals and they weren't careless enough to let it interfere with performance. His people were professional, one thing he didn't worry about.

Amidst that pride, he caught the low sound immediately, a dull buzz of warning dragging across his sensors as an early alert danger was incoming and he cursed before finding his focus, moving his gaze to the long-range scanner.

"You pick up on that, Wing One?" Box asked. "Looks like thirteen… No, fourteen incoming ships. No ID's active. Assorted makes."

"That's never good," Wing Four said. "What's the order?"

Wolfmeyer said nothing, studying his interface briefly before sighing. He knew it had been going too well. "Stay sharp. Box One, if they continue to approach, hail them and advise them to turn back. If they continue their course, warn them their continued advance will be met with reprisal."

"We're a bit outnumbered here, Wing One," Wing Two said. "Might be tight."

"You out of practice Wing Two? We might be outnumbered but not entirely outgunned." Wolfmeyer glanced at his screen and then out of his cockpit. He could see them in the distance now, several specks approaching fast, growing larger by the minute. He could hear Box hailing them, giving them the warning to turn back.

No answer. Still they didn't retreat. Wolfmeyer sighed again. It looked infinitely likely this wasn't going to be the simple trip he had imagined a few minutes previous. The banter had faded in those few short seconds, he was pleased to hear. "Okay, Wolf Squadron. This is going to be rough. We can do this though. Don't hold back, pick your targets carefully and try to keep them off Box. We don't want them getting too close."

"You worried, Wing One?" Wing Four asked. "Nothing's getting through Box's shields. I'd be more worried about us."

"You're worried, Alex?" Wing Five inquired. "Now I'm terrified. Okay, somebody take the five on the left and I'll go after the five on the right, someone meet us down the middle. Easy. Be home for lunch, right?"

Once more Box hailed the oncoming aerofighters and once more they declined to comment, prompting Wolfmeyer to activate his comms. "Unidentified aircraft, this is the commander of UAD taskforce Wolf Squadron, advising you to desist from current flight plan and find another route or you will be considered hostile."

No response, he drew a deep breath, hands already moving to his weapons systems. "Final warning, unidentified aircraft…"

"Commander!" Wing Three's voice came through urgently. "I think it's the Dark Wind."

This time curses broke across the communication frequency, notably from Wings Five and Six. Wolfmeyer felt like joining them. The Dark Wind, the aerial fringe of the Vazaran Suns, notable for crack pilots who didn't care if they lived or died provided the payments kept coming. An interesting ideology, Wolfmeyer had to admit. He'd always preferred the idea of surviving to the end. Still, that rumour continued how part of the profits for each mission the Suns were involved in were kept back for the families of those who'd been killed in action. Mercenaries with a heart, he'd believe it when he saw it.

As the unidentified ships got in closer, he saw what Thwaite had said rang true, they were an eclectic mix of ships of all ages and design, all painted in the dark grey not quite black colour the Suns favoured. As they moved in closer, he could swear he saw the logo on the side, a sunlit skull against a desert background.

"Okay, Wolves. This is going to turn nasty. Assume targets are hostile immediately. Permission to engage granted. See you all on the ground and happy hunting." With that, he kicked his thrusters and his HAX shot off towards the oncoming crowd.

Already they were splitting as he approached, aware of the dangers of arriving in a tight-knit group. If they'd stayed that way, it'd have been easy for them. That many ships close together, all his squadron would have to do involved launching missiles into the maelstrom, the combination of explosions and flying debris would have done for them. Yet they weren't falling for it. Instead he hit the button to ready his forward laser cannons, glad he'd checked them over before they'd taken off.

"Pick your targets of convenience!" he barked. "Watch each other's backs." If command was listening in on this, how long would it take for them to scramble some backup for them? An accurate answer was impossible to predict but either way, it'd be way too long for them to get here. They'd have to do it all themselves.

Deep breath, Wolfmeyer put all thoughts out of his mind and yanked his HAX into the field of engagement, an enemy ship passing across his crosshairs just for a moment, an old Pash Runner and he let loose a flurry of blasts towards it, their rake smashing against the Pash's shields, yet the hull held as it veered and shot past him. He would have banked, kept on its tail but a Licus was already bursting towards him, lining him up in its sights and he jerked down, losing his line on the Pash but escaping with a few bruises to his shielding. Licus' never did have the most potent of forward armaments, he was grateful to recall. Seconds later the Licus exploded as Wing Three swept in, all weapons blazing with a series of direct hits overcoming its shields and armour in a matter of milliseconds.

"Good shooting, Three," he said before locking his HAX in on an ancient Vazran Kesi already accelerating away from him.

"One down!" Wing Three yelled. "Only another thirteen to go!"

Wolfmeyer heard her, caught the sound of a hull ripping open and saw the spectacle of igniting fuel seconds later his starboard side, Wing Five letting out a whoop of glee at the result.

"Make that twelve! One for the Navarro!"

He needed to get in on this, couldn't have his wings outscoring him here. The Kesi had decent speed, but so did he and he wasn't letting it get away. It had to fight the winds up here, he had power to force through them with belligerence, his HAX gaining every second, he'd be in a firing position in a moment…

"One for Wing Four!" Nkolou didn't sound as overjoyed as Navarro had over her kill, but he didn't allow it to distract him as he lined up his sights on the Kesi and squeezed the controls, scarlet fire spitting out his forward cannons and shredding its meagre defences, Wolfmeyer yanked his stick back and brought it above the explosion, punching the air with his free hand. Four down, ten to go and they were keeping strong.

"Lowest scorer buys the drinks!" Wing Two said, Wolfmeyer could see him jinking his HAX through a crowd of grey enemy ships, all weapons at full blast, none really landing a fatal hit but keeping them back far enough to avoid landing any telling shot. Wings Six and Four converged on him in a matter of seconds, sending their own assaults into the scattering ships to blast two of them into slag.

"Two for Four," Wing Four said.

"You tagged anyone yet, Wing Two?" Wing Six inquired, a note of sarcasm in his voice. Jiro, in response sounded just as sarcastic.

"Just lining them up for my teammates. I'm claiming partial scores and assists for kills here."

"You can claim all you want," Wing Five said. Wolfmeyer saw him out his port window swooping to evade the azure lasers of a Bura Ithora. As the grey ship chased past him, Wolfmeyer sent his own fire crashing into the Bura and moments later it was a ball of useless flaming metal falling to the ocean below. "Doesn't mean you're getting them!"

"Head in the game, Wing Five," Wolfmeyer warned. "Don't lose track of…"

A scream broke across the comms, then silence as he saw a great fireball erupting from the space where a perfectly good HAX had been flying passing across the starboard side of his window. An Ikari tore across his line of sight, he quickly readjusted target it, couldn't quite keep his mind on the job and his shots swept wide. Nor could he move his eyes away from his tactical readout where the tag designated Wing Three had vanished.

Thwaite…

If he lost focus now, he'd be joining her. He swept after the Ikari, trying to close it down, eager to ensure the rest of them survived. Ellen Thwaite would not have died in vain, he vowed. The rest of them would raise a glass in her honour later, they had to make sure that later came. The Ikari pilot was a skilled one, his craft small and agile, all he could do to keep on the same vector, much less get a lock. Three times he fired randomly without a certain shot at it, the laser bursts never close to landing a telling blow.

His sensors buzzed angrily, like a saw in the confined spaces of the cockpit and he jerked his attention back to his readout, an Elki lining up behind him, a lock confirmed…

"Wing One, that Elki just launched an incoming!" Wing Two yelled. "Watch out."

Wolfmeyer allowed a smile to play across his face as he punched his thrusters and shot away, already knowing the missile was locked onto him, it'd keep coming. Always a slim chance to hurry the process, he nudged a button on his control panel and his rear rotary cannons deployed, mini lasers designed to harry a pursuer. They weren't of a strength to be able to punch through any half decent shield, but it still took a brave pilot to keep following his course when fire came at him, no matter how deadly it may or may not be. Of course, hitting the missile would be a challenge. For a human maybe.

The weapons contained an automated targeting system, he glanced down, saw they were locked onto the missile and let loose the blast of cannon fire towards the streak of exhaust chasing him. A flash, a hit but not a decisive one. Or maybe it was covered. Some missiles had made their way onto the market recently to block such countermeasures. All they needed was a sheet of corrosium across the nose, the area most likely to be hit by counterfire. Corrosium wasn't even expensive, unfortunately. Although with the missile gaining, he suddenly realised he wanted to keep living in a world where that was the case.

He retracted his cannons, brought his attention back to the sky. Maybe he could evade it. Maybe wouldn't be good enough. He'd have to. He spun into a tight bank right and still the missile followed him through the carnage that the battlefield had become, locked on his HAX and still he ran, rising high above the rest of the battlefield until he could see the other four HAX's engaging the shrinking remnants of the Dark Wind. They'd done well, could have done a lot better and it still wasn't over yet. There was always the potential for it to get worse.

Still it was coming after him as he rose higher into the air, touching twenty thousand feet, still accelerating. He tried to remember if there was an altitude the missiles failed to function at. He doubted it, as his altimeter hit twenty-five thousand feet and still it came, he yanked his control stick back, bringing the HAX back across itself to drive in the opposite direction, sending it into a corkscrew spin, wide angled and hopefully unpredictable.

The Suns couldn't have that advanced weaponry, missiles capable of keeping up with manoeuvres like this were rare and more importantly, expensive. Already he could see it was struggling to keep pace with him, torn asunder by the twists and turns of his craft. Again, he spun it into a series of agile twists, zigzagging back and forth towards the battlefield, the Pash he'd started the battle against hovering a thousand feet below him and he grinned. Still the missile came, nine hundred feet, eight hundred, seven, six…

He fired his forward cannons, took the Pash completely by surprise as the craft exploded in a great fireball of debris and smoke. Deep breath, he glanced down at his sensors one last time and plunged through it, his systems screaming with the effort as he felt the heat in his cockpit, a thousand bits of wreckage buffering the ship, followed by the explosion several seconds later, his pursuing missile meeting a large remnant of debris, a remnant from the Pash's fuselage and he punched the air.

"Show off," Wing Two said dryly. "There had to be an easier way to do that."

In his cockpit, Wolfmeyer shrugged even though nobody would see the gesture. "Probably. But hey, someone's got to remind you all what standard's you've got to get to here. I consider it not just my duty, but my right." Still thinking of Thwaite, the words felt hollow and meaningless, but he couldn't let them drag him down. Not yet. That was what the post-mission drinks were for. Drowning sorrows in a way denied on the battlefield.

He glanced to his sensors, saw only a few Dark Wind ships left in the sky. They'd managed to whittle them down easily. Box One powered one ahead, unhindered and unharmed. He found himself wondering what the point of this had been. If it had been a random attack, then surely there were easier targets for the Suns to pick on. Was it a mistake? Or something else at work here.

Either way, it wasn't his job to try and work it out, not while in the air anyway. There were people on the ground far more qualified to do that sort of thing than him, all he had to do was ensure that Box got to their destination once the rest of the enemy ships were taken from the field of play.

The day wasn't out of surprises yet, he realised, something long and thin sweeping past his line of sight, something he had to check again he really had seen. Was that... Couldn't be, surely...

"Am I seeing this right?" Wing Four asked. "Because it looks like..."

"Wing Four, there is a dragon entering the field of engagement," Wolfmeyer said. "Until we have more of an idea what to expect, do not..."

It wasn't a regular dragon, rather a great serpent-like creature maybe twenty to thirty feet long with a thick chunky grey body, twin huge leathery scarlet wings and an angry pointed face complete with four horns raised out the peak of its skull, orange and gold spots mottling grey scales. Its underbelly was a cream colour marked with dirt and scarlet stuff that might have been blood. A quad of forelegs broke out of its upper body, spindly but likely incredibly strong, each ending with a quintet of ugly-looking claws.

"That a vos lak?" Wing Six asked. "Not seen one of them before. Not in the wild anyway."

One HAX got in close, Wolfmeyer guessed it might be Jiro in Wing Two in for a closer look but with definite intent not to spook it, and the creature opened its jaws to reveal a mouth of angry looking yellow teeth, each pointed like giant knives. Flames broke from its mouth, white hot and intensely bright in the morning sun and Wolfmeyer winced as he heard Jiro's scream, the HAX moving to evade but just barely. He could see the burns on its hull, heard Jiro swearing angrily as the vos lak came after him again. Wing Two shot off, the dragon creature having a good few meters on him as jaws snapped angrily after the rear tail of the HAX. Jiro's rear cannons came down, determined to harass the creature but it ducked beneath the first rake of fire, keeping pace easily with the much smaller ship.

"Engage!" Wolfmeyer bellowed, already mindful things could turn on the head of a pin here if the vos lak continued to attack with no regard for who it blasted. Except, it hadn't gone after the Dark Wind ships yet. Curious. "Wing Six, you're closest, try and keep in on Two to get that thing off his back. Wings Four and Five, try and deal with the remaining Suns. Keep them off us all."

The crackle of static hissing from Wing Six's comms hinted he might not have been impressed with his orders to go near a pissed off vos lak, but he obeyed. Wolfmeyer could appreciate that, besides, he wasn't about to tell somebody to do something he wasn't about to do himself. He went after the creature, Wing Six already there, harassing it with laser cannon fire, Wing Two's rear lasers still peppering the sky as well. Worse, a few of the remaining Dark Wind ships had gotten past Nkolou and Navarro and were closing in on Box.

"Wing One," Wing Six called. "I think there's someone riding that thing!" Wolfmeyer had to blink as he stared at the serpentine body below him, tracing its outline up to around the head… Holy shit, McCaffrey was right. Someone, either very brave or very suicidal, was sat on the neck of the vos lak, clutching it behind the horns. It explained much. Such as the tight manoeuvres the creature had been performing under fire, it'd take lightning quick reactions but if it was a spirit, it acted as an extension of the caller's being and could put them into practice a little quicker than a pilot in a ship could.

"Guys," Jiro said slowly. He could see what Wolfmeyer also had, the Dark Wind gunships closing in on Box. They probably couldn't do much against those shields, but neither was it worth taking chances they might have something capable of cracking them. "Go take those out. I'll try and shake this thing on my own. I can do it. Like some great fucking snake lizard with wings is going to take me out." He still sounded serious as he said it, but Wolfmeyer could imagine his grin. "I'll see you all on the ground."

"Good hunting, Jiro," Wolfmeyer said, momentarily ignoring comm protocol. "Go get it and we'll let you off buying the drinks."

More reluctantly than he'd liked to admit, Wolfmeyer broke off his vector pursuing the vos lak and after the twin ships going towards Box. Behind him, Wing Six sent a couple more harrying shots at the vos lak, laughing and whooping as he did before he made to peel off after Wolfmeyer's own ship. He didn't see the tail coming for him, laughter cut off as the vos lak's giant tail swept through the air and sideswiped straight into the cockpit of his HAX, crushing it immediately. Wolfmeyer barely caught a strangled sound across the communications, the last sounds of laughter being cut off and then the HAX started to fall, bent uselessly out of control amidst the winds. By the time it hit the water, the tag designated as Wing Six on his screen had faded out.

And then there were four...

Again, he tried to put it out of his mind as he went for Box, exhaling sharply, bringing his weapons to bear. He wasn't too worried about accidentally landing a shot on Box, the shields could take it, he let fly with a dozen blasts in the direction of the closest shit, a Santa May, the enemy pilot taking evasive motions almost immediately. He gritted his teeth together, focused on the other one, trying to get a missile lock. Do the same to them as they'd done to him earlier. A small beep, the sound confirmed and...

He heard another scream, turned his head back and saw the vos lak raise its head back to roar in ear splitting triumph, Jiro's HAX already losing altitude with its entire body aflame. Wolfmeyer knew then what was coming, it was only a matter of seconds until reality caught up. The explosion punctuated his train of thought as fire met fuel line and he fought the urge to smash his fist against something. Two, Three and Six, all gone.

He swore angrily, let his head sag against his seat and just for a moment, he felt a sense of failure threatening to overcome him. Just for a moment. Amidst that hail of darkness, he found the small island of composure again very quickly. He hadn't failed. Wolf Squadron hadn't failed. They could still complete the mission. They would complete the mission or die trying. Either way Jiro, Ellen and Beck would not have died in vain. With renewed vigour in his system, he gunned his thrusters and went after the two enemy ships with a new sense of purpose. Nothing less than their destruction would satisfy him. And then came the bastard on the back of the vos lak. He'd be the last and the most satisfying out of the lot of them.

Gunning the HAX into position, he sent a barrage of fire in the direction of the first ship, he saw both pilots peel out of his line of sight and he spun after one, finding their vector and following it. He didn't let up, peppering shots in on the shields of the Eli Sandoval model that was doing its best to stay ahead. Its best wasn't good enough, he didn't rate Sandovals at the best of times, they were little more than airborne buckets with an engine attached, and his shots found their mark repeatedly. He didn't feel any sense of elation as the shields collapsed and the body of the Sandoval was riddled. In seconds, it had gone down. A beeping alerted him to the presence of the other ship in his slipstream, another Ikari.

Unlike the Sandoval, he did rate the Ikari and he didn't appreciate one trying to get a lock on him. Their forward rotary cannons would make mincemeat of him given the opportunity, hence, he wasn't about to give them one. He punched a button, dropped his rear cannons again and sent the blasts in on the onrushing Ikari, anything to distract the pilot. The Ikari fired, his shots wild and Wolfmeyer pulled his HAX into a dive, the blue surface of the ocean suddenly onrushing at him, closer and closer and he let that feeling of falling fill him, moments of elation and giddy fear coming back to him, memories of the first time he'd done this. Deep breath, the Ikari had followed him into the same dive, at least the pilot wouldn't be able to get a lock, and he exhaled, pulled into a neat loop, rising sharply.

The Ikari did the same, a split second slower than him before the HAX dipped down again and suddenly Wolfmeyer was behind him. They'd swapped positions and he was lining up his own sights at the Ikari.

"Good night," he said, his missile lock beeping into confirmation. Without a trace of satisfaction, Wolfmeyer fired, saw the missile burst from his HAX and home in on the Ikari, the pilot pulling out all evasive manoeuvres one might expect from a skilled opponent but ultimately it just wasn't enough. A small explosion in the distance confirmed the kill and Wolfmeyer swung his HAX around to focus in on the vos lak. He blinked, not quite sure if he was seeing things correctly.

Up ahead, the great serpent had wrapped around Box like a constrictor, not stopping it from moving but hindering any attempt to escape. Not quite sure what it had planned, but certain it wasn't anything good, Wolfmeyer accelerated after the trapped Box, vaguely aware Wings Four and Five had formed up on him. Amidst everything, they'd managed to deal with the rest of the Dark Wind fleet. Neither of them sounded overjoyed by their victory. He didn't blame them, it had pyrrhic at best. Losing the rest of the squadron was a price he wasn't sure he'd be willing to pay again. Sure, it was what they were trained for, a sacrifice they might be expected to be made. It didn't make it easier.

"Oh shit!"

He heard Nkolou's shout, glanced up to see the source of her worry. His eyes widened, he glanced back to his sensors. Nothing. "Shit indeed," he said, trying to sound calm. This day just wasn't getting any easier. "Okay Wings Four and Five, assume it's hostile…"

"You know what that is, Commander?" Wing Five asked. "It's a jack-ship."

Wolfmeyer blinked. "It's a what?" More of it was coming into view now, a great black shape dwarfing any other craft on show. It even dwarfed the vos lak, maybe twice the length, easily. It might even have been as much as three times.

"Sorry," Wing Five sounded a little abashed. "That's what we called them back home. It's an interceptor. A trap ship for snatching other ships out of the air."

"I thought they weren't allowed to make those any more under Five Kingdom Regulations," Wing Four said with surprise in her voice. "Didn't the Senate outlaw them?"

"You're welcome to hail them and tell them they shouldn't have it, Wing Four," Wing Five said dryly. "I'm sure they'll appreciate your outrage. The point is, what are we going to do about it?"

His first impressions of the interceptor, and though he had seen them, it hadn't been for a very long time. And Nkolou was right, they didn't make them anymore. Even owning them was illegal unless you could prove that all the necessary weapons systems had been irrevocably deactivated. This one clearly hadn't, the stealth systems still active at the very least given its lack of presence on the sensors. It was a ship that gave the impression of being pregnant, a bulging dome sweeping down out of an otherwise slender taping body, a long grey V-shape cutting through the sky with almost lazy ease as it came out of the cloud cover.

"Only thing we can do," he said. "Try and stop it taking Box. That's what it's after, by the looks of it. By any means necessary. You have your orders. Get to it!"

The doors slammed shut below him and he dropped down from the neck of the vos lak with a less than graceful leap. His legs ached from the constant holding on through the flight, he'd made the decision he was never going to do that again unless he had to. Unless the

Mistress ordered him to. Chances were, he'd need to. But until then, he relished the idea he wouldn't. Realism and desire were two different things. And for the Mistress, there was nothing he would not do.

The battle outside had been short and sweet following the appearance of the Viceroy, the Interceptor-class ship the Mistress had moved out here at incredibly short notice. Credits made the kingdoms keep running and they'd certainly done a job here. Those last three ships had tried to swarm him, keep him from getting here with the prisoner transport but they'd failed miserably. He'd strapped heavy shielding to his spirit before leaving, keeping him relatively well protected.

It might have been argued only an idiot would fight gunships on the back of a spirit, but in return he could point out that all their armour and weapons had done the pilots very little good. Four of them had died. That final pilot had died moving too close to the mouth of his vos lak, a suicide run to drive him away. Domis smiled. He'd seen the look on his face as dragon fire overwhelmed his shields and melted through his hull, roasting him alive where he sat. Only a charred lump of meat had managed to eject from the ship, flames lapping at his remains. Even now, his remains were probably already being torn apart by sharks fifty thousand feet below.

The other two ships had been sucked inside with the transport, a pair of HAX's rendered useless by the pulse technology employed upon them the second they'd been yanked through the doors. The transport itself sat there motionless, three squads of armed guards pointing weapons at the new arrivals. Already mechanics were seeking to cut their way into the cockpits of the HAX's, a Premesoiran and a pretty Vazaran inside them, both looking shell-shocked by what had gone down around them. Domis hadn't decided what he was going to do with them yet, they weren't his problem. The transport was. He strode over to it, past the armed guards and rapped a massive hand on one of the doors.

"Attention Unisco," he said. "You've got one chance to surrender yourselves and the prisoner here. Give yourselves up and we'll treat you right. Resist and you'll die It's your choice but we're coming through that door in a minute either way."

They probably figured they were okay, he thought as he studied the door. It was thick, doubtless sealed tight. If he was in their position, he'd imagine he had more than a minute to stay safe.

How wrong they would be. A grin broke across his face as he took a step back, drew a deep breath and stepped forward smashing the sole of his boot into the door with a deafening clang. He could see the hull vibrate, he'd felt it give under the force of his blow.

Repeatedly, he kicked it, each blow getting results. Under the first few, it held but gradually more quickly his superior strength told, each blow warping the door until finally he felt it pop with the tenth blow, slamming it inwards and Domis was through the door, going low immediately as shots from Featherstone blaster rifles streamed over his head.

He was at the first agent quickly, caught him with a backhand that threw him into a bulkhead, neck bent back at an awkward angle, the second and third he grabbed in each hand by the necks and squeezed until he felt vertebrae crumble into dust beneath his clutch. They hit the ground hard and he turned his attention to the last. A burning sensation kicked him in the chest and he doubled over in pain, fire rushing through his body, burning away his shirt but he gritted his teeth together and stood up slowly. He saw eyes widen as the Unisco agent fired again and again, more and more fire raking across him step by step as he closed the distance and took the rifle from him, twisting it into useless wreckage.

Only then did he hear the laugh of the restrained Rocastle, arms and legs chained, caged like an animal towards the back of the transport. Domis took the Unisco agent by the throat, twisted one handed and absentmindedly dropped him to the floor as he took in the prisoner. The one they'd gone to so much trouble to get back.

"What took you so long?" Rocastle asked cheerfully. "You stop for a tea break? You want to let me out? Because as much as I enjoy the idea of prison hijinks, I think there's better things we could all be doing."

In that moment, Domis considered killing him and telling the Mistress that there was nothing else that could have been done. He sighed. As enjoyable as that might be, he couldn't. He couldn't lie to her face like that. She'd wanted him alive. And alive was how she was going to get him.

As much as it might kill him personally to keep this stain breathing, he had his orders and he could no more disobey her than he could fly under his own volition. It was with great reluctance that he reached for the lock of the cage and broke it in his bare hands.

"Come on," he said. "She's waiting for you."

Chapter Three. What Price Paradise?

"Sometimes, to act is the easiest bit. I've always found living with yourself afterwards that becomes tricky."
Alana Fuller in her private diary.

The eighth day of Summerpeak.

She hated this. Looking at herself in the mirror became little more than an unwilling chore, she hated what she'd become and yet she still endured. And why? Alana Fuller thought savagely as she rolled over to look at the great balding head on the pillow next to her, the taste still foul in her mouth. All because she wanted a place in her Mistress' great new world. She supposed, in the end, it all boiled down to the price you were willing to pay. What price paradise?

She was paying for it with her body, keeping this loathsome little man distracted, two words that described him aptly. She'd found his decadence so excessive she'd wanted to hurl her expensive glass of wine into his face, yet calm had stayed her hands. Her vision of the future in which she'd rule under the Mistress' divine word burned in her mind, the hunger for the power and glory satisfying her in a way Ronald Ritellia hadn't been able to. Their liaison had been briefly unsatisfying for her, he'd kissed her hungrily enough with a mouth tasting of ash and smoke, she found her nose wrinkling at the memory of those vile cigars he'd smoked.

They'd returned to her room, away from the prying eyes of the media and away from any thought of Ritellia's wife and she'd played her part, eagerly undoing his belt and dropping to her knees, pulling his boxer shorts down with her teeth. He stank down there, a stale odour of sweat and stress but still she'd kept her smile plastered on, took him in her mouth and hands to get him going, a task keeping her busy for longer than was good for her confidence. As she'd run her mouth over his cock, back and forth while he'd made satisfied little sounds, she'd told herself it was down to his age not her looks. What she might have had in the past had faded a little with time but not so much she couldn't still have had seventy percent of whomever she desired. Unfortunately, this one, she didn't desire.

Still she was nothing, if not willing as finally she'd gotten him approaching some semblance of hard, guided him to the bed and he'd ripped away her clothes leaving her exposed and naked beneath his beady bloodshot eyes. She didn't care that he looked at her like a piece of meat, so much worse for him if he underestimated her in the long run. When it came, he wouldn't see the knife that slipped between his ribs. His rough hands had brushed her entire body, making her shudder in ways she hoped he mistook for pleasure before finally she'd spread her legs and felt him enter her with a surprising sudden vigour that made her want to retch.

She'd kept her brave face on, thought of the rewards and had been surprised at the smile passing across her face, an approximation of dopey glee that had completely fooled Ritellia by the looks of things. He looked like he knew he still had it, like he could still bring her to climax with very little effort. She couldn't quite keep that little laugh out, hoped he mistook it for delight.

"You're getting better at this," she gasped quietly, privately pleased at her own acting skills. She could fake it with the best of them. Of course, it wasn't entirely devoid of pleasure, but it wasn't anything she'd write home about. Exaggerated was probably a better word than faked.

Still she could be doing worse. She could be doing a Rocastle. Fuller had to admit it had been satisfying, she'd been in the crowd watching as he'd been dragged towards a prisoner transport, his nose bandaged and wrist in a sling. She could only assume he'd been arrested hard and someone had decided to give him a few 'accidental' knocks. She really couldn't blame them; she and he were supposed to be allies and yet she'd frequently fought the urge to stab him in the kidneys. Kill him in as painful a manner as possible, but for the sake of the Mistress, she had held back.

Now, though, she wondered as to his future. If he went down, a likely outcome given the rumours about his actions, then he could ruin everything. If he decided to talk… She put that thought out of her mind. He might not. The Mistress might get him out. How she planned to do that from a secure Unisco transport that would undoubtedly have an escort, she hadn't been able to work it out at the time.

Now though, she still didn't know as her attention was dragged from her thoughts by the vibrations of her summoner. Padding out of the bed naked, she picked it up and set it to personal mode, she didn't want Ritellia overhearing anything.

"Fuller," she said quietly, looking around for her robe. She'd take the call out onto the balcony, enjoy some privacy. Her robe had been thrown aside, a sheen of pink silk cast into the corner.

"Hello Alana." She stiffened at the sound of the Mistress' voice, standing a little straighter without thinking.

"Mistress," she said, bending down to scoop her robe up one handed and clumsily she fumbled it over one arm. "Good morning. How may I serve you today?"

If Ritellia was awake, she noted, it'd probably sound strange. It'd probably bring all manner of question into existence about her and yet she couldn't bring herself to care as she switched hands with the summoner and pulled her robe over her, cradling it into her neck and tying it up around her. She needed a shower, she felt disgusting after the bedroom aerobics.

Stepping out into the hot afternoon air didn't help, the sounds of a crowd in the distance. It sounded like a second-round bout was either underway or about to get started. They'd started the previous day, but she hadn't kept track of what was going on. Right now, she couldn't care less, had bigger things on her mind.

"Talk to me. Are you aware of what happened with Rocastle?"

So, the Mistress had heard about that. Somehow, she was less than surprised as she nodded to herself. "Yes, I saw him being escorted off the island."

"Then you know at this moment in time you are my only remaining asset?"

Again, she bobbed her head, as she'd suspected to be the case. She said as much, and the Mistress chuckled.

"That mind remains sharp as ever, I see. Nice to know engaging with President Ritellia hasn't dulled it. How goes that by the way?"

"I assume you got the videos," Fuller said dully. This wasn't their first liaison, the previous ones all recorded for posterity. If ever they needed to politically destroy the President of the ICCC, this was the ammunition they'd start with. She wasn't keen on her upcoming fifteen minutes of fame but what the Mistress demanded, the Mistress usually got.

"You're doing well, my dear. I could tell you weren't enjoying it, despite your brave face. A woman knows. Ritellia looked satisfied enough. I can't thank you enough, not until our work comes to fruition. All will be rewarded."

It might have sounded vague and unsatisfying. Fuller didn't care. She'd been sold a story and she intended to see that the Mistress kept that word, no matter what. She might have been reduced to whoring herself out for some greater goal, but she'd still hold everyone else to their word. If they didn't do so, she didn't know what she'd do. It wouldn't be pleasant, for sure. She knew the endgame, if not all the pieces in play. It held her respect for the Mistress, she knew that much. To keep everything running smoothly was an impressive fete she didn't know if she could even start to plan, never mind complete.

"Tell me, my dear. What do you really think of the good Mister Ritellia and don't mince your words."

She smiled slowly, aware the Mistress couldn't see her. "I think he's a complete shit. I've fantasised about killing him. I'd rather walk naked through a scorpion pit than let him touch me again. How he got to be president of anything is beyond me. I'd say he's a buffoon but that's giving him too much credit."

The Mistress sounded like she was smiling. Fuller would have paid to see that. "You really don't mince them, do you Alana?"

"But," she said quickly, just in case. "And please take this compliment the way I intend it, it's a sign of how much I trust I have in you that I let him. I wouldn't do this for just anyone."

In the Mistress' voice, she was sure she could hear the smile growing larger. "I thank you for your candid honesty. Although not as much as I thank you for your faith. It's ultimately the efforts of people like you which shall see our goals to fruition. You haven't failed me, unlike some who shall remain nameless."

Alana smirked at the lack of mention regarding Rocastle. Doubtless that was who she meant, a shame she hadn't derided him further. That would have just about made her day.

"Tell me something else. What do you really imagine I have you doing out there? I've purposely left you out of the loop but now I think I owe you the whole story of your mission. You've sacrificed your dignity; it feels only right I reward you in some small way."

"You've got me sleeping with the head of possibly the largest independent political organisation in the five kingdoms," Alana said. "You had me discuss with him the nature of the future. I assume you're looking to replace him in some way…" She paused, remembered something Ritellia had said previously. "But you might not have too much of a say in things."

"Oh really?" The Mistress sounded politely amused and just for a moment, she found herself hoping horribly she hadn't overstretched herself. "Do carry on."

"Thomas Jerome. He's…" Alana paused, searching for the right words. "It feels like he's trying to make a name for himself out here. Here, there and everywhere, always shooting his mouth off to the media, he did the draw for the second round. There's something going on there. I'm surprised Ritellia hasn't slapped him down yet."

The Mistress laughed. "I'm waiting for him to try."

"Excuse me?!" Alana couldn't keep the surprise out of her voice. "Why do I get the feeling I just told you something you already know?"

"Never underestimate the power of being able to manipulate that which you can control," the Mistress replied softly. "If you intend to create a new world, the old one needs to be torn down. The ICCC does not work. It's had its day, men like Ritellia and Jerome and their cronies need to be kicked out. I can't just wave my hand and bring it into existence, would that I could. It takes effort from us all. The best reform always comes from reaction, I've always said that. The best way to get reform is to prove categorically things are going wrong is to lose the public's faith in that which needs them more than they admit. Individually, the man in the street is powerless. Throw them all together and things may happen. You change it by force, they'll protest it. You make them think it's their idea and they'll wave it through happily."

She paused, Alana heard the breath of laughter in her voice. "I leaked the tapes of your nightly encounters with Ritellia to Jerome."

That hit her like a knife in her heart, Alana subconsciously stood up a little straighter and took great lengths to keep the composure in her voice. "I see." She wanted to shout angrily, demand to know how the Mistress could do such a thing. "I assume you were going to tell me about this at some point."

"I am now. You know why they call him the Falcon, right? He knows when to strike at the best moment and with great haste. He has leverage over Ritellia. Ritellia can't slap him down once he knows that. Jerome comes more into the public eye, he's nothing if not a savvy operator. With public notoriety comes support, a man like Jerome can gather a lot of friends, a lot of support, he can make promises he wouldn't have been able to keep before. Kwan-Sun and Klaus Zynski... Pfft, Jerome will make a much more appropriate head of the ICCC for our purposes. The man would stab his own mother for a sandwich."

Alana got it then, once more had to admire the brains and the sheer nerve of the Mistress. "Jerome challenging Ritellia for the leadership? I get the impression Tommy Jerome would be a terrible leader. What his supporters in the ICCC would ask of him wouldn't endear him to the people in the street. There'd be public outcry."

"Exactly. Worst case scenario for us, Ritellia fights a long hard campaign, wins but everyone knows his fallibility, the chinks in his armour. He's too busy keeping his enemies at arm's length, he can't do the job properly. Best case scenario for us, Jerome wins hardily, and things get progressively worse to the point the public lose faith in the ICCC. When that happens, we'll hopefully be in position to see things get shaken up. The best way to fool the people is to make things so terrible that they'll take any sort of alternative with willing arms. It's quite a simple trick when you think about it."

Just for a moment, Alana found herself speechless. And worse, the Mistress seemed to know it as well.

"That's to be your initial monument in our new history. The woman who brought about the beginning of the end for the ICCC. It's impressive considering where you were just a few years ago." Alana had to admit she was right. "Although that's for the future. For the moment, I have another mission for you. My brother is on the island, competing. I want you to reach out to him, he won't talk to me, it's something I very much wish for us to fix. I want him to be part of this. That is your new job for the time being. Rebuild what's been broken between us."

In a way, Alana realised as she processed the order, it might be harder than some of the other assignments she'd been given. "I'll make every effort, Mistress," she said. "I wish I could guarantee it, but I think that would be unwise. All I can promise is I'll give everything I have to make it happen and hope it's enough."

She really did. It wasn't wise to fail the Mistress. Too many had found that out.

Across the street, she saw Fuller close her summoner and stretch her toned arms in the afternoon sun, a small smile playing across her lips as she watched the other woman go back into her room and Ritellia. Holding someone's trust was a curious thing. To keep it, you had to give something back. You need them to know you trusted them, and they were wise to retain theirs. Her little reveals to the other woman might offer some succour following her shameful moments with Ritellia. She didn't regret making her do it. Fuller had a job to do. She was doing it and would be rewarded. End of story. If she had regrets about what she'd done, that was her choice. She hadn't had to do it. She'd had the outlines, the directives and the rewards laid out to her. And she'd made a choice nobody had forced her into making.

She let her own summoner drop around her neck and stared at the island around her, the resort she'd ordered built. Nice to finally see it teaming with life. Just as she'd always imagined. Her trip out here had been sudden, and she'd felt the urge for some sun, as well as checking how things were panning out. Domis was still overseeing Rocastle's retention to her home, Dale Sinkins was still chasing down leads, the rest of her merry crew running about their business and for the moment, she felt content things would work out.

Maybe she should have spoken to Fuller face to face. Or to her brother. Now though, she didn't feel like it. Maybe, just maybe she'd take in one of the bouts, take her mind off what lay ahead long enough for her to relax. Ever since she'd put the plan into motion, she'd found herself on edge, and she doubted it'd get better before it got worse.

"So, Sharon Arventino versus Darren Maddley," Carlton Bond said, looking across his panel of pundits alongside the battlefield. "What thoughts do we have? Obviously, there's going to be a bit of history here, not between the two combatants but between the Arventino name and the Maddley name. Sharon was the first one to comprehensively beat young Darren's father in a bout. We all know that, we've all seen the footage of when Luke Maddley went into meltdown. Choksy, you were in the stadium that day, you were beaten by Maddley Sr a few times before his collapse as a credible challenger, can you see the father in the son?"

Choksy Mulhern considered it, making a big show of musing over the question before grinning. "Well obviously I'd say Luke Maddley was a much more experienced caller than his son at this stage. But we never saw Luke Maddley in the Quin-C, so we can't say how he would or wouldn't have performed."

"There's definitely something with the son," Pree Khan offered. "Maybe he's taken what happened with his father to heart, maybe used it to fuel him on. Maybe it doesn't affect him, you'd have to ask him yourself. The point is, the children of famous callers often need to live up to the reputation of their parents. And Luke Maddley's reputation, well I wouldn't want it. We saw this yesterday, sorry Terrence, when young Matthew Arnholt went out to Katherine Sommer…" Arnholt waved it off without a hint of offence at the comment. "Sometimes it can be hard. My mom was decent. I like to think I surpassed her. Some callers get swallowed by having a famous family name. Others take it as a challenge."

"If it was me in young Maddley's shoes," Arnholt said. "I would be desperate to win here, not to avenge the spectre of my dad, but to make a claim on my own future. That's what he needs to do. He needs to say, yeah, I don't care about the past. I care about the future. You can't change the past, but if he beats Sharon here, it doesn't change the fact she started the chain reaction that finished off his father, it means he gets more recognition and people start to whisper for the right reasons."

"Is it possible for him to do it? Darren Maddley finished second in his group, Sharon Arventino won hers, it looks a mismatch without seeing a spirit unleashed. Do you think he can win?"

"It's possible," Choksy said. "I think she is a very distinct favourite, but the favourite doesn't always win. Let's not forget it would be an easy job for us if they did."

"It's a cliché, but a good one," Pree said. "Unfortunately, I don't think he has a chance. She's too good, she won't lose to him."

"I agree," Arnholt said. "Not a chance Sharon doesn't go through to the next round."

Carlton Bond cleared his throat, gazed at the camera with his showman smile and rubbed his hands together. "Okay so we all know the drill now. Just before the start of the bout, we're going to get a close-up of the randomiser to see how many spirits the two combatants will use. Remember, it won't be less than three, it won't be more than nine. We saw a nine spirit start yesterday morning when Theobald Jameson and Wim Antonio Caine fought, we saw only five as Matthew Arnholt went out yesterday afternoon to Katherine Sommer. What's it going to be now? Sharon Arventino versus Darren Maddley starts in moments, we're all looking forward to what is surely going to be a fantastic bout. It's been many years in the making, a rivalry between not just callers but between families. We're going to see something special here. Join us in a few moments."

Both Terrence Arnholt and Prideaux Khan had been proved right in rapid fashion following the conclusion of the bout. The headline writers for all the media outlets found themselves enjoying a field day, all their work a variant on the 'Lightning Does Strike Twice' theme, she had a few of them on screen next to her as she looked down from her private box, finding it just as luxurious as expected, considering the credits she'd forked over for access to it upon arrival at the stadium, plush seats, a refrigerator full of expensive wines, even a viewing screen showing the punditry at the side of the battlefield.

With four spirits each, the battle had quickly gotten underway with Sharon unleashing Gamorra onto Darren Maddley's first spirit. And then his second. And then his third in quick succession. The fourth managed to get some licks in but it had been too little too late, the applause had taken Sharon and Gamorra off the field and into the next round. What hadn't been quite so neat was the argument that had taken place at the end, a furious Maddley rushing over to confront his conqueror in vociferous fashion.

She could see how angry he was, the fury and the sorrow and the rage and the despair mixed up in one delicious cocktail. How angry he must be right now. And angry people did desperate things. The poor lad, he'd inherited a poisoned chalice of a family name and now played his own part in dragging said name through the mud. Right now, she smiled, he could use a friend.

He hadn't been on Rocastle's list. But that man's judgement had proven to be flawed. Getting himself arrested had displayed his inadequacies. She would deal with him later, either bring him under the thumb further or have Domis take him out and break his neck.

Hmmm… A delicious thought occurred to her. Rocastle had tried to kidnap the daughter of the famous city champion Terrence Arnholt, the man on the viewing screen in front of her. Maybe she could destabilise the establishment further by seeing if she could link him with Rocastle's fate, take her plans for the fall of the ICCC further at an individual level. Pin it on him somehow. It was an interesting idea; one she'd like to develop further if the need arose.

For now, though, she had a job of her own to do. She could use a proxy for it, yet that didn't appeal to her. She could be persuasive when the mood took her. And besides, she'd never ask anyone to do anything she wasn't willing to do herself…

It would be a calculated risk exposing herself like this. But what was life without risk?

She'd found the room easily enough, although in hindsight she wished it had presented more of a challenge. Because she didn't want to get the impression this would be an easy mission. If it started off hard, she'd be more alert, focused on the task moving forward rather than starting easy and slowly ascending in difficulty, meaning she was facing an uphill struggle before she even started.

Alana Fuller sighed and knocked twice, leaning against the frame, her mind already examining the dozen or so potential ways to get inside and coming up blank. If he didn't want to talk to her, she couldn't make him.

He did look a little like the Mistress in the face, she had to admit that as he opened the door, an easy-going grin on his face. Divines knew she'd never seen any look like it on the Mistress. Maybe that was why they'd never gotten on, maybe he lacked the killer instinct she seemed to pride. He was balding and paunchy, where she was slender and well groomed. Either he'd let himself go or really didn't want to be associated with his past.

"Why hello," he said. Big smile. Friendly voice. Very much unlike her employer. "What can I do for you, ma'am?"

Another deep breath, why did she find herself so hesitant with this. He wasn't going to bite her, he looked like he might even listen to her. All she wanted to do was relay her message and leave. But something wouldn't let her. Call it professional pride, call it a desire to please, she couldn't just let it go.

"My name is Alana Fuller," she said slowly. "And…"

"Pleasure, Alana."

"Well I come bearing a message," she continued. "For you."

He cocked an eyebrow to the side, examining her with his gaze, any hint of self-consciousness she might once have felt lost. She'd done enough in her life that him examining her wasn't going to be an embarrassment. "For me? You don't look like a messenger, you know."

She looked down at herself in the clothes she'd chosen to wear, business casual still presenting the right impression of professionalism and met his smile. "I'm an executive messenger," she said. "Delivering the messages others can't be trusted to. And this is quite an important one."

"Important? For me? Surely not." He sounded mock disbelieving in a way that made her want to smile. For all her troubles, all her thoughts about what would come, here was someone she didn't want to envy yet there was something there making her feel wistful. To have that little care in the world...

"It's from your sister."

That got a reaction, she had to admit, his eyes widened, and he made to slam the door on her. She reacted too swiftly for him, jamming her foot into the door before letting out a scream of pain as it smashed shut on her, agony suddenly rushing through her body. She could feel it throbbing, hoped fervently it wasn't broken. Immediately the door opened again, and he caught her as she almost fell through, a look of concern on his face.

"Sorry, sorry, sorry," he said, suddenly looking genuinely upset. "My bad. I didn't mean to hurt you, you okay? You need an ice pack?"

"Wouldn't go amiss," she hissed through gritted teeth. If she was lucky, it'd only leave a bruise. "Ouch!" It didn't hurt quite as much as she made out, yet if he believed she was in agony...

If nothing else, he was a gracious host, he had an ice pack ready in minutes, breaking up cubes from his minibar into a sock and handing it to her, an apologetic expression on his face. She slipped off her shoe and held it against the arch of her foot, the pain subsiding quickly.

"Talk about your misunderstandings, huh?" he said, scratching the back of his head uneasily. "Sorry, ma'am. Again. The humblest from down the bottom of my heart."

"Listen," Alana said. "It's okay. But seriously, you need to listen to me. Just hear me out on this. I know you don't want to talk about your sister, but..."

"I don't," he said. "I really don't. Didn't like her when we were kids. Don't want to talk about her now. She sent me an invite to Meredith's wedding. Declined politely. Shame, I liked that kid before she grew up into a spoiled little madam. I blame her for that."

"Look..." Alana paused before she could even start, not even sure what she could even say to change his mind. Or at least make him think about it. This so wasn't her forte and part of her resented being put in this position. "I get that. Nobody likes family. They're a bunch of horrible, horrible bastards at time. But..."

He raised an eyebrow at that. "Strong words. You ever spoken to my sister?"

"Yeah. She's my boss." She made a point of rolling her eyes as she said it, bringing a grin from him.

"So, you're not going to say anything bad about her? That's okay, I got enough for both of us. You ever looked her in the eyes? I mean properly? There's just nothing there. She forgot what it was like to be human a long damn time ago and there's no way of her remembering that. She can fake it with the best of them. No wonder Meredith ended up so damn screwed up. And that whole thing about nobody knowing who her father is... A kid needs a father."

Something long ignored twitched in Alana's memory, she couldn't push it back down before it took root, a flurry of memories she didn't want to remember. "I didn't," she said quietly. "I'd have been better off without one. You want to talk about family issues, I'll match you. Your childhood can't have been worse than m... Some peoples."

He smiled gently. "You're right. I can't say it wasn't. Considering our fortune, it was a pretty comfortable time. You didn't like your father, did you Ms Fuller?"

She pressed her legs together and folded her arms, trying to keep her mind off her throbbing foot. "I often dreamed about killing him," she said. And she meant it as well. "Stab him in the throat while he's sleeping, poison in his beer, scorpion in his clothes. There were always options."

"But you didn't."

She shook her head vigorously. "How was yours?"

"Distant," he said. "A busy man. Cold. I think my sister inherited it from him. Me, I think there's too much of my mother in me. That's what they always used to say. The staff. I loved my mother. She did her best."

She did her best... Those words stabbed deep and Alana blinked back the thoughts that came with them. Could she honestly say that about her own mother? Thinking back to the woman once beautiful gone thin and haggard with the life she'd been dealt, she didn't know. Now she thought about it, she wasn't sure she even wanted to know.

"When they died, a part of me died with them. Of course, we were both left wealthy by their passing. But you know what, I didn't want it. I wanted them back and all the credits in the five kingdoms wasn't going to change that. It hadn't saved them, when their speeder crashed, they were still as mortal as anyone else. A few billion credits and majority ownership in a company wasn't going to bring me any happiness. Do you know what it's like waking up and just realising there's no point to life anymore?"

"I've woken up not wanting to," Alana admitted. "Back when I was a little girl, I… Everything was simpler when I was asleep. Sometimes I'd wake up with the bloody tears dry on my face and it'd all come flooding back to me. There'd be nothing I could do about it. Sometimes I thought about killing myself."

"But you didn't. And things got better?"

"Eventually," she admitted. "I was kicked out of home at fourteen. At the time I was glad. Later, not so much. I did some things I'm not proud of, things I really want to forget so excuse me if I don't talk about them."

"Hey, your choice." He nodded in agreement. "Look, I can't imagine what you had to do. And I won't if you don't share with me. I'm not disputing you had it rough. You know what I did with my inheritance? I gave it all away. Told my sister she could have it and I'd be going. I left with the clothes on my back and my spirit calling equipment. I pawned the expensive summoner and bought a cheaper one, changed my name with the remainder of the credits. I want nothing more to do with who I was. I'm more concerned with who I am and who I'm going to be."

Alana nodded slowly. "I can respect that, I guess. But all that's in the past. I mean, sure you might not like her anymore. Doesn't mean you can't get along. She wants badly to speak to you…"

He snorted. "No doubt she does. Maybe her guilt reflex is finally developing after all these years. You know, I seriously doubt she's capable of loving another human being, you know. Meredith was the one I pitied."

"I think she wants to make amends. Prove you wrong. Look, you seem like a decent guy, you really do. I seem to meet nobody but scumbags…" She thought of Ritellia and blanched a little, trying not to dwell on it. "Believe me when I comment on how rare that is. You've confided in me, a stranger about your past…"

"I have nothing to hide. I'm not ashamed of who I was. I was born to luxury and I turned my back on it. I don't think it makes me better than anyone else to have done it. What sort of man would I be if I did?"

"But," Alana continued, ignoring his interruption. It was a slight thread but one she wanted to grasp with both hands and pull until it unravelled. "Say you're wrong about her. Say she really does want to reconnect with you. If she's genuine, how can you turn her down and still look at yourself? What then does that make you?"

She winced a little as she sponged at her foot, smiled weakly. For the first time, he looked taken aback as he considered her words thoughtfully. "And as for saying you're not ashamed, Collison... You changed your damn name. What does that really say about how you feel about her?"

Maddley had been located easily enough, had sequestered himself away on the roof of his hotel, a beer in front of him, and she'd decided to make an entrance. She'd wrapped the scarf around her face to retain her anonymity, it was warm, but she pushed it away from the forefront of her thoughts. Her discomfort wasn't important. If her dreams were to come true, there'd be a lot more discomfort than a bit of warmth. Her anonymity was more important. The air was cool-ish, not the warmest part of the day which was a relief.

Her taccaridon spirit wasn't quite as impressive as the vos lak Domis favoured, but it had an unusual factor about it that frequently made people take note. Whereas the vos lak resembled a serpent dragon from the far side of Burykia but wasn't quite a relative, nether was the taccaridon quite related to one of the extinct ones that had existed so many years ago. A leather skinned aerial monstrosity, it could ride the winds like very few beasts she'd ever seen, not so much flying as gliding through the air.

It was a very smooth flier, no constant unpredictable jerking motions that she'd experienced across riding giant birds or even dragons, its giant head reminiscent of a wolf, tail like that of an oversized scorpion while its claws could grip anything with ease. Acquiring this spirit had been a difficult task, though it was handy in a fight. It was a clone. Just like the vos lak but the efforts to attain it had been even more troublesome. The vos lak started to vanish decades ago, the taccaridon had vanished centuries since.

At what point Maddley noticed she was there, she couldn't say. Maybe he was just doing a good job of ignoring her until the shadow passed over him. He hadn't cried, she was relieved to see. If he was to reveal himself to be weak emotionally, this whole thing would have been a waste of time. But still he looked angry, cheeks flushed and knuckles white where he'd clutched them into his palms.

"Mr Maddley," she said. "Hard luck earlier, I have to say."

He didn't reply, just stared defiantly at her. She could see the insolence in him and it intrigued her more than she wanted to admit.

"Still, live and learn, right?" she continued. "I'm sure you'll grow from it. Use it to build a better future out of your experiences."

"Perhaps," he said slowly. "What's it to you whether I do or not?"

Yes, he had fire. She could hear it in his voice. He'd be perfect. Under her instruction, he could well be an asset.

"Because well, you could say the future is something I have a vested interest in," she said. "Let's talk about it, shall we? You and I."

Chapter Four. Proposal and Fire.

"It's something you'll never be able to completely remove. Something wouldn't be right if there was one hundred percent improvement. The nature of the job means our people will get hurt, will die. But since I took over Unisco, agent casualties are down by twenty percent. I've been out in the field and I consider that a good thing. I'm proud of that achievement."

Terrence Arnholt in a report to the Senate on his Unisco tenure.

The eighth day of Summerpeak.

"So, before we start, how are you holding up? That was a bit of a beating you took earlier?" She knew he'd had time to calm down now, which was important. The hours had passed, it had taken this long to track him down and the main thing was getting what she wanted out of him.

He shrugged, a dismissive gesture she chose to ignore. If he joined, it would be something that would need to be worked on. He lacked respect and it grated on her. This was why she had Rocastle to do what he'd done ably for the most part. "Doesn't matter."

"I mean; it was what drew you to my attention. Nobody wants to see that in a contest. I'd feel short changed if I'd paid to see that."

He studied her with an appraising eye. Something was going on behind those eyes and she didn't know how to read it, an unideal situation yet not one she was at a loss to deal with.

"I lost. It happens. Nobody gave me a chance and I didn't disappoint. So there."

"Yes, well." She joined him in staring across the island, only a few years ago untouched by the rest of the world. She'd built this kingdom upon it, changed the way it would operate forever, a trial for her new future. If she could change the fate of this small island, it would only be a matter of time before the rest of it all followed suit. Granted, they were far from that now. But baby steps. Sometimes you took the time to line everything up so when it all fell into place, it fell damn quickly. "Bitterness gets you nowhere unfortunately."

Her taccaridon looked unperturbed at being left to its own devices as the two of them spoke, great teeth munching contentedly at the water tower, leaving gouges in the metal as it sought the liquid inside. She would have brought it back to its container crystal had the possibility she may need a swift exit not been a factor. It wasn't causing any harm, she'd made sure, before diverting all her attention to the sullen young man.

Darren Maddley had the stocky build of his father, his hair a dirty blond colour she vaguely recognised as inheritance from his mother, a particularly vacant trollop who'd latched onto Maddley Sr when he'd become famous and rich only to leave when it faded. Women like this young man's mother gave the rest of them a bad name. None of this she said aloud of course, it wouldn't do to alienate him before she'd started. Some people could get so attached to family, it seemed. Whether he'd be one of them or not, she couldn't say. And yet, if she'd read him right, he held some antipathy towards the woman who had ruined his father.

Who wouldn't in his situation? Did revenge drive him or success? Credits or creed? Power or position? These she'd need to find out and quickly. Offering him a role would be a wasted effort should he not prove to be suitable, right now every move she made was a vital one. No venture was without risk but the one she was spending by being here was feeling more foolish by the second. Still, she was nothing if not an effective worker. Either way, she wanted to have an answer in moments. If he hesitated, it was unlikely he'd have the conviction that she required. And that would be a shame for him.

"What about the future?" he asked slowly, his voice devoid of the sullenness it had held earlier. It would appear she'd gotten some interest at last. "What does it matter right now?"

"Potentially," she said. "Nothing. Actually? Everything. It's all linked you know. The past, the present and the future. What happened in the past goes on to affect the present and what we do now will shape the future. That's always been the curse of humanity, I feel. We change everything, and we very rarely take the time to consider the effects of our actions. Tell me now that it doesn't matter."

He said nothing, she took that as a cue to carry on. "The details don't matter now but I'm currently engaged in a venture that should everything come off, well, it would make the future a new and fantastic place. The way we're going, it… It doesn't look so good. Tell me, do you actually like the world we live in right now?"

"It's okay," Maddley said noncommittal. "Good and bad."

"Give me an example, then. What's so good about this place? And what makes it bad? Weigh them against each other and I wager that you'll find the bad outweighs the good. Just look at this entire process." She waved a hand out across the island beneath them. "Couldn't the credits have been spent so much better? Incurable disease might be one step closer to not being so. Homeless could have been homed."

It was hard not to laugh at the idea that might have been what she'd chosen to do with her credits. Every argument was a weapon until she found one to drive home a point. "And this whole tournament is a gross mistake. It has become a juggernaut unable to stop moving, growing larger and more unwieldy by the year. I know you competed and that's fantastic for you but take off the blinkers and tell me you don't think things could have been organised a little better. We're in Vazara for Divines sake, have you not seen some of the stuff happening since the tournament started? Storms, suicides and kidnappings. Shootings for Divines sake. Was this really what we wanted?"

It was what she'd wanted but that was beside the point. Maddley wasn't to know that. At some point he'd sat down again, staring disinterestedly over the island. Either the argument wasn't working, or he was considering what she'd said in silence. She hoped it was the latter. Or she really would be wasting her precious time. Ideally Rocastle would have been the one doing this had he not messed up. He had that touch with people, he might grate them, but he got them talking.

"Well I guess that's up to other people, right?" he said. "It's nothing to do with me. I can't change their mind. They'll do what they do, and I'll do what I do and... Well I don't know." He leaned back to glance at her. "Guess I never thought about it before. But if someone wants to build all this, why should they be stopped?"

Hmmm... "Maybe they shouldn't. Maybe that's the beautiful thing about this world that was created. Free will. The ability to do whatever whenever wherever you choose. But that's not what I'm talking about, removing that. That would be a grave abuse of humanity and I don't desire that. A race full of automatons and endroids would do nobody any good at all. There'd be more problems than before. No initiative, no creativity, no flair. Can you imagine..."

"I'm through imagining," Maddley said bluntly. "Either make your point or leave me alone."

She sighed, rubbed her hands together to try and remove some of the sweat and stood up a little straighter. "I've had someone here examining the callers in the tournament," she said. "Looking for ideal candidates for my new world. Because out of the chaos of this world springs the order of the next. There will always be a need for those who are strong to impose that order. You weren't on my spotter's list, but I think you have potential despite what that bout showed me."

"Only potential? I managed to get to this point, didn't I?" He looked annoyed more than anything by her comments, she brushed it off and smiled sweetly at him.

"You did and now you've gone out at the hands of someone with infinite more advantages than you when it came to it. She was stronger, you were weaker. It showed, she cast you aside without breaking sweat. That, my boy, is an achievement on this island. Except maybe it wasn't as clear cut as that, was it? What were your thoughts when you stepped on that field?"

He took one long blink, rested his chin in his hands and exhaled sharply. "I wanted to win."

"Just that? You wanted to win and that would be the end of it? What would victory accomplish? A good feeling? Closure for your family…"

"You know what?!" He suddenly yelled, rising to his feet in anger. "I'm sick of people bringing up how she beat my dad. Yeah, you know what? She did. That's not going to change. I could have beaten her, and it'd still be there. The past can't be changed. I'm not even trying to do that. I wanted to win for me, not for him! I wanted to win this whole damn thing, I wanted the prestige and the trophy and the credits. Is that so fucking bad?! I'm not different from anyone else here! You can turn it all into some noble thing about how I want to destroy the bloody witch, but I just want to get ahead in this whole great game!"

"And I can help you with that," she said smoothly, not even breaking stride. "I'm offering you a way out of where you are. A nobody living in your father's shadow to somebody. Take my hand and people won't remember you as Luke Maddley's son. They'll remember him as Darren Maddley's father."

More than anything, she suddenly realised that might have got through, his eyes lighting up with consideration. She could almost see the cogs moving in his head, she rubbed her hands together in glee. Nearly, nearly…

"Maybe I just want to be me," Maddley said, her elation suddenly deflated. "I mean why does everyone have to have some grand divine purpose? I mean, you sound ambitious wanting to build your own new world and well, don't get me wrong, it sounds nuts. How are you even planning that? I mean, it's a good dream but you almost sound delusion…"

She wagged her finger at him sternly, cutting him off. Her heart pounded angrily in her chest, but she kept her voice calm. She didn't like people questioning her sanity. It was rude. "Now that's a secret I'm not about to share with you at this point. All I want from you is your devotion and your faith. That's all. I ask for that; I give you everything you could ever want."

He shook his head. "I doubt that very much." She was losing him, she could see that, just as she'd thought his interest was on the rise a few moments earlier, it was suddenly fading again. She could taste the first seeds of failure and they were bitter.

"I can't give you back your family, admittedly but…"

He cut her off before she could carry on. "You know what always gets me when they talk about my family? Nobody who tells it ever actually knew my mom or my dad. Because those who did had more respect than to go along with the frenzy. Everyone loves knocking someone down who rose higher than them."

She conceded that was true.

"My dad was a winner; it just took a while for people to realise. But when he lost, they couldn't wait to jump on him. You know what it's like being a running joke in a profession you love? But winner or loser, he was still my dad and I loved him! I loved my mom too! They loved each other, despite what the stories say about them. You know nothing so don't talk about stuff!"

She could see the anger in his eyes and nodded smoothly. "You want to enlighten me?"

"No, I don't. I want you to leave me alone," he said angrily. "I don't know what you want with me, I don't know what you intend to do but leave me the hells alone! I want no part of it. You don't want me to know who you are, which tells me everything I need to know." He gestured at the scarf covering her face. "Now goodbye!"

With that, he stood up and made for the door, halfway across the roof before she let out a sharp exhale of breath. "That truly is regretful, Mr Maddley. You do know I can't let you walk away, don't you?"

He turned, eyes wide as if he'd just realised before the taccaridon lunged at him in a flare of wings and he let out a scream as claws went for his face. There was a snap and a flash, he'd gotten his summoner out and suddenly they weren't alone, an eagle buzzing around Tac's face. Should she be worried? No, she decided, she shouldn't. Maddley's strongest were doubtless still recuperating following his bout, the most she had to deal with would be with the best of the rest. And that eagle, as unusually shade of vivid bright blue as it might be, would struggle to deal with Tac.

Far worse would be the commotion caused by a vicious battle, if Maddley had any sense, he'd make it so. This wasn't a bout in an arena with rules and good intentions, this was a very public arena and a fight for survival. Already he'd managed to wriggle out from underneath Tac, eagle and taccaridon lunging viciously at each other. The eagle's hooked beak had yanked a clump of scales from Tac's face, she heard the screech and rolled her eyes. For Divines sake, she chided the spirit silently. Stop fottling with that thing and finish it!

With a snarl of anger, Tac lunged after the eagle who took to the sky to escape. She fought urges to laugh in derision. In the sky, the taccaridon was king. Tac went after it with a push off the ground, wings flaring into a flight position as it went after the smaller opponent.

Smaller, it might be more manoeuvrable but was it quicker? She doubted it. Tac was one of the fastest non-mechanical things in the sky. And large as it might be, it was agile as well. That wasn't her only problem though, Maddley was fleeing, already at the door and struggling to yank it open.

"You should have seen this coming," she said softly. Down below, she could hear screaming and shouting and she winced. Of course, Tac's presence in the sky was going to cause some consternation. Howls and screeches from the great grey mouth were drowning them out but it meant she was running out of time. "To spurn me is to…"

She heard the shriek of agony, glanced back and saw Tac had won, the eagle in its jaws as it flew towards them. There was a thump, and the bloodied remains of Maddley's spirit hit the ground between them. She took no pleasure in it, folded her arms as Tac landed.

"Are you sure you don't want to reconsider?" she asked, reaching up to stroke Tac behind the skull, her nails catching on rough leather skin. "I have been known to forget insult in the past. Granted, it doesn't happen too often."

He shook his head, brought back his eagle to a container crystal. She let him do it, antagonising him by prevention wouldn't help anyone. "I'll never join you, psycho bitch! What the hells is wrong with you?!"

Wrong? Wrong? It echoed through her head, she shaped out a repeat of the word through her lips. "Wrong? You think I'm wrong? There's nothing wrong with me. Your lack of foresight betrays you as it does the rest of them. I'm truly sorry it must end like this, I am. But compassion has no place in the world I'm trying to build. You won't be the first blood spilled in the foundations of the new. But every transformation has its casualties. It has been so since the dawn of time and will continue. There's no shame in a death so others can thrive. Goodbye, Mr Maddley. It's a shame we couldn't work something out."

Something dark flashed across the rooftop and she froze on the spot, the sound of beating wings in her ears and slowly she raised her head to look at the sky. There was no mistaking the two dark shapes hovering above, she felt a sinking sensation in the pit of her stomach as she turned to look at the dragons.

Not just the dragons. In fact, one of them wasn't a dragon on inspection, rather a shark lizard, streamlined and spindly like a fighter ship. The other was a vivid orange and bigger, a lot bigger. If the spannerhead was a fighter, this was a dreadnought, almost docile-looking as it hovered on giant wings. There was something simple in its face, from rounded snout to large green eyes. Cream coloured scales swept from its jaws to its thick tail, four muscular limbs tucked in for flight.

They weren't alone, she realised very quickly with dismay. They had riders, one on the back of each, clothes indescribable and their faces little more than blurs. She knew then what that meant, and it terrified her, she wasn't afraid to admit. Unisco! Not here! Not now! She let out a little moan and looked at Tac. Two against one, this wouldn't be easy. She'd done a Rocastle, let her judgement be clouded and it could cost her everything.

No!

I will not fall! I will not submit, and they will die before I let them take me!

Brave words, she knew, but she believed in the weight behind them. She had to. She had survived through worse, she wasn't going to let a few men… She thought they were men, but she couldn't quite be sure… who thought they were doing the right thing get in her way. Their motives didn't match up, they had to be dealt with. A little violence was good for the soul, Domis had once volunteered to her. It had been the first and only thing he'd ever said to her on his beliefs and it felt strangely appropriate. Sometimes, you needed to cut loose and live a little.

"Attention!" The voice was distorted, warped beyond humanity into a deep bio-mechanical drone. "You down there with the big bird-wolf thing. Recall your spirit now on the grounds of public disturbance and unauthorised bouting in a residential area without a licence. Kneel on the ground and prepare to be detained."

She fought the urge to roll her eyes. Suffice to say that wouldn't be happening. At least they were being polite about the whole thing.

"And step away from that kid as well," the other said, the difference in the voice distinct but still unrecognisable as anything human. This time she couldn't keep the sarcasm out of her gesture, she turned and nodded to Tac. The taccaridon rose onto its hind legs with one sudden motion, jaws snapping open and both enemy spirits had to quickly take evasive action at the uniblast careening towards them, the energy blast sailing wide. Before they could recover their composure, painfully aware of how exposed she was on this suddenly very small rooftop, she sprang to Tac and was on board as the great beast took to the sky.

She was under no illusion that this would be the end of it. Already the orange dragon was closing in on her, pushing itself through the air after Tac with ease. A quick mental command and Tac lashed out with its tail, swiping through the air at to its face. It didn't go quite close enough to land but the danger was there, enough to stagger the charge. She'd learnt that a long time ago. When facing dragons, always aim for the eyes. A small target but a sensitive one. The spannerhead swooped over next, bursting past the dragon and she saw the hint of a uniblast charging up, lingering gobs of energy already forming around the mouth and she pushed Tac into a dive, the blast screeching wide and dissipating.

Down and down the two of them went, she and the spirit closing in on the ground, she could see the people far below them, realisation dawning slowly. Some of them pointed, others ran, she just heard the beat of wings. Still she fell, she wondered how good the two Unisco agents were. Better to overestimate them than otherwise. Still Tac fell in the dive, she allowed herself a glance back at her pursuers and slowly, she counted one, two, three, four...

Up!

She felt the tug of the wind dragging her hair behind her head as Tac evened out, curving harshly back into the air and suddenly where they had been falling, they were rising. She didn't allow herself a look back, she could still hear them, heard mechanical curses from behind her and smiled. An annoyed opponent was a reckless opponent, her father once said.

A sudden roar, her smile was wiped away as something hot and acrid whipped past her cheek, she froze and almost fell from Tac's back in shock. Her knuckles went white as she gripped the skin, desperate not to lose hold. Her cheek burned, she resisted the urge to clap a hand against it. That smell... She'd never smelled her own flesh burning before. Didn't like it. She wasn't worried about it, there were treatments for it, far more pressing was the need to get out of here as quickly as possible, so she could have the treatment. Silently she urged Tac on that little bit faster, the spirit already working to the maximum.

Still the two Unisco agents kept coming. She could fly with the best of them and they were matching her. She stole a look back, this time the orange dragon was charging up a uniblast to aim in her direction, she took evasive manoeuvres back into the mezzanine of buildings far below. This would have been better amidst the skyscrapers of a major city, here the buildings barely came up above two storeys at most but if she could stop them taking long range shots at her, that'd be an improvement. While she fled, she was defenceless. The most she could do was...

Hmm...

A stray thought flashed across her mind as Tac raced along barely six feet above the surface of the ground, the dragon riders still above and behind her but holding back now. Her cheek stung, she tried to put it out of her mind as she stared ahead to the gleaming building so out of place with the rest of the island. They'd insisted that it be built first and be among the finest of them on the island. What more could you expect from the ICCC? Their building was just as monstrous and grotesque as some of the egos inside it. Egos she'd cajoled into holding a prestigious tournament in one of the most dangerous regions in the five kingdoms.

Sorry boys, she mouthed at the building, a grin passing across her as she realised truly how little she meant it. You knew the risks. And if this didn't distract them, nothing would.

They couldn't have expected the potency of the uniblast that ripped from Tac and crashed into the ICCC building, punching straight through with explosive force, flames already feeding, screams and wails of terror filling the void of silence left by the blast. Laughing manically, she kicked Tac into the air, the taccaridon rising at her urging. Come on, come on, come on...

Something flashed in the corner of her eye, something large, she could feel the orange dragon closing in on her, wings pumping vigorously and still it looked comfortable, like it wasn't even breaking a sweat. Did dragons sweat? It threw out a claw, tried to nail her, would have done had Tac not woven out the way with a screech of outrage. That outrage turned to retribution, Tac swung its head and bit down on the dragon's foreleg. Only the density of dragon scale kept it from biting straight through and even then, she wouldn't have bet against the teeth winning out, given time. But the spannerhead was incoming and reluctantly she drove Tac to let go. The orange dragon, a species she couldn't place amidst the heat of battle, didn't give her the same respite and body checked Tac, favouring its wounded foreleg. She could see blood, the last thing she saw before she was nearly thrown from Tac's back by the impact, she felt the spirit waver beneath her and she dug her nails deeper into the skin, chest hammering. Her scarf whipped about amidst the sharp twists and with a rip, tore away from her face, she couldn't pull it back, needed to hold on. If she fell...

Instinctively she mentally screamed out the command to duck and Tac wove beneath the flail of the spannerhead's claws that might have taken her head off if she hadn't. Tac lunged, went for the serpentine neck with the teeth and it took a sudden reverse back from the spannerhead to avoid it, the motion nearly pitching the rider off.

The strangest thing she had to admit was, she was enjoying herself. Glee flooded her system and although she was breathing hard, it was exhilaration pumping through her lungs and her blood. She could feel Tac's emotions through their connection, a mirror of her own. Only Orange remained close in, Tac swung a wing to drive spirit and rider back and hissed angrily through bared fangs before lunging and suddenly the orange dragon was on the run from her, fleeing past her, past the smoking ICCC building and she followed, the adrenaline singing in her veins. Where the spannerhead was, she couldn't say. She didn't care, this was intense. Suddenly chasing rather than running, Tac easily caught the orange dragon, this time going for the rider. Or that would have been the plan, if the mount hadn't twisted out the way, protecting its caller with every motion. Even that worked for her, if it was defending, then it couldn't attack. At these speeds, one of them would make a mistake. She just had to hope it wasn't her.

In close, Tac raked a claw across Orange's haunch, drawing blood and a roar of outrage, enough to bring the orange dragon rounding on her. Orange smashed its skull into Tac's side, barely inches from her leg locked around the neck and she let out a strangled sound halfway between disbelief and joy. Nearly but so bloody far away! Tac shook itself, not a decisive blow but one aimed well. Perhaps movement wasn't as fluid as seconds ago, maybe some rib damage, but still enough to escape.

Escape... Somewhere amidst the thrill of the battle, the fight for survival so long missing from her day to day life, a little voice clamoured at the back of her mind. Escape. Need to escape. Get out of here. You can't win this fight now. Maybe you never could. The important thing is survival. Just run now!

She wasn't sure escape was an option as things stood. Not with Tac's movements suddenly laboured and clumsy. An evasive motion that might have been pulled off with ease moments ago suddenly became a near miss as the spannerhead closed in at speeds almost parallel to her own and only just missed clamping down on one of Tac's wings.

Time to end this. She directed Tac down, then up again in a sharp motion, it might get the spannerhead off her back for the moment. But not Orange. No, that'd need to be her distraction. She wondered if the two agents were good friends, if they were devoted to duty or if they'd behave like human beings.

Time to find out. The spannerhead dived, the orange dragon rose with her and that was the opening she needed as Tac span and slashed a claw at its throat. It was a good slash, she had to admit, it did exactly what she intended, made it jerk back to evade. She'd seen that coming and it gave her the opening as the rider steadied his mount.

Game over!

Too late he noticed the orange energy forming at Tac's jaws, a fleeting half second to charge and the blast struck Orange hard in the chest, she saw the rider throw his arms in front of his face as he lost his grip on the falling dragon, both rider and spirit suddenly falling.

She didn't even look back as Tac shot away from the scene of engagement, if the spannerhead followed her, she'd have to deal with it but hopefully, it would have more important things to deal with.

Nick Roper swore angrily and directed Carcer after the falling Wade, his body limp as he tried and failed to find something to cling onto. Maybe he was trying for his airloop, but with his cloak aflame, it looked a losing battle.

He should go after the woman and her creature, but she was already gone. If he didn't react, Wade would die. The wind tore against his face, through his hair as Carcer bulleted after the falling man and he took a deep breath.

Almost there…

Nearly…

Nearly…

Now!

He jumped, the realisation as to how dumb the idea was flashing through his head before he left his mount and swung out his arms, the feeling of falling catching him quickly. Grabbing Wade with Carcer moving at top speed could cause irreparable damage and it was a chance he hadn't been willing to take.

Nope, now he was risking his own life. That was infinitely better. He was falling too quick to be dry with his wit, desperate to grab Wade, his arm inches from his hand, the ground quickly approaching them, he couldn't delay any longer. He pushed himself, his muscles screaming against the wind resistance and caught an arm, grimacing as flames licked his legs and clapped his fingers against the button on the inside of his palm, not a strong slap but enough to achieve the desired effect. His own cape flared out, stiff against the wind rushing to meet him, catching the draft and gradually he felt his descent slow. By the time the two of them hit ground, it was only with a bump rather than a crunch.

For the whole time, he'd been holding his breath. Back on solid ground, he finally exhaled and dropped to his knees, the adrenaline slowly slipping away as he let Wade gently down to the ground. Not easy carrying someone as tall as you, even if they weren't as heavy. Already he heard the klaxons of emergency speeders approaching and he brought a finger to his ear. Trying to maintain portable comm contact amidst a high-speed chase was hard. He hadn't bothered, lest he be distracted.

"So, Will," he said slowly. "You want the good news or the bad news?" He licked his lips, tasted the coppery tang of blood. "You might want to get a speeder over here right now. Emergency one. Agent down!"

Leaning back in his seat, Scott tried to ignore the sounds outside. It likely wasn't important, someone had probably gotten a little too merry and had an impromptu spirit bout in the street. Some places that was more legal than others but nowhere was completely happy with it. The general rule of thumb went, the more civilised a place was, the more they tended to be against it happening. It was only when he heard explosions and sirens he sat up and took note. Already he was starting to arrive at the conclusion this tournament was becoming memorable for all the wrong reasons. Not least just for him but for everyone involved. Storms to psychos to break-ups to explosions. Maybe he'd made a bad choice coming here. It should have been one of the proudest moments of his life so and he'd found himself wondering if things were going to calm down.

Either way, all he could do was keep on going and hope for the best. If it didn't affect him, it was fine by him. Mia was out of hospital, but she hadn't let him see her. Bang went another dream. He sighed again, looked back to the screen. Wade Wallerington had won earlier in the day, Sharon had also gone through. Maybe they'd be drawn against each other in the next round and he'd catch a break there.

Somehow, he couldn't quite picture it. All he could do though now, was focus on Steven Silver and the challenges in front of him.

Chapter Five. Silver and Sight.

"The family Silver... Yeah they used to have credits. Rich as the hells. Now, not so much. Tends to be the way, you know. You have that many generations of frivolous relatives frittering away the credits... Yep, they get frittered right out of existence. They were pretty much royalty in their part of Serran. The Unifications War hit them hard. Steven Silver's true title is Baron Silver of Calism. Doesn't use it much anymore."

An oral account of his next opponent heard by Scott Taylor.

The eighth day of Summerpeak.

The atmosphere was heaving, almost as hot as the midday sun bearing on the battlefield, stone and gravel heating beneath its rays. It looked crumbly and Scott imagined the first impact would kick dust into the air. He'd need to watch out. A lot of spirits still needed to be able to see and introducing dry dust into the air would be a problem. Still, at least it'd hurt his opponent as much as him. Steven Silver stood across the arena, almost regal in his pose, hands in the pockets of his suit trousers. They went with his waistcoat, dark grey with pinpricked white stripes the length of them. Beneath it, he wore a cream coloured shirt and a scarlet tie, his hair as silver as his name.

Scott wondered if Steven Silver was really the name he'd been given at birth by his parents. Changing names wasn't an uncommon thing, he'd seen many times before. He didn't know much about him other than him being from Serran, he was supposedly a bit aristocratic, if he believed that guy he'd heard talking about him, and had a reputation as something of an explorer and expert in rare stones? Did that mean golems? He hoped not. He'd had enough of them with Santo Bruzack earlier in the tournament. The fewer golems he saw, the happier he would be. Some callers went through life without seeing any and knowing his luck now, he'd probably see several in a few weeks.

Five spirits. Not too short, not too long. That had been the instructions from the video referee and he could deal with that. He liked that they didn't tell you how many spirits you'd be using until the last minute. It prevented prior strategies being used against you by those who really liked to think things through. There was a certain simple delight to be had in taking it on the hoof. And sure, Scott noted, he did like to see what his opponent might use against him spirit-wise. And tactics-wise. But that was the extent of it. To come up with solid tactics to counter someone's best wasn't something he felt comfortable about. Some callers swore by it. He knew there was probably something in it.

If he was honest with himself, there was probably a lot in it. He missed the days of 'you bring your best and I'll bring my best and we'll see who comes out on top.' Those felt a long time ago.

All the pleasantries came and went, he'd heard them so many times now they felt etched into the matter of his brain. Scott smiled politely at Steven who nodded and tipped him a wave. All very nice and civilised. Not like that bout between Pete's sister and that weird kid the other day. That had been nasty. Nothing like seeing an arrogant piece of shit get what was coming to them and seeing Sharon smack him down had been decidedly pleasurable. Now if Theo Jameson would go the same way, he'd be happy.

Still, no time to reflect on that now. Steven's first choice in spirit was a bird the size of a four-person speeder, skin covered in a grey metallic sheen. As it landed on taloned feet twice the size of human hands, it opened its beak and let out a horrible mechanical-sounding squawk which made him want to cover his ears. How manoeuvrable could something like that be in the sky? He got the impression he was going to find out as he summoned Sangare to the field, the dragon proudly spitting out a burst of flames as he appeared, wings kicking up dust.

This would be an interesting matchup. If Steven was worried, he didn't show it. Come on, five to go. Knock those five out, he'd be through. No doubt it sounded so much easier than it would be. Still, if he was going to do it then he'd need to do it now. The signal to get going sounded, already Sangare was in motion at his behest, a gout of fire erupting from his jaws to engulf the iron bird. Yet it appeared Steven was no slouch with the commands either as his spirit took two haltering steps and then hopped into the sky, flaring out its wings to take flight. Scorched earth remained where it had stood a moment ago. Already Sangare was into the sky after the bird. It did fly well, he had to admit, but that wasn't going to save it.

At his silent command, Sangare struck again with a pillar of fire ripping through the air with vicious intent. Once more the attack failed, the iron bird ducked under the flames and cut through the air in a lazy dip picking up pace as it came towards Sangare. Scott caught the sight of the flames fizzling out on the barrier out the corner of his eyes, before he reacted, Sangare thrusting upwards to evade the pointed beak directed towards his scale covered heart.

He didn't doubt the strength of dragon scale but too many bouts had proven it to be not quite as impenetrable as widely believed. He'd had it disproven in one of his own bouts, not that it mattered now. The iron bird was in sight, in range and he gave the command. Sangare obeyed, still a new enough occurrence to make him feel a tingle of pleasure at his own efforts, reaching to grab broad iron wings with his forelegs, thick claws digging into sturdy metal and once more he heard that horrible screech as the iron bird struggled to get away.

He exhaled as Sangare coughed a great fireball into the bird's face from point blank range, the squawk going from outraged to agonised in moments. By the time the fires died, the iron bird was still in the dragon's grip, though its face now resembled a pile of twisted slag. If it could see, Scott didn't know how, its eyes had either been melted shut or had exploded under the heat, one of the two. Still it twitched and struggled, small but he knew it was done for. Silently he urged Sangare to finish it and with minimal effort, the dragon heaved his forelegs powerfully towards the ground, the iron bird hurtling into battlefield like a broken metal bullet. Dust and stone rose up as it crashed, a great groove churned up by its impact as it scrawled limply through the dirt, half buried and unmoving.

Holy shit…

Scott blinked, not quite sure he'd exactly seen what had just taken place. Sure, Sangare was most likely his strongest spirit in terms of pure power. But he'd never expected it to go down that easily. One to him. Four more and he'd be victorious. This might be easier than expected, or maybe Steven was just testing him. He shot a glance at his opponent as he brought back his iron bird. He didn't look too concerned by the matters that had transpired. Scott saw the disinterested look on his face and that, more than anything worried him. Either he was as cold as ice and he genuinely wasn't worried, or there was something else going on here he couldn't see yet. The first phase of some unforeseen strategy? Or maybe a common one. It wasn't unusual for callers to start long bouts with their weakest and finish strong.

I think I've got you worked out, Steven, he thought as the silver haired man locked in another crystal and prepared option number two. This was going to be by no means as easy as it looked like it might be. He couldn't allow himself to get complacent.

She'd gotten a very interesting message that morning, Darren Maddley offering apologies for what he'd said following their bout, admitting he was out of order and shouldn't have done it. There'd been words towards about it being heat of the moment and rushes of blood but at least he'd accepted responsibility overall and she couldn't fault him for that.

On the balcony of her room, she sat cross legged and barefoot, eyes closed as she meditated. Her former teacher had always pushed it on her, told her when things felt murky, it was always wise to stop and think things through. On the move, things became jumbled and hurried. Here, she could mull over them properly. A deep breath and she opened herself up to the universe of her thoughts, the family Maddley at the forefront of them. Darren already looked better than his father, he composed himself in a far more appealing manner. Now she remembered back to Luke Maddley, she remembered the man he'd been and the revulsion she'd felt. So arrogant, so full of himself, she'd been glad when she'd crushed him...

No, that hadn't been right. She hadn't cared at the time but looking back she felt disgust. That shouldn't have been her way, revelling in his defeat and considering herself invincible was as bad as he had been. Yet at the same time, he'd had a family. He hadn't been a bad man, somebody had missed him despite his obnoxious attitude to those he'd deemed weaker. Darren had obviously loved him, just like she loved Nick, even though she knew there were things he wasn't telling her. Yet didn't every relationship need its secrets? The past was the past and there was no changing that. There were things that she hadn't told him about herself and didn't intend to. The past was a long way gone and it was going to stay that way.

Sometimes she thought about the past, what could have been and what had happened. It could all have been so different but here she was. A champion. Soon to be part of a union. So why did she feel that little hint of regret? A question she might never answer on her own. Sometimes she wished she could still talk to her former teacher. He hadn't always had the answers, but he'd made her feel better about not knowing. He could do that, he'd had the gift. But he'd been long since lost out of touch, ever since the last Quin-C. Nobody knew where he was, but she was sure he wasn't dead. If he had passed on, somehow, she was sure she'd know. As it was, she felt uncertainty and doubt in regards of him.

Still he didn't want to talk to her. He'd made that perfectly clear. Her life was her own to lead and he wanted her away from his. She absentmindedly pulled at the bracelet around her ankle and just for a moment, she thought she caught something on the wind, something jerking her eyes open.

... Sharon...

Somehow that closed it for her. She couldn't find her focus after that. It couldn't have been. She was imagining things, had to be. It didn't even sound like him. Not at all. She sighed, reached down into her bag and scrabbled around the bottom for a moment. The memories prodded at her as she withdrew the metal cylinder with the rubberised grip from the bottom. It was about eight inches long, easily long enough for her to get both hands around it. Nick had seen it before, had inquired about it. Another half-truth. She'd told him it was a useless memento she'd picked up in Serran. True, of course, if not the whole story.

He wouldn't believe the whole story. Nobody would. She didn't want to remember it herself, too much time had passed for her to go back to that place, even in her memories. It was all gone now. Never to return. That was for the better. Her life had changed, and she wasn't unhappy with the way it had turned out. But always there'd be questions over that part of her life she would always wonder about. The past was like a river, currents spreading to affect the future, ripples producing tidal waves, Ruud Baxter had told her. At the time, she hadn't known whether to believe him or not. Looking back in hindsight, she got the impression he might have been more correct than he would ever know.

Sangare had fallen. As had Herc and Seasel but Scott wasn't too worried. They'd proved themselves to be evenly matched by now, despite earlier misgivings, Sangare had dispatched the bird of course and weakened the next spirit, a large mollusc covered in a spike-ridden shell before being overcome by crushing jaws smashing through dragon scales with ease. Herc and Seasel's combined efforts had done for said mollusc before Seasel had fought out a draw with Steven's next spirit, a huge steel snake that had dwarfed him many, many times. Still, Scott had been pleased to see Seasel hadn't been intimidated and ultimately the watery weasel had done well. Next choice? Crush. His giant orange crab appeared on the field while Steven's next choice was a huge rhinoceros covered in what resembled steel battle armour, he'd noticed the recurring theme here. He liked a heavy defence, it would seem but at the same time he could deal it out. Herc and Sangare had found that out in their clashes with the mollusc.

"Let's do it then?" he said, grinning at Steven. With each of them having two spirits left, it felt like they were slouching towards sudden death. But at the same time, he was enjoying it. The most fun he'd had since Mia had been attacked… He rejected that thought violently. Now was not the time to be thinking about her. Already the rhino was charging, and instead he was thinking of ways to counter it. He could worry about Mia later. The ground beneath Crush's feet churned as six hooked feet dug in, the crab bracing for impact. This likely wouldn't be pretty but it was his only option. Somehow, he doubted Crush was quick enough to run a race with this thing. At this point, he didn't want to draw the bout out. He needed it over quickly, stand and fight without taking risks. Not stupid ones. The sound of impact made him wince, neither of the two spirits were lightweights but he'd seen Crush being forced back by the power behind the charge.

That, he found unsettling.

"You do seem to have been a busy man since this started."

Nick looked up at the voice and fought the urge to salute as Terrence Arnholt strode past in casual clothes, his gaze towards the room where Wade lay unconscious, bandages across his face. They'd been coated in alska-salve, the hospital pulling out all the stops. Guess there were some slight perks to nearly being killed in action, he thought bitterly, trying to keep a lid on it.

"Just doing my job, sir," he said, proud of his efforts in sounding civil. "Besides, we got the call to action."

If he heard any bitterness, Arnholt didn't acknowledge it. "What happened?"

"Okay so Wade and I were talking, and we got a call from Agent Okocha saying there was a sighting of… Well something in the resort area. We were the closest, could we go have a look. Anyway, we went over, saw it and then it turned violent, looked like it was going for something else up there, we decided to investigate. And it escalated."

Arnholt nodded. "Things frequently do seem to escalate where you're concerned." It didn't sound overtly critical, not until Nick played it back in his head. "At least you didn't murder anyone this time."

"Heh." Nick didn't sound amused. Bringing up Blut didn't help his mood. It was starting to feel like no matter what he did, it would linger around his neck like a bloody millstone. It had happened in the past. He'd been dealt with over it. They could let it go now. But no, people kept mentioning it. They always missed the point as well. Sure, he'd died. But it had been a key sacrifice, so others wouldn't. He'd only been thinking of the bigger picture. Doubtless that was what had saved him, it had achieved results. So why did he still feel uneasy about the whole thing?

"Yeah. He'll be fine. Just needs a few days of alska treatment for burns. That bitch hit his dragon with a uniblast at point blank range, it took him out. Nearly hit the ground pretty hard but I managed to catch him."

"Yes?" Somehow, he knew what Arnholt was about to ask next. And he wasn't disappointed by it. "And you let the suspect flee the scene?"

"I didn't let her." He'd already considered this more than he wanted to admit, and it hurt knowing Arnholt had a point. Could he have… Maybe… So many variables had come into play. The woman had had distance on him and her spirit was no slouch. Could he have caught her? No way of saying. "I made a decision under fire. There were a thousand other things I could have done and whatever I decided to do, we'd have been having this conversation. If I'd let him fall and failed to catch her, it'd have been worse. If I'd let him fall and caught her, it'd be the death of my partner on my conscience."

"And now you've let her go, what happens next is on you? How does the weight of her future acts hold on your conscience?"

"I'll let you know when the future comes to pass," Nick said solemnly. "I don't hold guilt for maybes. I've got enough for stuff I have done without worrying about maybes. Even if we had caught her, what's the penalty for unauthorised spirit battling in the street? A five hundred credit fine at most? What difference would it make?"

"It's not your job to decide what should be enforced and what shouldn't," Arnholt said severely. "And it wasn't just that, was it?" He left the rest unsaid, something Nick was privately relieved at.

"I know. I know."

"You talk to the victim?"

"Not yet," Nick said. "Truth be told, I'd rather not. But I will."

"Rather not?" Arnholt raised an eyebrow.

"Luke Maddley's kid. Been saying some stuff about my fiancé. Might find the temptation to give him a smack in the mouth a little too tempting."

"I trust you can remain professional?" Somehow Arnholt managed to keep the linger of a threat there in his voice and Nick smiled.

"Always professional," he said. "It's me. Don't worry about me keeping my personal feelings in the way of duty. I'll talk with Maddley, see if I can catch anything that'll get us to this bitch." To that, he couldn't miss the small smirk on his boss's face.

"Hence why Wade's in the hospital rather than the morgue and our cells are empty rather than having a perp in there."

That stung a little, but he held his tongue. Anyone else, he'd really have toyed with taking a swing at. He'd have enjoyed that. Especially if it were someone capable of fighting back. It had been too long since he'd taken a punch.

"Good trade I think," Nick said. "We don't have so many agents as to throw them away on stuff like that. I think you're right. It shouldn't have escalated the way it did. Maybe we could have handled it differently."

"It's a bit late for recrimination," Arnholt said stiffly.

"Not a lot I can do about that," Nick replied.

"You know; I'm starting to worry about your judgement while out here. Your decisions lately, they've been questionable."

"If you don't want me in the field," Nick said. "You've only got to say. You want me to resign, Director?"

That changed the atmosphere. Nick sighed and leaned against the wall, looking through the window. Of course, Wade was going to be fine. A few burns, nothing serious, Will Okocha was already concocting a story about how he'd been hurt in the explosion at the ICCC building. If anything, he was glad that Arnholt hadn't brought THAT up. Because that was the real crux of the matter. That woman on the leather bird-thing had only fled and attacked because he and Wade had charged in. If they'd done things differently, it might not have happened. And right now, he felt worse about that than he did Wade's injuries. None of it should have happened.

"Terrence," he said slowly. Because it wasn't just this. It was the whole Blut thing as well, those memories hadn't left him and even knowing it was the right thing t didn't help. In a fight, it was easier. You didn't remember the faces when you shot at someone in the dark. You could shove it all down. Blut, there'd been no clear threat from him, just babblings he'd interpreted. It all felt worse given he'd gotten away with it. Knowing you'd done right didn't make things easier.

"I don't know what you want me to say. For once in my life, I don't know what I'm doing. I'd follow my judgement, but we've seen where that's been getting me lately." He sighed again. Arnholt said nothing. "Look I mean I don't know how much longer I can do this."

"The job? Or everything with it?" Arnholt's question cut to the crux of the issue and he had to admit he was right. Which was it? He'd never had a problem with the job before. He knew there was a chance he might be killed in action. And yet it had never bothered him like the other stuff did, living with the consequences of action, the idea his identity might be compromised, maybe it just wasn't worth it.

"I don't know anymore. When I see Wade like that, I think it could be me. On another day, it might have been. I'm getting married in a few months, Terrence and…" He paused, shrugged his shoulders. "I don't know how you did it. How you managed to sustain a marriage and kids for all the time you have."

Arnholt nodded. "It is a sad fact in our line of work that men and women with no attachment make the most effective operatives. Those who have nobody to live for. It doesn't always apply but the few times it doesn't are often the exceptions that prove the rule. Those who have something to lose are never quite as fearless in the face of the unknown. Yet I always looked it a different way, you know. That fear makes you faster, stronger, sharper. You have something to cling to. A reason to keep going when everything seems hopeless. Because it's never hopeless. You have a job to do and it needs doing no matter the odds. Do or die. You should know by now that those are the choices."

Nick nodded slowly. "I'm still not entirely sure, you know. I've been doing this a long time now, recently it feels like the job is… Not getting harder, that's the wrong term. But I can't quite explain it. It's like carrying a great weight. I knew it wasn't going to get easier to deal with the longer I went on."

"Nick," Arnholt said. "You're a good agent. I don't want to lose you. But if you're no longer able to function properly in the field…" His voice took on a hard edge. "You're useless to me. Consider yourself on leave. Get your head sorted out and if you don't wish to stay then don't. But I think leaving would be a waste of your considerable talents. We need you. We will continue to need people like you."

That had never occurred to him. Leave Unisco? Could he do that? Would he want to? The rumours about the crucible exit existed, sure, though he doubted they were true. Not if Arnholt was giving him an ultimatum. He didn't want to leave. He owed them more than he could pay back But, given the events of not just the last few weeks but the last few months, he wasn't entirely sure if he wanted to stay either. The Hobb incident had nearly done for him, seeing what had happened to Lysa in the build-up and nearly dying so many times over at the hands of people he should have been able to trust.

"I know you do. And I've never walked away from a fight. There's no need to send me on leave. I'll…"

"Only until the tournament is over. Think about it. That's all I'm telling you," Arnholt said. "No need to surrender your weapon and your badge. I just don't want to see you again after you deliver your report on this incident. Nick, this isn't punishment. It's necessity."

Just because that might be the case didn't stop it feeling like it was punishment. He sighed and offered a hand. "I know. I guess this is goodbye for now then." Arnholt shook it and smiled sadly.

"For now. Remember, I don't want to lose your services. But you must do what's best for you. Distractions will get you killed. It's all or nothing. Either you're with us or you're not. Think about that, Nick."

As he turned to the room where Wade lay unconscious, Nick inwardly blanched. To be removed from active duty for the time being, even if it wasn't permanent felt a kick in the balls, no matter how Arnholt might deliver it. He stood up and made for the exit, not looking back at his boss. Besides a holiday from work might be just the thing he needed. It had been too long, he knew that much.

The rhino went down, one of Crush's claws embedded into its skull and Scott punched the air. Four down one to go and for the first time in the bout, Steven looked a little concerned as he watched his spirit go back to its crystal. This could be fantastic. He was on the verge. All that stood in his way was one final hurdle. He could do this, scratch that, he would do it. No excuses.

Steven's final spirit hit the mangled ground with a thud and as Scott took it in for the first time, his heart fell. Oh crap!

He might not do it after all. Whatever it was, he'd never seen one before, though it was huge. Its body fashioned out of a dark blue metal, it stood towering above him on five legs the size of tree trunks around an oval-shaped body, as it stood there staring at him through eyes twice the size of dinner plates. Two of those legs stuck out either side of the giant eyes, one at the back of its body. When the mouth opened, he could see it was filled with giant triangular teeth, almost shark-like. It looked like a giant five-legged metal spider and he gulped. Crush wasn't a small spirit by any means, but the crab was dwarfed by the enemy. As it thundered to the ground, he could see each of the five legs was tipped by a trio of pointed claws cutting into the earth like butter.

"The mighty cavern crusher," Steven said proudly. "Very rarely seen, very difficult to damage and this is where it ends for you." They were the first words he'd said all bout, a vaguely aristocratic inflection to his voice, snobby pride in his words. It made Scott want to smash him in the face. "Very few opponents can conquer this creature. Can you?"

He didn't have time to consider the answer as the referee's buzzer went and he cursed mentally, Steven had out-psyched him with the question. He'd spoken, distracted him and Scott had been too busy considering his words to contemplate a strategy. Stupid, stupid...

He was doing it again, the crusher tensed its legs and sprang into the air with a clumsy leap, Scott quickly traced the trajectory with his eyes and blanched, screaming for Crush to get out the way. He responded just a little too late, the crab did duck but not fast enough, one giant leg smashing into his back with crushing force. Smashed to the ground, Crush let out a shudder, utterly pinned by the weight. Sudden panic running through him, Scott tried to keep a lid on it, the claws whipped out at his command and flailed impotently at one standing leg. Unable to get much momentum behind them, they clanged off with a desolate sound. He wasn't even sure if they'd left a scratch on the skin.

At the same time, he heard a cracking sound, for a moment he let his spirits rise that maybe they'd done something, all until he realised the source. It wasn't coming from the crusher, it was coming from Crush, the weight still on the crab's back and ever so gradually his thick shell was coming apart. If it broke, it would be all over.

Guess he didn't have any choice in dealing with it then, he'd have to take his chances with what he could do for now and hope his last spirit could take it home. Now though, Crush's jaws slowly slid open, the tell-tale vivid sheen of orange energy already forming. Maybe it'd be more effective if he could fire one down its gullet, burn it up from the inside. Pushing that strategy aside for the moment, he saw Steven's eyes widen and as the uniblast erupted from Crush's jaws, the cavern crusher sprang up into the air as if fired from a springboard, the blast sailing wide. But it was off Crush's back and he needed that.

It took a great effort for the crab to rise to all six unsteady feet, only now could he see the cracked carapace where the crusher had dug in. It didn't look pleasant, he forced himself not to look. Crush was wobbling, free or not he didn't think he'd last much longer. Coming in on its three rear legs, the crusher went for the crab like a boxer, using its front legs like fists and it was all Crush could do to stagger out of reach. Another blow came. And another. And on the third blow, Crush caught the fist in a powerful pincer and Scott could see the exertion running through the shattered body as he dug in, trying its hardest to crush the arm in his grip.

He never saw the other arm coming and suddenly Crush was airborne, hurled into the sky by a vicious uppercut, rising and rising until suddenly he was falling and suddenly Scott could feel the connection between the two of them fading. Crush was dying, might already be dead and there was nothing he could do about it.

Except… There was something there still, a faint hint of a spark and he seized it instantly, silently urging the crab on. One final blow was all he needed, it might be key in the fight. For a moment, he held his breath as he studied the cavern crusher. It had to have a weak spot somewhere but…

Where?

He followed the outline of the body all around, nothing he could see…

The orange blur hit like a comet, he knew he was out of time and in absence of a specific target, Crush had done the next best thing and driven heavy claws hard into the cavern crusher's face, the crash deafening him as the echo of the impact rang around the arena. If it had done anything, he couldn't say, Crush slipped down the face limply, falling at the feet of the opponent who had conquered him.

It was over, and he wasn't any closer than he had been at the start.

So, what now? It was a question he wasn't entirely sure he had the answer to.

Chapter Six. The Bowels of Her Castle.

"It's about more than just society. That's the whole, I want to think about the parts which make up the whole. Because without the sum of the parts, the whole is nothing. Think of a machine. A dozen tiny pieces all working together in concert to ensure everything works perfectly. If just one goes wrong, the whole thing will come grinding to a halt. That is the truth of society. Introduce just one flawed element into the way the whole thing works, and it churns to a halt. Change has been conceptualised. Be it permanent or only temporary, there it is. An actual difference exists with the potential for better or worse."

John Cyris pushing his Freedom Triumphant philosophy to listeners.

The tenth day of Summerpeak.

Had it been the right thing to do? She'd considered the question for hours now, constantly demanding the whole thing kept to the forefront of her mind. The first line in the sand had been drawn. She'd attacked, made the first move. She'd declared war on Unisco in the name of advancing her goals. Had it been the right thing to do? Perhaps not. Maybe she could have stretched out the first inevitable confrontation for further down the line. After all, she had made her move and it could have backfired spectacularly. She could have been killed. By all rights, on another day, she would have been.

She'd been lucky. Aerial dogfights, weapons, all things she had people to do for her. She leaned back against the wall, heart pounding in her chest. So why did she feel so alive? She had more credits than she ever knew what to do with, but it was the first time she'd ever felt this rush. She knew it had to be bad for her, doing it too often would be to invite catastrophe. Unisco agents were trained saboteurs, investigators, killers, to go up against them on her own would be suicidal. Sooner or later, it would backfire, and everything would be for naught. She was lucky they hadn't identified her and weren't already at her door.

She couldn't risk it again. Not yet. Things would soon change, circumstances permitting. All it took was patience. It felt like a dirty word in her mind, yet she knew the value of it. Waiting might be infuriating but there was ultimately very little she could do. Suffer the tedium of the present to bear the fruits of the future. She drummed her fingers against the desk, stared at the report in front of her and forced herself to read. adrenaline in her system still hadn't quite faded, tough chore to ignore the way it screamed at her. This was important. Too important to ignore.

The report came from one of her people downstairs, for her eyes only and extremely sensitive. It didn't make for good reading. Too many potential excuses and complications for her liking. Perhaps running off on unplanned jaunts to Carcaradis Island wasn't the best idea; the evidence stacking up. Things needed to be kept an eye on here.

But who was going to keep an eye on her?

She'd already had the argument with Domis. Dear sweet Domis with his unshakeable loyalty and desire to do nothing but protect her from those who wished her harm. For a moment she considered setting him loose on Unisco and its agents but quickly decided against it. It would be a fool's errand. They were too scattered, too anonymous to be worth it. By the time he killed enough to warrant the mission, the rest would be in retreat. Sending him into one of their office buildings would be a waste, even should he survive it, the chances of his anonymity remaining were low. That was his great talent. That he didn't exist in any sense of the world. He existed on no database in any of the five kingdoms save the one inside her mind. A truly anonymous man.

She was the only one which knew the truth about him. With Domis, she had something quite remarkable she'd soon decided she'd rather nobody else knew about. Those who'd helped her with him in the early days no longer could talk about him. He was the closest thing she had to a son, she valued him more than she did her good-for-nothing daughter and the constant drain on credits she constantly found her to be. That was before getting onto the subject of this infernal wedding...

He'd been agitated when she'd returned, hair windswept from the flight, breathing heavy and smelling of smoke. Her own black knight, her bodyguard and closest confidant, she'd found him pacing her study as she strode in, the grin plastered over her face.

"Mistress!" he'd exclaimed as he'd clapped eyes on her. "You're alive. I was worried. I saw the news, there was an attack at Carcaradis Island." He paused, looking wary in his worry, like he knew he should desist but unable to. "And I recognised what the attacker was riding. Looked awful like..."

She cut him off. "Yes, it was me."

Two sides of him wrestled for control, she could see the twitch in his face. The one that was subservient, the one that loved her too much to stay silent. The latter won. "Mistress, I wish you wouldn't... I didn't know. If you'd been hurt, I couldn't protect you from here."

"I am alive, am I not?" she said. Had it been anyone other than Domis, they'd have felt her full ire at being questioned in such a way. This from a man who'd recently recaptured Rocastle, had flown his vos lak into a dogfight with a squadron of Unisco fighters for her. Yet she stayed her tongue from chastising him. He'd earned the leeway and she'd let it go. Bullying him into submission wasn't going to do her any favours. She didn't want to push how devoted to her he might be. Those big hands could break her into pieces as easily as any weapon. "Domis, don't question me. I am capable." It was a gentle rebuke, nothing more. "There was something I needed to attend to. It escalated. Believe me, this was never my intention."

"Mistress, should you have been killed…"

"I wasn't," she interrupted him. "Domis, I appreciate your concern. But you need to understand you can't be beside my side every minute of every day. You are my strong right hand." She took his giant hand in both of her smaller ones and smiled at him, craning her neck back to meet his eyes. No doubt he had to be one of the largest men in the five kingdoms, he loomed like a small mountain on the horizon, not just tall but thick as well. He looked like he had some cave troll in him, yet appearances were deceptive. He'd never be acclaimed for his intelligence, yet it was always a pleasure to see the surprise of those who met him, finding him to be deceptively articulate.

His resolve cracked, she saw the corners of his mouth tremble. She might view him as something like a son but more than once she'd wondered to the exact extent of his desires towards her. "When I need you, I know you'll be there. Sometimes I need you to be elsewhere. You, I trust more than anyone else. Everyone else is replaceable. Everything else is replaceable. What you are is beyond that. You are the most unique singularity in my life."

She'd seen him swell with pride and had patted his hand before withdrawing. "Believe me; sometimes you can be more useful when you're not by my side. Like when I send you on the little missions." It was true as well. Others might see delivery duty as a demotion. Domis took it all in his stride without complaint, taking care of anything she didn't want to come into the house through official channels.

She didn't expect to be attacked in her own building, but he'd gone with her into the labs to deal with the doctor. Maybe he felt a special attachment to the project. After all, study of him had led to the inspiration behind it. Like as not, he didn't care. If he had a life outside of her, she'd yet to see any evidence of it. He lived on her property, he kept his wages in a lockcase under his bed and never spent more of it than he had to. Food, clothing and maintenance, beyond those, he must have had a small fortune beneath his mattress.

Doctor Andreas Hota looked up as she entered his office without knocking, the colour going from his face as he took in his visitors. He was aging badly, and the colour fading didn't do him any favours. "Ah, Madam, you took me by thurprithe." His accent, thick from the western reaches of Serran left him with a lisp; she'd heard it before and no longer found it amusing. "I didn't know you would be coming."

She smiled her cold smile, saw him shift uncomfortably in his seat. "I wanted to surprise you. Looks like I achieved that. I read your report, doctor."

"Madam Coppinger, the proceth ith going thlower than expected," he said. "And we're needing more medical web by the day. I have faith the project will be completed. I jutht need thome more time. We have some pothitive rethults already. Pleathe, allow me to thow you tho far." He scrambled to his feet and started to open one of the cupboards, thumbing through a collection of flash drives. "We recorded thith during a tetht in recent dayth. Tho far it theemth to have taken."

Her ire replaced by curiosity, she let him slide it into a monitor and prepared herself for what he thought she might find so interesting. She'd seen Subject A before. Nothing unusual there. There she lay on the operating table, mask over her face to keep her sedated. Her skin looked pale and clammy, not a well woman. That wasn't her concern, keeping her alive was imperative. Keeping her comfortable was not.

"Here we have Thubject A," the Hota in the room said as the camera turned to another Hota, one on the screen wearing a blue surgical mask and gown. "And there we have a charming man ready to cut Thubject A up." The Hota on screen gave the camera a thumbs-up and it focused in on the test subject, zooming in to cover the left hand. It was contorted into a claw, the nails still showing some trace of manicure. "Thubject is right handed. Thuth we decided that the left would make a more ideal tetht. We tharted out thmall, you thee," the Hota in the room explained.

On the screen, the whirring sound of a viraknife charging up could be heard in the background. Some of the same knives were across the other side of the room, she could see them in a cabinet. They were an incredibly useful surgical tool, once heated up to the right temperature they cut remarkably easily through bone in mere seconds, through flesh in less than that.

"Thetting temperature to low," the Hota on screen said to the camera as he took one of the knives in hand, the blade glowing a dull orange. "Preparing to make initial cut. Thubject has been thedated, blood prethure ith low, breathing ith thtable. Firtht tranthuthion hath been adminithered."

She didn't avert her eyes as he cut into the palm of Subject A's hand, going at it with surgical aplomb, taking the skin away with broad but delicate strokes. Within moments, he had the palm stripped of skin from wrist to the base of the fingers. Blood flowed but it was slower than she'd expected, sluggish even as it slipped out of the wound. She didn't want to avert her eyes. This should have distressed her, yet she didn't even flinch, watching with curiosity. He took away the skin from the back of her hand next, before moving to the fingers.

"The trickietht bitth," the Hota in the room said thoughtfully. "But ultimately, a thucetth, I feel."

"I will be the judge of that," she said. "How were her vital signs through this test?"

"Thlow but thable. As expected. Thubject thurvived the occathion," Hota said in a patient tone clearly implying he wished to tell her to wait and see for herself. On the screen, the other version of him finished with the fingers and straightened out.

"Ath you can thee, the removal of the thkin wath completed within a few minuteth," he explained. "Exact time, two minuteth, fourteen thecondth. Now moving to apply medical webbing."

She watched as the on-screen Hota started the process of applying the small metal gauze-like squares to the bare muscle, an eyebrow raising as they clamped onto the flesh and started to spread out across the surface of the skinned hand. They really were a remarkable invention. Hota had become world-renowned for creating them, patches that spread out across wounds and promoted regeneration of fresh, healthy cells. Of course, normally they were placed above the skin. They needed something to knit together. Placing it on the bare muscle, to the best of her knowledge, was something that hadn't been done before. Or at least with any success. If Hota failed, it wouldn't go well for him. He wasn't irreplaceable. Of course, they did have a help here courtesy of the biochemists in another lab.

"All thith time," Hota continued. "Conthtant injections of the therum into her thythtem. We're hoping over time thhe will thtart to produce it naturally. Thelf-regeneration on every level, yeth?"

"That looks like it'd hurt," she said watching the squares attach themselves to the muscle. They were starting to spread now, interlinking with those around them to form a web over the flayed appendage.

"I can imagine it doeth," Hota said. "Thtill, thhe can't feel it."

"No, you can't," Domis said softly. So softly she hadn't even realised he'd spoken until he'd finished. "You can't imagine the pain here."

Hota ignored him. "Thethe webbing patcheth were oneth intended to deal with thevere woundth. Broken boneth and the like. It ith often uthed to thupport the bone while thimultaenouthly repairing it. It hath to be tough, yeth? It therveth two purpotheth, you thee. Jutht a little more protection."

Subject A shouldn't need more protection, she thought. Not if everything went to plan. Because after all, she couldn't rely on Domis for everything now, could she? He'd given some of himself to the project. Without him, it wouldn't have been possible. In the background, Hota was continuing to speak, seemingly more to himself than anything of use to her. Maybe his genius was growing more flawed as he grew older. Perhaps. Her eyes widened as she saw the recording. And perhaps not.

Yes!

Already the wounds were starting to heal before her eyes, skin was starting to reform above the medical webbing, paler than before but still fresh, virginal skin. She couldn't help but smile at the result. The whole process took maybe thirty seconds and the hand looked as it had before Hota's surgery. Other than the blood, nobody would have guessed.

"We need to work quickly," Hota continued. "Dawdle and the wound will heal before we can finithh applying the medical webth. Ath time goeth by, it will be harder. The more therum in her, it'll be harder to cut through her thkin. Her muthcleth will strengthen, they'll be harder to theperate. We rithk damaging her unnecessarily. What we do won't latht long. But it ith a thtart, no?"

"Doctor," she said. "You have done well. Make it so. Although there is still the matter of control to consider." He nodded in agreement. After all, what use was a weapon when one couldn't effectively direct it at your enemies?

On the way back up, she fought the urge to rest her head against the wall of the elevator and close her eyes. Her sleep had improved only marginally. Her dreams hadn't relented. Vivid as ever. She didn't want to think about them now. Instead, her thoughts drifted to Rocastle and the mess he'd inadvertently brought upon himself. Had he not been caught in the act, had he not been locked up, she'd have been a lot more secure in things. But no, who knew what Unisco had managed to deduce from his jaunt. He'd sworn he'd not said anything, but she hadn't been able to bring herself to believe him. She couldn't ask her contact. They might share an arrangement, but she couldn't be sure quite how he'd react given the operation to recover Rocastle had led to the death of four Unisco pilots and the capture of two. Better to keep it quiet. If there was anything that affected her drastically, she was sure he'd tell her.

But she'd risked a lot to get him back. The Vazaran Suns were crying foul over the loss of several attack ships, compensating them was going to be the least of her problems. She'd risked exposing the Viceroy to those who might spot it. She'd risked Domis. He'd been shot several times in the attack, not that you'd know from looking at him. The man had a knack for healing. He'd survived everything that had been thrown at him. Often questions as to what exactly he was appeared in her mind, but she hadn't been of the mood to seriously consider them. He was what he was, hers. That was all that mattered in the scope of things.

Without him, she would not have Rocastle back. Left to the Suns, it would have been a disaster. And Rocastle was going to pay her back for the favour, he just didn't quite know it yet. She couldn't let him rot in a jail cell. He might talk, he knew too much. However, much of a loathsome character he might be, he still had his uses. But he'd been warned, one more mess like the one he'd gotten himself into on the island and he'd be out. He might be a big guy. He might hate women. But she would send Domis to eliminate him if he took his toes off the line. However big he might be, however tough he thought he was, Domis would break him into a thousand little pieces, bone by bone if need be.

It was Rocastle who'd provided Subject A, the ideal sample for the project. Everyone had tried to find subjects. Rocastle had succeeded and in such an audacious manner she'd had to approve. Everyone was looking for her, but they wouldn't find her. He'd covered his tracks too well. Rocastle had made himself useful. He'd risen in her organisation and privately she was proud he answered only to her. More than that, she secretly loved discomfort when she yanked his leash. Why he hated women, she didn't know. She didn't want to know. But knowing that she could control him against his basest desires was a feeling wealth couldn't bring her.

Either way, until further notice, she was keeping a close eye on him. He wasn't to be trusted running loose on his own at this moment in time. Plus, when his disappearance was inevitably discovered, there'd be an all-out search for him. People would want a man they considered to be a dangerous lunatic found. It was important that he wasn't. She hadn't moved to get him out of jail only for him to be thrown straight back in there.

Back upstairs she removed her jacket, wrinkling her nose as she caught the smell of it. It was there, almost imperceptible but infinitely irritating. She knew it was there and thus couldn't abide it, the smell of the labs. She'd like to have changed completely but it wasn't an option. She had another meeting imminently.

Beep-bip-beep-bip!

That came as a surprise, the holocom brought her up short as she sprayed perfume over herself, enough to drown the scent of the sterile labs. She glanced at the ID on the image. It was inconvenient, but she needed to take it.

Damn you, Coshi. On the other hand, at least it wasn't Rogan. That man really was turning insufferable since she'd made contact. "Domis," she called through the door. "Inform those who've already arrived that I will be with them in a moment. Offer them my sincerest apologies."

"At once Mistress."

She sighed. This better be important. "Answer call."

The holocom burst into life, bringing up a miniature 3D image of Johan Coshi on the table, his features transparent. He bowed, clutched his hat against his chest. "Ma'am," he said softly. "Greetings."

"I can't make small talk for long, Mister Coshi," she said abruptly. "You've caught me at a bad time. I assume you have something important for me?"

"You'd be right," he replied. "I'll be quick then. It's about the Eagle's Nest." Given his position as the director of that project, one in its own way just as important as what she'd just seen in the labs, she was unsurprised to say the least.

"You have updates?"

He nodded. "I know we agreed on a set date for completion…"

"Mister Coshi, you better not be about to tell me that there will be further delays. I do not wish to hear that.

"No, nothing of the sort," he said looking aghast. "Ma'am, I wanted to report we are ahead of schedule. Next week at the earliest for launch. I wanted to give you the news in person but unfortunately…"

She cut him off. "That's wonderful, Mister Coshi." She felt the smile grow across her face. "You've made me very happy. But why the sudden upturn in fortune?"

"Can't explain it ma'am. Just luck, I guess. Everything went right; we didn't have the setbacks we thought we might. And there was a good crew working on it." Damn right there was a good crew working on it for what they'd cost to hire. Still, credits well spent. "Still needs to be field tested of course, but everything is ready to go."

"You'll find a bonus in your next wage," she said. "As will everyone on your staff." She made a mental note to divert a million credits as means of reward. Finding the best people was sometimes so hard. You wanted to ensure they stayed yours when you did. "And inform them that there's more of the same for every further Nest that they produce."

Coshi's eyes widened. "You want more of them?"

"Of course. What's a queen without her castles?" she said. A sudden thought struck her, and she smiled. "One more thing, Mister Coshi. I'm sending Rocastle to join you. To observe and report on the field tests. Perhaps even be on board when it takes to the air for the first time. Do you think you can accommodate him for me?"

"For you, ma'am," he said. "Anything. I'll await him."

"Thank you again, Mister Coshi," she smiled. "You've done well. Farewell."

"Goodbye, ma'am."

As the image of him faded, she rubbed her hands together in glee. Things were starting to come together. She was glad she'd taken the call now. It made going into the imminent meeting ahead that little bit more enjoyable. If she could pull the next bit off, it'd be a very good day indeed.

Outside the meeting room, she paused, considering the two men waiting for her. What she knew of them and how they might react to the situation they found themselves in. It was perhaps ironic that they weren't that dissimilar if she thought about it, yet they probably considered themselves complete opposites.

Antony Montella was a man dominated entirely by credits and power, he got off on the thrills it gave him, how he could use it to further himself. He kept a low profile but cast a long shadow. Not unlike herself. He had a face like it was cut out of stone, rough and silent, ugly and dark haired. He was a short man, his dark hair slicked back against his scalp without a hint of grey even at his considerable age. His suit was exceptional, she approved. He looked so much more professional than Cyris. Whatever he needed to achieve his goal, he bought or arranged to be bought. If someone stood in his way, he took whatever actions needed to move them. He no doubt saw himself as an irresistible force of nature unable to be tamed. A man who was a risk. Going into partnership with him was not something she had taken lightly.

She'd thought it through. He had the men, he had influence and it was always nice to have someone around her who could be labelled as a ring leader if need be. Despite that low profile, he was getting more and more known as the months went by. Law enforcement were slow, but they weren't stupid. All efforts signalled her organisation remained largely unknown and that suited her. He was a calm man, a supposedly reasonable man.

John Cyris also liked the money and the power. Yet he didn't seem like the type completely dominated by it. He would be the more easily persuaded of the two. He had designs on hitting the top, he didn't want to be a king or a president, but he did want to step down on a society while not being a part of it. Unlike Montella, he had an ego the size of a kingdom or two, a shaven headed man with a cheerfully pleasant face. He looked like your average friendly uncle, not that she'd ever had one. Not many friendly faces in her family. No wonder he'd charmed dozens of people around the years into giving him credits, working for him, joining his organisation as a believer in his own brand of tripe.

Yes. This project would suit him. He looked the more interested of the two. He was smiling, chatting animatedly in one sided conversation to Montella. The muscle in the shorter man's jaw looked locked tight in a grimace. Another minute or two, and she'd make an entrance. An entrance she'd considered for a while now. How to make her first impression? How to lull them into a false sense of security? How to ensure they took her seriously enough to listen and yet at the same time underestimate her so she'd have room to manoeuvre around them. Domis was already in the room, stood politely to attention in his own imposing way. At least they were prompt. A shame her own good news had delayed her from doing the same.

Finally, she entered, clearing her throat as she walked in, giving them both the Coppinger smile. Sweet but with a hint of concealed menace. Just in case they felt like interrupting her. Montella was from Serran, Cyris from Premesoir, they might feel the urge to be mouthy about the wait. She wouldn't have been impressed had she been in their shoes.

"Gentlemen," she said. "My apologies. I'm sure you've both had the same problem sometime. I trust my associate has kept you comfortable in my absence." Domis chose that moment to crack his giant knuckles. A trifle unnecessary, she thought, but effective.

Cyris spoke up first. "It's of no matter to me."

"Nor I," Montella agreed.

Interesting, she mused. They didn't look comfortable with each other. Even now they kept shooting furtive glances, almost sizing each other up. Neither of them looked like they wanted to back down and show weakness in front of the other. That served her. She'd chosen these two to meet at the same time for a reason. If neither of them wanted to show weakness, they wouldn't be thinking quite as clearly, they wouldn't want to back down "Ey, business is business, am I right? That's the problem being on top. You might think you're the boss but you're still at the mercy of others. Someone screws you, sure, you can get rid of them, but it don't change you've been screwed, ey?"

"Interesting sentiments," Cyris said. "Are you honestly telling us that is common practice in your line of business? Getting screwed?" He couldn't hide the contempt in his voice.

Montella shrugged. "Some things you can't control. Sure, you can let some of it go, sometimes you need to make an example and whack a few heads. Sometimes it's just out of your hands. You never had to do that?"

Cyris didn't reply. She replied for him. "Exactly what I was coming to! Sometimes it's just out of your hands."

"Hey, some shit you just can't control," Montella said. "I mean, sometimes you're playing by the will of the Divines, am I right?"

"Potentially," Cyris mused.

"And it's funny you should mention Divines, Mr Montella," she said, sitting down across the table and crossing her legs. "Very funny indeed."

"Yeah? What's the joke?" He didn't look amused. "You're not building a church, are you?"

"Maybe, eventually. For the time being? Nothing like that. I'm engaging in a little enterprise and well, as much as it pains me to admit it, I can't do it alone." She let a little note of desperation creep into her voice. That wasn't entirely true. She COULD do it alone, but it would severely financially cripple her. Of course, that was moot. If it came off, it wouldn't be a problem, for the rewards would be infinite. If it failed, she'd likely not live to regret it.

Both men were criminals. Very large criminals, not physically but in their notoriety. What drove them to crime? Wealth? Greed? Ambition? Desire? It would be interesting to see if they went for it. Of course, if they didn't, Domis wouldn't be letting them leave the room alive. They'd be too much of a security risk. After all, crime was such a risky business and sometimes you lost.

In her own opinion, you'd have to be an idiot to turn down this arrangement. But of course, you could never accurately predict how people react when faced with the facts. However reasonable a case you might make, they would find some potential flaw and use it as an excuse to cite failure.

"I fail to see how we can help you in whatever you have in mind," Cyris said. "If the reports are to be believed, you have more wealth than both of us put together."

"You said it, Johnny," Montella agreed. "No offence, but I'm not seeing it either. What's the game?"

"There are some things that wealth cannot buy you," she said. "This has always been the case. Some things strike down both rich and poor alike. There is no changing that. We cannot change the fundamental rules of the world. No matter how much we might strive to leave our mark on the world, it is beyond us."

Neither of them commented on that. She hadn't expected them to. "I aim to change that."

Now that got a reaction. A cool disbelieving smirk played over Cyris' thin lips. Montella let out a bark of laughter.

"Okay, okay, I was expecting that," she said. "But please, gentlemen, hear me out. Don't make the mistake of assuming I'm insane. I assure you I'm quite sound of mind. And I know exactly how to do it."

The expression on John Cyris' face didn't change. He made a pyramid out of his fingers in front of him and waited. Montella didn't. "Okay, so you got some insane grand plan," he said. "What you need us for then? I mean, you got the means, you got the designs... Where do we figure into all of this?"

"I told you I cannot do it alone," she said. "I need allies. I have people I trust here, an inner circle. Loyal in their belief in me. Below them, there are people paid to be loyal and no more. I need more than that. Your people are yours. They're tied to you for a reason beyond pure credits. Mr Montella, your people are like your extended family. Blood binds you. Mr Cyris, your people share an idea with you. A simple belief. You gave them your philosophy and they bought into it."

Cyris nodded. "Freedom Triumphant is more than just a philosophy, Madam, it's an actuality. Through casting off the laws of society, we truly find who we are. When we are knocked down, stripped of everything we think we know, we find that we are free. That freedom always comes at a price though. People don't like change."

"Save trying to convert us, Johnny," Montella said. "What of it?"

She leaned forward in her seat. "Mr Cyris, I'm a great believer in what you preach. I'm not wanting to throw off the shackles of society. I want to bastardise the entire laws of nature. I propose a partnership. Pool our resources. Between us, what could stop us?"

It was Montella who gave the answer she'd been expecting them to produce. "Unisco?"

She scoffed at that. "I've already had several encounters with them over this. I had an agent... Him, actually," She pointed at Domis. "Observed at a tournament by one of them when he was collecting something for me. I had a recovery team wiped out by two of them on Carcaradis Island. One of my lieutenants was recently arrested by them.

I myself clashed with some of them, it was on the news, you might have seen it."

"Then you're walking a tightrope there," Cyris said. "They'll catch up with you sooner or later. They've been harassing me for years. Ever since they first arrested me."

"Hey, wasn't that the time you tried to escape in an aeroship and one of them came after you on a dragon?" Montella inquired. Cyris glowered at him. "Right in the grounds of your damn own home as well. Embarrassing!"

"They will be a problem," she said. "They have been a problem. But what sort of numbers do you imagine them to have? More than what we can put together? Law is an illusion. It only exists if the people allow it. Unisco agents die just the same as anyone else."

"If you can find them," Montella said. "They keep their identities pretty secret. That's the problem."

"And problems are meant to be overcome," she said. "Can you picture it, gentlemen. Our resources together. Our people. Our intelligence. My grand plan. What can stop us? Join with me for together we can be legion. We will be many. Join with me and I can give you something nobody else can."

"And what's that?" Cyris asked.

"The future," she replied. "A very long and very profitable future. Now, what do you say to that?"

It had precisely the sort of effect she had expected. To say both looked interested would have been an understatement.

Chapter Seven. Seeing It Coming.

*"Foresight of the future is a remarkably difficult skill to master.
Any idiot with half a brain can see what's coming. Making sense of it
however, is harder. Some people have the knack for it. Many don't.
Some can cut through the bullshit with ease. A lot can't. I've never
managed to work out the correlation between those with and those
without. As much as anything can be in this world, it does appear to be
truly random. Breeding, heritage and family... They don't come into it
as much as you might think. One of the true mysteries we have yet to
unlock..."*

From the writings of Bedoul Ghi-Zal, on precognition.

The eighth day of Summerpeak.

He chose Palawi.

It was a choice he would ultimately succeed or fail by, he'd
come to accept that. He also knew should he fall, he'd be universally
derided for his choice. On the surface, it looked like there would be no
contest. If Crush had been dwarfed by the cavern crusher, then Palawi
was like an ant stood next to an elephant. Just for a brief horrible
moment, he felt regret tugging at him. Maybe he should have gone with
Snooze. At least they'd be on a par in the same weight class. Too late
now. Come regret or rejoice, he'd made his choice.

It's all up to you, Pal. If you can't do it, we're out. Don't let me
down. Silently he pleaded with the hound and he could see Steven's
eyes narrowing as he studied the scene in front of him. If he were in his
opponent's shoes, he'd be overjoyed. Maybe, just maybe he could use
his overconfidence against him. What people always neglected to
mention with that cliché was those who found themselves
overconfident usually had a damn good reason for said overconfidence.
Steven couldn't see himself losing this bout, Scott could see that from
here and it looked a tough ask to prove him otherwise.

"Oh well," he said. "We've all got to lose sometimes, right?" He
grinned, seeing the look of confusion on his opponent's face as if
unsure what Scott was talking about. That suited him fine. A glance to
the side, he could see the video referee ready to commence the final
round of the bout. The decider. Mentally he tried to find his focus, he
needed to be at his absolute best here, if there was to be any hope of
victory. No distractions!

"Irrow, let us deal with this rapidly," Steven said slowly. Did he
detect a note of uncertainty in his opponent's voice? If he did, it was no

matter. To win, his prerogative was not for his opponent to slacken but for him to shine.

He couldn't contain his surprise as Irrow rose without warning, right foreleg ready to smash down onto an unsuspecting Palawi, a smirk on Steven's face and Scott let out an involuntary yelp and recoiled. What the fuck!

He said as much, blinking rapidly as he took in the scene ahead of him. Nothing. Irrow remained as it had a moment earlier, Palawi was looking at him like he was sick in the head. What the hells had just happened? The buzzer hadn't even gone yet, he knew what he'd seen, the smirk Steven wore was the same...

Then the buzzer did sound and Irrow rose high, right foreleg ready to smash down on Palawi, a Palawi who still had his back turned. Still reeling from the image, Scott found the coordination to give the mental command and the dog rolled away from the crushing claw. Claws tore through the ground like it was water, showering Palawi in dust and dirt.

Something was messed up here. Last thing he needed was his head going kerplooey in the middle of the most important bout he'd had since... Well, the last one. He tried to ignore it, gave Palawi a command to zap the thing. If it was metal, then maybe it conducted electricity. That'd make it a very short bout. He doubted he'd be that lucky, and as electricity arced from Palawi and crashed into Irrow, the static dancing along the illuminated metal skin, he was right. It didn't look like it had been ineffective. But at the same time, the cavern crusher remained standing, an amused look on its face. It ground its teeth together hard...

...Came in hard and fast at Palawi, pushing off from the ground with a great roar of effort, ready to bite down. They'd snap the pooch in two pieces easier than breathing...

... lingered for a moment, studied the dog and then lunged, pushing itself towards Palawi with a great roar of exertion and this time Scott was ready, Palawi hurled himself off the ground with a yip of effort and sprang off one of the giant legs for extra height. Level with the gap between the eyes, Scott gave the mental command and Palawi spun, tail glimmering with silver as he drove the appendage hard towards one of the giant eyes.

Briefly, he felt a sense of elation running through him, this could be a decisive blow. Irrow, curse the thing, twisted below Palawi and managed to take the blow between its eyes, metal meeting metal with an ear-splitting scrape. He winced, the brutal keeee-skreee ripping into his head but didn't let it distract him. If whatever was going on with his head wasn't distracting him, the sound wasn't going to.

Irrow's eyes looked unfocused for a moment by the blow and then it snapped to attention, raising both forelegs…

…Smashing one down to the ground, Palawi dodged only to be crushed by the second one coming down even harder…

… Scott didn't hesitate this time, Palawi leaped out the way of the first one, barely dodged the second one, he saw the uniblast coming a few precious seconds before it left the jaws of the cavern crusher, Palawi already jumping high into the air before the blast tore into the ground cutting a deep groove through the dirt. He could see the stone glowing red where the heat had touched it, almost melting it into magma.

For the first time, Steven looked worried, adrenaline surged through Scott as Palawi dropped another blast of electricity onto Irrow. This time it looked good, all five legs looking unsteady as Palawi landed on the cavern crusher's head and fired off another blast in quick succession.

… bringing one of the legs down onto its head, crushing Palawi to a bloody smudge…

Already Palawi leaped free, as one of Irrow's giant clawed legs came smashing down into its own head, there was an explosive clang and Scott saw the grooves left in the metal by the blow, could see cracks spreading from the point of origin like a spider's web as it staggered. It didn't fall but for a moment he thought it might, at least until the eyes refocused, looking plenty mad.

This time he didn't get an early warning of what was coming but he didn't need it, he saw the attack coming from a mile away with his eyes, not his mind. All five legs went crazy, Irrow trying desperately to smash Palawi into the ground beneath it, crazily trampling stone into dust-sized chunks as it flailed angrily. All brute force and no finesse. He could work with that. Still he needed to observe Palawi's movements, giving warning when one large chunk fell dangerously close to the hound but following the tantrum, the dog still stood relatively undamaged, if in possession of a newly dust-matted coat.

As Irrow scanned the area, trying to search out Palawi, Scott gave the command and the dog lunged, body enveloped in a swathe of static and hit the giant iron spider between its eyes, not stopping there but carrying on running up and up the huge face until he was back on the head again, ready to unleash a blast of electricity down into the shattered skull…

…Rearing up, thrown back…

… Not enough time for the blast, Palawi was hurled into the air as Irrow rose onto its back three legs and let out a huge roar from within its huge body that made Scott wince. The entire stadium felt like it was shaking under the sound. The electricity rose impotently into the air, fizzled out into nothing.

Shit! Scott saw it all twice, first in his mind and then with his eyes as Palawi flailed at the empty air, falling towards the open maw ready to swallow him. So near, yet so far... He'd nearly done it and he'd blown it. Those jaws were big, it had managed to swallow Palawi without biting down, that was the only thing that gave him some slight relief. If it had bitten down, it would be all over, and he'd be out. As it was...

He'd had a strategy earlier, one with Crush he'd need to deploy now. It wasn't quite the same, but it would have to do. Just for a moment it flitted across his mind and suddenly exploded through him like a river of perfect clarity. Scott's face lit up with a smile, he could still connect with Palawi despite the six inches of iron between them and that was all he needed.

Everything you have, pooch, he thought. Right now. Don't hold back.

It couldn't be armoured on the inside, surely. He could feel Palawi struggling for oxygen, he hoped there was enough to get do what needed to be done. Irrow looked uneasy, like it was struggling with indigestion. That more than anything gave him hope it was working. Steven looked worried, doubtless he could sense discomfort through the connection he shared with Irrow. The cavern crusher continued to struggle, wobbled unsteadily on its back three legs, scratched at its body with the two forelegs. A deep moan escaped its jaws, just for a moment as its mouth opened, Scott saw a glimmer of light deep inside.

Pal?

Nothing. He couldn't sense Palawi anymore and that sudden lack of a presence within him hurt, he almost bent over and retched.

No! No! Not like this!

All in silence of course, all the better to hear the suddenly audible cracking heard around the arena, followed by the sudden bellow of pain. He jerked his head up, glanced to Irrow who was suddenly clawing at its eyes. As it lowered the forelegs, Scott saw the cracks down the pupils, just before...

...Cutting and shredding, mangling naked flesh...

... He threw a hand in front of his face to shield himself from the debris, blood and glass raining down on him, shredding his arm. If he hadn't, it would have been his face. Somewhere ahead of him, he heard a giant thud drowning out a howl, his arm stung in the sun and slowly he lowered it from his eyes to the sound of panting.

Scott dared to look. Palawi sat there, tongue lolling out, fur covered in a sticky black substance he'd rather not think too deeply about. Behind him, Irrow lay defeated, two great holes where the eyes had been. Even if it could get back up, it wouldn't be able to see and Palawi would have two targets to fire electricity into.

It didn't matter, because as the crowd rose as one in an ocean of rapturous applause, the video referee announced the conclusion of the bout and Scott bent down to scoop the victorious Palawi high into the air, all the pain in his arm suddenly gone and right there, he felt on top of the world, like no challenge was too great for him to overcome.

Oh yes!

It was the first time Peter Jacobs had found himself truly surprised in a while as he exited the stadium, almost walking into a familiar redhead in a scruffy black dress and oversized belt combination. In the stadium, you didn't notice the heat as much. Out here, he suddenly felt the need to mop his brow. Which he did as he contemplated several sarcastic comments he could hurl at the girl.

"So," he said, mentally high fiving himself. Way to go Pete, that's the highlight of wit. "Stranger."

Jess turned, glared at him. Ah, he hadn't missed that. Not even in the slightest. He folded his thumbs into the waistband of his shorts and shot her a grin to counter her glare.

"Oh, it's you," she said. Her expression softened a little. "I thought you were Scott."

"No, you really didn't," Pete said. "I look nothing like Scott. We're different colouring for a start. And I'm taller. That'd be like me confusing you for someone who isn't a complete bitch." Ouch, he mentally congratulated himself. What a burn.

For a moment, he saw the look on her face and steadied himself for the tirade surely about to come his way. He'd had a moment of bravado and he was surely about to pay for it. One simply did not just talk to Jesseka Blake like that without serious reprisals.

They never came. One moment, she looked ready to cut loose and then her lip trembled. Apparently, surprise was more contagious than he'd been willing to believe before. She turned her head away and just for a moment, he felt bad. Really bad. Maybe he should apologise… He should but that'd be giving in. He wouldn't put it past her to be faking just to wring one out of him. Or, he could just act like a human being. He gritted his teeth and sighed. This was going to be painful. "Ah, I'm sorry Jess. Been a long few days. Nothing personal."

She didn't say anything, he frowned and strode to her. Her eyes were red, she looked tired, suddenly he felt worse than before.

"You don't look good," he said.

"Way to state the obvious," she said. Her voice lacked the usual snarl. He thought she looked vulnerable, small and very, very worried. "What's next?"

"How about I ask you what's up?" he asked. "I thought you'd left the island when you and Scott..." She stiffened at the name. "...Split up."

"I've not..." She rubbed at her eyes, he could see they were wet. "I think I made a horrible mistake."

Slowly he placed a hand on her shoulder and gave her a reassuring pat. "Well it's a bit late now, I think." That didn't sound reassuring, he quickly realised as she looked even worse than before. "Although I might be wrong. It's been known to happen. Come on, let's get you out of here. I'm sure you don't want people to see you like this. My room's pretty private."

He wasn't quite sure he was comfortable with the way she linked her arm into his as they left the stadium. Sure, it could be a neutral gesture. At the same time, he was glad Scott wasn't here to see it. Last thing he wanted was his best friend to do something stupid like see his ex and feel pity for her, going back to someone who'd been completely horrible to him.

Even if he was putting himself on the line by putting up with her. He cut a rough smile, weary but ready on his face. They might not like each other, but they did have some history together. They'd known each other for a decent amount of time. Long enough for him to be a shoulder to cry on. And it wasn't like Scott was going to find out. He'd be sure of that.

She glanced around his room and gave him a sad lopsided smile he returned with a heavy heart. Jess Blake should not look like that. He'd never seen her cry, he'd always thought she was like a Vazaran and just got more pissed off. "So, this is where you've been living?"

"Yep," he said. "Sure is."

"Smells like it." Her grin perked up a little and she folded her arms as she sat down on the edge of his bed.

"You know, I'm rapidly running out of sympathy if you're commenting on my personal hygiene," Pete said, sitting next to her, slid an arm round her and sighed. "Look it's not important. I don't know what you want me to tell you. I think Scott's moved on." He felt her stiffen at that. "He went with someone to that..."

He felt her anger flare up as she jerked away from him, glaring angrily. "Was it that little bitch Mia?"

Okay, no easy way to answer that… He shrugged. "Not sure." It sounded like a lie as it left his lips. "Might have been. Might have been someone else built like her." And looked like her, with similar hair, also called Mia. None of which he said aloud. "I don't think it was though. I never saw her up close."

Something which had been tugging at him ever since Scott had first mentioned the arguments popped to the forefront of his mind and he looked at her with sincerity in his expression. "It was a bit of a weird night. A weird spirit dancer guy tried to kidnap…" Mia… "… Someone. It was a messed-up night." He'd gotten into the news over that. Him and Scott and Mia and Wade and Harvey Rocastle all part of the same article. Scott had saved one as the background on his summoner screen, apparently proud of it. He wasn't sure why, it had made the two of them sound like they'd cocked up. Now, it felt like one of the last things in the world he wanted to bring up. "Jess, I talk to Scott, right? He said some stuff, you know. About Mia and…"

He swirled saliva around in his mouth, wondering how to word it. She glared at him and he decided to come out with it. "Okay so why is it you went into a jealous rage every time he even went near her? I've never seen you do that before with anyone else. And even then, is Scott worth it? I mean, I'm at least twice as good looking as he is, and he seems to be having to beat the ladies off with a stick."

She said nothing, just tried to bore him through with the intensity of her stare, dulled by the smudged black around her eyes. He stared back. Nothing he wasn't familiar with. She wasn't going to get to him.

"I don't like her," she said. "Mia Arnholt, the little harlot has a bit of a reputation on the spirit dancing circuit."

Something twigged in Pete's memory. "Hey, that isn't why Rocastle wanted to kidnap her, is it?"

Jess snorted. "Rocastle is a fucking freak. All cock and no balls. Don't even think he leans towards women. Whatever he wanted her for, it wasn't to fuck her." It didn't surprise him, he'd already gotten that impression from the rooftop.

"What sort of reputation?" he asked. "I thought you were all sleazy as hells anyway?"

She ignored him. "Okay so she slept with a bunch of guys on the circuit."

"Yeah. Your point is?" Pete wasn't impressed. He'd expected a little more. That alone wasn't quite enough for stupidly irrational jealousy

"Couple of them weren't single."

Ah, that might explain it. He smiled and said as much. "So, you were worried she might steal Scott from you?"

Jess rose up to her full height, putting his eyes level with her breasts and narrowed her gaze at him. "No. I was worried Scott would fall for her I'm-such-an-innocent-little-cock-tease act. I mean, we'd had problems before…"

"Yeah you did a great job of trying to hide it," Pete said. "I only got the impression it was trouble in paradise once or twice a week. Just let me get this straight. You were worried she'd steal him from you, so you broke up with him. I love the way you think."

"Well what was the point?" Jess said with real anger in her voice. "He wasn't making things easy, we'd been fighting a lot, it wasn't going anywhere. He loved spirit calling more than he did me. I'm not going to be second fiddle to a damn sport!"

"Yeah, you're better than that," Pete replied. "And don't get me wrong, I think one day he might regret what happened between the two of you. But…" He reached out, put a hand on her arm and fished around for the right way to phrase it. "But, Jess, that day isn't today. It probably isn't going to be any time soon. You can do better than Scott. Don't get me wrong, I love the guy like a brother, but he annoys the hells out of me sometimes."

She raised an eyebrow quizzically and smiled at him, the sort of smile he wasn't used to seeing her give. It was almost friendly. When she'd walked in, she'd looked haggard and tired, like the world was wearing her down. Now, he could see reassurance in her eyes. She sat down, rested a hand on his.

"It's nice of you to say," she said. "Of course, you might just not want me back near your friend. I was never very nice to you, was I?"

"No, you were a complete bitch. And here I am being nice to you. What does that say about me?"

"You lack judgement skills," she murmured, ignoring the bitch comment. She glanced into his eyes, intensity still there but different. Her pupils were dilating, cheeks flushed with colour. "Or I've been reading you wrong for a long time."

"I think you might very well have been," he said. "Hey, we all make mis…"

Whatever he might have been about to say was lost as her lips met his, taking him by surprise as slowly he returned the gesture. She tasted like strawberries, he felt the twist of arousal in his stomach. Somewhere at the back of his mind, a warning blared out how wrong this was, and he wanted to listen to it. He really did. He could taste her as he crushed his mouth down on hers, her fingers fumbling for the clasp on his belt as he pushed her down onto the bed, one hand pulling up the hem of her dress to her waist. She wasn't wearing anything underneath.

By the time he'd gotten his shorts down his legs, he was rock hard and ready, their lips still in tandem as he teased her playfully, felt her body sense with anticipation. Even amidst ecstasy, he caught the look of exasperation and he sped up, entering her slowly at first and then gradually more vigorously. She was warm and wet, every motion bringing a strangled cry of pleasure as they became little more than a frenzy of pure animal emotion.

Amidst it all, the absurdity of the situation never crossed his mind, instead the moment caught up with him and all he could think of was her, in a way he never had before.

"Unbelievable."

Derenko sounded annoyed and Lysa Montgomery couldn't blame him. They'd met, the six of them in one of the cafes for an informal meeting. Her, Derenko, Fank Aldiss, Anne Sullivan, Jacques Leclerc and Al Noorland. No doubt it looked a strange meeting but hey, it was turning into that sort of tournament. Anywhere else, it might have looked even stranger for many recognisable figures to congregate. Here, they might just get away with it.

"I'm afraid that it isn't so," Leclerc said. "Wolf Squadron was wiped out." His knuckles went white as he gripped the table. His allegiances to the squadron were well known, he'd before he'd transferring to field duty. A lot of field agents were qualified to fly cross-kingdom aeroships, it didn't make him special. Warships were a different matter though. Only the best of the best found themselves behind the controls of those. Lysa had heard rumours that he bore the squadron's insignia tattooed on his back. Whether it was true or not, she couldn't say. "Could you back me on this, Alvin?"

"It's true," Noorland said. "I saw the reports. The transcripts of the radio transmissions from Wolfmeyer and his squad. They were wiped out, Rocastle vanishes into the sunset."

"This is worrying," Aldiss said. "I mean; do we think this is random?"

"I don't believe in coincidence," Derenko replied. "I don't think anyone else here does. Reports say it was the Vazaran Suns. I'm already making a case to the director we investigate this further. This sort of behaviour cannot be allowed to stand."

"Do you seek revenge or justice," Anne inquired mildly. "Wiping out the Suns will not solve the problem here. It will cause more problems than it solves, if anything. They do keep some semblance of order in Vazara. Without them, it'd be war in the streets."

"That's true," Lysa said. "I recently spent some time there. It's not uncommon to see a couple of Sun units in every city. They're probably the biggest employer in the kingdom. Going to war with them would be a messy affair. If we got rid of them, Nwakili would struggle to keep the same order on his lonesome."

"What we do," Derenko said. "Is a messy business. Sometimes it isn't, but always remember, we are required to make hard decisions."

"And sometimes," Leclerc added. "We have to make smart ones. I agree with Anne, I don't think it's a fight we can win. And the negative publicity would be a nightmare."

"And we'd be in trouble if we tied up resources dealing with them," Aldiss said. "I'd recommend caution. Maybe negotiate with them. See if we can make a deal with them to give up whoever paid them for the attack."

"Because they're so likely to be openly honest and welcoming with that information?" Noorland asked sarcastically.

"You can ask nicely, you know," Anne said. "At least do that before immediately going for Plan B. They might cooperate."

"With the greatest of respect, Anne," Derenko said. "Sometimes I think you don't have the stomach for this job."

Anne said nothing, just smiled at him, a tight little smile that started at and finished with her mouth. "Isn't it funny," Lysa said. "Whenever someone uses the words with the greatest respect, they're about to show you as little as possible." It was Derenko's turn to smile, though there was no joy in it. "Vassily," Anne said. "I don't need a stomach for my job, I prefer to use my brain. It makes things so much easier, I suggest you try it sometimes."

Lysa smirked at that. Noorland and Leclerc joined her, both chuckling under their breath.

"For the very least, I think we should try negotiation first," Leclerc said. "I mean, not all our HAX's went down."

Aldiss blinked at that. "Excuse me?"

"He's right," Noorland said. "We got the satellite imagery for the entire area during the engagement, we have radar readouts, thermal imagery and the telemetrics from those that did go down. Captain Wolfmeyer did manage to transmit before he was shot down. We've even considered sending an investigative team out to study the wreckages, but the battle took place over fifty acres of ocean and it might be a while before we get them all found. But the fact of the matter is, there's two HAX's unaccounted for. Ross Navarro and Alexandra Nkolou. They weren't shot down, they just vanished into thin air."

"There were reports of a rider with a vos lak entering the field of play," Leclerc added. "Any of you know anything about them?"

"They're rare," Lysa said. "I've not seen one for a long time."

"They're extinct, aren't they?" Noorland asked. "That was my impression. It's not really my field of expertise."

"I suppose," Anne offered. "You'd probably be better asking Wade."

"Shame he's in a medical coma," Derenko said. "Or we would."

"I knew a guy who had one," Aldiss said. "But I doubt it's him. He has kinda a solid alibi."

"Yeah?" Noorland asked, sounding more than a little offhand. "You sure? Because that'd make things easier."

"Not unless he's gone massively off the rails. Plus, he used to be one of us."

"Am I the only one not missing the point here?" Anne asked. "These two HAX's… How'd they even vanish anyway? Our ships aren't fitted with cloaking devices, right?"

"Some are," Leclerc said. "These weren't. Doesn't mean something else wasn't."

"That'd be my guess," Noorland said. "We have fourteen odd enemy ships, six HAX's on screen and one vos lak which shows up as a large unidentified object. Nothing else. Not on our radar, not on our thermals, nothing."

"So, if something grabbed them, it was something we couldn't see," Derenko said.

"An old interceptor, perhaps?" Aldiss asked. "Do they even still make those?"

"Not wholesale," Lysa said. "I wonder if the Suns have one."

"It's more a pirate thing than a mercenary thing," Noorland replied. "But's it's not impossible."

"It'd definitely be something worth checking out though, I think," Anne said. "There you go, Vassily, something for you to bring to the director." She picked up her cup and drained the contents. It tasted lukewarmly sweet against her taste buds. "Looks like you might get your action against the Suns after all."

"I don't want this," Derenko said. "But I think it is necessary. We can't let this action stand. We're supposed to have a truce with the Suns."

That was news to Lysa. "What?!"

"Yeah. They don't go after us; we don't go after them unless they dip their hands in the dirt. Then they're asking for it."

"Didn't Nick and Dave kill some Suns not long back?" Noorland asked. "Maybe it's a revenge killing."

Derenko didn't look convinced. "Maybe. Maybe not. There's easier ways for revenge."

Unbelievable.

He had an in after wondering about how best to interrogate Darren Maddley. The trick was getting information from someone without them realising they were being interrogated. Of course, if he showed up and started small talk, they'd work out something was up, unless the witness was a congenital idiot. And they tended not to make the best people to ask.

In this instance, he had Sharon to thank for the excuse. She'd told him about the apology and Nick had jumped on it. It was only polite, he'd said, to go and thank him in person. She'd taken a bit of bringing around but that was then, and this was now. They'd found themselves outside his room and mentally he was congratulating himself on his ingenuity as he rapped on the door, grinning at Sharon.

"Still don't see why you're making such a big deal about this," she said, a little sulkier than he found attractive.

"Hey, it's only polite," Nick said. "You'd appreciate it as well, wouldn't you?"

"I wouldn't have started an argument with someone if they beat me on the battlefield."

"That's because you're unbeatable," he quipped. She blushed, punched him lightly on the arm. He could have caught her blow before it met him but that would have led to more questions he didn't have answers to.

"I'm not though," she said. "Stop spreading that rumour about me... Hey you hear about Wade?"

"Course I heard about Wade," Nick said. I was there when he got injured, he added silently. "I went to see him earlier. Still in a medical coma. They were sorting out his burns when I went up."

"Poor bastard," she said, just as the door opened and Darren Maddley peered out through a crack between rim and door. He didn't look a well man, Nick had to admit. Small wonder. Last time he'd seen him, he'd been about to piss himself with fear.

"Who is it?" he asked. He didn't sound well either.

"Darren, it's Sharon Arventino," Sharon said. Nick hid a snort. Not like he doesn't recognise you, love, given the argument you had. "Can we come in?"

The door slammed shut, he caught the sound of chains being removed and that puzzled him. Apparently, this hotel was more security-conscious than his own. Eventually it opened all the way and Maddley stood there, eyes a bloodshot. His hair looked wild, he smelled like he hadn't taken a shower for a while. Sweat and fear, as well as something probably overpriced from the minibar.

"What do you want?" he asked, his voice slurred.

"Just wanted to..." Sharon started to say, before halting, running an eye over him. A manicured brow furrowed as if she was trying to work something out. Nick had already known what to expect. Maddley's part in the whole thing was thankfully being downplayed by the media. Their priority had been the destruction of the ICCC building, the ineptitude of Unisco agents and the injury of Wade Wallerington. Darren Maddley had been mentioned only once briefly towards the end of the article. No surprise Sharon had missed it. He might have, had he not been looking for it. "What happened to you?"

"Don't want to talk about it," he said. "What do you want?!" This time it came out bluntly and Nick wondered if maybe he'd overreached with his cunning genius. He'd gotten them in, it wouldn't be any good if Darren refused to talk to them.

"I wanted to thank you for the apology," Sharon said. "It takes a man to realise when they're in the wrong and say sorry. Truly. I want to look you in the eyes and offer you my respect. Sometimes it's not enough to be a great spirit caller. Sometimes it's better to be a good person as well. Your father would be proud of you."

For a moment, he thought Darren was going to slam the door in their faces again. Yet Nick was to be surprised. "It's no problem," he said. "I was out of order. I didn't want my family legacy tarnished I'm the last Maddley. I nearly died the other day, it got me thinking."

Nick seized his chance. "You nearly died? Do tell."

He nodded. "Some crazy woman on a... Think it was called a taccaridon, I've only seen pictures of them...

"They're extinct, aren't they?" Sharon interrupted. Nick cursed silently, although he had to agree he had heard the same thing. Darren glared at her.

"Apparently not." He couldn't hide the sarcasm. Nick couldn't blame him. He'd seen the spirit in question and it did look like a taccaridon. "But yeah, this woman, she was insane. She wanted to recruit me for some quest. Some babble about a new world and how she was going to rule it. Wanted me to be part of her chosen people or something."

"Takes all sorts, don't it?" Sharon smiled. "What did you say?"

"Given she attacked me," Darren said. "What do you think? Told her where to shove it, didn't I? I know when I'm being manipulated. She was taking advantage of my mood to get me to go over. I don't play for anyone's tune."

"She didn't give you her name, did she?" Nick asked, realising it might be too much to hope for.

"Nah, but she looked a bit important. I got the impression she was wealthy. But the same time, I think she was quite disdainful about what's going on here. It was weird."

At the very least, he had some stuff to report. They'd stuck around another fifteen minutes, Darren had invited them into a room that had probably been nice until recently. For the moment, it looked like housekeeping hadn't been let in for a while. They'd made small talk, Darren had mainly asked Sharon what she could remember about the famous bout she'd waged against his father and she'd been diplomatic over it. He'd tried to prise more out of him about his attacker but other than a vague description of long brown hair, about mid-forties and expensive clothes, which was marginally more than he'd managed to pass on himself, he'd been disappointed.

Still as they left, he couldn't help feeling he might have done more. They were further than they were at the start, but something was going on here that worried him. He didn't have all the pieces. But as they came together, he got the feeling it wouldn't be good news.

Fortunately, it wouldn't be his problem for the time being. He put an arm around Sharon's shoulder and grinned. Off the clock for the next few weeks. So why did he feel so unsettled?

Chapter Eight. Secrets.

"If you have a price, then you're willing to do a deal. Simple business economics. I find however, you should always make sure the price and product match up. Otherwise you're going to end up with a very unhappy consumer. And an unhappy consumer is one who won't come back. If they don't come back, can't take their credits from them. That is the simplest truth of them all."

Christian Coppinger in his book, Credits! Truth and Myths.

The eighth day of Summerpeak.

Having medical webbing wrapped around your arm, Scott could testify, was not a pleasant experience. The stuff, administered by a sour faced medic in a sweat soaked white uniform, clung tight to the cuts across his arms, already closing them shut, sealing them with its regenerative qualities. He knew the discomfort would last a few minutes longer. It wasn't the first time he'd been patched up with the stuff, likely wouldn't be the last either.

He couldn't abide the smell in the tent either, a potent mix of the chemical and the biological. Despite the cooling air, the Vazaran medic had managed to sweat profusely, the smell getting to him. He tried to smile it out, make out it wasn't bothering he could ignore the constriction in his arm, but it was a losing battle. Slowly his grin faded, replaced by the grimace of pain. The adrenaline of his victory was slowly trickling from his system leaving the remnants behind, painful and confusing.

As much as he'd relished the final moments of his bout, he had questions he wasn't sure how he could answer. If he approached it logically, then he'd been able to see things before they'd happened. Every movement Irrow had thrown against Palawi, he'd seen it and countered it without so much as breaking a sweat. Before Palawi had been swallowed, they had gotten through the round without taking a hit. Even after being swallowed, the most the pooch had suffered was being drenched in what passed for cavern crusher blood. Somehow, he doubted that was a pleasant experience but at the same time, it was better than being beaten, crushed, stomped, eaten, any of the truly bad choices.

He glanced around, closed his eyes to try and cut out any sort of distractions. The medic wasn't paying him any sort of attention now, he had the chance for some scant privacy. In the heat of the moment, it had come to him, beyond his control and now he had no idea how to do it again. For several moments, he sat there, his mind wandering. About the only thing that came to him were thoughts about who he might face in the next round. He tried to blot them out. What had he been doing when they'd come to him before?

Okay, he'd been involved in the bout. He'd been heavily focused on victory… Maybe it was a connection with one of his spirits. Maybe Palawi had developed pre-cognition and he'd been getting a loopback from the dog. Maybe. It was, in theory, likely. A lot of things were possible in theory. At the same time, reality often didn't match the possibility. It sounded absurd but there was a miniscule chance it might be the case.

Or maybe, more likely, it was him who had done it. But how? It felt like the most important question he might ever ask and even thinking it inside the confines of his head was enough to send echoes rippling to the corners of his mind. How. A small word but behind it, there was enough mystery to be getting on with. If he could do something like that, then why had he never done it before? There were plenty of times when it would have benefited him…

Except he had. He remembered that dream all too well. That had turned out to be sort of true, an omen that he hadn't ignored and thus been rewarded for. At the same time though, that had been a vague dream. These had been crystal clear images that had benefited the situation at hand. Every attack Irrow had thrown at Palawi he'd been able to react to.

Wasn't that cheating? That question hung in his mind and he hesitated. Whether it truly was or not, he didn't think so. It wasn't something he'd planned to do; he wasn't even sure he could do it again if the situation required it. Therefore, not cheating. It felt a little hollow as he repeated the words in his head.

One final effort to recreate it, one final failure and he got to his feet, tottered on the spot for a moment and then bent over double and spewed the contents of his stomach.

Pete felt lousy.

Or at least he should have. He didn't feel it physically, his body felt pretty good considering. Weary, taut from the preceding actions but still he felt satisfied. Mentally was quite another matter. Seeing Jess's arm draped across his chest, her head in the crook of his arm wasn't something he thought he'd get used to. Maybe he wouldn't have to. On the other hand, now he'd shot several loads into her and the clarity was returning to his mind, he had questions. Only the thought he might not like the answers had stopped him from voicing them. He wasn't even sure if she was awake or not. He could see her back gently rising and falling as she breathed, her eyes not open. Did she just not like to talk post sex or…

Scott would have known.

Oh Scott… Somehow, he had a feeling his friend might be… Well if not okay with it, he might not make a big thing about it. After all, he and Jess had broken up. It had been pretty messy the way he'd read into it. Really messy. The sort of mess which meant he didn't want to be suddenly in the firing line.

Yet at the same time, she knew what she was doing between the sheets. It was undoubtedly the best he'd had for a while, perhaps in his top five of all time. Seeing her like this was an experience, he'd never seen her look so at peace with herself. With her eyes closed and her gentle breathing, she looked so small and innocent.

Part of him felt fucking brilliant. The other half wanted to run into a corner and groan. Nothing about this felt a brilliant idea now Yet back when it had been happening, he couldn't have gotten enough of it. Way to go Pete, think with your crotch, look where it gets you.

He must have stiffened at that thought, for she brought her head up to look him through sleepy eyes, stifling a yawn.

"Oh, hey," she said. "Thought you were asleep."

"Same," he said. She furrowed a brow at that.

"You thought you were asleep?" she asked before grinning. "I know, I know. So…"

By the look on her face, Pete would have sworn she was just as uncomfortable as he was. Maybe she hadn't planned it. Not that he'd think her capable of planning something like this. That hadn't occurred to him until right now.

"So…" he said, genuinely lost for words. If there was anything he could say to break the ice, he wasn't sure what. "That was… Nice, I think."

Yeah, that wasn't it. He flinched visibly, more so as she focused her eyes at him, colour flushing into her cheeks. Not in a good way either. He'd seen that face before, it usually meant one thing.

"Nice?" she asked incredulously. "That was nice?!"

"Well I enjoyed it," he said, his cheeks flushing. "You were pretty good. I hope you got something out of it." Her expression was a picture and he genuinely didn't know how he could keep looking her in the eyes. "Yeah, I'm not going to bullshit around the truth here. I'm feeling a little uncomfortable."

"Why?" she asked, wriggling up closer to him. He could feel she was still naked under the sheets. Somewhere during the whole thing, she'd lost her dress. Despite what they'd just done, he wasn't sure he'd be able to bring himself to sneak a look when she got up. Some things you didn't want to see. Suffice to say if they'd ever been friends, they were no longer.

"Gee, why do you think?" he said, a lot more abrupt than he'd expected it to come out. "Which part of what we just did do you think makes me feel uncomfortable? Was it the first, second or third time?"

"It might have been the fourth," she said, grinning at him. "Got to say, you've got more endurance than Scott…"

"Yeah you just killed any chance of round five," Pete said. "That really makes me in the mood for it, I got to say. Being compared to my best friend in bed."

"Why? You measure up a lot better." She winked at him and snaked a hand across his body, toying with him. "A lot better. Think I might be walking funny the rest of the day."

Nice! He smirked sardonically. "What can I say? I'm a blessed man. Some guys get length; some guys get girth. I got it both. Gilgarus loves me."

"I think Gilgarus has more on his celestial mind than the size of your cock," she said dryly. "Me on the other hand…"

"Hmmm…" Pete said, suddenly not quite able to suppress a grin. "I never had you down as a nympho."

"Nah, I like fucking," she said, her hand teasing him to hardness. He tried to control his breathing, finding it harder by the second. Her hands were so soft. "Really, I do."

"That why you played me?" he asked breezily, felt her hand stop at his words, fingers still around him but not moving. Maybe having this conversation while she had her hand on his cock wasn't the best idea.

"What?" She looked confused, more than a little insulted and he got the feeling it wouldn't take long for her to catch on. "You think I planned this?" Anger was creeping into her voice. He wondered if he could yank himself free of her grip before she got it into her head to start squeezing.

"That thought had crossed my mind," he said lightly, trying to roll away from her. Maybe he could make a break for the door. And go where exactly? This was his room. Running naked into the corridor wouldn't be the best idea he'd ever had. "I mean; you can't stand me…"

"Yeah and now you're reminding me why," she said. The tiniest amount of pressure started to give on his cock and he tried to bear it without flinching. "Just for the record, Pete, don't think you're a Divines gift to women and I'd go to all this effort to try and entrap you."

The tiniest flicker of affront crossed his mind and he glared at her. "Not the reaction I was expecting. You seemed keen on it, you initiated it. Can't blame you really." His glare faded, and he returned her wink from a few moments ago.

"Can you be any more self-absorbed?"

"I think I could," he said. She'd stopped squeezing, thankfully. She hadn't resumed other activities though unfortunately. He leaned his arms back behind his head, tried to make himself comfortable. "So, it just sort of happened then?"

"I think the correct term," she said. "Is taking advantage of a situation." She saw his face and grinned. "No, not like that. I'm not about to shout rape. I was low, you were quite kind, for you and I just thought why not. You didn't exactly say no, did you?"

"I couldn't. My mouth was busy." He wasn't exactly without charm and he turned it on, grinning at her. "I'm glad it was." He blew out his cheek and sighed. "But you know what? I can't help but wonder where we go from here?"

"We?" She sounded incredulous. "There is no we, Pete. Don't ever forget that." She threw the covers back, he did the gentlemanly thing and averted his eyes. He could hear her getting dressed. "This was a onetime thing, I'm sorry to say."

"That bad huh?" he asked. She finished adjusting the straps of her dress and he met her eyes. "Kinda adds credence to my 'you planned this whole thing' theory' doesn't it?"

"Well I didn't," she said. "Pete, there's a thousand reasons why we wouldn't work. Scott and I weren't really... We didn't work, okay. You'd have to be blind not to realise. You and I would be even worse together. Give us a month and we'd be throwing punches at each other. And I don't want to put you on your ass. Besides, do you even want to date me?"

He couldn't lie when she put it like that. "No offence but no, not really. Like you said, we'd grate each other too much. You think this sounds like the quitter's way out?"

She shrugged. "It's not quitting if you never started. It's avoiding it. And plus, if we did start something, it'd be a bit awkward around Scott, right?"

Ah... She'd brought it up. "I wouldn't mind keeping it quiet actually," he said slowly. "You know; he might take it the wrong way."

"Or he might rib you for getting his sloppy seconds," she said. No part of the smile as she said those words looked real. "He can't say anything to you about it. He and I are finished. I was missing him earlier, I wanted him back, and part of me still does I think, but I've got to remember that it wasn't always good. A lot of it wasn't."

Pete nodded. "You know; I don't think of you as sloppy seconds."

"That's sweet of you to say, but you know how Scott's mind works. It starts at the bottom and goes a little deeper every time he opens his mouth."

"That's true," Pete replied, relief going through him. She was right, he hadn't technically done wrong, but you couldn't always work out the way people were going to react in any given situation and this was one of those. Scott's mind did work in a funny way; she was right about that. Things any normal person might find offensive, he laughed at and stuff the same person might brush off, he had the potential to get in a state about. He hadn't done it much since they'd gotten to the island, but it remained beneath the surface.

"You know…" She'd gotten her shoes on now, her eyes meeting his with a mixture of sadness and relief. "If I'd seen this Peter Jacobs more often, our travels together might have been more pleasant. Bye, Pete. I'm sure we'll see each other again someday. Until then, enjoy. Good luck in the tournament."

And with that, she was gone, the door slamming shut behind her.

The meeting had finished, and Anne had originally planned to walk out with Lysa. Yet like all plans, it had been subject to failure at the first part of human interaction. Lysa had made some excuses about last minute practice she needed to engage in, Anne hadn't detected anything in her emotions beyond a sense of overwhelming apology that wasn't fake, at least in her opinion.

She'd done what any friend would have, smiled and said it was fine. If Lysa had other things to do, then that was fine with her. Anne would find something else to do. They'd missed the Steven Silver bout; it had been on in the background of the bar, but she hadn't been paying attention. She knew he'd lost but that was about the full extent. Maybe she'd try and track down the highlights package, see if she could see what had gone wrong for him. She knew of Steven Silver and he wasn't a pushover. Irrow on its own was a formidable opponent. His conqueror must be a fierce competitor.

For a while she wandered the promenades. From the night the people had started to arrive on the island, the sideshow attractions and vendors once so prominent were slowly starting to fade. Still people milled but the marvellous was starting to become mundane, it would appear.

A shame, for wonder came in many forms, yet it appeared only that which became spectacle drew on the hearts and minds of those who could appreciate it. For many minutes, she strode the streets until she found herself at the Clinton Abedi Training Complex. She'd been by a few times, never entered. She'd met Clinton Abedi in the past and had been impressed with the force of nature he'd been. A Vazaran spirit caller turned politician who had fallen foul of the Vazaran Suns for openly condemning their acts. He'd called them a blight on the sands and made every effort to get them outlawed.

It had been an act of defiance which had ultimately cost him his life, but he'd made his point. Had he not made the sacrifice, the Vazaran Suns might be running the kingdom by now. At least with Nwakili in charge, he wasn't going to take any shit from them. It was good to see even though you might be gone, you still got recognition in some small way. Would Abedi have liked it? She couldn't say. She hoped he would have. He'd given his life for his beliefs. No doubt they'd thought they were honouring him by naming this for him. Maybe he would've hated it.

She'd like a building named after her. The Annabeth Sullivan something for something-something. That'd be awesome. She pushed the door open, grinned at the thought. Was too long since she'd had the chance to practice her technique. Her crystals were getting a little too dusty for her liking Besides, she had a good feeling about it. Somewhere beyond the doors, she could feel the tug of a familiar mind.

Him.

She'd have laughed were it not so unexpected. He hadn't noticed she was there yet, his back to her and an anklo out in front firing sharp leaves at targets. They'd really put their all into developing this centre, a state-of-the-art place for callers to work on techniques in a controlled environment. She'd always felt that a bit of a misnomer. You couldn't have controlled environments where spirits were throwing around attacks. The best you could do would be put in safeguards and hope for the best. Wade had told her the story of that boat ride he'd taken over here, how one of them had failed and he'd nearly been hit by an unconscious gytrash. Even now as she watched him with his spirit, she could see those leaves were capable of cutting an opponent in half with a clean hit. Without shielding and thick walls, a miss could smash through the building and ruin someone's day.

Still, Theobald Jameson looked like he knew what he was doing. He'd beaten the boss's kid to go onto the next round, but he was keeping his eye in. He wasn't resting on his laurels. Training hard to stay sharp. She came to a halt, had to steady herself in surprise as she watched him. For once, she couldn't sense naked anger in him. That was new. This time, it was more controlled aggression. Focused. Useful. He'd listened to what she'd said.

Somehow that pleased her. It was a feeling she couldn't explain, a little surge of warmth deep in her stomach. He'd listened to her. She'd never fancied herself as much of a teacher before but then again, she'd gotten the impression Theo never fancied himself as much of a student. He'd seemed like the sort who'd take a dozen kicks until he worked out how to stop it on his own, rather than be told after the first one. Stubborn. Really stubborn. Never backing down. Never admitting defeat.

If she was honest, she found that an attractive quality. What did that say about her? She liked people who stuck to their convictions.

Why had he agreed to let her give him some pointers? It wasn't something he'd been willing to share with her. She'd not been able to get an answer off his emotions, for empathic abilities only went so far, or maybe she didn't want to know the answer. Sometimes things had a way of working out. He'd been here practicing. She'd been stuck for something to do. They'd been drawn together. It was unlikely they'd be friends. They'd never associate in the same circles. She wasn't even sure if he did have friends. And the strange thing about that was he seemed happy with that.

"Ms Sullivan," he said without turning around. "Are you going to stand there all day?" She stiffened. How'd he known she was there? She made a habit of being stealthy. His emotions didn't change one bit. Part of her was disappointed by that. He could at least be happy to see her. "Or are you going to come over here and show me what you're capable of."

This time his aura twitched, and she smiled, pulling out her summoner as she strode forward. He turned to greet her, the corners of his mouth shifting as if he wanted to smile but couldn't force the expression out.

"I should be saying that to you," she said. "How about you show me what you're capable of instead."

"Standard bout?"

"How about we make things interesting?" she smiled. He caught her expression for a moment, then looked away.

The tenth day of Summerpeak.

The breakthrough had come. Sinkins was there, as were Domis and Rocastle, the four of them studying the man sat in front of her. He didn't look well; he had clearly suffered for some time. Dark skinned, his hair long and unkempt he stared back at her with eyes far too bright. They were mismatched, one brown and one a brilliant electric blue. His clothes were stained and torn, the oldest she'd ever seen. His jacket was missing a sleeve and she could see his toes through the left of his mismatched shoes. Several months-worth of beard marked his face, his entire body shook every time he moved.

His voice sounded hoarse, yet it rang with the faintest lingering traces of authority, a rich accent whose origin eluded her. The call had come in not long after her meeting with Cyris and Montella, one of her operatives had managed to trace the payment Jeremiah Blut had made regarding his inquiry to the Kjarn. That operative had been heavily rewarded for bringing the destitute before her. If he'd been paid well for the information, he looked to have squandered it. Yet for all the grime and filth that had accumulated about him, there was something she couldn't quite place.

"Your name," she said. He stiffened and didn't reply, yet still stared at her like he could see through her. "What is it?"

Still no answer. She resisted the urge to order Domis to slap him around until it loosened his tongue. As pleasant as it might be, she doubted it'd make him chattier. He looked like he was made of stern stuff. To survive on the streets of Xandervool, one of the more unsavoury cities in Canterage meant he had something about him.

Time to try a different tactic. If the stick wouldn't work, then perhaps he'd bite down on the carrot. He looked gaunt enough to eat a field full of them.

"If you don't want to talk," she said. "Then don't. That's your choice. But it's all I wanted to do. Nothing more at first. Are you hungry? You look hungry."

Still no reply. He hadn't even blinked as she'd observed him.

"Strong silent type, huh?" Rocastle said. Speaking of people whom she wouldn't mind seeing Domis slap around, she thought with a small smile. That was something long overdue. Again, she held the order against her tongue. "See plenty of those around here. But they're never usually that…" He wrinkled his nose as if searching around for the right term. She knew exactly the word he wanted to use. But he wouldn't. Rocastle had a thing about him, he'd never use a basic word when a more cutting one would suffice. He dug under people's skin that way. "Odorous, I must say."

The smile that broke across the dark-skinned man's face might once have been majestic, but now the teeth had yellowed and broken, his lips black and cracked inside. She shuddered inwardly with revulsion, her stomach twisting. If he noticed her discomfort, he didn't comment on it, but more words did come her way.

What was that accent?

"You'll have to forgive my appearances of dishevelment," he said. "Times have been hard, and I am perhaps not as formidable as once I might have been." He didn't sound like your average street bum. And given what information he might have, she somehow hadn't expected him to. "But, my dear ponce, never mistake the surface as a true reflection of what lies below."

Rocastle bristled at that. "Scratch your surface, honey, I think I'd have to spend a week cleaning my fingernails."

"Domis," she said. "Please remove Mr Rocastle from the room." She'd grown tired of his presence; she didn't want him aggravating their guest. Domis was already rising to his feet, Rocastle already opening his mouth to protest. "If he can't be civil…"

"Let me the hells go!" Rocastle snarled at Domis. "I'll be civil. I want to see what happens!"

"We're all reasonable adults here," the man said, as she nodded at Domis to let him stay for now "And let me guess, if you want to be a queen, you need a court jester. Think you should acquire for him a hat with bells on."

That interested her. "Queen? What makes you think I want to be a queen?"

That smile again. "You've got that feel about you. I can see the ambition in you. You already have so much," he swept a hand around the room. "And yet you want more. Much more. Maybe to the point that I'd almost say you want it all."

"You're a perceptive man, Mister…" She left it blank, hoping to tempt him into a revelation. He didn't bite.

"Not really. I've seen your type before. People like you."

She laughed. "There are no people like me."

"There are always people like you," he said. "I'll give you credit though; you've gone to great length to get me here. I almost wonder what I could do for you in this grand scheme you're no doubt plotting. Little old me. Humble me. Not a credit to my name and yet you need something from me no doubt. Life likes its little ironies, does it not? Even the highest occasionally has to wait on the lowest."

"Somehow, I doubt you're the lowest," she said. "Or you always were. I think you used to be someone else."

"Everyone like me used to be someone else," he said scornfully. "Everyone who hit bad times has a story. Every single cautionary tale. Best consider that. It could be you one day."

"Maybe. But isn't it better to reach for the sun than stay in the shade. You might get burned but at the same time, you might hold the sun in your hand. And then…"

"You hold the sun in your hand, you WILL get burned," he said. "No two ways about it, I'm afraid to say. Every action has a price. I'm sure you didn't get me here to bandy philosophy though. I'm waiting to hear what you do want."

She nodded. "Do you remember a man named Jeremiah Blut?"

"Should I?"

"He paid you a great sum of credits some time ago for some information regarding the Kjarn. I want to know what you told him."

He shrugged. "You want to know; why don't you ask him?"

"He's dead. That makes it rather difficult to hold a conversation."

The man leaned back in his seat at that, a sudden wide grin on his face as he flexed his fingers out in front of him. "Well I guess that means I suddenly have an excellent bargaining chip. Price just went up. A lot."

She returned the smile. "That's good you feel that way." Her own smile grew as she saw the confusion flash across his face. "If you feel you have a bargaining chip, it means we can bargain."

"Or we could torture it out of you," Rocastle piped up. Sometimes she wondered if she'd erred in not having him killed when it would have been convenient. At the very least, he was skating on thin ice as for remaining in the room. She'd shown him mercy once.

"You could try," the man said. He didn't look too bothered by the comment. "But you want to be privy to a little secret? Won't do you any good. I'm a dead man anyway, reality just hasn't caught up with me. Torturing me, well how long you think my body will hold out? Then where will you be? Shitbag!"

"If you're a dead man," Sinkins piped up as Rocastle's face went bright purple with rage. Only the fact that Domis had moved his shoulder stopped him from lunging forward and grappling with the dishevelled man. "Then why not share the information with us, all so it doesn't die with you."

He ignored him and Rocastle and looked her square on. "You want to know what I told him? It has a price."

"Name it." She didn't hesitate.

"Save my life," he said. "My name is Wim Carson and if you save my life, I'll help you with whatever you need."

It likely didn't have the effect he'd desired. She blew on her nails and stared him down for a few moments. "Okay, I hear you. How do I know you have information that can help? Give me something showing you're genuine."

Wim shrugged. "You said he asked about the Kjarn. That's true. The Kjarn is a part of us all. We all touch it, we all channel it, we're all part of it. It cannot exist without us; we cannot exist without it. It is what enables us to capture spirits, it is what makes us more than a bunch of individuals and turns us into a collective people. And it is what makes us capable of the spectacular."

"Do you refer to the Vedo when you say this?"

The dishevelled man smiled. "What do you think you know of the Vedo, ma'am? I'd wager whatever you think you know has a number of fallacies attached to it."

"I heard they were a cult…"

"And I'm proved right," Wim smirked. "The Vedo were not a cult. Far from it. Cults indoctrinate. They are a blight that swallow all before them and move on without facing the fallout of their actions. Consequence is nothing to them. They do things in the name of religion no sensible Divine would ever ask of humanity. The Vedo… They didn't do any of that. Far from it. They did only what they needed to. Nothing more."

"You seem to know a lot about them," Sinkins said suspiciously. "Where did this extent of knowledge come from?"

"First-hand," Wim said nonchalantly. He couldn't hide the faintest trace of a smile. "I used to be one."

That brought silence to the room and he smiled that black broken smile again. "That's got your attention, hasn't it? Now if you want more, I've named my price. It's a steep one but I think what I know is worth it."

She studied him for several moments, sifting over the options in her mind. If he could shed some light on what remained in the dark to her, it might be credits well spent. The least she could do was assess his condition, see what was wrong with him and take it from there.

"Mr Carson," she said pleasantly. "I think we might be able to do business…" Her words tailed off as he rose to his feet and wandered over to one of her walls, attention apparently elsewhere for the moment. Domis moved to halt him, she gave him a glance stopping him in his tracks. Wim's attentions were taken by the paintings on the wall, numerous artworks from a long time ago. Each of them supposed pictures of the Divines, he studied them all for several long seconds.

"You have an interesting taste in artwork," he said. He glanced around, squinted at her through watering eyes. "I'm sorry, what were you saying?"

"I think we might be able to do business," she said, brushing down her irritation. Getting angry with him wouldn't solve anything. When dealing with one who looked like they had nothing to lose, you had to tread carefully. "I'd like to have someone examine you, see exactly what is wrong with you and take it from there. If you have something incurable, you might have to accept that there is nothing we can do to save you."

"Well you might have to start investing in miracles if you want the cure," he said. "Best pay special attention to my brain. There's something not right there, I can feel it."

"Magical Vedo powers?" Rocastle scoffed. "As if!"

Wim ignored him, instead fixated his gaze on her. "You know something, ma'am, I think I've got you worked out. I might be a shadow of my former self, but I still know how to connect the dots. I know how to see the connections. All this work. All this hunger for knowledge of the Kjarn, pictures of the Divines, all by the same artist…"

Are you going somewhere with this? She wondered silently, yet said nothing, waiting for him to get to the point/

"You wouldn't happen to be searching for the Gilgarus Heart, would you?"

For the second time, his words brought silenced the room and she rose to her feet with a face like thunder. Shock and anger flooded through her, she had to clamp her hands together to stop them shaking.

"Who told you that?!" She demanded. He didn't wilt before her, only grinned and settled back in his seat like he didn't have a care in the world.

"I put it together." He sounded so smug it made her want to vomit. "I know things, you see. And well, I can help you. Help me, I'll help you. Partners?" He stood up and offered her a grimy hand. "It'll be worth your while. If you help me, I'll owe you my life."

Reluctantly, she moved around her desk and faced him. He wasn't a tall man, their eyes met, and he showed that smile one more time. His hand felt filthy beneath hers, but she didn't flinch as she shook.

"Well here's to partnership," she said casually. "And a friendly warning, if you disappoint me, I'll kill you myself." She smiled at him. "No pressure then."

Chapter Nine. Cause and Effect.

"Everything you do has a counterbalance. To act is to create a reaction to that balance. To react is to try and restore. If we could predict the reaction, I think we'd do things differently. But at the same time, knowing the future is something maybe we shouldn't be privy to. Nothing good comes out of knowing what happens next when you shouldn't."

Doctor Dale Sinkins on consequences.

The eighth day of Summerpeak.

He didn't believe them when they'd said the vomiting was a reaction to the medical webbing around his cuts. It had come off now, his arm pretty much healed but their words hadn't rung true. For one thing, he hadn't felt nauseous beforehand. It had just come over him when he'd stood up. He'd been ill before, and it hadn't felt like this. When you were ill, you felt it for at least a few moments before it overcame you. He hadn't felt that, far from it to be him to diagnose his own condition but he knew it felt wrong. Really wrong. It hadn't been like sickness; it had felt something else

Rot in my stomach, bile, blood churning…

His head buzzed, he'd been given some pills, but either they were taking their sweet time to kick in or weren't doing any good. His tongue felt furry, his throat delicate, but he didn't want to surrender. It had been a long day, maybe he was tired. A good night's sleep and he'd probably feel better in the morning, he hoped. It felt a very long time since his victory and wandering back towards the hotel, he could already feel the call of his bed. The sun was fading, the air was warm on clammy skin, he couldn't stop sweating. He ran a hand over his forehead and it came back drenched. He swallowed, and his tongue felt so heavy and dry. His lips felt like sandpaper and he couldn't stop shaking.

What… What's happening to me? Even as he asked the question, no answer came as he nearly tripped and fell, had to steady himself on a passing person. He heard their complaints and muttered a clumsy sound of apology. Then he felt their hand on his shoulder and he doubled his fist just in case they were going to turn violent.

"You're Scott Taylor! Oh wow! I was just at your bout; can I have a picture with you?"

He shrugged the hand off. "Maybe… Maybe later. Just need… Not feeling well. So… Sorry. Really." He felt the look of exasperation on their face as he shuffled away. his breath catching in his throat and he had to rest against the side of a store. His face was on fire and he felt his stomach churn again, vomit spattering down the side of the building, brown and red and black. He couldn't look as he turned, exhaled a groan. That was when he saw her, a vision amidst the fog his eyes had become. She was like a beacon of light in the darkness, golden and bright, so harsh he couldn't see beyond the radiance.

"Wha…" He managed to say clumsily. A hand on his shoulder, her radiance only grew brighter and as he felt the grip, he heard a voice, low and urgent. Why did it sound familiar? He knew it. Wasn't Mia. Wasn't Jess. Who was it? It wasn't even like he could hear the words, more experiencing them as they were thrust into him like a dozen little swords and he could no more ignore them than move.

Breathe. Breathe. Just close your eyes and shut it all down. Let the pain go. It'll pass. It's only feelings. They're all in your head. You can conquer this.

He couldn't. A whimper slipped out the corner of his mouth as fresh migraines assaulted him, a million hammers crashing at his mind and his legs almost gave out. If he fell, he doubted he'd get up.

Shut it all down! You can do this. Block it all out.

Can't!

You can! The voice in his being went silent, until he heard it again, loud and strong. This pain is an opponent. Like the one you just faced. Your pain is Steven Silver and once more you must conquer him. You've done it once. You're stronger now. Are you going to let some posh bastard finish you off?

What are you talking about? He couldn't fathom the meaning behind her words. They just… Pain was pain. Steven was Steven. They were two separate things.

Only in your mind. Everything is connected. What makes up one thing makes up another. You are limited in your world view. If you don't do this, you will die. Or worse!

What's worse than death? He asked silently.

No answer.

I don't know if I can do this.

You must. The voice in his mind was suddenly cold, brisk and professional, not a hint of emotion. If you don't, you live with the consequences. Likely not for very long admittedly.

His entire being hurt, like he was being chewed on and he felt himself drop. Scott threw his hands at the onrushing ground, felt the sidewalk bite his palms and fresh pain shot through him. His stomach churned, he knew a fresh wave of nausea was about to assault him.

Like a punch. He had to try. She sounded like she knew what she was talking about. He giggled to himself. He didn't even know who she was. Might be someone or nobody, he wasn't even sure there was someone there.

Visualising the pain as a punch was harder than it sounded, he'd already thought it sounded nigh on impossible. As it struck his gut, he tried to imagine it that way. He tried to picture it as someone throwing one into his stomach and laughing as he doubled in pain. It took a few tries as fresh sensations clawed his insides and he wanted to scream. Slowly that person turned into Steven and his cavern crusher. He could see their faces, feel their malice and he tried to back away from him. Irrow looked mad enough to go on the hunt, ready to kill, ready for revenge over the way Palawi had defeated it.

Palawi!

Somewhere amidst the buzzing mix of images and feelings his confused mind had become, he heard his summoner activating, felt a tongue on his face and somewhere amidst it all, the hound forced his way into his vision. Not just out in the real world but in his mind as well. He could see Palawi in there just as much as he could see Steven and Irrow, he could smell them now. The metallic tinge on the cavern crawler, the sweat and musk from Palawi, even Steven's cologne, harsh and bitter in his nose.

Again, Irrow came at him, he felt the first precursors of pain and instinctively he commanded Palawi to attack. The blast of electricity erupted from the dog and struck Irrow dead on. The crawler roared in pain, so did Steven and just for a moment they flickered out of existence and Scott felt fresh relief pulse through him, a boon of everything good that had ever happened to him. He felt bruised lips form into a smile, felt the laughter ripple from him and he sat up on his knees.

Still they returned and once more Palawi let a rip of thunder into them and he saw them both cry out in pain and vanish. The third time they returned, he didn't even need Palawi. He stared them both down, Steven and Irrow, grinned at them and folded his arms. "Your move, boys. When you're ready." He felt simultaneously light headed and confidently elated, his head buzzing, dizzy but fired up for whatever they had.

They charged, and he clenched a fist, his hand hopelessly small compared to just one of Irrow's legs never mind its whole body. If he landed the punch, he knew his hand would break. Flesh and bone against tough iron wasn't a contest.

Except…

This wasn't the real world. It wasn't going to make a damn-diddily difference here. His grin grew, suddenly Irrow was there, suddenly it was just Steven and the pain intensified as he stepped towards the silver haired man, each footstep an agony trying to drag him down. H

He wouldn't let it. Step by step he moved closer and closer until he stood nose and nose. It felt like his entire body was bleeding as he raised a fist and punched the figure hard on the nose, he felt his knuckles crack under the force of the blow and he saw Steven recoil, his nose shattered...

The pain vanished, and this time Steven didn't come back. For several moments, he wasn't quite sure what had happened until he felt cold breeze against his burning skin. All the higher sensations he'd experienced vanished, slowly he felt the mundane returning to him. The sounds. The smells. The sensations.

He opened his eyes. Everything looked better already. He blinked several times just to be sure. Still on the island. Alone in some alley, a stream of vomit down the side of a building. Palawi was sniffing at it, curiosity on his doggy features as he started to lap at it.

No sign of the woman whose voice he had recognised but unable to place. He felt better. Maybe the pills had kicked in at last. Or something else he couldn't explain. He'd felt like he was about to die, his entire body about to go kaput and now he felt good. He felt better than good. Sure, his face and his arm still ached but there was nothing wrong with that. His palms were bloodied but they didn't hurt like he thought they might.

Scott stood up and stretched. Palawi turned his attention from the vomit and gave him a curious look. "Don't you dare think of licking me with that tongue," he warned, unable to hide his grin as he reached to scratch his furry head. "I know where it's been."

That was when he caught something out the corner of his eye and he tensed up. Palawi's fur rose on edge and he heard the growl rippling from deep inside the hound. The air felt just that little bit colder, the sun was still just about up but he knew it shouldn't be this frigid. Slowly he let his muscles react, Scott glanced down to Palawi and saw the dog hadn't relaxed. He was prowling about, sniffing the air in search of the source of the discomfort. He knew something wasn't right here.

"What is it, Pal?" he asked, glancing about to try and seek the source. He might have just been seeing things. After all, he had just gone through a traumatic experience. Somehow, he doubted he was imagining it, unless Palawi was sharing in his psychosis.

Scott exhaled, saw his breath in front of him. It must really have gotten cold. Already it was fading, and he heard something behind him, just a small tic of metal on stone and he turned, the growl from Palawi sounding again.

Nothing. He was alone. Good. He visibly relaxed, shaking his head at the dog next to him. "That was weird, Pal." He reached out to scratch the ears, grinning at his own skittishness. "Next time I do that, just bite me yeah? Tell me not to…"

Palawi howled, too late he felt the sudden rush of something grazing the top of his skull. He'd never known he could move so quickly, hurling himself out the way with a yell of panic. Something ice cold brushed against his back, the chill rushing all the way to his inner being and he fought the urge to shudder. His teeth wanted to chatter, he bit down and did his best to stop them, felt them fight to almost breaking point in his mouth. He looked back, saw the cause seeping down into the ground. Blue, purple, black, all the shades of smoke he saw, and he kicked himself. Someone had told him there were a few native ghosts loose on the island. Looked like he'd disturbed one, something he found both surprising and delightful. He'd been after a ghost for a while. He'd known someone once who used one, it had been powerful. Scott looked at Palawi and grinned. "Let's go and get this thing!"

No sooner had the words left his mouth, he felt something shove him forward, the same cold feeling rushing through his shoulders and he fell once again on injured hands. Palawi snarled and lunged forward at his command, electricity crackling through his teeth, only to snap down on empty air. Scott rolled over onto his butt and swore as Palawi landed.

"Okay," he said. "The minute you see it, zap its ass."

Palawi let out a yip of confirmation, started to sniff the air again, ears twitching as he sought any sign of their slippery spectre. Whether he could smell it or not, Scott hoped it'd give them a chance to find it before it attacked again. That was the thing with ghosts. They were good to have, but an absolute bastard to get. Presumably because of shit like this.

You could get specialised equipment for hunting them, he'd heard, but that felt like missing the point. Besides it was expensive to rent and, to the best of his knowledge, nowhere on the island sold it. He hadn't sought it out, but it was the sort of stuff you tended to notice.

No, if he was doing this, it would be the old-fashioned way. A spirit and an empty container crystal. He'd done it this way for all his spirits, wasn't changing now.

He glanced to Palawi, hoping for some sort of clue. He didn't want more cold shocks. This always was a risk when trying to claim spirits. Sometimes they did go for the caller rather than the other spirit. The trick would be avoiding that, hope it went for Palawi.

Scott saw the look in the pooch's eyes, felt something screaming at him to move and he threw himself aside, the blast of electricity rupturing the space where he'd been stood a moment earlier. He heard an ethereal shriek, felt mixed emotions, worry and relief mixed together. Worry he'd nearly been fried on the spot, relief he hadn't.

"Careful Pal," he muttered, the thought already dying away as he saw the twitching ghost where he'd been stood, not down, not defeated but affected. "Next time try not to take me out as well."

That was all he planned to say on the matter. At his command, Palawi hurled himself at the ghost, the same electric bite attack he'd utilised earlier and bit down on the spectral space, Scott heard the shriek and let out a mental cheer as Palawi growled, shaking the spirit as sparks streaked through its smoky body. He reached into his pocket, digging deep. He had a spare container crystal somewhere if he could find it.

His distraction a factor, the ghost suddenly jerked to life, twisting wildly and he heard the yowl as Palawi was thrown free and crashed against one of the oversized trashcans lining the alley. The pooch lay in a pool of his own blood, whimpering in pain and Scott felt a twist in his heart at the sound. Still Palawi tried to get up, legs unsteadily supporting him. A chunk of fur had been torn from his back, blood everywhere. He thought he saw bone protruding, he tried not to look, glancing around for a sight of the ghost.

This was starting to become annoying.

A thought exemplified as he caught another cold blow about the face and he went down, half blind from the chills rushing through him. He couldn't feel the left side of his face, numbed by the blow and he flailed impotently. Vision slowly crept back, the flashing darkness replaced by a jumble of images he could just about bring into focus. Where was it?

It rose in front of him, large and powerful, he could see it wholly for the first time. Ghosts did have a shape when they chose to. This one looked like a short fat little imp with four pointed ears and a mohawk sticking all directions out of its head, what passed for skin all blues and purples and blacks. It had a mouth out of proportion to the rest of its body, large enough to see the void inside when it smiled, behind stubby white teeth. That tongue was huge and slimy, flecked with silver spittle that stank of death and decay. The three eyes it bore were yellow and malicious, the brows heavily protruding, giving it a judgemental look.

It laughed, not a pleasant sound and he steadied himself for a blow that never came. He sensed the static in the air a fraction of a second before the blast hit the ghost and Scott saw Palawi had stood up, three legs still quivering and as he had with Irrow, the current was still being generated. The pooch was dropping hundreds of thousands of volts into that one space. And it was working, despite its incorporeal body, he could see the ghost was feeling the effects, reeling on the spot. Knowing he might never have a better chance, Scott took a deep breath and went for it, clumsily tugging the empty crystal from his pocket. He slammed it against the permeable cloud of smoke passing for skin, felt it penetrate the ghost. Immediately his arm felt like he'd dunked it in a bucket of cold water and the shivering ran up his body. Inside, he reached out with the very essence of his entire being, found the ghost's presence and reached for it.

If before had felt like dunking his arm in a bucket of cold water, going in for the capture felt like he'd jumped in head first. Not only did his skin shiver with clammy cold but he felt the sensation of a hundred little pinpricks moving over him, fought the urge to recoil as he tried to keep a grip on the slippery presence. Here, they were evenly matched. It wasn't seeing, not as such, more being everything and everywhere, just a small part of the whole and at the same time not being able to care. He'd done this too many times and each time was different, the duel between potential spirit and future owner.

The ghost wasn't letting go easily, scratching and biting, attempting to suffocate him, smoke in his mouth and nose, ears deafened, and eyes blinded. All he could feel and see was the objective. The ghost he'd come this far for and he wasn't about to let it get away. The scratching and struggles were annoying, but he knew it wouldn't leave any permanent damage. Nobody knew quite the explanation behind this state, the best way he'd heard it described was as a higher state of being, an acknowledgement that life is connected. As exists you, so exists the potential for a connection.

Strangely enough, that quote hadn't come from a scientist but rather a priest of Gilgarus. Go figure that one out.

The fighting was a two-way street here, he brought back a metaphysical fist and smashed the ghost between the eyes. They always fought and always it was a challenge. Claiming Palawi had been the easiest but even he'd snapped and bit and howled, he'd not gone out easily. Sangare had been hardest, the dragon of Threll had nearly engulfed him completely. Three times he'd attempted that. As the ghost went down reeling, he made to jump on it. The sooner he got out of here, the better. His body passed through empty space, the ghost no longer there and he rolled onto his back, a wave of panic going through him.

The blow slugged him right in the heart and he let out a wheezing gasp, doubling up into a ball. He nearly blacked out, nearly lost the connection but even as some of it slipped away, he clutched down and managed to retain enough of it to keep hold. The ghost stared down at him and laughed, a malicious bellowing sound amidst the darkness and the shit did something he'd never have expected, something he'd not heard before and doubted he ever would again.

"You keep fighting, bagmeat," it said in an eerily high masculine voice. "What?"

The fucking thing had spoken.

It had fucking spoken to him. He was so shocked he let the connection fail, he let go and suddenly he was back in the real world, light and life coming back to him. He blinked several times, his eyes dry from the trance and he saw the ghost fleeing, leaping up the side of the building and away over the roof, gone into the night by the time he'd had the chance to stand up.

Scott looked at Palawi, still not quite sure what had just happened. The dog cocked his head in bemusement.

He was good looking in a dark sort of way, Anne thought as she studied him. She could read not just his expression but his emotions and for the moment he was radiating cold, calm curiosity. Anything but that aggressive anger that normally came from him was good.

"Explain again," he said. "You want to make it interesting how?"

She shrugged. "Anyone can fight. You fight best when there's something at stake. Like now in this tournament. Would you say you've done your best because of a bigger prize?"

It was his turn to shrug. "I go out to win every time. It's nothing unusual."

"Except it's all in your head," she said. "It's the way you view things. You can't keep going at things a hundred miles an hour and hope to overwhelm like you've done so far. Sooner or later you'll meet someone who can weather it and then you'll be in trouble. Or you'll burn out long before the final. That which burns twice as bright burns half as long and all that stuff. Don't get me wrong but you haven't fought anyone top notch here so far. How do you think you'd do against Sharon Arventino? Or..." Thinking of Wade hurt, so she quashed that example down inside her. "Or... Nick Roper."

If he'd been calm before, the wave of rage that struck her at that name was like a hammer and she had to steady herself, regain her composure before speaking again. That was interesting. Something she hadn't heard about, it would seem. Maybe she'd try tempting that out of him soon, see how keen he was on sharing. Now though, he wasn't going to. She could only push him towards the door. He still needed to walk through it himself.

"I can take anyone on my day," he said grimly. "Anyone."

"Yes," she said. "You might be able to. But the key is to ensure every day is your day. If you're at your best and your opponent is at their best then the key is to ensure if you don't win, you don't lose easily either. It's not always about pure power sometimes. Sometimes a little guile and craft goes a long way. You miss that from your game." She leaned over to one of the targets that his anklo had shattered with a leaf and rapped it with a knuckle. The wood was three times as thick as her hand, she noted.

"I'm going to prove this to you," she said. "And here's the deal. If you win, I'll shut up about it and let you chase your own path down to victory."

He looked moderately interested, although she didn't detect any radical switch of emotion. Maybe he liked the idea, or maybe she didn't. She didn't know which she'd prefer.

"And if you win?" he asked. His voice was bored, listless. Completely out of sorts with his being. She could sense intrigue.

"You keep a tight rein on your emotions," she said thoughtfully. "Don't you?" He didn't reply, and she flexed her fingers out in front of her. "Tell you what. You lose, you buy dinner. How does that sound?" Been too long since a good-looking man bought me dinner. She didn't say that aloud, almost wished she had, would her cheeks not have flared up like fireworks if she had.

She felt the stab of emotion run through him, curiosity, surprise, bemusement... Got you, she smiled.

"Good thing I don't intend to lose then," he said. "Isn't it?"

"You can intend all you like," she replied as the spirit emerged from the crystal locked into her summoner. "Intentions are the cheapest currency you'll find unless you act on them." Paws formed out of the energy and stretched out her lithe body with a little yawn, powerful muscles flexing as she extended her claws. Purple and white spattered fur covered her feline body, tail twitching lazily in the air-conditioned room. A trio of silver jewel-like protrusions emerged from her forehead, shiny in the artificial light of the training room. Anne had caught Paws up in the Fangs in Serran, a native snow leopard she'd done some tweaking with. Compared to Theo's giant anklo, she looked small and slight. Weak. Insignificant.

Paws was none of those things.

"Is that your choice?" Theo asked, a little note of curiosity in his voice. She sensed the cocky confidence radiating from him, she fought the urge to smile. Those who underestimated their opponent had already started on the path to defeat. Maybe he would win. Maybe she underestimated his abilities. It would be interesting either way.

"Of course," she said. "Whenever you are ready, we will commence."

He attacked first, she'd seen it coming a mile off as the leaves shot from the back of his anklo and swept towards Paws. She could see them spinning through the air, like mini-saws, just as she saw the light glinting off their edges. She smiled, a mirror reflection of the expression passing across Paws' face as the leaves halted mid-spin, not falling, not moving.

Though she couldn't see them, she knew the crystals would be glowing, unlocking the full potential of the upgrades she'd given her spirit. The look on Theo's face was something to behold, surprise etched into every pore of his skin as she smiled sweetly at him and gave Paws the silent command. Almost immediately the leaves lunged back towards the anklo, digging deep gouges into its face and shell. The roar of pain shook the room and she felt the anger emanating from Theo and fought the urge to smile. That wouldn't improve his mood.

"Getting angry doesn't solve anything," she said. Atlas looked just as pissed as his caller did and she mentally cajoled Paws to remain vigilant. If the anklo suddenly attacked, it wouldn't be good to get caught beneath those heavy feet. Whatever Paws' telekinetic abilities might be; she wouldn't want to wager on her being able to stop the anklo in its tracks.

"Who's angry?" Theo sounded nonchalant, but she didn't buy it. Not even for a moment when she could see past his words. Not that he knew that. "I'm calm."

You're not though, are you? Again, she fought the urge to smile. Paws' forehead protrusions shone again and from their epicentre, a beam of pure white light striking Atlas face on, Theo's attempts for the anklo to block just a fraction too late. This time she did feel the rage like a hammer blow and she subconsciously took a step back. She swallowed, found her composure and this time she did smile. "You're easily distracted. And that can be…"

Atlas roared and the uniblast tore towards Paws who didn't miss a trick, springing lazily aside of the destructive blast and Anne commanded her to counter-fire with the same white light, the attack she'd informally christened the mind beam. It was quite a twee name as they went but it did what it suggested. It was a beam of energy and it came from the mind. What more did you want from a name?

The aim wasn't as good this time with Paws off-balance, but still the blast caught a glancing hit off one of the stubby legs. Several layers of scale and muscle were torn away, blood gushing out in thick pools. Maybe she'd hit an artery. She didn't know enough about anklo physiology to say she had or not. If she had, it'd be over very quickly. One thing she knew was where to hit to cause maximum damage.

She fought a wry smile. Not for nothing had she been trained as a Unisco sniper. And it'd be churlish to not use that training in her battling abilities, not to mention a waste of talent. Those who didn't utilise all their advantages tended not to get very far.

If the blow was fatal, then Atlas wasn't letting it show. She didn't even have to look at Theo to get a read of his emotions, she kept all her attention on the giant bleeding spirit. As she stared, she saw the glow of illuminous green energy shining through it, starting from the centre of its being and radiating outwards like a shockwave. And before her very eyes, the torrent of blood slowed to a trickle, skin healing as if it had never been wounded.

She couldn't miss the wave of smugness falling off Theo as the anklo roared proudly. Anne sighed, saw the leaves coming and once more she gave Paws the command to halt them. If she had Theo read right, she knew what would come next. Ninety percent of callers who she employed this tactic against went with the same counter attack next time round. They thought they were being original, only to be proved hopelessly wrong.

Halt the leaves. Send them back. Send more leaves to shoot down the returning leaves. If you try that, Theo, I've got you worked out.

The leaves slowed to a halt, she winked at him. Atlas' mouth opened and another uniblast tore out, burning straight through the halted leaves and Paw took the blast full on in the face. Anne's mouth fell open as she felt the backlash of pain burn into her very being.

Ouch. She clutched her heart, hoping the agony would cease soon. Not likely. Only way that would happen was if Paws went down, she'd conditioned the leopard to take more than this.

It wasn't pleasant. Most of the fur on her face had been burned away, one eye taken out and she smelled like cooked meet. The gems had remained undamaged though, her teeth remained pearly white between the overcooked mix of black and red her face had become.

Well played, Theobald, she thought. Nice move. But it's not over yet.

The tenth day of Summerpeak.

Okocha slid the chip across the desk and Arnholt studied it before sliding it into his summoner. He'd been waiting for this, slightly longer than expected coming, even now he found himself tapping his desk impatiently as he waited for it to load. Roper's report on the incident a day earlier. He skim-read through it at first to get the general gist and then read more thoroughly a second time, Okocha sitting patiently while he did.

He didn't say anything. Arnholt didn't expect him to. By all sounds of it, Maddley had been willing to cooperate but what he'd offered hadn't been helpful enough. Roper had offered suggestions, such as getting him in for a composite scan of the woman who'd attacked him and getting him to go through surveillance footage images from the stadium since she'd mentioned she was at his bout but neither of them looked sure bets for answers.

It didn't help Maddley had stated unequivocally he hadn't seen her face. Roper said he had, but from a distance and not clearly during pursuit. He'd added he wasn't confident he'd be able to identify her irrevocably, but he was willing to go through any processes that would help. He didn't sound thrilled about it though. Sometimes doing something for the sake of it was a fool's errand, none of them wanted it. The only perk for Maddley was he was a footnote in this investigation. His attack was playing second fiddle to the attack on the ICCC building, deliberate or not as it might have been.

Even if it had been just an accident, something caught in the crossfire, that wouldn't save them from the full extent of the law. Three people had died, more had been seriously injured. It was a serious crime. Both Ritellia and Tommy Jerome were shouting their feelings from the rooftops and Arnholt was just about sick of hearing them fighting for attention in the media. They were like a pair of posturing peacocks squawking for the sake of it. He wondered how long before one of them brought up supposed incompetence of Unisco in the whole investigation.

"What do you think?" he asked, not looking at Okocha as he spoke.

The dark-skinned man didn't say anything, just removed his glasses and buffed a non-existent spot on them, his eyes locked in concentration.

"Initially I thought about how I wished we'd brought more people out to help deal with this," Okocha said. "But then I reconsidered. Getting more boots on the ground to deal with this thing, it's not going to help. This wasn't a planned terrorist attack; it was a spur of the moment thing. We're not going to get far with investigating the attack on the ICCC building without identifying the woman. What she did with Maddley, I think was her true goal. And her identity, or at least the clues to unlocking that mystery is locked away in Maddley's head. We need to get it out of there."

"How would you recommend that?"

"Sit him down with a technician, get him to give a description of what he has, match the result to the databases, see if we can get some hits. Either way, without his help, we're not going to get the answers that we want. Same with Roper. It's not much but it's all we got."

"I find it unfathomable he wouldn't want to help," Arnholt said. "This woman nearly killed him by his own words. This might be the only thing to stop her trying again…" He tailed off as Okocha spoke aloud the words passing through his head.

"… Especially if she knows he might be able to identify her." Already Arnholt was reaching for his summoner, he dialled a number and waited a moment.

"Leclerc. I want you and Fagan to go to Darren Maddley's room. Track him down, bring him into Unisco protective custody. His life may be in danger. We can't take chances."

"Of all the creatures in this strange and wonderful world of ours, none are perhaps as rare and fascinating as the kirofax. Whereas some creatures remain drastically unchanged through the stages of evolution, the kirofax has adapted dramatically though perhaps not for the better. Why something would evolve such a volatile DNA structure, it's hard to say. But the environment we find ourselves living in today, where caller is king, it is surely the reason they are now almost extinct in the wild."

Professor David Fleck on the kirofax.

The eighth day of Summerpeak.

There were a lot of different places Kyra Sinclair would rather be right now as she gripped the length of rock and tried not to look down. Her fingers ached but she tried to ignore them, digging her boots just a little further onto the outcrop beneath. At the Quin-C for one, if only things were different. Instead, here she was in the middle of Serran going hand over hand up the Trabazon in the midday sun, dangling from a rock like an oversized bogey.

The mountain was the highest point in the south, not the highest in all the kingdom but still a formidable obstacle to overcome. There were mountains in the Fangs to the north which dwarfed it but thankfully she was nowhere near them. At least here, she was sweating from the oppressive sun, the rope digging into her waist and she was already anticipating reaching the peak and flopping down in exhaustion. This hadn't been her smartest idea. But hey, since when had she let that stop her in the past. If she stopped to consider possible consequences of her actions, she'd never get anything done. In with both feet and to hells with consequences. It had been a spur of the moment thing, one she doubted she'd regret.

She'd heard the story down in the town below, she'd been passing through aimlessly wandering through the humid south of Serran, intent on keeping her mind off the tournament she'd failed to get to. It was nice down here, plenty of sun, just enough rain to halt it from being overbearing and about. Since the south of Serran and the north of Vazara were only split by fifty miles of open water and a few islands, plenty of locals were of Vazaran ancestry. It had been one such man, a tall fisherman with a shucked eye who'd told her the tale. They'd been in one of the bars, a rough place she wouldn't normally have been found dead in. Yet there'd been so little choice and she'd fancied living dangerously.

Yeah, she thought bitterly, feeling the crumbling of a dozen little pebbles beneath her fingers. Living dangerously. Whose brilliant idea had this been again?

Despite his ruined eye, he'd been friendly enough. He stank of overbream and sticklefox and various other types of fish she couldn't start to name. She'd only guessed at those two down to the copious amounts of the stuff stinking up the Latalya waterfront.

Not a bad town but it looked about ten years behind some of the less advanced parts of Serran, themselves about twenty years behind the modern parts. So, thirty years from the present and she'd found herself thinking maybe she should have taken a left turn at the crossroads rather than the road she had. Next time, she'd avoid taking the right turn.

There was a Willie's here, but she'd avoided it. Compared to most of them, even the normally pristine restaurant looked shabby and unkempt. If this was thirty years ago, this was the stage of the violent Willie O'Rourke, not the respected businessman and restauranteur of the present. She'd always wanted to see him offer to fight someone. Unfortunately, the number of people who'd seen that in person were decreasing day by day. The only thing Willie was fighting these days were various diseases.

Still, the bar hadn't been bad, compared to the rest of the town. Latalya wasn't a place she'd ever come again given a choice. But while she was here, she might as well enjoy it. It was too dark to head out now, not with the threat of creatures outside. She didn't fancy renting a speeder either. No, she could wait. Rest for the night, experience an actual bed for a change.

Generally, there were enough small towns dotted across this part of Serran she'd not had to pitch the sleeping bag out often. It was always a gamble, all it needed was something to come across her sleeping place. She had her safeguards, at least one of her spirits kept out to defend her while she slept but you could never eliminate risk. At least here in the town, there wasn't much chance of being eaten alive.

Also, she had to admit as she studied the bar around her, it did have a certain rustic charm. She'd realised it the moment she'd seen the sign announcing its name. The Fish and Fist. What a name, she'd smiled when she'd seen it and was still grinning now. Normally the only place she saw names like that were towards the north of Canterage where the accents were thick and the locals quick tempered.

It hadn't been a surprise to discover the man behind the bar was from Canterage, thin and weary with what little hair remained on his head the colour and consistency of old wool. He'd bowed his head to her, taken special care to ensure her glass was clean and poured her a glass of amber coloured liquid that smelled of hot honey. She hadn't asked for it, but she'd been taken by the smell and paid regardless, sliding a credit chip across the counter.

It had felt warm beneath her fingers; they were already chafing by the time she sat down in the corner. It wasn't as full as she might have expected, maybe a dozen and half people dotted about the room. She felt a little conspicuous, but nobody was paying her any attention. Not the men, certainly not the women.

Ah well… One day when she reached the elite she'd probably look back on the quiet moments like these and be envious of how her life had changed. She relished anonymity if she was honest. You could get away with so much more when people didn't know who you were. You had to relish the present no matter how mundane because things wouldn't always be this way. There'd be times of hardship and times of bounty, both would have their ups and downs. You had to take what you earned in life.

Her master had told her that. She felt a brief stab of hurt thinking back to those days He was gone now. She didn't know where or how or even if she'd ever see him again. All she had were her instincts to go on and they told her one day she would. She had to trust them.

Speaking of her instincts… He'd dropped down across from her and grinned through uneven teeth. For a moment, she'd been worried, something about him felt off and then she relaxed. He didn't seem to be an immediate threat, she smiled at him, returning his gesture. She leaned back in her seat and crossed her legs. His one good eye didn't leave hers. The smell made her want to wrinkle her nose, she disguised it as a twitch of the face and hoped he didn't cotton on to her discomfort.

"Can I help you?" she asked, taking a sip of her drink. It was hot and strong, like a firework in the pit of her stomach. She felt the heat spreading through, couldn't help but let the woozy grin flash across her face. Maybe this place wasn't so quiet and friendly after all. She drank no more, just let it warm her hand.

"You're new in town," he said. It was more a statement than a question and she nodded.

"I am. Just passing through. Be leaving in the morning."

"Caller?"

Among other things. Kyra nodded. "That's right."

"Not a famous one though. I don't know your name. You don't know mine either. We're even on that. Back across the water, they got a saying. Names is for tombstones."

"That's true," she said, folding her fingers together. "They are. I don't do names. Not for strangers. It complicates things."

He laughed, a sound like bark being ripped off a tree and she fought the urge to flinch at the sound. She wouldn't. It might sound unpleasant, but nobody had ever been killed or harmed by laughter. Not physically. Some emotional wounds took a long time to heal but those people usually had their problems to start with. "I like what you say." For a long moment he studied her, and she kept her face impassive. "You want to know a local secret?"

"Should I want to know a local secret?" It was a genuine question. Some people were very insular about local traditions, especially places like this where everyone knew everyone else's name and habits. Most of them time they knew what everyone else was guilty of too.

He laughed again, this time it didn't take her by surprise. She was trusting him less and less by the second though. Never trust a man who laughs too much. The master's words again. What are they hiding behind those gestures? Either way it had taken a longer to prise the secret out of him than she'd initially thought. He hadn't been quite as forthcoming as initially hinted She'd smiled, flirted, laughed at his jokes and even arranged a few drinks that, as time went by, hadn't been so much as drunk as sloshed down a vest growing grubbier by the minute. Privately her disgust grew too.

Yet the secret had been worth it as he'd told her what could be found atop the mountain and she knew precisely why he'd hinted and then been reticent to reveal. If it got out…

All this for a damn kirofax.

That was unfair, she immediately corrected her mistake. It was all for a kirofax, but she shouldn't write it off as a waste just solely for that purpose. A kirofax was a rare animal indeed, highly sought after by callers and as a result, they'd nearly been hunted to extinction. On their own, they weren't anything too special. Small dog-like creatures they were naturally but what made them valued was their volatile DNA structure. Because it all came down to what you could accomplish with a spirit in the lab. Most creatures could be tinkered with, the more mundane a creature, the more you could work it. Birds, rodents and traditional household pets were usually the first spirits of new callers, there was a reason for that. They were easy to tame, they were in plentiful supply and all sorts could be done with them.

All animals are complex. Some are more complex than others. Some creatures, like dragons to name an example, could resist modification to the point it absolutely would not work under any circumstance. Then there was the kirofax down the other end of the

127

scale as anything worked on them. Anything. The volatile nature of their DNA meant they could be reconfigured easily and quickly. She remembered a caller with one ten feet tall and two headed, one spitting fire and one spitting ice. In the wild it would be a horrible freak of nature, destined to die soon. In the hands of a spirit caller, they would survive and thrive.

The extent the people of Latalya were willing to go in keeping that secret had been apparent the moment he'd spilled it, uncomfortable silence had fallen over the bar as he'd laid over the table and started to snore gently. She could see the barman on his summoner, dirty looks coming her way and she knew why. If people knew there were kirofax on top of the Trabazon, this sleepy little village on the waterfront wouldn't remain peaceful for long. There'd be a massive influx of callers from all around the kingdoms coming here, the closest settlement to the base of the mountain. The ugly feeling about the bar told her a swift exit was in order, she'd skedaddled before anyone could say anything to her.

Outside, on the other hand, had been a different matter. She'd barely gotten a few hundred yards from the bar, many more from her inn when a palm had grabbed her, only minimal warning alerting her, and she'd been thrown unceremoniously into the alley, pain shooting through her as she landed clumsily amidst a heap of garbage bags. The light wasn't good, but she could make out three figures stood above her. Malice radiated from them.

"What the fuck do you think you're doing?!" she demanded, trying to keep their eyes on her face, rather than the fact she was rooting through her bag. Come on, where was it!

"You bitch," one of them said, an accusation that stung. "Come here, sweet talk the secrets out of our drunks... No. Not on ours."

Another laughed, a wheezy high sound out of place in the darkness. "Let's cut her. Make her squeal."

"She'll never tell them. She'll forget."

Three different voices. She'd been right. She couldn't see them well, they were still bathed in shadow, but she didn't need eyes to know where they were. They left a great greasy stain in the air around them. She could touch their minds, their small insignificant minds and she wanted to vomit. Anger coursed through her, a fire being fanned in the pits of her stomach and she savoured its sticky smoke radiating across her muscles as she gracefully rose to her feet.

"The bitch rises!"

She cocked her head, still furious with herself for failing to sense this coming. Right now, they thought she was an easy target. They had basic knives, she could smell the fish on them. Fishermen. If she never saw another one of them for a month, she'd be happy. They didn't know who they were dealing with. They thought her someone small. Someone weak. Just a nobody.

Good! Use that to your advantage!

She heard her master's voice in her mind, the memories bringing back painful emotions and she felt her face crack into a ghoulish smile. Those who saw it usually didn't tell anyone. She withdrew the cylinder of metal from her bag, mentally chastising herself for not carrying it before, held it to her side.

"I will warn you now," she said coldly. Her voice radiated danger, she put every emphasis of the Kjarn into it. The words felt potent in her mouth. "I haven't seen your faces. You can walk away right now, and I'll forget this." It didn't even sound like her voice anymore. She sounded older. Crueller. "If you don't, I assure you that nobody else will see your faces ever again. Anonymity isn't always a blessing, boys, sometimes it's a curse."

She felt their hesitation, their sudden rush of fear and uncertainty. That was all she needed, she savoured the emotions and drank it in deeply.

"She's lying!" One of them finally said. Whether he believed or not she couldn't say. He sounded like he did, his emotions too jumble like he was messed up on narcotics.

"She doesn't…"

"Get her!" The all-too overconfident guy almost shoved his two buddies forward at her and she sighed, leaping forward in one graceful motion the same time she thumbed the button on her kjarnblade.

With a crackle and a hiss, the pink and silver blade of energy erupted from the tip of the cylinder, illuminating the alley in its brilliance. By the time they'd reacted, the weapon was already little more than a blur as she swept through them, her mind barely processing the motions as it cut through them with minimal effort. The weapons used crystals to focus pure Kjarn energy into a formidable blade capable of cutting through almost anything.

Because the Kjarn links all things. Master Amalfus' words once again came to mind. Those two hadn't been a trouble at all, she'd wondered if drawing her blade was the best way to deal with them, before she'd decided she wanted to make a statement. Already the third guy had started to run, she'd gestured with her free hand and the invisible force of the Kjarn had yanked him back to her, as if a hand had grabbed his collar and pulled, he'd fallen at her feet and she crouched next to him, her fingers shimmering with energy.

Up on the mountain, she'd wondered if her drawing her blade in anger had been as much about the way they'd easily gotten the drop on her as punishing them Her master would have been furious with her. Her rival would have had a field day with her petulance. Nobody knew. Nobody would ever know. The dismembered remains of the first two men were hidden in the cellar of their leader, his mind a shallow fraction of what it once was. Even now the law was on its way to his home following an anonymous tip.

As clever as she had been, it still didn't change the fact she'd abused her powers against the grand scheme of Master Amalfus. He'd taught her caution and vigilance to temper the formidable power he assured her she would wield one day.

Sometimes she missed his teachings. More than that, she was sure Gideon Cobb knew where he was. Cobb had been claimed by the master the same time as her. They'd been trained together. They knew each other inside out. And he'd told them that one day, one would kill the other to become his rightful heir.

She'd often thought about that. Killing Cobb. Not that she thought she couldn't. She could, it'd be just the case of ensuring everything was right. Maybe that was the only way to bring him back to her.

It wasn't good to think about this at a time like this. Memories of her time with Amalfus were bringing her into a cold sweat, refreshing but at the same time uncomfortable. She just wanted to get to the top.

Kyra looked up, saw the few ledges above her head, sturdy enough to hold her weight. So far, she'd been trying to make it under her own steam. She felt she'd done well. It'd be a simple matter to leap the last few hundred meters, using the Kjarn to augment her body.

That'd be cheating. She didn't like that thought, it made her feel unclean. She'd made it this far on her own and that she'd gotten so high only to balk and rely on the Kjarn for the final push would devalue the first nine tenths of the trip. That'd be what Gid would do. Not her. It was through gritted teeth she pushed the urge down and slowly began to scan the immediate environment for the next best handhold. She would do this!

Personally, she'd always felt stubbornness a good characteristic. To keep going through thick and thin no matter what was what split the strong from the weak. But at the same time was it not a form of weakness to fail to admit futility? Perhaps. There would appear to be a thin dividing line between admirable determination and senseless recklessness.

Finally, she reached the top, tipped herself onto the flat of land of the peak and lay baking in her own sweat for long moments, a surge of triumph ripping through her. Plenty of times she'd considered her course of action. Every time she had conquered negativity. She was strong. Stronger than Gid. He was nothing more than a nasty overgrown boy with an inflated sense of his own power. If he was in contact with their master, it was only because he needed more instruction. She was the one he'd sent out into the world. Gid was being kept closer to home, not trusted. Maybe it wasn't true. It was her read of an unrelished situation, but it would be the one she stuck with. To acknowledge it as anything else would sincerely damage her faith in the great scheme.

Thus, the character of Master Amalfus was summed up. You give a mission to a politician, they achieve what they can through politics. You give a mission to a violent man, they do it through violence. Her master was a schemer, a good one as well from her understanding of him, limited as it may be. Under his guidance, she'd learned to manipulate the Kjarn, she'd built her kjarnblade and he'd turned her loose in every sense of the word.

It felt good to feel her muscles ache from the exertion, her short boyish hair caked in sweat and dust as were her coffee-coloured arms and legs, yet that didn't matter. She'd conquered the Trabazon. As she lay there, she closed her eyes and let her mind wander into the area around her, seeking any trace of what she'd come to find. If there was a kirofax on the mountain, she'd find it. The Kjarn would make sure of that.

Yet it was the Kjarn that told her she wasn't alone long before her eyes picked out the ship docked in the distance, not a big one but certainly packing a very thick hull. She paused, sat down on a rock shadowed by larger rocks, out of the way of potential onlookers, and took up the meditation pose, legs cross-tucked beneath her. She didn't normally enjoy the act, but it did have its uses.

One does not always need to enjoy. Consider it a tool, its use to be neither loved nor hated but vital.

Through that single act of concentration, she found the ship powered down, by her guess it could take up to ten people. She could smell dog amidst metal and the oil, a pair of black clad guards left to watch over it. Both were armed, she could smell their weapons.

She inhaled sharply at the realisation. Not because she feared them. Fear was for the weak. They didn't worry her. No, she worried at what their presence might mean. Should she seek out the kirofax rumoured to live up here, they'd be less than willing to show themselves in the presence of so many strangers. She pursed her lips angrily. Why, then?

Curiosity is a sin. To sin is to be human. To be human is to be curious. That had been another lesson endowed to her. This one she'd not gotten the meaning of at first. It had taken time coming to her. And ultimately, it had, although in different words to the ones Amalfus had used.

We can't deny who we are.

So yes. She was curious, especially given the locals were keen on keeping what was up here a secret. So maybe it wasn't the local kirofax population they were interested in. What could prompt armed men to come here in force? If she had the answer, it wasn't coming to her. Still perched in the shade of the rocks, she let her consciousness expand further into the...

Aha! Cave.

Shocker. Up here in the mountains was the last place anyone would expect to find a cave. She rolled her eyes beneath her lids and continued to probe further, past the lips of the cave, down and down and...

Kyra sensed the sudden emotions, violent auras of battle and involuntarily she recoiled. Whatever was going on down there felt savage. Something strange was going on here. Maybe they were Unisco. Maybe. They didn't feel like an official presence though. She could touch the minds of the two guards from here and they felt furtive, shifty even. Like they didn't want to be here. Like they shouldn't be here.

We can't deny who we are. She smiled and dropped off her rock, wrapping herself in the anonymity of the Kjarn as she strode into the space between the edge of the mountain and the ship, halving the distance between herself and the armed men in a matter of moments. Gently she grazed their minds, just enough to keep them from noticing her and secure in her confidence it should be enough, Kyra stepped past them, close enough to smell them. It had an astonishing effect on the weak minded, especially when they were lulled to boredom.

She preferred the subtle stuff to raw displays of power, being honest with herself. Gid had once ripped a moving ship out of the air to prove a point, something that had infuriated their master. She felt she could do the same, rather chose not to. Far easier to manipulate the pilot into landing. A mind was easier to manoeuvre than a machine, for her anyway. And as Amalfus had pointed out to Gid, what if the ship had been damaged by being ripped off its vector? He'd looked chastised, she'd felt a surge of glee until he'd rounded on her and inquired of her what if the pilots mind had been too strong to control?

Often your first thought of action was also the most dangerous. Far more than that, she'd had impressed upon her the dangers of inactivity. The worries of choosing the wrong path to the point that in the end you did nothing.

That had never been her problem, she thought as she strode into the darkness of the cave. Just as she had in the alley the previous night, she didn't need her eyes to see the twists and turns of the tunnel, the Kjarn guiding her footsteps as the sensations of violence grew ever closer. Just as a precaution, though she intended not to use it unless the situation was dire, she drew her kjarnblade from her bag.

Before long the tunnel led into a cavern and she found traces of light ahead, light, the faint auras of heat in the air. She heard yips and growls, howls and roars and she couldn't shake that pervasive feeling of unease seeping through her. Still she walked on, spirit summoner in her other hand. Just in case she needed to fight.

It's good to avoid a fight. Sometimes it's impossible not to. She hoped she didn't need to fight here. Curiosity had brought her in here, but she'd need to get herself out if the situation was not to her beneficiary. Nothing worse than a fight which couldn't be won. Or even one avoidable in the first place. The walls were cold around her, she couldn't sense any life within them. Odd. Normally when she opened her senses up to the subtle whisperings of the Kjarn, she could 'hear' all the things that nobody ever saw. The vermin, the insects, the parasites might not leave much of a presence but a trace of one regardless. For it to be completely devoid of life was curious.

Reaching the mouth of the corridor, she leaned against the wall and craned her neck into the pit below, curious as to what she might find. A rough path had been cut down the side offering a way below. It didn't look manmade, she followed it with her gaze, tracing its path around the voices and the flames.

Men. All of them armed with assault weapons, all firing off in the direction of something she couldn't quite make out. Ice blue bolts, meaning stun blasts if she had it right. They'd been one of Master Amalfus' favourite training tools. Oversized wolves lurked in front of the men as well, all black furred with very prominent claws and teeth, a pair of curved horns emerging from their heads.

Despite her best efforts, the gasp slipped from her. Devil dogs. It was unusual to see them in Serran, they were a bad omen. Some said they harvested the souls of those deserving to die. Her eyebrow ascended higher, she grimaced as she fixated on them. The Kjarn was distorted through them. Like an echo repeating through the cavern, impossible to pinpoint anything about them. Even their exact location came out vague. She could see them with her eyes, but should she close them and rely solely on the Kjarn, it'd be unlikely she'd be able to lock them down.

Exactly the reason she should walk away. They were launching blasts of fire into the shadows, bathing the darkness in sticky orange heat, she thought she saw something in one of the corners in the half-light, their target not quite cowering but clearly taking cover.

She should walk away. This wasn't anything to do with her. With fire and stun blasts converging in on whatever was trapped down below there…

Woah!

Whatever they were after, it didn't have a sense in the Kjarn like anything she'd ever experienced before. When she touched it, she got one impression at the forefront of her mind and one impression only. Possibly the same reason eight men and twice as many devil dogs were trying to pin it down.

Power!

It was power tinged with something else but that didn't matter to her. She'd long since failed to acknowledge weak emotions so she didn't care much that this thing was frightened. It was powerful. And it was alive. It didn't feel human.

She fingered her spirit summoner, a small grin playing about her face. Maybe she'd see the way this played out. An invisible force ripped one of the devils up, hurled it against the pit wall less than twenty feet below her and she heard a spine crack. Involuntarily she flinched and then cursed herself. Idiot!

Unusual. It was very unusual for a creature to be able to employ telekinesis in the wild. Normally they could only use it following genetic augmentation. Not many knew, but it was the Kjarn in full force, making the modifications not only possible but workable. All life was connected. Through the Kjarn, humans and animals became connected, through the Kjarn spirit calling became possible, though very few knew the truth behind it.

She was so caught in her thoughts she almost didn't see the pillar of flame erupting towards her, a few of the devil dogs had caught wind of her amidst everything else. They had very strong olfactory senses, she remembered suddenly, leaping to evade the flames lapping at the rock. It had suddenly gotten too hot to stay and she was over open air, tumbling towards the ground. Simultaneously she activated her kjarnblade and her summoner. Ravalix materialised the same time as her blade, a great snake fashioned of copper and silver coloured rocks. Unharmed, she landed on the giant head, took in the surroundings. The black-clad men had already turned their attentions to her, rifles now pointing in her direction and she sucked in air and gave Ravalix a quick command. Deal with the hounds!

She had to fight. No other option.

The first blast came towards her and with great difficulty she batted it back the direction it had come with her blade, the force almost tearing the weapon from her hands. Laser blasts were a form of energy. The refined focused Kjarn making up her blade was a superior form of energy. Simple effort to repel it away from her. She saw the refracted blast hit a man, not the firer and he crumpled in on himself as he went down, she dropped into a roll across the floor, feeling blasts chip stone behind her as she took the legs off the goon closest to her and he went down screaming, his last shots flailing wildly into the ceiling. He wasn't dead, she could still hear his screaming through her Kjarn-fogged mind and she thrust her blade backwards, cutting him off mid-sound before striking back two more blasts, the force of their assault pushing her back inches.

She gestured with her free hand, watched two of them suddenly fly backwards, drank in their shock and fear as they hit the wall and went down, she felt the snapback through the Kjarn as their life left them. Suddenly breathless in the pit of her stomach, she silently cursed and swept her blade up in front of her in a defensive formation, anything to keep back the shots until she could catch her breath.

Behind her, Ravalix was ripping through the devil dogs with all the lack of subtlety one would expect from a twenty-foot snake made of minerals. She felt more shots come at her, only just managing to push them aside, her lungs gulping stale air as stun blasts hammered at her, her features bathed in pink and silver light as she struggled to keep them back, both hands on the busy blade.

All the air was suddenly kicked out of her as something hard struck her in the small of the back, immediately flat on her face, limbs refusing to respond and kjarnblade dead in her hand. She could taste blood in her mouth. It was all she could do to stay conscious, keeping her eyes open a tremendous effort. Above her, she could hear fresh footsteps from on high. Footsteps and laughter. Her mind felt a mess, she couldn't gather the Kjarn.

Three of them above her. She could sense them, sense but not touch. Not affect. She ground her teeth in her bloody mouth. Come on!

Three separate stun blasts hit her at close range, cut through any resistance she might have, defiance the last thought to come to her.

The tenth day of Summerpeak.

135

His face hurt, his eyes were sticky with disuse and he didn't know where he was. For several long moments, Wade Wallerington blinked repeatedly. He was laid in a bed, he knew that much, surrounded by white. He almost sat up with a start, felt the cables attached to him, as he shifted in his bed and grimaced. Almost unconsciously he moved to scratch the discomfort at his face, fingertips brushing against cloth. The room stank of disinfectant, horribly sterile. Hospital then. He hadn't died. That was a relief. Though at what cost. Every blink was like a pinprick to his eyeball, he whined as the tears threatened to poke their way through the membranes, salt stinging the sore muscle.

He hadn't come this far in life through overreacting when things were out of his control. Beyond the white, he could see shadows, hear muted voices until a bright light snapped into his vision, forcing him to squeeze his eyes shut, blocking it out.

Chapter Eleven. This Flesh Is Fragile.

"When you have examined every option, when you've run down every possibility, when you think you should have the answer, but you don't, you're missing something obvious. Don't be afraid to think outside the box. Sometimes lateral thinking is needed to solve a puzzle with no immediate answer. Don't be afraid to ignore the improbable. Remember, your enemies are trying to get away with it and will stop at nothing."

Prideaux Khan lecturing Unisco trainees on investigation techniques.

The eighth day of Summerpeak.

Neither of them waited after the silence that had greeted their knock. Leclerc and Fagan had looked at one another, then drawn their weapons. Neither of them wanted to take chances. Casual inquiries at the desk had told them Maddley hadn't left his room. He had to be in there.

Twice they'd knocked. Three times. Again, they glanced at each other and then Fagan stepped back, leaving Leclerc a run at the door. He sized it up, brought his foot viciously into the door, it gave a little but not relenting on its hinges. Once more he kicked, this time it flew open and they entered the room, mufflers active and weapons up. Main room empty. Closet empty.

The bathroom wasn't.

"Fuck!" Fagan yelled, backing out of the room, face contorted with disgust. "We're too late."

His heart heavy, Leclerc stepped past him and glanced into the bathroom, saw the body on the floor and groaned. "Damn." He said, more curse words in native Serranian and shook his head.

"That's Maddley all right," Fagan said, already past him and standing over the body. He leaned down, placed a hand on the body. "Huh, not been dead long. Still could pass for human." He continued to look down at the body, Leclerc turned tail and took in the main room. The door had been locked, the key card was still in its slot powering the room. The viewing screen across from the bed had been cracked, rendered inoperable. He could feel cold air blowing in from the machine on the wall, could see the window open.

On a hunch, he checked the open window, looked out onto the promenade beneath, he could see dozens of people milling about, all oblivious to what was going on above them. Well, maybe not all oblivious. Someone knew somewhere.

"Nicer than our digs huh?" Fagan called. "No sign of any visible entry or exit-wounds. I'm not sure what killed him here."

Leclerc didn't hear, still studying the scene below out the window. If someone had killed him, it wasn't impossible they could have exited through the window. Maddley had kept a room only three floors up of the Oceanside, high enough to make a nasty splat if you hit the ground. And if the assassin had left via a spirit or something, there was always a chance someone saw something. Especially if it involved a bird large enough to be able to carry a person. Even shimmying the side of the building would have left some witnesses, even this time of night.

So how had they done it?

He could still sense the ghost.

It was the second surprise he'd found involving that thing and even then, not the biggest shock of the day. As Scott wandered back to his room, he felt something, a presence in the distance, not an exact position but a vague sense of location. It felt stronger, like a pressure in his head if he faced the right direction and started walking, weakening if he turned away.

So how was he going to use that? He'd been impressed with the potential raw power of that ghost. It had nearly done for him, run rings around both him and Palawi. But that was the problem. It had run rings around him and Palawi. There wasn't a guarantee come the next time he'd be able to prevent it from doing the same thing again. Admittedly he hadn't been prepared. But was there much more he'd be able to do under the same circumstances?

Maybe he should look for some special ghost containing equipment. It obviously had its merits. And there wasn't any shame in doing something the easy way if it worked. It all boiled down to a point of view. Doing something the hard way didn't score you any extra points, didn't make you better or worse. Being a martyr wasn't for everyone, it was a hard path and not one he really wanted to walk. Sometimes he craved simplicity.

He'd strode into the lobby of his hotel, aware of how much worse for the wear he looked, and he saw her, exactly the last person he wanted to see looking like this. It had been too long, and he suddenly found himself despising fate for throwing them back together at the worst possible time.

Last time he'd seen her; she'd been beaten up by that freak-of-nature Harvey Rocastle, her nose smashed, covered in her own blood. He could remember feeling helpless as he'd watched it happen. They'd managed to fix her nose, only a slight crook remaining where she'd taken the blow. Strangely, it didn't make her less attractive, he couldn't help managing a smile as their eyes met. He could see her taking in his dishevelled appearance, the blood and stains covering him, and his smile grew a little more apologetic. She approached, he smelled her as she sashayed up to him, a little odour of the heavens. Judging by the wrinkle of her nose, she could smell him as well.

"Whew... You been rolling in garbage?"

"Had a..." Best way to describe what had happened? "A minor incident on the way over. Nothing too serious. Bit ill is all. Might have had a reaction to medical webbing." Not true but it'd do for the time being, given he didn't have any other explanation that made sense. "Never mind me, how are you?" He looked pointedly at her as he saw the hesitation, a look of worry on her face at the question. "Been avoiding me?"

That got a reaction. "No! Never." She looked hurt by his comment and immediately he felt bad. Really bad. Like it was the worst thing he'd ever said. "I've not been avoiding you."

"I was joking!" It burst out of him and he was aware how lame it sounded. Mia looked a little startled by it, an eyebrow rising.

"I got that," she said. "But I'm hurt that you think I'd be avoiding you. Why would you even think that?"

"Because I've not seen you for a few days," he said. "You remember what happened last time we were together in the same building?"

"Yeah!" He couldn't miss the sarcasm. "Probably better than you. Scott..." He could hear it fade from her voice and he exhaled sharply. "Can we talk? In private? Not down here."

It took him half a second to answer and he gave her a grin. "Sure. Step into my room."

Okay, with hindsight maybe it wasn't the best idea he'd ever have. His room had been left a bit of a sty recently, ever since Jess had stopped coming, he'd kinda stopped giving a shit. Housekeeping hadn't been in for days, he'd purposely locked them out, and mentally he blanched at the underwear he'd left on the floor. The words Jess would have uttered if she'd seen it came to mind, the second uncomfortable twitch more noticeable than the first.

Can't take you anywhere nice, can I? It was like hearing her voice and he grinned at the memory. Wasn't like he had to put up with that any more, thankfully.

Still it wasn't the ideal thing he'd liked Mia to have seen on her first visit to his room. He wondered if he could kick them under the bed before she noticed them. Unlikely, knowing his luck, he'd forget they were there. Be a bit embarrassing when he suddenly remembered it a few thousand miles away, it'd probably mean he wouldn't be returning to the hotel. But then again, if it hadn't been heavily subsidised by the ICCC, he wouldn't be here anyway. Coming back soon wasn't an option. No point missing what he'd never have again.

He shot a grin at Mia, a little unnerved by the circumstances. "Yeah, sorry about the state. Didn't know I'd be entertaining."

Fair play to her, she made a point of avoiding looking around, despite the twitch in her eyes as if she wanted to peruse. "I've seen worse. Should see the dressing rooms some of the guys have on the spirit dancing circuit. They can be right divas about stuff. Things get thrown about. Sometimes they break stuff." Scott, remembering his most recent encounter with a spirit dancer, only smiled politely.

"Yeah I can imagine."

"Pair of pants on the floor?" She asked, before scoffing politely. "You're an amateur in the trashing places terms, flyboy. Sorry to tell you that."

"I've never been so happy to hear that," he grinned. He was surprised to find he genuinely meant the words as well. "Hey, we're all human right. All do stuff sometimes."

She grinned at him. "Oh yeah." Mia sniffed at the air, her nose wrinkling as she did, as if she could smell something on the air. What it might have been, he couldn't say. "You have many other people up here?"

He shrugged. "Not recently. Just me. And I've not been spending much time here. Just sleeping." Don't mention old sweat, don't mention old sweat, he urged himself quietly. "You know how it gets, I imagine. Sometimes it's hard to settle somewhere so you just make yourself comfortable how you can. If tossing some clothes around makes it feel more like home, I say do it."

"Home," she said with a chuckle. "You never lived at my house growing up. My mom'd have gone nuts if we'd left clothes on the floor."

"Heh." He wanted to add that his would have as well, but the truth was he honestly didn't know if she would or not. Maybe if she'd been there for him more often, he'd have had the chance to find out. "Nice for some freedom, eh?"

"Definitely," she said. Now she was looking around easily, running her eyes into every corner of the room and at the turn of the head, he could see the crook in her nose more prominently.

"Hey, can I ask you something," he said. "You know when you've tried claiming a spirit?"

"Yeah." She looked a little taken aback, like she'd expected something else but nodded regardless.

"And you know when it gets away?"

"No but go on." Big cocky grin as she said it.

"Oh, it doesn't matter then," Scott said, watching her sit down on his bed, she tested the springs with a motion that made her breasts bounce pleasantly. He could see she still had the look about her, figured he should get it back on track. "Yeah, sorry. I guess you didn't come up here to talk about the trade though, huh?"

"Nope," she said. He shot a glance towards the bathroom, then back to her. He could hear the shower calling following the endeavours of the day. Maybe burn the clothes as well. They'd seen better days, it'd be cheaper to buy new than get them repaired. Shame. He'd liked these jeans. Now they were shredded and stained with blood and alley filth.

"Mind if I hop in and get cleaned up first?" he asked quickly. "I mean, sorry, but…"

"Sure," she said, grinning. "Go right ahead."

Scott, not hearing her and expecting an argument carried on as if she hadn't spoken. "I mean I got injured earlier, I'd…"

"Scott, it's fine."

"… Don't want infection, I mean what?" He gave her a surprised look. "Okay. Sorry. Didn't expect that. Was expecting an argument."

"Does you wanting a shower usually devolve into an argument?" she asked. "Limited hot water?"

Well, he'd sometimes wound up in it with Jess. "Mia, m'dear," he said, tipping her a wink. "You don't know the half of it. I'll be a moment and then we'll talk. Sorry."

"No need to keep apologising," she smiled. "As cute as it might be."

He came out, clutching the towel around himself, saw her turn her head and take a long look at him, her eyes drinking in every detail. He fought the urge to slip back into the bathroom, instead he met her eyes and gave her a grin.

"Like what you see? Take a picture, it'll last longer."

He hadn't expected her to oblige, but she drew out her summoner, one of those models with a picture box on and before he could react, she'd snapped several images.

"Cheers," she said. "Always glad to get permission. Nice abs. You work out?"

"Nah," he said. "Not especially. Just do a lot of walking about the place. Sometimes we got to run from stuff. And climb up stuff.

You?" He corrected himself. "I mean are you one of those spirit dancers who goes everywhere by private hovercar?"

She raised a thin eyebrow in bemusement, her mouth crinkling up with mirth. "I don't know anyone who does that. Not off the top of the head. Hey, I think you're getting caught up on the result. We still claim spirits just like everyone else. You should know that."

Yeah, I should. Scott grinned at her. "So, what did you want to talk about then? Come on, let's do it. You and me... Talk! Talk, I mean." He felt heat stroking his face in cruel amusement at his slip. She didn't have to sit there looking so alluring. Worse part was she didn't look like she realised he was doing it. He looked around for a fresh pair of... Well anything. He felt a little exposed right now. She didn't seem bothered though. He straightened up, relaxed a little. He got the impression she truly didn't care.

"Yeah. I haven't seen you for a while and..."

"Well I assumed you were in hospital for the last few days. I came to visit." It was true as well. He had. That was when he'd found out she'd checked out. "More than once. First time you were in surgery.

She opened her mouth to interrupt, he didn't let her. "I mean; they did a cracking job I've got to say. Can barely tell you had the shit kicked out of you. I mean, he was like what? Three times the size of you and you come out of it well." He was rambling now, he knew it and he couldn't bring himself to stop. His mouth had gone onto autopilot, his brain keeping pace but barely. "Had the feeling he was a bad 'un. Could have told you that. You know you should be careful about who you trust..."

"Scott!"

"I mean look at you now. Sat there alone in a hotel room with a mostly naked man you barely know. No wonder you get into trouble like that. What's next? Skinny dipping in the lake when there's a maniac on the loose? Because I'd be up for that. Hey, I'm already dressed for it..."

"Damnit will you listen to me!" She exclaimed, the surprise enough to silence him. He almost dropped the towel in shock but held on. It probably wouldn't make the situation any better, letting her see what lay underneath. "I know. I got out and well, I was shaken up. Can you hold that against me? Have you any idea what that feels like? I didn't want to be in that position. I didn't want to be someone you and your idiot sidekick felt you needed to rescue! I'm glad you did it but... Just drop it okay. I'm not a fucking damsel, okay?"

The anger she'd given off at first had slowly dissipated with every word and now she was calm, resigned but calm. "I didn't want to be like that. You know who my dad is. He insisted Matt and me both took self-defence classes. Me especially." She scoffed bitterly at the words. "Because I'm his special little girl or whatever. But only when he wants me to be. Only when he's not doing other stuff like working miles away or coming home with laser burns or… You know I fought. I fought Harvey and I'll not let you get away with… Whatever it is you think."

Her eyes were glistening in the corners and Scott felt a tinge of pity for her, easily overwhelming the amusement he'd felt at hearing Pete described as his idiot sidekick. He'd have appreciated that if he was here to hear it. "I didn't abandon you. I had a nice time on our first date. I really did. Apart from… Him. You were perfect. Which is why I felt so crappy about staying out of touch."

"Why did you then?" he asked softly. He dropped onto the bed next to her, careful to keep his modesty intact. He could smell her perfume, an exotic mix making his own eyes water.

She pointed to her nose. "This. Scott. They couldn't fix it. Not all the way. I… I couldn't face you with it." She trembled as she said it, the realisation behind her words dawning on him as she spoke. "I mean look at me. I'm hideous. You know how many times I almost walked out of the lobby while waiting for you to come back? Loads. I saw it so many times you'd turn your back on me and I couldn't face it. I didn't want your scorn."

He couldn't help himself, under the circumstances. It was probably the wrong thing to do but Scott Taylor burst out laughing and even with the look on her face, he couldn't stop.

"Mia… Have you been taking drugs?"

"Yeah, they gave me some strong painkillers, why?" she started to ask before catching his meaning. "I mean, no, but…"

He placed a hand on her shoulder, looked her in the eyes. "Mia Arnholt. You have just said without a doubt the absolute dumbest thing I've heard in my entire life. Truly. You can barely see that thing. And it kinda… trust me on this, it kinda suits you. Who was it who said that beauty flourishes more in the face of its flaws?" He might have just made it up on the spot, but it sounded good.

"It's not bad. It gives you character. It says you've taken knocks and you don't care, you've got back up and carried on. I don't think any less of you because you had your face smashed in by a messed-up whacked-out crazy freak of nature. And if you think it messes up your face, you're wrong. And besides, you've got more than just being fit as…" he nearly said fuck, choked it back. "Something different from what I was just about to say. You've got a vibrant personality. You're single minded, you're not afraid to go after what you want. I mean look at the way you were chasing me."

She raised an eyebrow. She seemed more at ease now, relief pouring out of her. "I wasn't chasing you."

"Yeah… You really were," he said with a grin. "You might not have been doing it intentionally but believe me, you've been doing something. J… my ex really had a thing about you being around me."

"Ah dear Jesseka. The angry one. Least I was never that insecure," she said with a smug grin. The angry one summed her up nicely. Pretty much in the same way as describing the sun as the hot one. "I'd have expected you to throw me out if I ever got that self-absorbed. She's an idiot, you know."

"Really?"

"Yeah. Because I wouldn't have let you go." She sounded like she meant it as well. He could tell in her voice, not even a trace of deceit in it. "But I'm not going to lie. I have wanted you ever since I first met you. Longer. Ever since that time you fought my little bro. I saw you and I was like, wow."

That took him by surprise. "How come?"

"Maybe I've just got a thing for half black dudes," she replied flippantly, he couldn't miss how she was avoiding the question. If she had a better reason, she wasn't about to spill

"Well we've got it out in the open," he said. "Mostly. Anyway, with that in mind, what are we going to do about it?"

Apparently, she already had something in mind as she leaned over to brush her lips against his before playfully pushing him down to the bed, his towel falling away from his waist. She glanced down and smiled. "Yeah, I can work with that."

"You better be able to," he said as she wriggled down to kneel on the floor at the bottom of the bed, her hair tickling his stomach. "It's the only one I got."

She grinned at him, winked and blew him a kiss. "So glad to hear it. I'd be running out screaming if you had two."

He made to reply, it was lost in his throat as she took him in her mouth, working away with sudden tender vigorousness, the surprise shutting him up. Jess had never been a fan of it. She'd said it made her feel unclean. Mia didn't have any such hang-ups, she worked away, and the pleasure waves threatened to overcome his sensibilities, a dopey grin on his face and there she was, bobbing away, her lips teasing back and forth across his shaft, she knew what she was doing, and he was getting closer and closer…

A bang on the door and he was snapped out of it, sitting bolt upright at the same moment her efforts came to fruition and her eyes widened as salty fluids filled her mouth and he let out an involuntary yell of delight.

"Scott! You in there!"

Pete!

Mia, still with part of him inside her looked at him with a surprise in her eyes and slowly she let him slide out of her before running into the bathroom. He heard her spitting violently and that killed some of the illusion, especially as she returned rubbing her mouth.

Already he had the towel back around him, limping towards the door, not quite sure what to say to Pete. It was for damn sure he wasn't going to let him in, he knew that.

Right now, he just didn't want to share what had just happened. He would need to talk to Pete eventually, but he wanted to savour the moment while it lasted.

The tenth day of Summerpeak.

He couldn't see right out of his eyes. Everything cast unusual shadows, the lights bright and the people blurry. All efforts aside, Wade had panicked the moment he'd first realised that, only calmed down when one of the doctors had told him it was only temporary. It would heal up and he'd be back to normal in a few months or so given frequent treatment. Suddenly he was relieved he would have been able to afford it, even if Unisco weren't footing the bill. As they should, considering he'd been injured in the line of duty. Considering everything that had happened, it could have been a whole lot worse as well. He'd nearly hit the ground having fallen off his mount and when he'd heard the full story, he couldn't help but feel a little bad Nick had chosen to grab him rather than catch that woman.

That woman… She'd been a wild one. There'd been something about her which worried him, he wasn't quite sure what she'd wanted with Maddley. Because as he'd laid here, he'd had the chance to think and he was sure it was about more than an illegal fight in the skies. People didn't react that badly to what was a minor crime. They didn't blow up buildings just to cover their getaway. That was like trying to get away from a parking violation by robbing a credit depository. It just wasn't done. Not even in the slightest.

That fucker hadn't helped. He really hadn't.

It had been earlier, he'd been laid with his eyes closed, trying to ignore the sharp pains in the side of his face when he'd slowly became aware of another presence in the room, breathing not his own and the smell of an all too pungent cologne. Something about him looked familiar, the light shone off his bald head and he had a beard surrounding a face that was distinctly piggy. Not fat but the composition of the mouth and nose had that feeling about him. He wore a suit that must have been warm even under the conditioned air of the hospital.

"Can I help you?" Wade inquired. His throat felt dry, he scrambled for the bottle of water on his bedside table. Even as he slopped some of it over his chin, it felt good. Cold and wet, the way he needed it.

"Oh, I think you can, Mr Wallerington," the man said with an air of sarcastic cheeriness. "I think you can. My name is Mallinson and I work with the inquisitors. I've been wanting to talk to you about the attack on the ICCC building."

"Think I should debrief first," Wade said quickly. "You're literally the first person I've spoken to since I woke up who doesn't work here. I want to talk to either Brendan King or Vas Derenko. They're the ranking agents here." He purposely didn't mention the director. Even in times like these, you kept some sort of protocol going on.

"And I want you to talk to me." Mallinson didn't sound impressed with his response. "Never mind those two. You're mine for the time being, I intend to treat you that way."

Already Wade was wondering how best to end the conversation given he couldn't get up and walk out of the room physically. "Well I'm not sure exactly what I'll be able to tell you, Agent Mallinson..."

"That's Inquisitor Mallinson!" the bald man snapped. "Not agent."

That resonated a little and he suddenly remembered where he'd seen the man and heard the name before. Mallinson. The man was a legend for all the wrong reasons. All Unisco agents had heard of him, very few wanted to meet him. He'd anointed himself the guardian of Unisco integrity, a role he took all too seriously. There were other inquisitors, dozens of them, but this asshat had a rep for being the worst of them all.

"And you're going to tell me everything that you know. I don't want speculation, I don't want evasion, I want answers to my questions. You comprehend?"

"I'm happy to help," Wade said slowly. That piggy face contorted into a sarcastic leer at him and he would dearly have loved to have given him a smack.

"I don't care if you're happy or not. Tell me about the incident in your own words. What were you and Agent Roper doing up there in the first place."

"Do you have a statement from Agent Roper?" Wade asked.

Mallinson glared at him. "I'll ask the questions here, Agent Wallerington. You might be some big shot out there but here, you're mine so don't forget that."

It had continued in that vein, Wade had answered them to the best of his ability, some of the events were blurred and he said as much to the clear displeasure of the inquisitor. He didn't know how long they'd gone on, but he'd been permitted some rest eventually. And Mallinson had gotten up and departed, leaving him alone with his thoughts. He'd wanted to get up, test his body out but the nurses had flat out ordered him not to even try it yet.

He hadn't remained alone long when he'd been granted yet another surprise visitor, President Ronald Ritellia himself striding into the room like he owned the place, a couple of aides in tow as well as Tommy Jerome and a strange woman Wade didn't know behind him.

"President," he said respectfully. Ritellia might be becoming more unpopular as time went by but for the time being, he still held the title and he'd show him according respect.

"Wade Wallerington," Ritellia said. "How are you?"

He wanted to laugh and laugh and laugh despite the circumstances. There was just no easy way to answer that after all.

The fourteenth day of Summerpeak.

The same stadium the whole thing had started, Scott noted as he found himself in the crowd once more. The second round had finished earlier with Simon Shaw edging out Edyta Bryckov with considerable difficulty, but he'd triumphed at the end. Scott had seen him on the way in, sat smugly on his own. He had a face like a rat he'd noticed, pointed and twitchy. Yet even one potential douchebag didn't kill his mood as he drank in the atmosphere of the stadium around him.

It felt like every time he came here, it got emptier and emptier as people went through and went home in equal numbers, spectators coming and going, the old replaced by the new and he couldn't help feeling relieved he'd at least gotten this far. The third round. The last twenty-four. He wasn't sure who was going out as worst winner, but he had a good feeling it wasn't him. The rumour went around that the ICCC did at least inform the unlucky guy beforehand, so it wasn't a shock. If that was the case, he could sit pretty knowing he'd be at least in for another match. Only four from the final. Third. Quarter. Two semi matches... He was starting to believe. Somehow, he felt more confident now than before.

Still he could feel the presence of that ghost clamouring for his attention. Pete hadn't known. Nothing he'd looked up had been able to explain it. Depending on when his bout was, he'd make his best efforts to go chase it down. He'd never felt obsession like this over a spirit before. Maybe it was the fact that he could feel its presence. He wanted it to stop, if claiming it was the only way, then claim it he would. Whatever it took. He wanted it out of his head.

Mia came in with Pete, the two of them sitting next to him. He fought an urge to put an arm around Mia. All the time they were there, he couldn't help but keep his attention on Pete. Somehow, he had a feeling that this might be the round they were drawn together. Should that happen, he honestly didn't know if he'd be able to beat him in a straight-up, no-backing-down fight. He couldn't say for certain he could, knew it would be tight.

He wondered if Pete was thinking the same thing. It felt so long since they'd last clashed in battle, way back in Burykia. And he'd been with Jess then… Weird thought. He hadn't thought about her for a while. Why should she pop into his head when he looked at Pete? He shook himself, got a strange look from Pete who rolled his eyes. Things had been strange for a while. Mia leaned over and whispered in his ear, lips bare millimetres from his skin. He could feel her breath. "Dinner after this?"

"Sounds good," he said. He couldn't help but grin. "Let's hope it goes better than last time." He saw the slight crook in her nose and knew she got what he'd meant.

If it had been Thomas Jerome to announce the second-round draw, the spotlight was back with Ronald Ritellia this time, the fat man waddling up with great glee as he announced his presence onstage with a harsh clearing of his throat.

"Good ladies, likeable gentlemen," he said, a furrow creasing his brow at the words. Scott wasn't surprised. It sounded wrong. Maybe some speech writers would be getting fired. "Once more I find myself here before you all and I think to myself, has it really been just a few weeks since I first stood before you with Premier Nwakili and announced the tournament underway? And I always come up with the same answer. Yes, it has. But it's not over yet, there is more and more to come. We find ourselves at the third-round stage, twenty-five contestants victorious and through…"

He tailed off. "Except that isn't the case. Because we find ourselves at the point where twenty-five becomes twenty-four. It has been emotional, yet all journeys must come to an end. Sometimes it must happen, sometimes it is beyond our control and today we must say goodbye to a great champion. As everyone knows, the International Calling Competitive Committee building came under attack days ago from parties unknown. Although our home may have been tarnished, our will grows stronger and we refuse to be intimidated by faceless cowards who would attack innocents."

His face grew black like thunder, but his voice stayed strong "However, one of our number must leave due to said attack. Wade Wallerington, you all know his name. Due to injuries suffered in this senseless attack, I spoke to Mister Wallerington yesterday myself and he has withdrawn to focus on recovering from his injuries."

He cleared his throat. "I would like to read aloud a statement from Mister Wallerington in relation to this." Ritellia tapped down on a pad on the podium in front of him and cleared his throat again. "In the light of circumstances beyond my control, I have respectfully chosen to withdraw from the competition due to the nature of my injuries, feeling I will not be able to give a good account of myself from my hospital bed. I thank the staff of the hospital for their help and apologise to everyone who may feel I've let them down. However, I feel it would not be fair for someone else to go out under these conditions when I would likely falter in the next round. Therefore, I give my place to whoever originally had been due to depart. It is the least I can do."

Scott looked at Pete. Pete shrugged.

Any touch of solemnity Ritellia might have held for the moment was lost as he raised his head and grinned at the crowds around him. "A noble sacrifice. With that out of the way, shall we see our draw for the next round?"

"Well, we had to come up with a good way of containing ghosts, of course. It might get nasty eventually with thousands of them running amok. A good craftsman always has a plan. With this particle barrier, they can at least be contained over a small area, giving the caller chance to claim them. It finds the frequency the critters operate on, blocks them, stops them from running, even renders them somewhat corporeal for the time being. All completely illegal in professional bouts, for obvious reasons."

Thomas Rogan, inventor of the Ghost-Containment Particle Barrier, on his greatest invention.

The eleventh day of Summerpeak.

Alana studied the holoprojector in front of her and steadied herself. This was it. If her theory was right, she'd be lauded beyond her wildest dreams. If she was wrong, it wouldn't be a hammer blow to her career, but it certainly wouldn't help. But she had the hunch and it needed to pay off. The pieces were there, she was amazed she was the only one who'd fit them all together.

Wade Wallerington. Injured. Dragon. Mistress. Uniblast. Close range. When you had them all together like that, it sounded all so simple. Alana didn't agree with what the Mistress had done on her jaunt to Carcaradis Island. It had been a bad reckless move. Put aside privately and given the option to do so gracefully, even the Mistress might admit it wasn't the smartest thing she'd done.

It had fallen to her to be the one to take care of the witness. Darren Maddley had to die, there was no way around that and she'd been the one nominated to do it. And do it she had. The Mistress had ordered everyone be outfitted with the ideal weapon for assassination, the pegaserpent, a winged snake with a solitary prominent fang capable of delivering a deadly dose of poison. Through his window it had gone, it had gotten him and out it had come again. She wondered if he'd been found yet. Not that it mattered. There was nothing to tie the murder to her or to a spirit she owned or even to who she worked for. The perfect crime.

And if she reported in her suspicions, she'd be complicit in another. If Wade Wallerington was one of the men who'd chased down the Mistress, he too would need to be dealt with. It would unlikely be her who did that, not when she'd discovered it. Taking someone by surprise was one thing. Killing a suspected Unisco agent was something beyond her specialities. She'd been there with Ritellia and that loathsome Thomas Jerome when he'd told them he was pulling out due to injury. The irony, she had to note. He'd had to pull out of the greatest opportunity of his life because he'd sought to interfere with something that didn't concern him. The Mistress' dream trumped the vision of one puny little spirit caller.

It would make everything better. And that was all the justification she felt she would ever need as the projector fired into life and she heard the dial-up tone.

Here we go…

It felt like an age as the image of the Mistress flared into life in front of her, a neutral look on her aristocratic features. She was always hard to read, today her emotions were almost opaque.

"Yes?!"

She didn't sound impressed. Unscheduled communications were her forte after all, not those of her underlings. Alana steeled herself, kept her own face neutral. Showing too much emotion would be her undoing, would make the Mistress question what she was hearing. She could see the Mistress' manicured hands tapping impatiently on her desk, she made the choice to just plunge right in.

"I have a report, my Mistress," she said slowly. She wasn't worried about being overheard in the slightest. These lines had the best possible security to keep out eavesdroppers.

"Then report." She didn't just look impatient, she sounded it as well.

"Your last order was carried out," she said. Even if nobody was going to hear it, it wasn't wise to utter the words 'I killed' and 'Maddley' in consecutive order where it could be recorded. Even less of a good idea was owning up to it. She didn't want the Mistress to have that sort of evidence against her. "But there's something else. Something I think you should be aware of." She paused, teasing the words silently around the inside of her mouth to make sure they felt right. She couldn't afford to slip.

"Something I should be aware of, Ms Fuller?" She could hear the amusement. "Do tell, please."

That was when she went right out with it. "As you know, I've been keeping close to Mr Ritellia as per your orders. And recently I went with him to the hospital to visit someone injured in the recent incident when the ICCC building was attacked here on the island." The building you blew up, she didn't add. It wouldn't add anything to the conversation other than the Mistress' ire. "And there's something that just keeps playing about in my head. Are you aware that Wade Wallerington pulled out of the tournament?"

The Mistress bobbed her head briefly. "What of it?"

Oh my... You really don't see it? Are you really that clueless on this? Or is there something more to this? Alana wondered about it silently. Unisco did wear those devices that obscured their identities, maybe it left some sort of permanent psychological block on the mind of anyone who saw them.

"Wade Wallerington says he was injured when the ICCC building was attacked. I've seen some of the footage of that attack. There was... Someone being chased and two chasing on dragons. Wade Wallerington owns several dragons. Someone got blasted at point blank range. His injuries match up with what you'd expect from that. Burns. Partial vision loss. I asked a doctor innocently, I managed to coax it out of him that the injuries were anomalous compared to the others injured in the incident. He put it down to bad luck."

The Mistress had stopped tapping her fingernails on the desk, she sat with her chin in her hands, deep in thought. For a full ten seconds she didn't say anything, and Alana found herself curious as to what was going on inside that head.

"Sometimes I find it hard to believe in luck," she said. "Thank you for bringing this to my attention."

As the words came out, Alana wondered if she'd just signed the death warrant of Wade Wallerington. If he was what she'd just voiced her suspicions as, the Mistress couldn't let him live. It was unfortunate, but she'd made her choices and would have to live with them. That didn't bother her as much as she thought it might. Killing Maddley and being ready to eliminate Ritellia if the order came, had changed things. She found herself wondering how things had gotten so far out of hand so quickly. This wasn't what she'd signed up for. But it was to be what she'd ended up with. A means to an end. That was all it was.

Paradise would come. And she would be there in the upper echelons of that paradise, if not a queen then perhaps a duchess or something similar. Everything would be worth it.

It had to be.

She assumed that would be the end of it, at least until the Mistress spoke again. "One more thing. My brother made contact. Well done, Ms Fuller. You make me very happy. Thank you. My eternal gratitude goes out to you."

The fourteenth day of Summerpeak.

"I'm sorry," Pete said. "Just explain this to me once more. I still can't get my head around it."

"I've told you like five times now," Scott replied, his temper rising. Okay, so it was hard to believe but that wasn't the point. It was true, he'd experienced it for himself and if people couldn't come to accept that, then there was something wrong with them. "It spoke to me. It called me bagmeat and ran off."

"I believe him," Mia said. She was perched on one of the chairs, legs folded underneath her while she fiddled with her summoner. Pete rounded on her almost immediately, determined to call her on it. Inwardly, Scott blanched.

"I'm sorry, you're disregarding everything you've seen over the course of your life and just accepting his word on it? Really? Are you sure that's the best idea?"

"I also think it's worth accepting sometimes things happen in life that are new," Mia snapped. "I mean just because it hasn't happened doesn't mean it won't. Are you really so confident we've seen every new thing this life has to offer?" She continued to stare at him until confident he wasn't going to reply, then went back to fiddling with her summoner.

"Forget the fact whether it spoke or not," Scott said. "It's not actually important right now. The important thing is capturing it. I need to do it. I really do. And given I tried once and it gave me the run-around, I need another way."

"Best way to trap ghosts is to use a particle barrier," Pete said. "It stops them from, like you said, giving you the run-around. I mean I've never been a particular fan of using them to hunt spirits but if needs must, I'm sure we could rustle up one from somewhere."

"Yeah because particle barriers are really that common," Mia offered. "They're specialist equipment..."

"They are but you can rig one up from other stuff," Pete said. "I've been told."

"Can you rig one up from scratch?" Mia asked. Pete shook his head reluctantly. "Then why are you even bringing it up?"

"Because there might be someone around here who can," Pete retorted. "What are you even doing here anyway?"

"Pete?!" Scott exclaimed. "No need, my man. No need. I'm taking any help I can get right now."

Besides, he wanted to add, she's here because I want her to be here. He didn't say it out loud. It brought up too many questions he didn't want to answer yet. Not that he was ashamed there was something forming between him and Mia, he just wanted to enjoy that privacy while it was still something intimate to be celebrated. In time he'd be shouting it from the rooftops. Maybe when he won this entire thing. He had a chance now, he could feel it. He was getting closer. The third round was starting shortly, with Pete's sister in the commencing bout. They all knew who they'd be facing now, it didn't get any easier.

In a way, it was why he wanted the ghost, he supposed. It'd be a powerfully addition to his squad. The way it had run rings around him and Palawi, if he could bring out its best, it'd make him harder to beat.

Of course, even if he did manage to track it down before his bout with Weronika Saarth, there probably wouldn't be any point in sending it straight into battle. Those who used untested spirits straight at the deep end did tend to regret it. It was a chance he just couldn't afford to take.

He was confident about it any way. He didn't know much about Saarth. But rather her than Katherine Sommer, Pete's opponent. He'd heard rumours about that woman, he'd seen her battle before and she was a merciless, Pete already looking worried. Scott knew he knew he had a tough fight ahead and while some part of him might be relishing it, he also knew Pete would have wanted someone easier.

Hey, you need to beat the best sometime, buddy. Might as well be now. Going out now would hurt. Going out to the same opponent in later rounds would be even more painful.

"Okay," he said, suddenly startling himself out of his thoughts. "There has to be someone on this island who can rig together a particle barrier out of basic stuff. What say we go find them and ask them for their help? But on the sly, like. Because I don't want this getting out. I don't want someone else catching my spirit."

"It's not your spirit until you claim it," Pete said. "Remember that."

Scott felt a flush flare in his cheeks and he clenched his fists together, the action surprising him. That was a bit of an excessive involuntary reaction. He was right. It wasn't his. He still needed to claim it. But… It felt like he was almost halfway there, was his in all but reality. He could still feel the traces of their connection, he could remember how it had spoken to him and there was a part of him that felt it no matter where he was.

"Not yet," he said softly. "But it will be, Pete. I promise you that."

The fifteenth day of Summerpeak.

"And Theobald Jameson will be facing Sharon Arventino… Arventino… Arventino… Arventino…"

That memory was going to haunt him, he knew it. The morning after the draw, he'd woken up with the words echoing through the mind. Sharon Arventino. Possibly the single toughest caller remaining in the competition since Wallerington had quit. Theo had snorted when he'd heard. So much for being tough. He'd walked away when the going had gotten tough. It hadn't sounded like his injuries were that bad.

He hadn't mentioned his thoughts to Anne. Not a chance that he was doing that. Not that he cared what she thought, of course. It just wasn't relevant to any sort of interaction they'd had since then, and he wasn't about to waste words on something that didn't matter. All that mattered was that a tough opponent had been removed from the fields of play without him needing to face him. Because Anne Sullivan's training or not, he doubted there'd have been much he could do to stop Wade should he come out in full force. In the five matches he'd won so far, Wade had been imperious, in a way, Theo felt it was a shame he wouldn't be able to try his strength against him. Except he was also relieved that he wouldn't have to.

Besides he'd been training with Anne. And as sceptical as he'd been that it was a good idea, he had to admit it hadn't been the worse one he'd agreed to. Anne was a deceptively skilful caller, she'd have to be given her history, already he'd agreed to visit her home town after the tournament to see her preside over one of the local competitions.

Back when he'd been in the café having breakfast, she'd come over with that friend of hers and he'd been in a less than welcoming mood. Still she'd persisted, and he'd caught sight of her several times over the next days. He didn't think she was stalking him. The way she moved, so graceful and delicate, he got the impression that he wouldn't see her if she didn't want him to. That thought was even more impressive when you considered she had such a distinctive appearance with her soft silvery hair.

And then there'd been that one day that he'd turned, and she'd been there talking to Brendan King of all people and something had shifted in him. What they'd been talking about, he hadn't been close enough to hear but it had looked a serious discussion. He'd waited until it was over, and they'd split, watched her come towards him. It felt like she had that uncanny ability to know who was in her surroundings, she'd homed straight in on him and given him a smile as he'd stood with hands in pockets feeling uncomfortable.

"Theobald Jameson," she'd said with a smile. "Hello."

He'd seen the twitch as he savagely corrected her, anger flooding him at the use of his full name. Nobody used his full name. He hated they used it on the draw for the competition, despite him insisting that they call him Theo. Theobald was the name his father had given him, and he despised it almost as much as he despised the man. He'd already changed his surname to break associations with him. Nothing to connect them now. "Don't call me that!" he'd spat. "Theo, please. Just Theo. Nothing else."

When the shock had faded, he'd seen some trace of amusement on her face and if anything, it was quite soothing. When he reacted like that, people tended to avoid him, all part of the reason he did it. If he didn't want to hear what people had to say, he didn't listen to them. Period. Sometimes it was over before it even began.

Was it a little stupid? Not at all. He didn't think so. He only had so much time to become the best and he wasn't going to waste it on niceties. That was for the weak. Those who wanted to be liked more than they wanted victory. He wasn't one of them. Sure, there were those able to capture the hearts and minds of those around them, be adored and admired for not only being strong but for being a bleeding heart as well. Yet he'd noticed something about them. They were growing increasingly few. You could be one or the other, he honestly felt, and he wasn't going to waste time on being liked. After all this wasn't a popularity contest. It was a series of brutal battles and you couldn't waste time with pathetic emotions like desire to be popular.

His actions would bring him admiration.

It wasn't surprising Anne seemed to disagree with his outlook. A lot did, not understanding victory took sacrifice. She said she respected his single-minded desire and sheer stubbornness. Those first few training sessions had brought amusement more than anything else. He hadn't seen the point, hadn't wanted to see what she was on about. She had a pedigree as a caller, he could respect that, but what she was getting at here escaped him.

He didn't even know what had possessed him to agree with doing it. He'd done fine on his own for so long and why he should need it now... Except he'd remembered the bout with Nick Roper and it had put him into a cold sweat. He wasn't ready for the best of the best. They could still beat him through a mix of sheer power and experience, tactics and willpower, all of which he could possess in theory but wasn't there yet.

His strategy had always been strong attack, strong defence, press the psychological advantage. Intimidate the opponent. He'd always considered it a good starting point, but Anne had put it to him another way. What happened when their defence was stronger than your attack? Their power greater than your ability to resist it? What happened when they weren't intimidated by you? Only then did he start to understand the thinking behind what she was getting at. Sometimes, you need an alternative plan in case things weren't going your way. And despite her slight figure and her youthful face, he got the impression she really wasn't intimidated by his attempts to psych her out, he'd need to adapt to bring her down.

Those first few battles with her, he'd played his usual strategy and he'd won. Then she'd slowly stepped up her game, adapted her own style each time so previous engagements were useless to draw upon. If he pushed, she pulled back, bringing him up short. If he hung back, she did the same, drawing on his dislike of defensive tactics. If he set up to counter attack, she didn't give him the opportunities to hit back.

The point, she'd told him, was that following the same strategy every time makes you predictable. And when you're predictable, you're easy to beat. She'd pointed out some of the other callers in the tournament and showed despite their lack of power compared to him, their unpredictability and guile made them a lot more formidable than they first appeared.

Training with her, he had to admit, was dare he say, fun. She'd come out of nowhere and throw him a challenge, maybe put it in the form of a contest or a bet like she had the last time. Take me to dinner. He'd been amused by that. He'd had to do it, of course. She'd found the key to bringing down Atlas once again and that didn't annoy him as it might have done. When he'd realised that, he'd almost felt physically ill with himself. What effect was she having on him? Before he would have been furious with a loss and now he was accepting it.

Unsurprisingly she'd had words for that. Maturing. Sometimes, Anne had said, you need to accept things, that sometimes you can't do everything. Sometimes you need to accept the loss wasn't anything to do with you, the opponent was just that little bit better. It doesn't do you down any less, use it as a spur to work harder in the future. Make sure it doesn't happen again. Only if you refuse to learn from it, should you be angry and only with yourself.

He didn't want to take her to dinner. Theo didn't know what she wanted out of him or why she insisted on helping. He hadn't asked, she'd volunteered, and he'd often wondered about her intentions Either way, be they noble or selfish, she was the closest thing he'd had to a friend for a while. Someone he had a connection with.

Normally he saw people in three ways. Potential rivals. Actual rivals. Everyone else. He needed a fourth space for her. Maybe she had a crush on him, that thought alone enough to make him feel acutely uncomfortable. He hadn't spent much time alone with the opposite sex and in a way, he didn't see Anne that way. He'd have beaten himself up a few weeks ago for even thinking something like this, but he didn't want to ruin what had emerged between the two of them. Friendship. That word wouldn't ever have entered his vocabulary then, yet it had snuck into his life without his permission, leaving him powerless to do anything about it.

Theo had already made his decision though. A deal was a deal; his father had always drilled that into him. You make it, you follow through. He'd take her to dinner following his bout with Sharon Arventino. He'd honour the arrangement they'd had. He owed her that much. They'd continue to do what they did, then they'd see what the future held for them.

The tests had been done and he'd felt their scepticism. He'd heard them tell him there was nothing wrong with him, but he'd insisted they go deeper, that they check his bloodwork again. They didn't know what they were looking for, even if they did there was a chance they might not be able to heal him, but he'd done his best to make damn sure that they did everything they could. Their employer had certainly a big enough carrot dangled in front of her. It hadn't taken long for him to work out her angle. She wanted what she wanted, he could help her with that if she helped him. It was a risky move, granted, he could still sense just about enough of her intentions to know serving her up the sort of power she sought would likely be a bad thing. What she would do with it would fail to benefit people beyond her and those she surrounded herself with. She would be the worst type of ruler should that day arrive; she would make Vazaran despot dictators seem like kind thoughtful men. She preached paradise but what she promised was domination. He got the impression it wouldn't take long for the balance to tip from the benevolence she spoke to the cruelty she craved.

Unfortunately, Wim Carson couldn't bring himself to care. That was not part of his thinking process now. He had too many problems of his own to worry about what she might do. It was possible he may have misjudged her. He'd been faulting his own judgement for far too long, he couldn't keep doing it. And he had his own agenda to pursue.

Nothing good comes of great power being handed to those who'd misuse it. At least by entering in partnership with her, he could attempt to keep a check on her. It might not work, he had to try. And he might as well put into fruition his own plans from a comfortable base until he got back onto his feet. The times had not been good. Not since the Fall. He didn't know how many Vedo were left. He might be the only one and until they helped him, he was only a half-Vedo. Not even that. All the knowledge and memories, what good did it do him?

Now here he was, wearing one of those horrible blue gowns and awaiting them to finish prepping up their cocktail of drugs. Blue clad doctors and nurses swarmed around him, all looked busy, they were all going way too fast for a simple thing like this, only then that Wim Carson realised the drugs were kicking in. He didn't like drugs, not normally. But this was quite a pleasant feeling, made it hard to care about things. Things that should be towards the forefront of his mind just danced away out of reach. Hard to think. But not impossible.

Back in the day, he wouldn't have needed this. He'd just have slipped into a calming coma, let the Kjarn accelerate the natural healing process of his body and he'd have been fine. Ever since the Fall, that had no longer been an issue.

The most maddening thing, he had discovered since then, was being able to sense something but not touch it. Not utilise it. Not embrace it the way you had for so many years. He had once been so much and now he was so little. Even cleaned up and shaved, given fresh clothes and a room by his benefactor to sleep in, he was still a shadow of his former self. A pale reflection. Without the Kjarn that had guided him since he was a child, he was less than nothing. They'd taken it from him and he wanted it back. No matter the cost.

They'd found the cause, of course. He'd urged them to look into his bloodwork, he'd been able to feel them there inside him for a long time, and only then had they had results.

That strange doctor with the lisp, Hota, had come to him with a passive look on his face and Wim had been intrigued. When the men with knowledge had that expression on their face, it generally didn't bode well. Either they were excited and trying to hide it or they were terrified and trying even harder.

"Mithter Carthon," he'd said primly. "I have your tetht rethulth." He held out a data pad in front of him, slender fingers dancing across the buttons, bringing it to life. Wim locked his eyes on him as he did.

"Is it bad or good?" He asked before realising it might not have been the right question to ask. "Can you heal me? Or not?"

"We will heal you, Mithter Carthon," Hota said. "There are jutht quethionth to be athked firtht. I have never failed."

"There is a first time for everything, you know," Wim replied, stretching his fingers out in front of him uneasily. "And pride will always be the undoing of those who wear it as a badge of honour."

"There ith." Hota didn't sound like he was disagreeing. "Your proclamation of imminent death appearth to have been exaggerated. According to thith, you are in perfect health. Too healthy."

"That's what they want you to think," Wim said. "They're keeping me healthy. They don't want me to die. Not while they're feeding on me."

"Ath you inthithted," Hota continued, his face registering annoyance at being interrupted. "We examined your blood thampleth and it wath there that we found the anthwer." A holographic image flashed up in the space between them with a red tinge, a dozen red and white disc-like objects running across it and Wim realised it was a cross section of his own blood stream. "Ath you can thee here, everything lookth normal, ath can be expected, yeth?"

Without replying, Wim just nodded and folded his arms. "But if we look clother, then we can thee thith ith not the cathe." He hit a button and the holo-image began to expand, zooming in on one of the platelets. "Thith ith a hundred magnification. And thith ith where the problemth come into play you thee." Wim narrowed his eyes and stared at the image, trying to take in what he saw. More than that he found he was trying to process what he saw into something could understand.

"How small are they are?" he asked, still not quite able to believe it. Even at a hundred magnification, they were still little more than dots on the platelet.

"Beyond microthcopic," Hota said. "They're tho thmall that outthide the human body, they would ceathe to exitht. The light falling on them would cruth them. But in you, they thrive. Magnify a thouthand."

Even now they still looked small, but definition was coming in. It was like looking at an ant on a table. You could see the outline but not quite every little detail, Wim noticed. Way too many legs.

"Magnify a hundred thouthand," Hota continued and Wim recoiled at the sight of the ugly little creature biting onto his platelet, a hideous microbe with a thousand hairy little legs and three sets of jaws, the body covered in milky blind eyes and as the platelet rotated, he could see it was dug in with a single spike stuck into the cells.

"That's disgusting," he said.

"I agree abtholutely," Hota said amicably. "And you're filled with them. What doeth that make you? Other than medically interethting."

"Your bedside manner is terrible," Wim said dryly.

"Tell it to thomeone who careth," Hota replied. "You want curing or not? Oh actually, you want to thee thith?"

Still focused in on the creature, Wim watched as the platelet rippled suddenly with a faint sheen of blue energy and the creature went into frenzy, he could see it sucking the stuff in, growing bigger and fatter although the effect didn't last long. Within moments it was back to its normal size.

"Want to explain?"

Wim didn't. But what he'd suspected might just have been confirmed. When they'd been doing the tests, several times he'd reached for the Kjarn and several times, just as before, he'd failed. And now he knew. The things were feeding off it, off him. Knowing it to be true didn't make it better. The opposite, more likely.

"They're called tesicre," he said. "They're a rare type of energy parasite. They feed off the Kjarn." The former home of the order used to crawl with them. But they were never like this. They were harmless. They had been harmless.

"Don't thuppothe you know how to get rid of them," Hota said, closing the image. Wim grinned at him, looking more cheerful than he felt.

"Not even in the slightest. They were never like this. I never heard of them doing this. They shouldn't be able to..." Unless they were affected by the Fall. It had driven the Vedo mad. Caused them to turn on each other. Only those who had been away from the temple had been spared the worst effects. They'd come back to find the bodies. Even worse, they'd found the survivors. Something had corrupted the Kjarn if only briefly. Even unable to touch it, he'd been able to sense the film that covered it if he focused hard, like finding salt in sugar. Normally it was sweet. Every so often it would take on a different taste.

"Fortunate for you that I have thome ideath then," Hota grinned. "Not for nothing doeth the Mithreth rely upon my work. I will thave you, my dear Mithter Carthon. You'll awaken a new man."

His entire body ached as he awoke, felt bruised and battered like an oversized crash doll. The first thing he saw was her staring down at him, a tube in his throat preventing him from speaking. Hota, still wearing his scrubs was stood behind her, arms folded.

He could feel them both. Hota was smug, she was impassive. It was different than before. Beyond the pain, he couldn't feel anything of his body. But if there was pain, then at least he was still wired up right. His body still worked. That was good. Nothing broken. Nothing damaged. He let out a groan and Hota came over, gently easing the tube from his mouth.

"Thteady, thteady, Mithter Carthon," he murmured. "It wath a routhing thucceth. How do you feel?"

There was only the one way he could answer that question, his body on fire with agony and his mind still catching up with the waking state. Focusing in on the tube hurt. More than that, it was an effort. More of an effort than anything he'd done since first learning how to touch it. He had plenty of practice to get back in. Just for a moment, he thought it'd failed. More than once, he thought it would continue to fail. No matter how much he focused on the tube in Hota's hands, it failed to respond to his mental command.

Come... Come on!

Still he focused. The fires screaming through his body roared ever louder, he almost blacked out from the pain. He wouldn't. He couldn't. He needed to do this, he wasn't going to give up until he made it happen.

Had it twitched? He couldn't tell. His stomach churned. Being hungry wasn't a new experience for him. He could go longer, he just needed to feel it again. The first time of many. He needed it, then he could rest.

It twitched. It did more than that, it hovered up out of Hota's palm, a paltry inch into the air before it fell. Compared to what he used to be able to do, it was pathetic.

But it was a start.

And for the first time in years, Wim Carson felt settled as he lapsed back into unconsciousness. The hardest thing he'd ever done and the most peaceful he'd ever felt merged in one fleeting moment as the blackness rushed to claim him.

"Yeah, I remember Phillipe Mazoud. Ruthless bastard in every sense of the word. Whatever you do, don't underestimate him. He might not look like much, but he's a man who will put you in the ground given reason. You won't see it coming either. Always be reasonable with him, never turn your back and never let him see you bleed. He'll find a way to use it against you. I can't imagine a more dangerous man in charge of the Vazaran Suns."

Terrence Arnholt to Premier Leonard Nwakili upon Mazoud becoming head of the Vazaran Suns.

The fifteenth day of Summerpeak.

The image flickered in front of them, it wasn't a high-quality transmission but there was no mistaking the identity of the man. Phillipe Mazoud looked predominantly Vazaran but according to his file, he had some Serranian blood in him too. Stood watching in the background, Terrence Arnholt found himself wondering which side of him would be more reasonable. Vazarans were known to be hot headed and reckless. Serranians had a reputation for being wild and hot blooded. It wasn't a good combination in the slightest but Mazoud had to have some savvy. He wouldn't be the leader of the Vazaran Suns if he wasn't. Mercenaries with honour didn't follow just anyone. They'd kill anyone for credits, but they weren't suicidal.

It was an interesting model, one that worked for them. If you wanted them, they were the best, Mazoud had cultivated a not undeserved reputation for being reasonable just as much as being capable of wanton brutality. It was a lethal combination. Small wonder he held the sway he did in Vazara with more than twelve hundred highly trained mercenaries at his immediate disposal. And those were just the ones that they knew about. Arnholt had often wondered about the unaccounted ones. At what point do mercenaries become a militia?

He wanted to remain unseen for the moment yet still observe the discussion Allison Crumley was holding with Mazoud. As communications director for Unisco, it was her job to be with him in situations like this. Crumley was a matronly woman in her forties, her hair neat and equal parts ash blonde and grey, but the days of sitting behind a desk were slowly starting to catch her up. She'd flown in a few days earlier, along with Inquisitor Stelwyn Mallinson and Arnholt felt confident there would be a positive outcome to this conversation.

"Anything for Unisco," Mazoud said. "What can I do for you?"

"Mister Mazoud," Crumley said, her voice strong and authoritative in the silence of the room. "We would like words regarding certain actions your organisation recently found themselves engaged in."

He held out his hands and smirked. He had a turned down mouth like a slit, his eyes menacingly hooded. Long black hair hung down his face in oily ringlets. "Ms Crumley, I assure you everything we do is entirely within the legal limits of the operation zone. It may not be ethical, it may be immoral but believe me, I can say it is certainly not illegal."

Crumley didn't blink. Arnholt nodded to himself in approval. Being unfazed by bullshit was always a prime commodity not enough people appreciated. His old superior had described it as a key leadership quality. "I am afraid I may have to dispute that with you. Have the Dark Wind been out on patrol recently?"

"Perhaps. We recently lost quite a few of our ships on a training exercise." If he was bothered, Mazoud didn't show it. "There are always more of them."

"This training exercise wouldn't have taken place above the Elkan Ocean, would it, by any chance?" Crumley asked. The Elkan Ocean split Vazara and Premesoir, the area in which six HAX gunships had either been shot down or gone missing in a recent engagement, along with a prisoner transport and the staff crewing it. Not to mention the prisoner. Arnholt had a desire to see that it was found before that individual was back walking the streets unchecked.

Mazoud shrugged. "I don't have the details in front of me. That exercise you refer to was set out by someone else. Why do you ask?"

Crumley said nothing, just stared at him with a smug smile for a moment. "Because if this exercise consisted of what we believe it did, then not only did you break the rules of the five kingdoms, you broke your own code of honour. Six of our HAX's were shot down. They were escorting a prisoner transport."

Mazoud shifted on the spot, shrugging his shoulders again. His hangdog expression took on a pursed look that didn't fool Arnholt for a moment. "Sounds like you need to train your pilots better. I can recommend someone if you like."

"We know the Dark Wind was there," Crumley said. "What we want to know is why? Who sent you after that prisoner transport?"

"If you seem to know that we were there, regardless of whether we may or may not have been," Mazoud said smoothly. "Then you should also know it is largely beyond our abilities to hijack one of your prisoner transports. I'm not saying we couldn't do it. I'm saying it wouldn't be worth it. We never touched it. I can assure you that much."

There was something he wasn't saying, Arnholt knew. But as to what he was hiding, he couldn't say.

"But you know who did?" Crumley asked, raising an eyebrow. Mazoud tutted angrily and waved a finger playfully at her.

"Ms Crumley, this is not our first dance. You know I can't divulge that sort of sensitive information. It goes entirely against our organisations principles. We can't share it with you of all people."

"It goes against the principles of your organisation to start fights with Unisco," Crumley said angrily. "Remember, for all the people of Vazara might see you that way, you are not the law. You're not even close. You're just thugs for hire."

"Thugs for hire who have you outgunned five to one," Mazoud replied, his voice as oily as his hair. "Ms Crumley don't make threats you aren't capable of carrying out. Don't insult my intelligence by thinking I make my decisions lightly."

"Mister Mazoud, you don't have to be against us on this. We look after our own. You look after your own. Surely we can come to some understanding."

"I'm sorry, Ms Crumley but I'm sure it would be highly inappropriate for an organisation of our status to associate with you. Some of our clients are the unsavoury type. A conscience is nice, but business is business. I do not want to war with you. It would be bad for both of us."

"All we want is a name," Crumley said. "Just point us in the right direction."

Mazoud shook his head. "I will not give up our clients. You assume too much I respect your organisation. How long do you think you can continue to go on when your leader won't even come out and face me? Your days number far fewer than ours."

That settled it, Arnholt thought, striding into view. Time to make an executive decision, especially given something was bothering him about this whole thing. "Okay, Mazoud, I'm here." He saw Mazoud's face light up with delight and carried on speaking before he could come out with some sarcastic comment. "Answer me one question and we'll let you get back to your day. All this time you've overseen the Suns, you've never hassled us before. For that, I respect you. It makes both our jobs easier. We don't want to go to war with you, just as you don't with us."

"I am not giving up my client," Mazoud repeated. "Director Arnholt. So nice of you to make an appearance."

"I'm not asking you to give them up," Arnholt said. "I respect your integrity. I find it infuriating but I respect it. I'm going to give you it in a different way. For as long as I can remember, you've not hassled us. But you had to have known what you were getting into here. HAX gunships are easily recognisable. Someone had to have radioed it in, if it was a surprise. But I'm curious. How many credits did it cost to make you attack us?"

For a moment, he thought Mazoud might disconnect the line in disgust before the thin lips broke apart revealing yellowed teeth and he heard the bark of laughter across the line.

"A good question," he said, folding his arms. "Director, I want to correct you on something. Our order was never to attack. Only to delay. The order was given to only fire in self-defence. It wasn't the case, but in these situations, you can never plan everything. To answer your question, five million credits. The single biggest job in our history. I'd have been crucified if I'd turned it down. We have our honour, but business is business and there's no changing that. I am sorry for the loss of your pilots, I truly am."

"And I for yours," Arnholt replied. "If you'd turned it down, we'd all be better off. You know who the prisoner was who they took back?" Once again, he didn't wait for Mazoud to reply. "It was Harvey Rocastle. Only a few hours earlier, he tried to kidnap my daughter. When did it become Sun policy to aid pieces of scum like him?"

Mazoud said nothing for a moment. "We all have jobs to do, Director Arnholt. I can't turn back the clock and reverse the decisions made. Neither of us can. But that is our burden. We put people where they will be hurt. You're making this personal and it is unbecoming of you, I have to say."

He was right and that stung. Arnholt drew a deep breath and took a moment to regain his composure. "It's never personal," he said. "Not even slightly."

"Yes, keep telling yourself that," Mazoud frowned. "What you don't seem to understand, everything about our jobs is personal. Professionalism is nice but no matter what we do, it comes back to us. Success or failure are fine lines and I don't know about you, but I savour every victory as much as I lament every failure. Sometimes I feel we are little more than cards in a game of Ruin being moved in some never-ending game for supremacy. The only winner is the one who backs all sides at minimum cost. The least possible risk for maximum reward is the favourable outcome."

"I assume you're going somewhere with this, Mister Mazoud," Crumley said. Stood in silence, Arnholt had almost forgotten she was in the room. He was too busy pondering the words, his chin resting in the cusp of his hand.

Mazoud inclined a head towards him. "If your director doesn't understand now, he soon will. In some regards, you lack both foresight and understanding, Ms Crumley. Don't contact me again. I cannot see a future in which our goals will be the same. I advise you to keep your agents out of Vazara too, for it may soon become an unhealthy climate for Unisco."

With that, the line went dead, and he heard Crumley sputtering with unrestrained anger. "Who in the hells does he think he is? Did he just threaten us?"

Arnholt said nothing, still pondering what he'd just heard. It sounded that way. Mazoud hadn't issued a threat in so many words. That wasn't his style. A man of his position and disposition didn't issue threats. The first sign you got he was annoyed with you was when the door came crashing in and his soldiers opened fire. No, that wasn't it at all. Privately he was disappointed with Crumley. More to the point, he was disgusted with himself. He shouldn't have brought Mia into it, he'd let Mazoud see what was under his skin.

But it wasn't a threat. That much he was certain of.

"He doesn't think we can win," he said softly. "Whatever comes next, he's playing his cards close to his chest. He thinks we're going to be wiped out and he wants in bed with the victors. It wasn't a threat. It was a warning construed that way." He sighed. "I've known Mazoud for a long time. I know how his mind works and this is classic from him. He thinks he's cleverer than he actually is, unfortunately which doesn't do anybody any favours."

"And him giving us that information," Crumley said, the light dawning in her eyes as she realised. "He's keeping his options open. Just in case. He's not fermenting outright betrayal but just giving us enough to avoid declaring him an enemy."

"Exactly." Arnholt frowned at the thought. "Five million is a lot for a holding action. Someone really must have been desperate to get the Suns onside. Rocastle's employers?" He asked it more as a question thought out loud but Crumley nodded in agreement.

"Reims," she said. "Once more, it boils down to them. How long before it all stops being circumstance?"

Honestly, Arnholt didn't know the answer. Reims were hiding something. The questions were clear. It was the answers giving them all so much trouble. "I think I'm going to send someone to talk to the CEO of Reims," he said. "See if we can halt this from escalating any further." Now, what was her name again? He had it on a file somewhere.

"Sir?" He looked to Crumley, solemn in the confined space of the cabin they'd set up as their communication hub. "Thank you for summoning me here. I'm glad to be able to help."

Arnholt nodded. "Think nothing of it. Think you could go talk to the Lady Reims for me?" That wasn't her name, he was sure of it. Crumley nodded. "You might just be the only one I can trust."

She raised an eyebrow. "Excuse me?"

That might not have been the best thing to say. "I worry sometimes, you know, Allison. And given my job, the things I worry about are a lot scarier than most. It's enough to make you paranoid. But I do wonder how, if it was Reims, they knew how Rocastle was being transported off the island and their travel vector."

"You think we've been compromised?" It was a scary thought. "Is this why it's just you and me here?"

Arnholt nodded. "I'd like to not take the chances on a thing like this."

"Okay, this is the last place on the list that might be able to sort us the parts out," Pete said as he shoved the door open and heard the bell chime an announcement to their entrance. He rolled his eyes at the pleasant little ting, held it open for Scott and Mia to follow in. He wasn't sure why Mia was coming along for the ride, but Scott seemed to want her around. In the times since they'd been to that bloody dance, he hadn't seen her and neither had Scott, he'd heard the resentful moaning enough to know he'd been hurting over the whole thing.

Mia wasn't looking as good as she once had, if he was honest. He could tell her nose had been broken and part of him thought of Jess when he saw it. Jess had had an imperfection as well, those scars on her arm and he'd wondered if she was jealous of the way Mia pulled off a sense of flawlessness.

Why was he even thinking about this now? Jess was in the past, he'd seen her leave the island a few days after their tryst. In hindsight, he wasn't entirely sure what to think about it. He'd enjoyed it, sure. But he'd also spent more than a few moments with his fingers crossed Scott wouldn't find out. Pete wouldn't have put it past Jess to inform on him, just to screw up their friendship as a final fuck you to them. He was glad she'd gone now. He'd just about gotten over the difficult decision of whether to pester Scott to change his contact details just in case she got in touch and felt like dropping the bombshell.

Maybe he would. Just in case. It couldn't hurt.

Still it felt good to get his mind on something else. He'd help Scott here, focus on Kitti Sommer from a distance. Pondering the possible bad things that could happen wouldn't help him any. And besides, a little ghost hunting might not be a bad idea. He knew for fact she had at least one ghost and some practice against one of those slippery bastards could benefit him. They weren't entirely common to face as a species and had Scott not already set his heart it, Pete might have put a move in to try and claim it for himself. Especially if it was as unusual as his friend had said.

He's talking rubbish. No way a ghost speaks, it's impossible. About the most you could get back off a spirit was an occasional flash of strong emotion. Never actual conversation. Then again, there always had to be something new out there. He didn't know why that worried him more than it should, but it did. There was something comforting about the familiar. The idea that everything he'd known wasn't quite right, Pete wasn't sure he wanted to wake up in a world where the shields had been shifted.

"Yay!" Mia said dryly as she took in the store around them. "Junk." In classic Vazaran style, some of the stuff had been old five years ago. To call it junk would have been a compliment. Broken summoners lay in a pile to be salvaged for parts. Shattered container crystals stood in a mortar dish ready to be ground up and recycled into new ones. All various bits of equipment that had long reached the end of their life but not yet deemed unusable. Yet it was not the only stuff available, Pete could see a much smaller section filled with newer stuff. Compared to the prices on the old stuff, the mark-ups on the new stuff were eye-watering.

"One man's junk is another man's older junk," Scott said, glancing around. It might have been a surprise to find a place like this amidst the swank of Carcaradis Island, but Pete privately thought the owner had the right idea. Spirit callers were notorious for holding bits of valuable bits of junk, at least until they could either get rid or get it repaired. Added to the fact this place also did repairs, it wasn't as farfetched as it might have sounded. The sign did promise expert repairs at low prices and short waiting times. It was appealing to the skinflint living inside every caller, the equipment was expensive, and warranties short. Sometimes you needed good repair jobs, that it was a trade in which few were masterfully skilled meant they could charge whatever they wanted. A bad repairman went out of business very quickly. Maybe this guy was chancing it for the two months while the tournament was on. Even then, Pete couldn't imagine he'd have gotten away with it this long if he was terrible.

Both Scott and Mia were making a show of perusing, his attention moved to the guy stood behind the counter talking to the one other customer, a big guy who moved with the grace of an athlete and looked vaguely familiar. He didn't look like someone who'd be in here for kicks, maybe the owner had done some bad repairing for him and was about to get his ass kicked.

He did feel a little like a spare part lately, seeing those two hunched close together, muttering stuff in each other's ears, the way Mia let out a little giggle every so often when Scott said something surely not as funny as the reaction warranted. He'd not been around when it had been the start for Scott and Jess. It surely couldn't have been this annoying. Not with Jess anyway. Hearing her laugh had been rare and it usually had been at someone else's expense, never the girly sound that came from Mia. Or at least if she had, it had never been something he'd heard. Jess in private… Well you couldn't get much more private than what they'd done, and he'd still never heard it.

Why was he dwelling on this? Must be the constant reminders. Still if Scott was happy, then good for him. He was less inclined to be a total tool when he was in a good mood. Although if Pete was honest, he wouldn't have been looking to start a relationship right now with all the stuff going on in the tournament. He'd re-watched Scott's bout with Steven Silver and but for an almighty effort in the last round when Palawi had put down that giant cavern crusher, he would have gone out. He'd have won their bet about being the last one standing, claimed bragging rights

Now where were they though? Pete himself had to face Katherine Sommer, bumped up to one of the favourites since Wade had bowed out. Odds compilers had her as one of the top five winners along with Sharon, Nick Roper, Reginald Tendolini and Lucy Tait, although where those last two names had been pulled from, he didn't know. What he did know was he had a tough bout ahead, potentially just as tough as the one he'd waged against Sharon in the group stage. That felt a very long time ago, a good few weeks that felt like months. Time was getting deceptive here in the middle of the goldfish bowl this tournament had become. He'd heard it before but had never quite understood how in the middle of something like this, time could simultaneously drag and fly at the same staid pace.

It was the waiting around between bouts that did it, he decided. You were the first one to fight in the round, you'd have at least a few days to sweat before you even knew who you'd be fighting. Even then there was no guarantee you'd be the first to fight the next round along which would make things even more stressful. That, he decided, might just be part of the challenge. Not only must you conquer your opponent but also the threat of inactivity.

Up at the counter, the customer finished his debate with the owner and turned, a big box under his arms and seeing him from the front for the first time, Pete recognised him. He was a hard figure not to recognise. Things made sense suddenly.

"Al?" he asked, surprised. "Alvin Noorland?"

Alvin Noorland, renowned spirit caller and world-famous inventor looked tired as he blinked at the sound of his name but quickly regained his composure and slid an easy smile across his face. "Hello," he said warmly. "You, I know from somewhere. Paul? Parry?"

"Peter," Pete said. Inside he got a warm feeling of glee. Al Noorland remembered him from their last meeting. He'd held a tournament for his birthday, the Alvin Noorland Birthday Invitational. Pete had entered and gotten to the semi-final, hadn't gotten close enough for the chance to face Noorland himself but he'd gotten some consolation words from the man himself. "I met you a few years ago. At your invitational."

"That was a good tournament," Noorland said, nodding his grizzled head in agreement. "Must do it again sometime." Already Scott and Mia were coming over and Pete wasn't surprised. It wasn't every day you got to meet someone on the level of Noorland. Well Scott wouldn't. Mia did every time she went home. Heh, he imagined Scott probably thought he did every time he looked in the mirror. Neither of them was at that level yet unfortunately. Pete grinned. He might be when he won this thing and got international recognition for his achievement. "Must do it again sometime. And you're Scott Taylor."

"You know me?" Scott asked, and Pete rolled his eyes. Duh!

"I know of you," Noorland replied. "Seen a few of your bouts here. I enjoyed that last round against Steve Silver. That was intense. Real intense. You fight like that again; I might bounce a few creds on you. Not everyone can take down a cavern crusher the way you did." His gaze slid across to Mia and the smile grew. In Pete's eyes, it was a smile screaming of sleaze, but his words were courteous and well meaning. "Ms Arnholt, a pleasure."

"Alvin," she said. "Call me Mia, please."

"Gladly," Noorland said. "Got to ask, what the three of you doing in a place like this? Summoner trouble?"

Scott shook his head, a look on his face of comprehension and Pete thought he got what his friend might be thinking.

"Well we're looking for a particle barrier," he said, trying to sound offhand. "You know, for trapping ghosts. But there's nowhere here on the island that sells them. So, we tried here to see if there were any we could…"

"Or build one," Mia offered. "How hard can it be?"

Noorland paused, then burst out laughing. "Mia, you have no idea. To build not just a working particle barrier but an effective one is not easy. Everyone talks about building one, but the trick is doing it, so it won't blow up on you. They're finickity bits of equipment at the best of times. You won't find one here you can fix. It'd take more time than I imagine you have to do it up to standard. It'd be quicker to build a stop-gap one from scratch."

"Which we were sort of trying to do," Scott said quietly. Noorland studied him with an amused look as he took in the words.

"Kid, I like your spirit. You got any experience of protoplasmic-repellent designs? Automated frequency modulators? Phase shift oscillators? You got Thomas Rogan's contact details?"

"Wait, what was that first one again?" Scott asked. "Thought that was a brand of deodorant." He grinned a little as he said it and Noorland shook his head.

"Thought so."

"Well," Pete interrupted. "I'm sure what he meant to say was we'd find someone with experience of all that stuff to knock one up. Someone with mad engineering skills. I mean there has to be someone on this island capable of doing that, right?"

"Lik?" Noorland glanced back behind the counter at the owner of the store, the heavyset man pricking his ears up. "You want to build them a particle barrier?"

"Could. Got stuff on though. Might take a week at least. Need some fresh parts. Going to cost you." His voice was slow and ponderous, he rubbed his thumb and forefinger together as he mentioned cost and Pete hid a smirk. Oh, how had he guessed that was coming? He didn't know how much Scott wanted to spend but he had a feeling he might be about to be fleeced here.

"How much?" Scott asked. By the wary sound in his voice, it appeared he'd had the same thought, Pete noted.

Lik pondered for a moment, his lips moving soundlessly as he muttered a few sums to himself and then grinned, showing several missing teeth in his smile. "You want it quick?"

"As soon as possible," Scott said.

More silent mutterings, he moved onto counting on his fingers. Lik gave him a grin. "Thousand credits and I have it done by the end of the week."

That was the point Scott stood up straight, turned around and walked out the store, hands in his pockets. Mia glanced after him and shrugged. "Think he means that as a no," she said apologetically. "I'm sorry, he could have…"

"That didn't take long," Pete grinned. "Before you started apologising for him. Welcome to my world."

They found him leaning against a street light, hands in pockets when they emerged, whistling a casual tune. For a few long moments, Pete listened, then straightened up in surprise.

"Thought you hated Kayleigh Stafford," he said.

It was Scott's turn to shrug. "Meh, I got it stuck in my head. And I don't hate her, I just don't like most of her songs."

"That wasn't the best way to do things, was it?" Mia asked, looking at him. "Walking out like that."

"Hey, screw that," Scott said. "I'm not paying that. I'd pay a thousand credits if it was done by the time my bout was over. Not for the end of the week. Someone else might have claimed it by then. I can't wait that long."

"Has anyone ever told you about the virtues of patience?" Noorland smiled.

"Yeah. But you know what else they say about the bird and the worm," Scott retorted, folding his arms. "I can't let this go. I won't. I'll go try catch it without a particle barrier if need be. I nearly did it before."

This time Noorland laughed out loud. "Dear me. You know what, kid, I like your spirit. World needs more callers like you. I think sheer bloody mindedness counts for a lot. I tell you what. How about I fix you one up. Think I might have something for the job. Might need repairs but…"

"And you're just doing that out the goodness of your heart?" Scott inquired. "I mean, not that I'm not grateful for the offer, but…"

"I'm not giving you it for nothing," Noorland replied. "I'm loaning you it. I want it back. Plus, payment for the trouble."

"How much?" Scott asked. "And how quickly?"

Noorland didn't make near as much of a show of considering it as Lik had. He stared Scott down and smiled. "I don't want your credits. I want a bout with you. No holds barred. Been too long since I had a good fight and I think you might give me one."

Scott didn't blink. "Well I got a bout tomorrow. I don't really want to fight you before then…"

"That's okay," Noorland replied. "Take me a few days to spec it up to standard anyway. When I've finished, we'll engage in a bout. That's my price. Take it or leave it?"

He'd have to be an idiot to turn it down, Pete thought. Although why Noorland, a pretty tough spirit caller would want to fight someone like Scott was beyond him. Still, good for Scott getting a deal like that. He wasn't too dumb to turn it down as he reached out and shook Noorland's hand.

"I accept," Scott said. "We going to be in touch then?"

"Count on it."

Mallinson was back and Wade was already sick of him. More than that, he was tired of the same repetitive questions only seeming to be used to provoke a reaction, Mallinson's extensive brand of sarcasm being wielded in great flourishes like an oversized knife.

"Right, I see, so Agent Okocha informed you that... Let me get this right, someone was disturbing the peace on something that looked like a pterosaur... You do know those things have been extinct for a while, do you not, Agent Wallerington?"

Through gritted teeth, Wade nodded. He wasn't too bothered about Mallinson picking the holes out of that part of the story. There were no holes to pick. Unless he was going to ignore about a hundred plus people who'd all seen it, upon which case he wouldn't be around much longer to carry on the investigation.

"I guess extinction isn't quite as permanent as it once was," he said. His sight was slowly returning, it had been bathed in alska treatments three times now, all at tremendous cost and he could now make out Mallinson in glorious blurred detail. He wished it was faster, but all things considered, he was making remarkable progress apparently.

"Try not to be flippant, Agent Wallerington while we're in the process of investigating a very serious matter, will you?"

No wonder people often wanted to punch him in his piggy little face. Wade settled back in his bed and tried to focus on the sounds from the viewing screen in the background, the opening bout of the third round was getting underway and he wanted to hear what was happening beyond that tormenting drone. Sharon Arventino and Theobald Jameson were about to go at it and he was interested.

Interested and sad. Quitting the tournament had been the hardest choice he'd had to make in a long time, he hadn't wanted to do it. But circumstances had been what they had become, he hadn't had a choice. He'd made his decision; he knew it was the right one but that didn't make it any less painful. It could have been him standing on that battlefield going at either Arventino or Jameson and he'd have loved nothing more. Sometimes that was the price you had to pay. What you loved sometimes came second. Every Unisco agent found that out sooner or later. It wasn't the first time he'd experienced it. He would have to again no doubt, just as sure as the sun rising in the sky.

"Flippant? Me?" He did his best to sound nonchalantly insulted. "I don't know the meaning of the term."

Mallinson glared at him. At least he imagined he did. He fought the urge to smile. Just keep calm, don't aggravate him... At least don't show him that you're enjoying making a fool of him. He then moved in front of the viewing screen, to Wade's irritation.

"I don't know how seriously you're taking this, Agent Wallerington but let me tell you this, you might be in trouble here. Choke on that, smart guy. You did some dumb things, and someone has to pay."

"I did my job," Wade said. Sounded like the two callers had drawn, sent out their first spirits, he couldn't hear what they were. "I always do."

Out in the corridor, he could hear something. Footsteps. Sounds of commotion. It was probably nothing. Maybe an aggrieved relative. Maybe someone was getting violent. Either way he felt the hair prickling on the back of his neck. A warning? His stomach twisted, he suddenly wished he had a blaster in hand.

"You doing your job endangered countless innocent people this time though," Mallinson said, his attention slowly turning from Wade. He could hear what was going on in the corridor as well. His hand reached inside his jacket, pushed it aside to reveal the X7 holstered at his waist. Wade might have missed it had he not caught the scent of blaster oil. "I imagine you didn't consider that when you were rushing around…"

He was interrupted by a scream. Two screams. The burst of blaster fire out in the corridor and Mallinson drew his X7, swearing quietly.

"What's going on out there?" Wade asked. Mallinson didn't reply, moving over to the door, weapon out in front of him. More blaster fire, he could hear people screaming and running. "Damnit, Mallinson, what can you…?"

"Quiet!" Mallinson hissed as he put his hand on the door and twisted the handle, slowly tugging it open. He advanced out slowly, his head and his blaster out, taking in the environment ahead.

Wade heard it more than he saw it, the sound of the blaster firing and the impact of laser into skull, Mallinson didn't even scream as the body hit the ground, the X7 skittering across the floor into the room. He could just about make it out through the haze of his vision and he knew he had to react quickly.

Several seconds later, they reached his room following the crash, emptied their power packs through the door in the direction of the overturned bed.

"The darkness of the unknown often weighs light in comparison to the weight of wickedness in human hearts."
Proverb. Author unknown.

The tenth day of Summerpeak.

She rose from darkness into further darkness and the sudden vicious snap of electricity at her wrists threatened to send her once again into the abyss. Not expecting it, she let out a yelp, flailed helplessly as the spasms in her arms subsided. She wanted to rub them, get some feeling back but they wouldn't respond. She blinked several times, trying to take in her surroundings but they were hidden amidst the inky black permeating the area. Wherever she was, wherever they were taking her, it wasn't going to be in style. It rather reinforced the point home as to her predicament. She was a prisoner.

A prisoner. Her? If Kyra Sinclair was honest, that simple little fact annoyed her. She wasn't supposed to be a prisoner. Not her. She struggled against the cuffs binding her wrists, felt them crackle with their debilitating charge and involuntary spasms sent her head cracking into the floor. She yelled in pain, realised she wasn't going to be doing that again soon.

"Shit." It didn't sound angry, rather lost and lonely like a terrified child alone in darkness. Her head felt wet. Maybe she'd cut herself when she'd struggled. The pain made it hard to focus, she could feel the sharp throbbing clamouring for attention but not for nothing had her master insist on her training in discomfort. He'd used the Kjarn to induce headaches in her more than once, some mild, some skull splitting migraines that made her want to curl into a ball and cry.

But she hadn't. And he'd told her until she did what he'd expected of her, then the pain would carry on. Come the end of some sessions, her brain felt like a mangled sponge, but she'd had the techniques down and the relief was almost as potent as the pain. Nobody could ever say pain wasn't an effective teacher.

Of course, you needed balance. Couldn't just solely rely on it. Her master had understood that, even if his teaching ratio had been heavily weighted that way. What was the saying about catching more bees with honey than with a stick? That wasn't right. The metaphor applied. If you have a big enough stick, you can keep the honey for yourself.

She wanted to giggle, would have done had it not been an embarrassing situation. Honey and sticks. Who thought that up?

Somehow that thought was more distracting than the pain as she closed her eyes and tried to focus through the Kjarn, just to take stock of her surroundings. She could see more through the Kjarn than she could with her eyes. They were the most prominent of the human senses, the ones most likely to lie to her. She'd trained blindfolded in the past, gone blade to blade with Cobb while relying on nothing but her other senses and the Kjarn substituting in. She still bore the burns, but he'd failed to come away unscathed too.

Scrabbling for concentration wasn't easy at first but the closer she got to it, the more some of her old poise returned and she found herself attaining the desired state within minutes. A painfully long time, it had been a while since she'd been this ineffective, but at the same time she'd not trained for these circumstances. A lot of the time, her touch of the Kjarn was instinctive. Reacting it instinctively was a lot easier than planning it beforehand.

She hadn't trained for these circumstances, but she was in them now and there was no point complaining. She needed to do what she had to, the only other option was to lay there and do nothing. Somehow that would feel like more of a betrayal than failing to rise to the challenge. She would not be crippled by inaction. She would get herself out of this situation.

She was in a cell, laid on a cold metal floor. Through the Kjarn, she could picture the rivulets that made up its pattern. She could sense the few droplets of her blood where she'd nicked herself. The bars were thick metal, she might be able to pull them away with the Kjarn, but it would take time. Easier with her kjarnblade, which she couldn't sense anywhere in her immediate presence. Past the bars, she could sense another cell, this one strangely impermeable to her senses.

Curious, she moved on for the moment and sensed human life far beyond her, her captors no doubt. They were uneasy but professional, no sense of doubt or fear burning through them, rather a sense of calm rationale about them. They weren't thinking about what they'd done. How many? She couldn't differentiate between their minds, like staring into an interlocking set of puddles all mingling together, unable to tell where one began, and another ended. She frowned, filed that bit of information away and moved past them out to the metal shell surrounding them all and…

Her breath caught in her throat, she almost lost focus and had to bite down to keep herself from gasping in surprise as beyond the shell, she felt the force of the atmosphere outside assaulting her senses. The rush of air, the roar of engines, the force of the pressure buffeting against the side of the ship all hit her as if she were experiencing it in person. Still she persisted, expanding her senses outward to get a further glimpse. She couldn't hold on much longer now, her head was screaming with pain, she'd have to relax and let go or risk further damage.

Just a little more!

Further and further she expanded her mind, farther than ever before and she could feel it, sensations of going past her limits as her breathing became ragged, she wasn't sure how much longer she could continue before blacking out, her eyes burning from the strain.

There!

She saw it and her heart fell. Almost immediately, she let go and snapped back to her suddenly fragile body, sensations of being everywhere and all-encompassing gone in a heartbeat. Suddenly she was just herself again, painfully limited to her own senses. She'd suspected but to have it confirmed was disheartening. The same ship she'd seen on the plateau. Escape might have to be delayed for there was no leaving this place now.

Even if she did get out her cell and dealt with the guards, she couldn't land this thing. Pilot training was something her master had omitted from her curriculum and right now it would cost her dearly. She cursed him silently. If she did it out loud, no matter how alone she might be, past experiences had scarred her with thoughts he might hear her.

No, she'd see it out until they landed. Patience. If she acted now, the chances of her survival were slim. For a few moments longer, she lay huddled on the floor in a puddle of her own sweat and blood, recovering from her exertions until she felt her curiosity slowly returning. She couldn't see the cell, not through the dark, but she gave it her full attention.

If there was anything there to see, it wasn't apparent. She tried to shift herself, get more comfortable and managed to a point. She lay on her back, head tilted back in the direction and coughed. Her mouth and lips felt dry. How long since she'd drunk? That mountain had been humid, she'd been parched before reaching the top and the mouthfuls of liquid she'd swallowed hadn't cut it. She could draw sustenance from the Kjarn if need be. It could be done but it wasn't the best idea. Doing it could cause long term damage because while it might be all encompassing, it couldn't substitute for actual food and water. If it got worse… When it got worse. Somehow, she doubted this would be the end, she might have to though.

She tested her arms, felt the warning crackle of electricity. Brilliant. Long as she didn't want to scratch her nose, she'd be fine. Just thinking it made her itch but she bit it down. She had to. She could resist temptation. Just don't think about it. Think about that cage. She'd not experienced anything like it ever before, something completely impermeable to the Kjarn. By rights, that shouldn't happen. The Kjarn was a part of all things, connected to everything and everyone and yet it remained a blank slate to her.

Maybe her grip on it wasn't as secure as she'd like, but there was no way she should be sensing nothing from it. She let herself fall into it again, felt energy fill her weary body and reached out, letting her mind touch it. It felt smooth to her touch, like stone, yet still she couldn't tell what lay beyond. Curiously she circled it, feeling more than seeing and found it a large square shape, all as impervious as first appeared. Through little effort, she rose and checked the top, found it just as secure. How they got the contents in and out, she couldn't tell. Nor did she want to. If it was as impermeable on the inside as the out, she wouldn't want to be locked in there. She should thank whatever Divine was listening she hadn't been. Of course, right now the real prison was the altitude. No getting out of this until they landed.

"Hello?" Kyra called, making her choice. "Anyone in there?"

If it was sealed up, it was unlikely they would hear her. In her examination, she'd found nothing she could use as leverage to prise it open, no knobs or levers, nor any sign of protruding machinery she could manipulate. She hadn't seen what the men had been chasing earlier but it must have been something they were worried about given their numbers and the firepower they'd been packing. She'd not seen that many weapons in one place outside the viewing screens, to have them shooting at you wasn't a pleasant experience. All the preparation in the kingdoms couldn't help you with that when it came.

The important thing was she'd survived. Another amazing lesson her master had imparted on her. Survive. If you survive, it is the first step of retaliation. If you are dead, then you are of no use to me and I will have wasted my time with you. I will be required to waste my time training another apprentice. She could almost hear his cold dead voice in the confines of the ship, echoing through the cargo hold.

There'd been no answer. Twice more she called with her greeting, twice more she met silence. She felt frustration, let her head fall back to the ground and closed her eyes. Maybe she could sleep. Restore some of her strength. The pain in her head had devolved to a dull thump demanding attention but not a lot of it.

Yes.

That sat her bolt upright on the spot, the snap of her stun cuffs a distant sensation as she heard the voice. Except that wasn't the right term for it, was it? They were words, but speech wasn't the best way to describe what she'd heard. It was more like she'd heard it directly in her head. Impossible… Well not quite. She knew what she'd heard.

She'd heard of Kjarn users being able to pass rudimentary messages to others via a similar method but not like this, even the most powerful of Cognivites would have struggled to pass a word like she'd heard. All lore said most common were strong emotions and their ilk rather than actual words. What that meant now, in these circumstances, she didn't know.

"Are you okay?" she asked. "Are you in that box?"

Several more beats, she wondered if maybe she'd imagined things. That would be about right. Here in a short space of time and she went crazy. That'd do wonders for her reputation.

I am unharmed. What is this box?

Okay so maybe she wasn't imagining it. Or maybe she was. Either way it was something to while away the boredom.

"Okay, that's good," she said. "I don't know what it is. I've not seen anything like it before. It's weird."

Whoever was in there, they weren't a rapid talker, she had to give them that as she waited for a reply. Several long moments passed, she tapped her feet impatiently on the ground, beating out a lonely dull sound that never would have passed for a tune.

What is weird?

The question took her by surprise, of all the things she could have been asked, that wasn't one she'd been expecting.

"Weird?" she asked. "You really want to know what weird is right now?" She sighed. It probably came out harsher than she'd intended but in the stress of the situation she thought she'd be forgiven. After all, she wasn't used to being locked up and it didn't do wonders for her disposition.

"Weird is when stuff is strange. When it can't be explained. When you know something is going on and you can't work out what that something is, and it just drives you nuts. It's when you see something you know is wrong and shouldn't exist and yet there it is." Silence. As if she hadn't seen that coming, she thought with a sigh.

You use a lot of words to explain.

"I do," she said. "Do you understand?"

This time she counted the beats before her answer, one, nothing, two, nothing, three, nothing, four...

I think so. I think if I am in this box then I must be weird.

She said nothing, didn't voice her suspicions aloud about this whole thing. It wouldn't be worth getting into the minefield it'd undoubtedly bring up.

And if you can hear me, then you must also be weird.

"Hey!" she protested. "Don't call me weird. Not nice. And unjustified. How are you doing that anyway? It's like I can hear you, but I can't hear you at the same time."

Her arms ached through that last shock, she tried to ignore it while wondering if she could jimmy them loose with the Kjarn, give herself a reprieve.

I do not know. I simply am.

It wouldn't be a good idea. Once she got them off, there was no guarantee she'd be able to get them on again when they came for her. And when they came for her, there might be more of them. Without a weapon, her chances grew smaller with the greater their numbers. No, better they thought her beaten and tamed. A docile animal is regarded as less of a threat than a feral one. Everyone expects a feral beast to bite you. Everyone is surprised when the domesticated one does it to you.

"I'm not weird," she insisted. "I'm just… well, I'm just me. Nothing else."

I do not know. I do therefore I am.

"Uh huh." It had come out of the blue, she hadn't expected it but there was just no way to answer that. She wondered what was in there once again, the whole thing a question burning through her very being. So curious and yet no way of assuaging it because of the distance between them. So near and yet so very far from answers. They could at least have given her some light. "I need to know. Who are you?"

Beat.

I do not know.

It felt like the unseen speaker was getting the hang of the whole conversation thing gradually. The gaps between answers were growing shorter every time she heard that booming voice in her head.

"Everyone has a name. Everyone."

If I do, then I do not know. What is a name?

She hesitated, closed her eyes and sucked in stale breath of air. Before all this, she'd felt carefree. Now look at her. Talking with someone for whom strange wasn't just an option but a choice by the sounds of it. "Are you genuinely asking? Or are you being philosophical?" Kyra decided very quickly to just assume he… Was it a he? She decided very quickly to just assume he was genuinely asking. She didn't want to start explaining or debating philosophy right now. "A name is a brand. It's how we identify each other. It's what makes us who we are, if you get my meaning. My name is Kyra Eve Sinclair. It's the name my parents gave me." Well, it wasn't, but she didn't know her original name. Nobody in her position did.

I see. I think. You didn't choose it yourself?

She shook her head. "No. Nobody does. It's like the first gift you ever get. It's who you'll always be no matter what happens. You're born, and you get a name, welcome to the world."

You talk a lot. I don't have a name.

That was a little rude, she thought. Being told she talked a lot was a bit impolite considering all she was doing to answer his questions She still didn't know if it was a he or not. Questions, questions and not an answer in sight.

Have I angered you?

That caught her by surprise. He had, but… There was no way he should have been able to know. She couldn't get anything off him and yet he'd just read her even through that Kjarn-proof cage. With that there, she wasn't getting anything. Weird. Very weird. There was that word again.

"No, not really," she said. "I'm just surprised. How did you get here? Do you know?" It might have come off a little sarcastic, perhaps unnecessary but her patience was hanging by a thread growing tauter by the minute. She tried to flex her fingers, felt them growing numb and winced as a smattering of static danced across her skin.

I awoke. I was caged.

Amnesia? Maybe he couldn't remember. It wasn't impossible. If he was who they'd being shooting at in that cavern, it was likely they'd had to incapacitate him the same way they had her. Waking up, she'd found it a struggle to compose her thoughts. If he'd been hit with several stun blasts, it could have caused untold cognitive damage. Stun blasts interfered with mental functions, especially when those shooting were under the impression more is better. Her body still ached where they'd hit her, felt like being kicked by a wild roo.

I was caged until I wasn't. I reached out into the world and everything broke. The walls, those small weak apes, nothing could hold me back. I tasted freedom and it was sweet. The air was delicious, I've never felt anything so beautiful. I flew through worlds unimaginable, but they followed me. They hounded me to a hole in the sky and I fought them for a long time, but they overcame me eventually. I was exhausted inside and out. Now I am caged once more.

Oh… They were the most words she'd heard him speak at once and she felt they were also the most illuminating

"You're not human, are you?" She couldn't help herself, the words just came out. She knew they lacked tact, at the same time she didn't care. Thinking back to the cave, she tried to remember what she'd felt when she'd cast her mind towards whatever those guys had been trying to lock down. If there had been something, then she couldn't recall but it hadn't been anywhere approaching human. She knew what a human felt like in the Kjarn and she knew what an animal felt like in it. Yet that aura hadn't felt like either. What was going on?

Like those who attacked me? Caged me? Flesh and bone? No. Never. I am not like them. I would wipe more of them out if I could.

That hurt like a slap and she recoiled, shuffling back along the floor to the other side of her cage, keeping going until her spine was pressed up against the opposite end. The bars dug into her flesh. "Erm... Okay. You definitely can't get out of there, can you?"

She tried to sound offhand. Failed miserably, the implications of what was going on in front of her too staggering to ignore. Not human. Not animal. But existing regardless. Capable of actual speech. Emotion. Intelligence. This really wasn't right. Something messed up was going on and she didn't know what.

For the first time for as long as she could remember, Kyra felt staggered. She hadn't felt this way since the first day she'd met her master and he'd told her about the Kjarn. That had opened a raft of new worlds to her she'd never even dreamed of and it had changed her life forever. This could change everything forever. Across the darkened room, the impervious block rattled faintly, then all sound ceased.

No. It remains sealed to me. But I will escape.

Oh goodie... That was a relief. Maybe she could sic this thing on her captors and flee in the confusion. That wouldn't be a bad plan. At least until you considered the two downsides. One, he might just as easily take her out, two, there was still the matter of them being airborne.

They cannot hold me. They failed once. They will fail again. I will await my time. It will come, and everyone else's will run out.

"I hope you don't include me in that," she said, regretted it as she physically felt the void of sound erupt from the direction of the block ahead of her. Oops...

You are one of them, Kyra Eve Sinclair?

The voice sounded surprised and she didn't know if that was a good thing or not. "Yes. I'm human. Very human. Super human in fact. Can't get more human than me." She was babbling now, maybe with nerves, she couldn't stop her mouth moving. All her training was threatening to bleed through her ears, she privately hated herself. She shouldn't feel fear like this, but there it was, a big void in her stomach sucking in everything else.

For the longest time, he didn't respond, and she wondered if he was plotting her demise. She wondered if he'd made up his mind to no longer speak to her because of that discovery, if his hatred had now extended to her despite the conversation they'd being having. They'd been getting on so well as well. Probably never be best friends but they might have become prison break buddies together. Now who knew?

She didn't know how long it was before he spoke again. Might have been minutes. It felt like hours.

I did not know.

That stung a little, caught her by surprise as she stared thoughtfully into the darkness beyond, wondering more than she wanted to admit at the revelation. Eventually she couldn't keep it in and she let it spill out.

"What?! What the hells did you think I was then? Some sort of talking machine? I mean, we've been talking for… I don't know how long."

I thought you were like me. Different.

"Yeah, you're different all right. But so am I. I'm not like those guys who caught you. I tried to save them. I fought them, don't you remember?"

I know that violence will begat violence. Where there is some, there will always be more.

"You wouldn't have been complaining if I'd…" Killed them? She had done just that. Didn't seem prudent to mention it. "… If I'd saved you now, would you? You wouldn't be here. I wouldn't be here…"

And neither would they. I did not fight them. I have no desire to fight.

"Are you saying you didn't fight back?" That felt like an incredibly selfish attitude if she was honest, though she held her tongue. She couldn't imagine not fighting for her freedom. Even now, she was just waiting for the moment to strike when she could be free, and they couldn't stop her.

I did not. Nor did I ask you to for me.

"I didn't plan to. It happened by accident. I was in the wrong place. I couldn't have known what would happen. I was looking for something else and I found all this. I was unlucky. I only struck back."

What is unlucky?

That question took her by surprise, she considered the answer before debating whether to give one or not. They didn't have time for this, she didn't know how long before they landed, and it could be spent better. Kyra also took a few seconds to consider this as well. She was having a conversation with something that freely admitted it wasn't human, it hated humans. Now she knew that, it was easier to think of it as an it than it had been to think of it as male.

"It's when something favours you fortunately or unfortunately in a tight situation," she said tersely. "It goes for you, it's lucky. It lets you down, it's unlucky."

I see.

"Well good for you," she said. Her master had always encouraged patience, but it was wearing away now, and she was considering escape plans. Already she'd ruled out doing it here but was it possible? Maybe. Perhaps in the right circumstances.

Perhaps I was lucky in my escape.

"You didn't seem so hesitant to kill then," she said. After all, hadn't it moments earlier more or less said it'd cheerfully kill any human it came across. And now it was talking about refusing to fight back and hating violence. "You're one messed up creature, do you know that?"

Perhaps that, I am.

The voice took on a solemn note and just for a moment she felt guilty by what she'd just said. A little. Not a lot. "Then again, I think we all are to a point," she added. There wasn't any point in being cruel for the sake of it, you won more friends with honey than whips. She doubted they'd be friends now. They'd gotten on okay at the start before words had been exchanged and identities compromised. "You're not alone in that regard I think."

The response that came back to her sent a cold tinge through her skin and she had to draw several deep breaths to keep her composure.

I don't believe I'm alone in this room in that regard when I talk to you.

"What?!" Even with her composure, it still came out sharp, couldn't keep it from her voice. She didn't want to, didn't care if it knew the words had struck a nerve, she was having it out. "What did you just say?!"

Kyra Eve Sinclair, you profess to be human, but you don't feel it. You claim to be different from those who hounded me and yet somehow you are just the same. I can feel the darkness in you. You are different from those men in there. You are worse. I can see inside you and you know what I can see?

It was almost shouting now, she cringed at the volume of the words splitting her head and tried to reach for her ears, anything to shut it out. Everything just went straight to her brain like white hot needles, no chance of preparing a way to shut it out. The Kjarn left her, any thought of control lost to her, like snatching at thin air and she wanted to weep.

You are rotten from within, worms in your meat, parasites in your blood and sins in your soul. You mock my status; you are the worst of the worse.

All this was making her sick, she thought she heard the engines, was the ship descending? She didn't know, all she could hear was the booming voice and the anger flowing through her, not just her own anger but that of the bastard in the impervious cage. It made her insides crawl, she couldn't stop shaking, even as the cuffs discharged into her. She barely felt them, electricity arcing about her fingertips, sending them into uncontrolled spasms. At least one snapped, she heard the faint crack of bone. The pain was intense yet felt like it should be a thousand times worse amidst her spinning mind.

There is no hope for you. When you die, it will be in an empty grave, people will spit on you and say here lies a nameless nobody... Worthless, weak, pathetic...

She blinked, a brief schism in the torrent of anger rupturing through her, tearing her entire being to shreds and she tried to focus on what had just been said. Wasn't easy. But easy wasn't what she did. She did hard. She did so very hard and she was too damn stubborn to do anything else. Still she felt the anger, but it no longer demanded every fibre of her attention as she quashed it for the moment, despite it bubbling beneath the surface of her being.

What had been said to her? Dying alone. Unknown. Scorned. All the things she'd feared. All the things her master had promised her categorically would not happen to her if she took his hand. She focused on the face of her master, or what little of it she could remember that wasn't hidden beneath his cowl and mask and her lips broke into a cruel smile.

"I don't know how you do it," she said. "I don't know how you can read me when I can't read you. But you've overreached yourself. Badly. You don't know shit about me despite what you've being doing."

What is it I've being doing?

The anger in the voice had been replaced by faux innocence that didn't fool her for a moment. Slowly her own anger faded, her fingers and hands and arms chafed sore from excess electricity and she flexed them, ignorant to the stun cuffs' discharge. Maybe there'd be some permanent damage inflicted, it hadn't affected her dexterity. Even her broken one felt unhampering. She'd fix it in no time.

Good. Her master had displayed similar abilities, had been able to deaden himself to pain, an ability he'd trumpeted as handy but dangerous. Pain was there for a reason. For the next several seconds she took the opportunity to scratch a spot on the side of her head until the gradual sensations of pain came slipping back, spiking through her skin without warning.

"All the questions, all the chatting, the way you got handier with words as the conversation went on… You're a psychic. You've been in my mind, you know what I am and what I can do. You knew my buttons to push. You found them, and you thought you'd use me to break you out. Maybe I could have done." She let out a burst of laughter, it felt good to clear her lungs of the staidness she wasn't aware had been filling her. "But you know what? You'll never know now if I could have or not. And you know what else?"

Kyra let her voice drop a few octaves, just so anyone listening outside couldn't hear her. But she knew the thing in the box would. "The first chance I get; I'm going to kill you for it. You know what I am, you knew what risk you ran and yet you did it anyway. I am the future heir to the Cavanda, you poor deluded son of a bitch and you just made my shit list. You better watch out while you can."

With that, she dropped to a sitting position and closed her eyes, slipping into a meditative stance. If there was anything else for it to say, it chose not to.

When the lights came on and they came to drag her out, Kyra rose to her feet in a docile manner, doing her very best not to look threatening. For the first time she saw the impervious box and wasn't impressed, it looked little more than a white featureless cube. Certainly nothing special. They didn't unlock her cage, just surrounded her, and she glanced around, not seeing her kjarnblade with them. If she had, she might have called it to her, cut her way free and made a run for it. But she didn't, and she couldn't.

"Errr…" she said instead, glancing nervously around. Play the part. Lead them into assumptions. She'd learnt that lesson long before her master had come along. If people underestimate you, then so much worse for them. "Whatever I did, I'm sorry." She let a note of panic creep in, the volume and the urgency rising as she continued. "I mean it, I'm sorry, I don't know what it is I did, I was just out looking for something and I didn't mean to… Please let me go… Please?!" She even added a sob to the end, a convincing one she thought and even toyed with prodding them mentally with the Kjarn to lead them down her path. She rejected that idea. It wasn't her strongest skill. And with this many, it wasn't a good idea.

Kjarn or not, they weren't buying it. They continued to stare impassively at her and she got the same impressions through the Kjarn she had before. The overlapping puddles. Hard to tell where one began, and another ended, too many parts of a same whole.

She considered pleading again. What harm could it do? Except to her ego and that was far from important here compared with her survival.

Chapter Fifteen. Siege.

"We're getting breaking news out of Carcaradis Island, our sources there are saying there's been some sort of attack, another one. Unidentified figures have taken control, we're hearing, of the hospital there..."

Five Kingdoms Media anchor-man, Jarvis Timothy breaking the news.

The fifteenth day of Summerpeak.

"Okay," Brendan said, already clad in a composite carbon vest and an X7 holstered at his waist even though he wasn't going to be anywhere near the shooting. Wilsin had to give him the kudos for making the effort to look the part. "Here's what we know. An hour ago, a group of armed hostiles entered the hospital and opened fire. There are between ten and twenty hostiles in there, all armed with what looks like BRO-60 assault rifles."

Around the room, everyone was hung onto his every word. Arnholt stood arms folded with grim determination on his face while Okocha worked away at the viewing screen, his fingers dancing across the keyboard with urgency. David Wilsin sought to block out the constant clack-clack-clack in the background and instead focus on the images being projected out onto the wall ahead. He'd need to know these. Floor plans of the hospital, blurred stills from security footage, outside images of the hospital. This wasn't going to be fun.

They had to intervene. The call had been made to Arnholt, a plea from the chief of the local police force on Carcaradis Island, citing their inability to effectively handle something like this. By the time a response team arrived from the mainland, it could be too late. Allison Crumley had been despatched to the front line to coordinate the effort, Fagan going with her at Arnholt's urging. Just in case. Between the two of them, they were doing an effective job, but the hard part was still to come.

Around him, everyone was just as focused on the briefing as he was. Mel Harper and Lysa Montgomery checked their Featherstones, both kitted out in the same type of vest as Brendan. They had been Noorland's idea a few months back, extra protection as well as light-weight and something easily identifiable in the confusion. In conjunction with the personal shields, they meant that their protection was more effective than ever. Just a damn shame they couldn't outfit the hostages with them until they'd finished the inevitable firefight.

"Most of the staff and able-bodied people present did manage to flee," Brendan continued. "Reports tell us that the hostiles bore no identifiable features on their uniforms and were masked. Armed, dangerous and unknown. Permission to terminate on sight is authorised. Priority is the safety of the hostages involved."

"Do we have thermal imaging of the building?" Anne asked. She was in the process of putting her vest on over her street clothes, she'd hurried over from the stadium when the call had been made. As far as Wilsin knew, people were being urged to stay off the streets and in the stadiums until the danger was passed. She had her Saga laid across her knee, checking it carefully, the rifle nearly half her size and just as deadly sleek.

"It would appear our hostiles are encamped in the administrator's office," Brendan said. "There are a number of hostages with them, making exact numbers hard to determine."

More images snapped up of the administrator's office, a neat room with a couple of bookshelves and a large desk. All very fancy, Wilsin thought, noting the plush purple curtains covering the huge window towards the back of the room. It had a decent view over the island, he could see the shelves were filled with various medical tomes. It looked like the sort of office where someone who didn't do much beyond its four walls might work. He could tell it had that worked-in look. He didn't know much about the administrator but considering how short a time it had been open then he must have done well to get it like that in such a short space of time They were official images, promotion material. He'd heard rumours the Carcaradis Island hospital was hoping to become one of the most prominent in Vazara. Given most of the hospitals in Vazara were allegedly one step slightly above being left to die in the gutter, he didn't think that would be hard. The next images that came up were shots of the same room but from outside, he could see the window frame and into the room, no mistaking the men stood there with the rifles.

"This shot came from across the recorder across the street, we've done all we can with it, made it the best we're going to get." Wilsin had already noted the grainy quality of the image. If Will said it was the best they could get it, it was the best they could get it.

"What's the plan?" Derenko asked. He stood at the back of the room, his face etched with disinterest but Wilsin guessed it wasn't. Based on experience, this was just the way he readied himself for the fight. He didn't like to dwell too much on what needed to be done, did Derenko. Aldiss next to him on the other hand looked thoughtful, like he was considering every word from Brendan or Okocha. He was cleaning off a knife with an oiled rag, examining it for any traces of rust.

"We have a number of options," Brendan said. "Thermal imaging has shown sporadic patrols through hospital corridors. So far, they show no specific pattern we can lock down with what information we have. I want to send two teams into the hospital, one goes high and one goes low. The Administrator has his office here on the fifth floor. One team goes in through the basement and ascends. Our second team hits the roof and descends. Hopefully we can pincer them. Nine floors, between ten and twenty hostiles, they can't hope to keep an eye on that amount of space all at once. Disable surveillance, blind them and we should be able to take them. Agent Sullivan, I want you on the rooftop opposite with your rifle, I want you keeping an eye on the situation in there with the hostages. Take a spotter with you. Any preferences?"

"I'll go," Noorland offered, striding through the door. He provided no apologies for his lateness. "I'm probably the best with the tech we've got anyway."

"I did toy with the idea of pumping knockout gas into the room," Brendan said. "But it is not without its risks. We don't have any here…"

"Big problem that," Leclerc remarked. Someone snickered, some of the tension eased out of the room. Some, not all. They did have a dirty job to do after all. Brendan ignored him.

"We don't have any here and by the time we could get some, it might well be too late. So, of our two teams, the air team will use spirits to get to the roof and land silently. Already the area is cordoned off below in the parking lot, but there are people there. And the media."

He said the last word with distaste. "If they have a viewing screen active, it'll blow our cover if they see our assault coming and those consequences could be disastrous. Go from the back. Come from the north of the building, stay low and ascend when you need to. Given Agent Wilsin's intimate knowledge of this island's sewage system…"

One trip below, Wilsin thought dryly, and you're tagged for life. I don't even remember much from that night. Trust Nick to be suspended for this fun job. Even if he hadn't been, it'd be debateable if he'd even show up, not with his lady currently fighting across the island. He'd been amazed Anne had shown really given the closeness he'd seen her displaying with that Jameson kid. Maybe he'd read the situation wrong.

"He will lead the team down there, along with Agents Montgomery and Leclerc. Agent Derenko will lead the air team with Agents Aldiss and Harper. We mobilise in five minutes. Any questions?"

"What about Wade?" Aldiss asked. "Any word on whether he got out or is he still in there?"

Arnholt and Brendan looked at each other silently. Neither of them looked like they wanted to answer the question until Brendan reluctantly spoke up. "He's not been reported sighted. Nor has Inquisitor Mallinson We believe they're still on site. Agent Wallerington is still incapacitated and is not to be considered an active asset. Checking on him is not your priority. Save the hostages. Eliminate hostiles. Anything else is secondary."

"Have they asked for anything?" Mel Harper asked. "The hostiles? They must want something. There had to be some reason they did this."

"Furthermore, how do they intend to get out of it?" Derenko wondered. "Because they must know once they set down this path, it ends violently. There's no going back now."

"Maybe they didn't want to," Lysa said softly. "Maybe it's a statement."

"Or maybe it's just some assholes with an outlaw complex," Wilsin said, shrugging. It made no difference to him.

"Nothing has been released," Brendan said. "On a further note, Agent Noorland, I want you to equip everyone with the stun grenades we brought. They could come in handy."

"I've got just the thing," Noorland grinned, moving to one of the storage boxes littering the room. "These things pack a nasty punch. They'll do the job nicely. Completely gums up the nervous system. They get hit with these, they won't even be able to hold a weapon never mind fire one. Range about ten feet from impact, potentially greater in an enclosed space." He smacked a fist against his open palm and chuckled. "No permanent damage though. I remember testing these. Fun times. Now we don't have many... I know, I know, hindsight is a wonderful thing, so we best split them up nice and even like."

"Will, requisition some more from the mainland," Arnholt said brusquely. It wouldn't help now but the way this whole thing had gone from the start, Wilsin was starting to think they had the right idea, prepping for things to get worse. If it was up to him... Well him as someone else, not him the competitor in the Quin-C, but him the administrator... he'd call the whole thing off, split the prize money twenty-four ways and offer sincerest apologies. Things had been getting too dicey recently. Two murders in hotel rooms, both nowhere close to being solved, the attack on the ICCC building, attempted kidnap, flooding... There came a point when you just had to give something up as a bad job.

"On it," Okocha said. Wilsin looked up and nodded at him before opening his mouth to speak. If he was going to be commanding the ground entry team, he was putting his credits into the pot.

"Split the grenades two to each. Anne and Al won't need them being out of harm's way."

"I'm out of harm's way," Anne said primly. In her words, he could hear a certain coldness he found surprising. He'd never gone into the field with her before, he couldn't have been the only one who'd never expected to hear those words from the silver haired waif's mouth. "Whoever I point my weapon at won't be." It could have sounded like the words were full of bravado, rather an iron certainty in them telling him she meant what she said. She believed it. He'd never been able to work her out completely.

"Anyway, we'll have six between the two on-site teams which will be plenty if we stick together. If they're all congregated together, we'll have them despatched in no time."

"That sort of confidence won't help you none," Derenko said coldly. "If you think this is going to be easy, Agent Wilsin..."

"I don't. I know it's going to be hard. I don't think anyone would be dumb enough to line up where we can pop them at will," Wilsin interrupted. "If we get through this without losing anyone, then I think we'll have done well."

"He says it well," Arnholt said. "Listen up, teams. You have your assignments. You know what you need to do. May your skills save you, and others around you today. You've all been trained well, you'll need every ounce of that training to see you through. Draw on all your experience and we'll get through this. I believe in you all."

And that was that, Wilsin thought as he checked his X7 and slid it into his holster. Moving around in full combat gear felt weird, something he hadn't done for a while. At least there were cooling pads inside to help with the temperature outside. It was lightweight but would be unbearable without the pads. Especially with the mask. He slid the balaclava over his face, it'd hide his features in case the muffler malfunctioned. All overkill an outsider might think, but protecting identities was something they'd gotten very good over the years.

"Wilsin, your team is Alpha," Brendan called. "You're Alpha One. Montgomery, Alpha Two. Leclerc Alpha Three. Derenko, Bravo One. Aldiss Bravo Two. Harper..."

"Bravo Three? Just a guess?" It was hard to tell if Mel Harper was smiling behind her mask. It sounded like she might have. Brendan nodded.

"Correct." He then carried on over to Noorland and Anne. "Sullivan, Chaos One. Noorland, Chaos Two."

"Well now we've got that sorted," Derenko said as Wilsin bent down to pick up his Featherstone. "Let's get this going. Longer we dawdle, the greater risk those people are at."

"Good hunting, guys," Arnholt said. "Good luck. Don't fuck this up or we'll never live it down."

As Wilsin walked past him, Okocha pressed a projector disc into his hand. "Your route to the hospital. Wouldn't want you getting lost down there, huh? Damn maze of tunnels."

Wilsin laughed. "Don't I know it?" He patted Okocha on the shoulder. "Thanks pal. Appreciate it."

"No problem." Will sounded a little too prideful at the praise, he had to admit. If it hadn't been him, he'd have been worried. "It's what I do. Come back alive, mate."

That was then, and this was now. Taking a speeder to the closest water station, they'd been permitted through without anyone getting a hint as to who they were. If he was honest with himself, Wilsin always liked this part more than he thought he would. The getting recognised thing was cool in small doses. It felt like he was just about getting to the point where people did bother him when he walked down the street. Being here in this tournament was helping increase his notoriety. He couldn't complain. The publicity was part of the whole being famous thing. You couldn't have one without the other.

They walked through the underground caverns in silence, Okocha's data leading them towards their destination. He envied Derenko and his team for taking the faster approach, even if there was more chance of being shot at than there was them. Not that he wanted them to be killed but it was always possible. Unisco agents did tend to have a shorter lifespan than those who didn't work for the agency, a sad fact of their lives.

Then again, he'd always figured you never knew how much time you had anyway. Might as well make the most of what you did have. There'd always be those who deserved less who got more and those who deserved more who were cut down before their prime.

"You're both quiet," Leclerc said. "It's disturbing. Really."

"Well I was going to sing," Lysa replied sarcastically. "But the fumes fuck up my throat and well, nobody wants to hear me coughing."

"Damn right," Wilsin said. "Especially them upstairs. Keep it down, folks. They might have someone on the basement."

"It's unlikely," Lysa said. "If there's only twenty of them…"

"It only takes one to sound an alarm," Wilsin said angrily. Of all the things he had to put up with right now, this should not be on the list. "If you don't feel up to this Agent Montgomery then turn around and leave. Or you can be the one who apologises to the families of those who we got killed."

Okay, that sounded harsh, he had to admit. At the same time, this wasn't a joke. "Maybe they won't have someone there. Maybe they will. I don't want to take the chances. There are already too many risks here to chance a misstep."

"He's right," Leclerc said. "We can't assume anything here without further reliable intel. It's risky and unprofessional."

Lysa didn't say anything further, he had to credit her for. That was good. He might have sounded harsh but that was taking command and he didn't want anyone to die here. It was on him, if they did. There was going to be death very soon, he'd rather it be on the other side. If there was another solution, all well and good. But violence had guided the hands of those who sought to end the lives of innocents and they needed putting down. Not because they should enjoy the act but because it would enable others to carry on living.

He glanced down at the data, creased his eyebrows under his hood and bit back a sigh. His first time commanding a mission and so far, it was everything he'd hoped it wouldn't be. Yes, he'd wanted this, he'd wanted the additional responsibility and it had been granted to him. The difference between him and those on his team was that while they might watch each other's back, he was in command and had to watch everyone. They were his to oversee, his responsibility. What had he got? Lysa was a decent agent but rusty from her time convalescing and Leclerc was competent enough, but he'd been a far better pilot than he was field agent. Ideally, he'd have preferred Roper and Wade at his back. Both were survivors. He'd worked with them before, he knew their capabilities under fire, both would have found a way through this. But they weren't here, and it was up to him to ensure this didn't go badly.

The device Okocha had given him directed their path on a mini holograph of a map, a thin red trail leading them through the maze to show them the right path. When they deviated, it turned yellow and let out a whine loud enough to be heard, faint enough not to echo through the inky black. One final glance, Wilsin saw the line had faded, he saw the ladder and grinned. He trailed the rungs up to the covering at the top and found himself suddenly feeling apprehensive. So, this was to be the first step. No going back once they went up there.

"Control, this is Alpha team," he said. "We're at the entry point."

"I always liked that rifle," Noorland said as he watched Anne rest the stand of her Saga on a pair of old crates and take careful aim down the scope, her silvery hair fluttering in the wind. She looked very focused, he was pleased to see as she focused in on the administrator's office. The curtains had been closed but still she glanced in on it. "It's a good one."

"Yep," Anne said. She sounded disinterested, her fingers moving to adjust the scope. "You get thermal on your binoculars?"

Noorland didn't even have to glance at them, they were his own model. He'd built them, he knew what they could do. "Yep. Probably better than the one on your rifle. Doesn't interfere with all that heat being stored in the bricks. Shows humans in a different colour to solar heat."

"I just aim for the window," Anne said. "Anyone walks past it with thermal on, they're getting seen, even with the curtains. You pinpoint anyone in there?"

Noorland brought them to his eyes, blowing gently out his lips in a dull hum as he started with the office and moved across the building. It wouldn't spread too deep into the bowels of the hospital, but he could see several distinct shapes in the office.

"Okay, I see maybe ten hostages in the administrator's office," he said. "They look secured down. Think there's four... No five guys keeping an eye on them. I see two in the corridor outside. There's another circling a ward a few doors down, he's pacing. Think there might be some more hostages in the room with him. Oh dear... This has the potential to be messy."

"We got this, Chaos Two," Derenko said. "Don't worry about it. Just feed us whatever you can get us, and we'll get it done."

"Roger that, Bravo One. Bring home the bacon."

"This is Alpha One, we're in the building. Basement secured. No hostiles down here."

If he squinted, Noorland was sure he could see something rising in the distance, but he didn't move his binoculars to look. He was sure it was Derenko and his team. They'd be using airborne spirits to get to the roof. They'd make their way in and hook up with Wilsin's team halfway. This mission just looked worse by the second.

"You're nervous," Anne said without raising her head. "It's distracting." She winced a little, he saw her flinch. "Sorry. That was unfair."

"I am nervous," Noorland said. "Not what I had planned to do today. How do you do this? I mean if something goes wrong, you'll survive, and you might even have to watch everyone die? I couldn't do this every mission I go on."

Anne said nothing for a moment but when she did, her voice was uncharacteristically cold. "You get used to it," she said. "Nothing lasts forever."

"Amen to that," he said softly.

The rooftop in sight, Derenko guided his thunderbird down and as claws dug into the asphalt of the roof, he hopped down to give Takaris a pat on the neck, glad to have his feet back on solid ground.

"Good boy," he said, just hoping that they hadn't been seen. He unslung his Featherstone, made to secure the area as Harper and Aldiss came in for landing, Harper on an oversized firemoth, Aldiss astride a winged torchmander. Both landed, unslung their weapons and dispelled their spirits. Derenko was glad to see the back of that firemoth if he was honest, something about a five-foot-tall moth he found intensely creepy. He had to admire Mel Harper's metaphorical balls to ride something like that. Its wings might be huge, but they looked so delicate as they flapped. "Okay team form up. We're going to enter through that door, make our way down." He pointed at the roof exit across from them, locked tight, but he wasn't worried. They could get in. Aldiss had the equipment. They all knew how to use it. Silent entry was something they all knew a little about.

"Might be alarmed," Harper said, adjusting her mask. "If it is, they're going to know we're here before we even have a chance."

She was right, Derenko knew, something he'd already considered. Okocha had already pointed it out. Al Noorland had come up trumps again. If he glanced out over the side of the building, he was sure he could see him and Anne atop one of the other buildings. He waved, just on the off-chance.

"Don't worry about it," he said. "It's not a problem." He reached down into his pocket and brought out the chunky grey box, tossing it up and down one handed. "Let's go, Fank. Time's an issue."

Vazaran fire doors operated on the principle when the door was opened, an alarm wired into the frame of the door would sound, everything tied up on a box on the right-hand side of the frame. It'd be a distinctive box, Okocha had described it in detail, should have numbers on it, always a pair of lights, one green and one red. When the light's green, he'd said, the system's active and opening the door will activate the fire alarm. When it's red, it won't.

Noorland had come to the rescue again with a gadget. He'd pointed out it wasn't meant to be used for this exact purpose but the weak pulse of electromagnetic energy it emitted should be enough to confuse the alarm enough to get through. The only problem was it would need to be physically placed on the device, which was on the other side of the door. The device Aldiss brought out from the bag across his back resembled a camera tripod, three heavy black metal legs with a thick cylinder sticking out the end of it. Aldiss dropped onto his knees and took a long look at the door, then at the penetrator. If the situation hadn't been so serious, Derenko might have smiled at the name. Only Al Noorland could have come up with something like this and then given it a name like that to boot.

"Should have just rappelled down from here," Harper said, glancing down at the edge of the roof. "Hit them through the window of the office, blaze away before they know what's hit them."

Derenko shook his head. "Too risky. We did consider it but without knowing who or what or how many is in there, it's very dangerous. If there were no hostages, I'd have gone with it. But their safety is paramount. If even one person dies, we've failed."

"Yep, we got probably every eye in the five kingdoms on this island right now," Aldiss said, hefting up the penetrator and sticking it to the door through suction cups attached to the legs. He waited, saw the blue lights confirm that it was secured before moving across the cylinder, twisting it and teasing it into calibration. "That was before this happened. Now, we're so exposed it's unbelievable. We fuck this up, we're going to get pilloried by every media outlet across the kingdoms."

"Maybe that's why they did it," Harper said. "Maybe they're just dickheads who want to show up Unisco."

Derenko said nothing. He was too busy watching Aldiss, double checking the calibrations of the penetrator. The laser needed to be at the right intensity, too weak and it'd fail to burn through, wasting valuable time. Too strong and it'd burn too powerful to control, the potent heat melting the lock and popping the door, which would ruin everything. Eventually they both were satisfied but still he held his breath as Aldiss thumbed the activation. The acrid smell of burning metal filled his nostrils, even filtering through his mask but already it was starting to give way beneath the focused beam.

Ten seconds later, a hole had formed. Now for the hard part, he thought. Harper brought out the spray, depressed the nozzle and dashed it around the ragged hole. One of them was going to stick their hand inside that hole, feel out the alarm control. Hence the coolant. None of them wanted to scorch themselves on jagged metal. Even through armour, it'd hurt like a bitch if it touched them. He was tempted to tell Harper to do it. She had the thinnest arms. Still he wasn't prepared to ask anything of anyone on his team he wasn't prepared to do himself. Aldiss removed the spent penetrator and dropped it back into the bag. They weren't taking it with them. Unnecessary weight would slow them down. They didn't have many of them on the island, it'd need to be retrieved later. But right now, they needed to ensure there would be a later. Derenko stepped over to the hole and glanced through it, checking the corridors on either side through the gap. He couldn't see anyone.

He could see the outline of the control box, the faint reflection of green light off the far wall. Drawing a slow breath, he removed his glove and put the chunky box into his bare hand, easing it through the hole. It was tight, the edges of it scraped the box but it'd cope, and he grit his teeth as he had to force it through, rotating it around until it was facing the alarm control. The box was magnetic, that was good, meant he didn't have to worry too much about securing it in place. He removed his hand and put his eye to the hole. Still the light remained green. Just for a moment, he felt doubt rush through him. Had they found the right one?

"We in yet?" Aldiss wondered. "Is it working?"

He said nothing. Already he was thinking about alternative entry strategies should this not pay off. Still it remained green.

"Bravo One, what is your status?" He could hear Brendan in his ear, he still hadn't exhaled, he realised and let it go sharply. Come on, work, you bastard!

It was faint, but he saw the glow change from green to red and he felt the relief flood him. Hand back through the hole, he twisted the bar and the door swung silently open. He stuck his head through, sure there was nobody around but set to check anyway. If there was someone there, they'd surely have been alerted by previous acts. Never assume. That way led to death and pain. He wasn't about to get killed in action by something so basically dumb.

"Control, Bravo team has entered the building," he said triumphantly as the three of them stepped inside. That had been the easy part, he thought. The tough bit was still ahead.

Like all plans it was doomed to fail at the first sign of action and as they left the basement, Wilsin saw the guy stood down the corridor, back to them and smoking. He had a Broxtie resting at his side on a strap, plumes of thick noxious smoke filling the corridor. He raised a hand, halted Montgomery and Leclerc in their tracks, wondering if they could get around him. He didn't want to start taking opposition pieces out of the game too early. There had to be a reason the guy was down here. If he'd been despatched here, all it'd take would be one unanswered hail and he'd be missed. Someone would come looking for him...

Drawing numbers away from the rest of them and into easy ambushes. Or they could start killing the hostages, assume they were under attack. If that was the case, best get it done before they could make any such assumption. He raised one finger, gestured towards the guard and tilted his head, silently telling them he'd get him. Pushing the door open, he started to slowly move across the floor, keeping his breathing shallow and controlled, quiet as a mouse until he was within striking distance.

For a moment, he held position, fought the urge to cough over the odour of smoke growing ever stronger the closer he got to the guy and then he struck, lunging and grabbing him from behind. He felt the jerk of surprise before he got one arm around his throat, one hand on his head.

Stun him only... Cut off air, let him pass out, he can be jailed later...

The thought that went through his head, it was what he should have done. Instead he twisted hard and violent, the thoughts of what had taken place upstairs running through his head and he couldn't stop himself. The crack of his neck breaking filled the hall and the strangest thing Wilsin realised upon letting the body fall, for the first time making a kill, he didn't feel regret. He could justify it to himself. He didn't deserve to live. He'd been complicit in attacking a building of sick people and taking hostages. Furthermore, if he'd been knocked out, he could have shot them in the back. He'd removed a risk. Maybe that was the reason

Leclerc and Montgomery were behind him, Leclerc stepped past and removed the mask from the corpse's face. Wilsin didn't stop him, just raised his Featherstone in case he needed it. He glanced down at the face below, tanned, a bit Serranian, curly black hair and the faintest hint of moustache on the upper lip like he hadn't shaved for a day or two. He could smell olives. Bit good looking, he supposed. Now he was dead and for what?

Leclerc was still studying the body as he and Montgomery made to move on. Wilsin halted, glanced back. "Something troubling you, Alpha Three?"

For a moment, Leclerc said nothing and then looked at him. "This man. I know him. He is... I don't remember his name but he's a Fratelli family guy."

That brought a reaction. "What?!" Wilsin said.

"Say again, Alpha Three," Control said. It was either Brendan or Okocha on the line, Wilsin missed which as he stared at Leclerc.

"Are you sure about that?!" Montgomery asked. "What the hells is a Fratelli family enforcer doing holding up a hospital in Vazara?"

"One of the things that I'm proud to say we do make all attempts to do is ensure our agents are effective at fighting when circumstances are less than ideal. Low visibility for instance. Or when distracting stimuli are introduced into the mix. You can never plan for every eventuality, but we aim to try. Unarmed combat is always a funny one to plan. It means the weapons have failed and we don't like to consider failure. Yet sometimes, we must."

Tod Brumley, Unisco academy instructor, on training methods.

The fifteenth day of Summerdawn.

Wade wasn't dead.

It felt like he had, and his body was still moving of its own accord, but he hadn't yet. Which was good. The pain was good, kept reminding him he was still alive. It had happened when Mallinson had been shot, the blaster had skidded back into his room and there'd been seconds to react. Yanking the drip from his hand had been the worst part, he'd yelled in pain as the needle had broken free. For a moment, he was worried it had snapped, left embedded in his flesh. Then he'd hurled himself at the weapon, tipping the bed as he caught it with a flailing foot, already sure a bruise was forming up where he'd made impact. But he was still alive, and no sooner had it crashed to the floor had he scooped the weapon up and stood behind the door frame in time to see laser fire rip into the room and demolish the bed where he'd lain moments ago, shredding the wood and fabric with impunity.

He could just about see it, his vision maybe at about sixty percent, he slid the safety off Mallinson's weapon by touch and as the first shooter stepped into the room, he didn't hesitate, just shot him in the back of the head at point blank range. Even if he'd had a shield up, it wouldn't have made a difference.

He went down, Wade went low and spun around the door, weapon ready to fire. He saw the second guy already aiming but before he could adjust, Wade shot him three times through the chest, springing to a standing position and past him before he could react. He wasn't going to be doing much else, he'd seen the entry wounds in the guy's stomach, he might survive only if he got help immediately. He was in the right place for it, he doubted there'd be volunteers. As he ran, not entirely sure where he was going, one thought came through his head clamouring for attention.

They'd come for him. They'd come straight to his room and attempted a hit on him. Someone knew. He didn't panic, that wouldn't help him get out of here. He'd been trained to keep a calm head in the worst circumstances and these were slowly approaching that. Compromised vision, unknown number of hostiles, a potentially huge number of hostages… He wasn't getting out of this one on his own. He still had Mallinson's X7 in his hand, he didn't know if he could hit someone at range with it. Those two guys had been easier; would have been harder to miss but he wouldn't survive a firefight. Best thing would be to hole up somewhere, keep an eye on the door, blast anyone who came through. It'd be about the only thing he could do. They'd find the two guys eventually. In a situation like this, you had half an hour absolute maximum following the first death before people realised something was wrong. As estimates went, he'd always thought it generous. He just hoped rescue mobilised soon. No way could the Carcaradis Island constabulary handle something like this. They'd be horribly outmatched, undertrained and underprepared. No, it'd be either get a team in from the mainland or, more likely, make a request to Unisco to deal with it. It'd be embarrassing in the short term, but it would be the best thing to do. He just needed to hold out until then.

The Fratelli crime family was renowned for being one of the largest in the five kingdoms but Wilsin knew, they didn't have much presence in Vazara. Their main influence spread through Serran, Premesoir and some parts of Canterage, hence no reason why they should be here. The local Vazaran criminals were crazy enough to resist any attempts to organise them, they liked doing their own thing and they weren't about to have anyone tell them how to do it. Their way was one of violence where the Fratelli's and their ilk preferred to at least talk about it first before moving onto dismemberment and actual bodily harm.

So, with that in mind, what one was doing in a hospital on Carcaradis Island? Wilsin didn't know, he could just hear Okocha's voice filtering through his earpiece, painfully aware of the seconds ticking by. They'd made the first kill, they didn't have long to get into position before he was missed.

"Yeah, got him, his name's Richie Capelli. Also known as the Chain."

"Lovely," Lysa muttered dryly. "Who names these people after hardware?"

"Several counts of suspected trafficking, suspected murder… Yeah pleasant reading. Going to add domestic terrorism to that dossier," Okocha continued, ignoring her. "So… I'm at a loss here as to what's going on."

"It's not important," Leclerc said, surprising Wilsin. "I mean, it's not. Worry about that later, we have bigger problems now than someone being where they shouldn't."

"Well said Alpha Three," Wilsin said. "Come on, let's move out. Worry about it later."

"Heh, what chance all of them being Fratelli family goons?" Lysa asked, a question Wilsin had already considered. Even if they were and by some glorious fluke of nature they could take them alive, getting them to admit Giacomo Fratelli had put them up to it would probably be a pipe dream too far. The people who knew stuff tended to be almost fanatically loyal and close mouthed. More to the point, they were probably miles away.

It took them no time at all to run into trouble and Derenko hissed a curse as they rounded the corner and saw three guys walking the same direction towards them, two of them joking and laughing, another cold and focused. It was that focused man who survived, he saw them and dived for cover into a room, the merry men going for their blasters and a trio of shots hammered into them, knocking them down dead.

Cover blown and now they really were pushed for time. He'd shot, Aldiss and Harper had too, and they'd been good hits. They weren't getting back up, he confirmed, as he traced the path the other guy had gone with his eyes. That had torn it. It'd be only a matter of seconds to send a hail and... Couldn't think. Had to act. He pressed against the wall, the door had been left open. He briefly flashed his hand across the doorway, withdrew it quickly and heard the shots flash by.

"Come on in, the water's lovely!" he heard the cackling voice roar. "I'm waiting for you."

Derenko glanced back at his teammates, gestured for them to go back. Find another way into that room, he mouthed at them. They both slunk out of sight and he kept a tighter grip on his Featherstone. There had to be another way to do this. His eyes went to the two hostiles they'd dropped, he checked them over, didn't see any sort of hailing equipment. Maybe it was portable. If he'd been in this situation, he'd have his people hooked up to heart trackers. The moment they were dropped; you'd know about it. Hopefully whoever was organising this thing wasn't as organised as him.

"I'll enjoy it from out here," he said. Maybe he could distract the hostile long enough for Aldiss and Harper to flank him. This wasn't the best place for a shootout. Too many places to be ambushed, too many hiding spots, too many innocents. Many might have got out before the shit truly went down but those who couldn't move still had to be here. The knowledge there might be someone in a coma in the room was the only reason he hadn't opened fire. He thought of the grenade on his belt and toyed with the idea for a moment. It still might cause some damage, but it'd only be superficial, more distressing than anything. He'd give them another ten seconds and then toss one in there.

"Shame, it's lovely in here. So nice of you to show up, Unisco! I always wanted to kill some of you scum!"

"Nice accent," Derenko said. What was it? Burykian? He couldn't tell above his heart pounding in his ears. He'd overheard Wilsin's team discussing their corpse with Okocha and Brendan, more questions were being asked by the minute as to who these guys were.

Come on Aldiss don't let me down now!

"What's the HSB doing here?" He shouted at the top of his voice the name of the first Burykian crime group he could think of, the Holy Sun of Burykia, not the biggest but the most well know due to a series of serials on the viewing screens.

"Ha! Holy Sun has set. There's a new sun rising…"

He was cut off, Derenko cursed the timing as he heard the roar of Featherstone fire and the unmistakeable sound of a body hitting the ground. He threw caution to the wind, stuck his head around the door and saw Harper stood with the weapon smoking in her hand.

"Took you so long?" he inquired. "Good job, Bravo Three. Now let's move out. We'll identify bodies later."

Wade thought he heard laser fire. He wasn't sure, in the darkness of the closet, sound was distorted. Maybe it was close, maybe far away or maybe not at all. It was the best thing he could do, even if he couldn't shake the feeling he wasn't about to live this down if someone found him hiding. He was a Unisco agent. He should be out there trying to secure the area and here he was. If he had heard fire, it was safe to assume his comrades had entered the building and were trying to defuse the situation. They'd have it in hand. Nobody would hold it against him if he sat this one out. After all he'd earned his injuries in a more dangerous circumstances which counted for something.

He just wasn't sure if he'd be able to live with himself if he didn't do something. He'd taken two of them out, more through fortuitous circumstances than skill He had an X7 with a half-depleted charge, vision that was spotty at best and he was walking around in a robe that left his arse hanging out. Not exactly the sort of situation that left you optimistic.

He didn't even have his summoner on him. Roper had it for safe keeping. He wondered if Roper was part of the team entering the building. If he was, Wade felt confident that it'd be sorted in no time at all. He'd be able to deal. A fully trained Unisco squad could take on anything short of a full army. In these circumstances, they'd be fine, he told himself.

They had to be nearly there. Twice they'd encountered resistance, the first Leclerc had tussled with before Montgomery had shot him through the throat while the second had been taken down with a Featherstone stock to the head. Wilsin's aim had been good, he'd gone down hard. Three down, plus three that Bravo Team had dealt with.

They'd seen two more hostiles dead in a room as well as another corpse that vaguely resembled Inquisitor Mallinson. He'd been preferable in death than he had been in life. Wilsin had met Stelwyn Mallinson before and hadn't cared for him. Still the loss of any Unisco agent in the line of duty was a tragedy. Very little had been made of the fact he was on the premises until Brendan had mentioned he'd been brought to the island to investigate the ICCC building attack. They'd not known he was at the hospital until recently. He'd also revealed the room was Wade's. With the bed overturned and shattered, Wilsin didn't know what to think. There was no sign of a body, not the one they were looking for anyway.

So maybe Wade had gotten away. He hoped so. If anyone had been able to take an opportunity, it would have been him. Wade had all his training behind him, Mallinson was missing a weapon with no sign of it anywhere. Maybe he was fine. The hostiles had both been shot with precision, one in the back of the head, one several times in the stomach. It looked like he'd died hard.

So, eight down. Wilsin wondered how many more they'd have to deal with before the day was over. Nobody knew exactly how many there'd been to start with. It was a question he vocalised to Chaos Team.

"Ah, I think there's at least three in the administrator office," Noorland said. "Maybe four. It's hard to make out. Isn't less though. Plan for more, you won't be disappointed."

"Roger that Chaos Two," Wilsin said. "Bravo One, what is your position?"

"Converging on target," Derenko replied. "Should be at the hot zone in five. You?"

"Copy and paste that. We'll see you there, Bravo One. Good hunting."

"You too, Alpha One."

So far it was proving too easy and Wilsin found himself worrying. They'd snaked their way through the hallways, keeping out of the main corridors when possible just in case. As Bravo team had found out by the sound of it, it was just too easy to walk into an ambush when exposed in the open. He'd insisted on it, neither Leclerc nor Montgomery had complained. They knew the score and wanted to stay alive, were also professional to the end. He was grateful. Some Unisco agents could be real pains. He was sure he was one of them back when he'd been under command.

The whole point was limits. He'd known how far to push it before it became insubordination. He knew how to keep it in line before he became a liability. Everything had a limit and sometimes you didn't want to test those limits. He'd found himself wondering what the limits would be here. Without knowing what these hostiles wanted, it'd be hard to gauge how quickly they'd start exterminating hostages. If they were after bloodshed, no time at all. They could wipe everyone out before they were killed themselves. If they were after something else and he had to believe that they were, they might not do it as rapidly as they might otherwise. They might only do it if they were forced. It took a queer strength of will to shoot an unarmed person. Someone who was trying to kill you, Wilsin could testify was an easy mark. Killing them would not be a problem. By that logic, he was probably far more likely to get shot than one of the hostages in the room. Those hostages in there were probably terrified, stressed and not a threat at all. If they kept their heads down, they'd be okay. That was the theory. Don't be a hero and you won't get hurt. Would they do it? Finding out could be an expensive way to call their bluff.

More to the point, he couldn't figure the logic behind their attack here. He didn't have all the pieces, putting them together would be impossible but there should at least be the start of a picture. Not that it was important right now. The details could be established later. Maybe when they had all those, they could start to put them together, a very faint hope.

He almost missed the hostile ahead, halting his team as the uniformed figure strode through one of the wards, rifle hanging loose from his shoulder and letting his hand trail against thankfully empty beds. He had his back to them. The Featherstone felt heavy in his hands and Wilsin toyed with the idea of giving him one in the back. Except that would bring him back to the thought before about shooting someone who didn't pose an immediate threat.

Maybe he could turn it to his advantage. Get some answers. It was a thought that flitted through his head before the hostile turned away out of sight and Wilsin held himself still, slowing his breathing. He still pointed the weapon towards the doorway the figure had vanished through, mind already half made up to go after him. He could smell a rank cologne in the air, as he went to follow him, it stank of a scent he couldn't describe but it had a distinct blend of sweat within it. Lovely. Exactly what you wanted to pass through your nasal passages.

He grinned, heard something in the distance and quickened his pace, rounding the same corner the hostile had followed at a slow walk. If he was about to walk into an ambush, it wasn't going to be blindly. His finger sat on the trigger guard, he didn't need to employ it. Nothing. Immediate area was clear. Leclerc and Montgomery were behind him, had every direction covered and as three they moved through the corridor in a tight circle, trying to get a lock on the position of the hostile. Leclerc tagged him first and Wilsin heard the tell-tale snap of Featherstone fire cutting him down.

"Hostile eliminated," Leclerc reported, before glancing around at his commander. Wilsin gave him a nod and thumbs up.

"Control, I had a thought," Montgomery said. "About how we could defuse this situation peacefully."

"Go on," Brendan said. "Let's hear it."

Wilsin glanced around to ascertain their location, just another spotless white stairwell and he didn't like this. They'd been up a few already and they made good places for ambushes. The higher ground was key, all it'd take was for hostiles to wait them out at the top and they'd have a clear shot as they came up. They were on the fourth floor. Bravo team would have more fortune descending from the roof.

"So, they'll be watching the door, right? Why don't we find another way in? Examine the room above, see if there's something we can exploit there. Or throw some stun grenades in through the window. Didn't Chaos Two come up with some wall crawling gloves?"

"Didn't bring any with me, Alpha Two," Noorland said. "Sorry. Nice idea though."

"We're nearly at the engagement zone, Alpha team," Derenko said. "What is your position?"

"Fourth stairwell," Wilsin replied. "Be with you when we get up there. Had a little fly in the stew, had to take time to swat it."

"We don't have time to check the room above, nor the equipment to silently breach the floor, Alpha Two," Brendan said. "Next time bring any ideas like this at the briefing."

"Sorry Control, it only just occurred to me," Montgomery said, sounding apologetic. "It doesn't matter. Let's get this done."

Doctor A. B Mwarumari. Administrator Director.

At least they were in the right place, Wilsin thought as he read the sign on the door across from them, shut tight and probably locked if they had any sense. Bypassing it would take time, time that the hostages wouldn't have if they tried to storm the room. When the shooting started, they'd be the ones most at risk. Six of them stood outside, more than a little uneasy. They'd regrouped swiftly, he couldn't help wondering how many they'd not accounted for around the hospital. Or maybe the last of them genuinely were locked in the office.

"Chaos team, we need numbers," Derenko said into his comm. "Can you get them for us?"

"Negative Bravo One, too many variables," Anne said. "For an exact number anyway. Best guess, five hostiles, twice as many hostages."

"I'd second that guess," Noorland offered. "My thermals are better than hers, I can make out at least four, maybe five or six sets of weapons in there. Double that number for the hostages. They're sat out in a semi-circle around the administrator's desk. Everyone looks to be towards the back of the room except one guy... Wait, he's coming for the door. He's coming out!"

"Take cover!" Brendan ordered, a redundant order by Wilsin's reckoning given half the team had scattered already, not out of fear but desire to keep their presence secret. He didn't rush, just pressed himself against the wall the same side as the opening door, he heard the twist of the key and hoped that the door would at least be closed before he had to do something to neutralise the threat.

Their luck was in, he saw the hostile exit, the door close behind him, heard the lock clicking shut before he was on him, hand over his mouth and dragging him away with great difficulty. Fuck, this guy was strong! His struggles threatened to break Wilsin's grip, he felt teeth tearing at his hand and he bit down a yell. Both hands were busy, one over his mouth, one around his neck and the hostile's elbows were trying to swing back and catch him in the side, like riding a thrashing donkey. He applied pressure to the neck, squeezed harder, trying to find the sensitive nerves that would pacify him all while taking blows to the side and the shins, the man not going down easily. Aldiss appeared from nowhere, sprang into view and clocked the struggling hostile square on the jaw with a vicious right hook that snapped his head back and brought it lolling to a rest across Wilsin's shoulder. Reluctantly he let him drop, stretching his arms as he did.

"Nice hit," he said amicably. "I had it under control."

"Course you did," Aldiss grinned. "Now it definitely is though." He shook his fist, flexed his fingers to retrieve the feeling in them. "You're welcome, mate."

"Think they heard that?" Wilsin asked, reaching to his belt for a pair of restraints. He took one of the unconscious hostile's wrists, secured the cuffs to it and then did the same to the other wrist.

"Well we haven't heard shooting or threats yet," Aldiss replied. "I'd say we're in the clear for the moment though I don't know how much time we do have. If he was due to report back any time soon, they may suspect something."

"Then we should move sooner rather than later," Derenko said, appearing from around the corner. "We need a plan to get in there now."

They turned, saw Leclerc crouched down next to the lock, examining it thoughtfully. If he had any thoughts on what they were talking about, he didn't share them. Montgomery glanced over at him, then back to Wilsin and Derenko with a bemused look.

"Not a complicated lock," Leclerc said. "Old style key. Not electronic. Probably for security purposes. Can't be hacked. Could probably be bust open with one solid hit. Makes it obvious if someone's been in there."

"At the same time, it does the job," Harper said. "There has to be a way…"

Wilsin broke away from the group, moved to stand behind Leclerc, glanced at the lock and stroked his chin behind his mask. She was right. There was a way.

"Chaos One, come in!"

Anne, lost in the moment staring through her scope, jerked out of her reverie and looked at Noorland, still focused on the same spot as before.

"Go on Bravo One," she said. "What do you need?"

"Can you see inside that room? What's happening in there?"

She sighed. That question or variations of it had been asked several times since the mission had started and it was starting to grate on her. This wasn't what she'd planned to do today. Not even close. "Same as before, just with one less guy. Curtains are still shut."

"Does the window look reinforced?" Wilsin asked. "Do we have any data on that?"

"Shouldn't be," Okocha said over the comm. "If it is, they didn't include it on the blueprints of the building."

"You want me to open fire into the room?" Anne asked. "I can't eliminate them all before the hostages get hurt. Couldn't do that even if I could see in there."

"We have a plan," Derenko said. "All we need from you is one shot. And it needs to be a good one."

"One of your best," Wilsin offered, slightly unhelpfully, she thought as she heard his voice. "You get it wrong and it'll be disastrous."

"What do you want me to do?" Anne asked, emotion out of her voice. At least she couldn't feel the terror of the hostages from over here. That'd be distracting. She wasn't going to feel any sorrow from them either because they were all going to be fine. Nobody was going to die, and she was going to do her bit in ensuring that was the case.

"We're going to supply you a target," Derenko said. "And we need you to hit it dead on."

"It's a small target," Wilsin continued. "If the curtain's closed, you won't be able to see it and you need to avoid the hostages as well. Think you're up to it?"

She almost laughed. "Could you do it? If you can, feel free to come over here and put your credits where your mouth is. If you can't, get that target for me."

For several long minutes, nothing happened. It didn't bother her. It was the sniper's lot. Sometimes you had to wait for hours, maybe even days in the same spot without moving. She somehow didn't think it would take so long this time. Whatever they were doing, they had to move quickly. She didn't hear anything over the comms, just kept her rifle pointed at the room, controlling her breathing. In and out, in and out, inhale, exhale, inhale and exhale. Noorland kept quiet but she could tell he was as agitated as her, trying hard not to feel. This whole situation was draining on everyone but that wasn't an excuse. It was something that they needed to get right.

"Alpha team, Bravo team," Noorland finally said. "What's happening down there? Are you nearly in position?"

"Nearly," Derenko said. "Should be on your scope in a few."

"Hey, you try scrounging up something like this in a few moments," Harper quipped. "Mind you, you'd probably be good at it, Chaos Two."

Anne could imagine the look on Noorland's face, the smug prideful look she'd seen so many times before. At the same time, he was entitled to it, given the abilities he had with mechs and techs. The guy was a genius, she had to admit.

Finally, she saw it, faint but slowly blinking into existence. At this range, it looked little more than a dot, but it was growing by the second, a small red smudge against the blue of her thermal scope. If she hadn't been looking for it, she might not have seen it.

"Think I see it," she said. "Want to tell me what I'm shooting at here, Bravo One?"

"The target," Derenko said. "You can hit it, Chaos One. Good hunting."

She wasn't worried about hitting it. Strangely enough, the idea she might miss never entered her mind. No, what worried her was what could happen if she did. What would come next?

"Back at you," she said. "Alpha, Bravo team, I'm going to take the shot. Move quickly, whatever you do. You won't have a lot of time. I'm going to take it in five. In four. In three. In two. And…" She squeezed the trigger, felt the kick of the oversized weapon against her shoulder and the flutter of hope her aim had been true.

Stun grenades in hand, Derenko and Wilsin heard the end of the countdown and looked at each other. Moment of truth. She was right. They would need to move quickly. They didn't hear the shot; they did see the door fly open in a manner it hadn't been meant to. It opened inwards, a shot hitting it from outside the building wasn't going to do much good. Anne's shot had been good, straight through the lock, but it hadn't been what had gotten it open. The small amount of thermal breach they'd spread over the lock had done that for them and it was that which tore the door open. Thermal breach grew hotter and hotter the moment it was applied; they'd spread some around the lock in hopes of giving Anne a target. Normally it simply grew hotter and hotter until it burned through the lock, but it was also incredibly volatile, given certain stimuli. They'd needed an instant reaction, no time for the breach to burn through the lock. Wilsin had set his grenade to explode on impact, he leaned around the doorway and tossed it in, ducking out the way as the disorientating sonic boom shattered through the space, Derenko doing the same, mirroring his movements. Then the teams were moving in, Montgomery and Harper, Aldiss and Leclerc firing with pinpoint accuracy on anyone holding a weapon.

By the time Derenko and Wilsin had retaken their Featherstones and entered the room, Aldiss was already shouting it was clear. Wilsin saw the hole in the window where Anne's shot had come through, saw that some of the hostiles had been facing that direction. That had served its purpose. A twin pronged attack on two fronts was better than a solitary one. As far as he could tell, nobody was hurt, the hostages all looked fine.

"Everyone! Remain calm!" he bellowed. "This is Unisco!" Just for the benefit of some of the people there, he repeated it in Vazaran.

Regardless of linguistic abilities, it was something they were trained to be able to repeat in any of the main languages of the five kingdoms. "You're safe now."

Weapons were kicked from the hands of their fallen wielders, pulses were checked to see who was still alive and only then did they start to free the hostages. All in all, David Wilsin decided, not a bad day's work.

"Unbelievable!"

The roar erupted from the crowd around the stadium and Theo stood in shocked silence as he stared at the battlefield, the carnage left lingering on the stones. Atlas was breathing heavily, covered in cuts and scrapes, the scales slathered in blood but at least the anklo was still moving, which was more than could be said for Gamorra. The spannerhead wasn't moving, eyes not seeing but so much less in death than in life. Sharon, to her credit, didn't bat an eye. If she was bothered, she didn't show it. Some part of that stung him.

She should be upset. Why was she not showing more emotion? The verdict was in, she was out of spirits and he'd beaten her fair and square, he'd beaten the favourite and yet she appeared unfazed as she strode out towards him, pausing only to kneel and pat Gamorra on the neck before bringing it back to a crystal.

"Well folks, that was that and what a result! What a shock on the cards! Theobald Jameson pulls off the shock of the tournament and defeats Sharon Arventino five spirits to six. On a day when it's all been put into perspective, given what's happened across the island, we've seen a fiercely competitive bout and perhaps it might not be remembered the way it should, but in this commentator's opinion, the match of the tournament so far."

She was in front of him now, close enough to see the sorrow in her eyes. Sharon offered him a hand and he took it to shake. She managed a weak smile at him. "Don't let anyone diminish this victory for you, Theo." At least she hadn't used his full name. That was a relief. "You deserved it. Good luck in the next round. May fortune guide you on your travels."

At least she'd lost with grace. He didn't even have the heart to rub it in. Against someone else, he might have tossed it back in their face. Yet with her, it felt churlish to do so.

The victory was what mattered. He'd won. Nobody could take that away. Anyone who tried would have seriously problems. Still, looking around the adoration and the sheer force of glee billowing down from the watching thousands, Theo decided he was just going to enjoy the moment for once.

Chapter Seventeen. This Dream We Have.

"When you keep having the same damn dream, do you really want it to come true? Feels like it spoils the surprise somewhat."
Ruud Baxter.

Time has no meaning in the land of dreams.

She'd had this dream before. Here she was again, same place she'd been a thousand times before, and for the thousand and first time she was happy to be here. And why shouldn't she? It was her special day after all. All eyes would be on her and her soon-to-be husband as they formally declared their love for each other. Her father wasn't here admittedly. Of course, he wasn't. She could barely recall Canderous Arventino's face, she could just remember the mindless rage and twisted fear contorting it the last time she'd laid eyes on him. Instead John Jacobs had her arm, walking her down the aisle, fulfilling the role of father of the bride as the music played around them, light melodic music from Burykian silver tamborlutes.

As the two of them approached the altar, it rose in its melody, somehow sounding in time with the click of her heels on the floor of the chapel. A great statue of Gilgarus and Melarius stared down above the zent and the altar, a single earth-fashioned urn sitting on it. The lion and the tigress, Melarius more prominent as the Divine of love, birth and marriage. Sharon allowed herself to raise eyes to her, silent prayer passing her lip as they moved through the throngs of adoring people. Friends and family of both her and Nick, people she knew well, people she'd love to get to know further and those with whom she'd love to reconnect.

The guest list read like a who's who of the spirit calling world. The groom and his best man were just two of them, Nicholas Roper and Wade Wallerington both in tuxedos, Wade grinning, Nick smiling as they awaited her. Her maid of honour, Gemma Holtby, a smiling sight in summer yellow stood waiting, Sharon knew she'd been trying to catch Wade's eye. He looked better, not like the pictures from when he'd been involved in that attack at the Quin-C, not a trace of scarring remained, his eyes vivid bright as ever.

Faces she recognised through the crowds as they made it ever closer included her brother Peter, David Wilsin, Vassily Derenko, Fank Aldiss, even Terrence Arnholt. Her own side, well some of those faces it felt like she hadn't seen for ages. Blank faces, happy for her but vaguely vacant as if they were devoid of something. That sent a little shiver up the length of her spine, she couldn't quite place it, even if she should be able to. Allison Teserine, Julius Hong, Arnaud Kroll, Luke and Darren Maddley...

But not him. She stole a glance, a little hurt he hadn't deigned to attend. She'd invited him, even if it had been difficult to arrange communication. Maybe he hadn't gotten it. He would have been here if he had, surely. Still he wasn't and that was that. After today she'd be closing that chapter of her life for good. Before the new could truly begin, the old had to go. For the final time, she looked down nervously at her dress, pure cream white with black and red trim across the hem and around the waist and conceded finally to herself she looked fine. It felt unusual with her hair up, twisted and teased into a three-foot-tall style held in place with copious amounts of invisi-pins and styling cream. At this point, she felt hitting it with a hammer wouldn't budge it.

Finally, she reached the altar and slowly turned to John. He smiled at her, she smiled back even though he couldn't see it underneath her veil and he let go of her arm.

"You look beautiful, darling," he said, before turning to the tall zent, the man resplendent in his purple robes. He looked at the two of them through thin spectacles and as he met the priest's gaze, John cleared his throat. "I, John Jacobs, hereby relinquish the responsibility of this woman from my household," he said. She heard the note of amusement in his voice. Yes, it was archaic but that was just one step away from traditional. Her father had been Serranian. Her mother was from Canterage, just like her future husband and so it had been arranged for a traditional Canterage ceremony. Which unfortunately meant that bit be included, but she didn't care. She felt giddy with excitement. It was closer to happening.

The zent... Stoatley, she thought his name was, too much to remember, nodded at her and Nick broke from next to Wade, descending the three steps and offered her a hand. She took it in her gloved one and followed his lead as they stepped to the altar.

"... And into her husbands," John finished, before sitting down to a smattering of applause, seating himself next to her mother who wore such a look of pride on her face.

Husband... it was happening.

As they stood facing each other in front of the altar, Nick reached to lift her veil, winking at her as their eyes met for a moment before they turned to the zent. He had a scar on his nose she'd never noticed before.

"Beloved friends and family gathered here today of this man and this woman," Stoatley intoned, his voice dry but powerfully reassuring. "We are here to celebrate the union of Nicholas James Roper and

Sharon Melissa Arventino in devoted matrimony before the eyes of both Divine above and man below."

So far so good. She'd read through what he'd say the previous night. Not because she'd wanted to know. Because she was bored. And nervous. And didn't want any surprises. Nerves. Yeah, there should be some here. But there weren't. She felt pretty good about the whole thing.

Nick was nervous, an alien feeling emanating from him. But they were the good nerves, she guessed, the sort you battled through, because you knew the reward was worth it. And what if he was nervous. Only an idiot wouldn't be nervous right now.

"Divines give, and Divines take away but to some they give more than others and when this happens, we find ourselves here in the presence of two who love each other," Stoatley continued. "To validate this marriage before the Divines above, I ask anyone here who may or know any such reason as to why it should not be blessed."

Nobody said anything, Stoatley kept his face impassively professional as he looked at them and spread his arms. For a crazy moment, she thought it would be over just like that. How wrong was she? "Let us all never forget that we are all just shade cast by the brilliance of the Divines above and that all we do may never be enough to earn their approval but that we hope it is enough to evade their wrath. Let us all hope that the fruits of this union hold ripe and prime for the future, a bountiful harvest that may never wither and die."

A bit bleak, she thought. But in a way, it felt nice. It felt reassuring hearing it out loud for the first time when it concerned her. Ahead of them, Zent Stoatley moved a hand over the earthen urn and she heard the trickle of liquid against stone.

"For the success of their new life together," the zent continued. "An offering will now be made from each of you to Melarius to bless what you have together. An offering that for all the new adventures that your life will bring you, you sacrifice something of the old for something new cannot be erected…"

Without the old being left behind, Sharon added in her head, fighting the urge to trace the words out with her lips. She'd never seen divine fire before up close. Somewhere amidst his robes, Stoatley struck a match and she caught the acrid scent of smoke. He dropped the match in the urn and it went up with a roar of blue and scarlet fire, the scent of jasmine and rosemary filling the chapel.

"Nicholas James Roper," Stoatley said. "Your words, please."

He cleared his throat. "I, Nicholas James Roper, in devotion to a Divine power far greater than I ever will be…" He probably meant it to sound humble, she thought it sounded like he was taking the piss. She'd never known him be especially devout. "… Hereby make a humble offering to Melarius, Queen of the Dei in hopes of recognition and appreciation for the love I hold for my future wife. Dei be praised."

He nodded at her, winked then drew a leather case from his jacket and tossed it into the fire, the flames rising with whooshing roar that brought sweat to her brow. Shouldn't have stood so close. It'd make her makeup run.

"Sharon Melissa Arventino," Stoatley said, turning to her. He looked satisfied with what Nick had said. No reason he shouldn't be. "Your words, please."

"I, Sharon Melissa Arventino daughter of Canderous and named for Melarius, Queen of the Dei, humbly plead to her, whose name I cannot do justice no matter how long I live, to bless my marriage to this wonderful man. In supplication, I close the book on a chapter of my life forever."

She drew the metal cylinder from her glove and tossed it into the fire. It'd probably take longer to burn than Nick's offering. She didn't have to explain what it was. Not to the watching masses. On the off-chance that Melarius existed and gave a shit, she'd known. Divine fire grew exceptionally hot, she had no doubt it'd destroy the item utterly. It hurt. But the good kind of hurt. She would miss it, but it was something she'd not used for a long time. "Dei be praised."

Again, Stoatley looked satisfied. There were some wet eyes in the crowd which pleased her. So far so good. Such a good feeling bursting in the base of her stomach surely wouldn't last forever. There'd be good and there'd be bad. There'd been both of those since they'd met. But even when you knew a feeling was fleeting, it didn't mean you couldn't savour it.

For several moments, they studied the fire until it died, leaving no trace of the items thrown in. Even the ash had been incinerated, thick black burns covered the stone, she could feel the heat radiating from it.

"The offerings have been accepted," Stoatley said in his dry imposing voice which had the audience so captivated. "In the eyes of Melarius, the union can go ahead. This man and this woman can be joined together in sickness and health, in trial and triumph, in life and in death. Where once there were two, there is now only one, united by love. Nicholas, can you repeat after me, please. I, Nicholas James Roper…"

"I, Nicholas James Roper…"

"Do solemnly swear in front of everyone present here…"

"Do solemnly swear in front of everyone present here…"

"To be there for this woman no matter what…"

"To be there for this woman no matter what…"

"To love and to cherish, to treasure and to value…"

"To love and to cherish, to treasure and to value…"

"Throughout the rest of my days."

"Throughout the rest of my days."

"Do you take her to be your wife?"

"Yes. I do."

There was a collective sigh of contentment around the room as Wade handed Nick something, she felt him tease away her glove and slip the ring over her finger. She smiled at him. He winked again, like he knew something she didn't. She wanted to kiss him but restrained herself. That time would come.

"Sharon, can you repeat after me please? I, Sharon Melissa Arventino…"

"I, Sharon Melissa Arventino…"

"Do swear honourably in front of those here to observe me…"

"Do swear honourably in front of those here to observe me…"

"To be wife to this man no matter what…"

"To be wife to this man no matter what…"

"To love and to cherish, to treasure and to value…"

"To love and to cherish, to treasure and to value…"

"For as long as I draw breath into my body."

"For as long as I draw breath into my body."

"Do you accept him to be your husband under the eyes of the Divines?"

Her throat tickled, and she didn't say anything, just rubbed at it with her ungloved hand, a flush of exasperation rushing through her. Of all the times for something like this to happen… She glanced about for water, didn't see any, tried to speak through the blockage in her throat to no avail. She coughed, felt the dryness scraping the muscle. Nick's expression didn't change, his face impassive.

I do… I do… Come on, why can't I say it? The words formed in her mouth, she moved her lips and no sound emerged, just coughing. Her head swam, almost tripped in her heels. Couldn't breathe, her face felt flushed, vision blurred under the shadow cast not just over her, but the entire chapel and she was the only one to see it.

Everyone on her side of the aisle was dead, eyes emotionless and impassive, some had their throats cut, some bore penetrative burns through them, some missed limbs and in one case, a head. Her hand had a distinctive grey pallor to it, she saw it out the corner of her eyes as she clawed at her throat, her expensive manicure drawing rivulets of blood.

Finally, Nick reacted, he smiled, and his entire visage split straight down the middle, something else emerging from within, something spectral and shadowy. It spoke, a masculine voice she heard even above her own coughs. Her legs couldn't hold her any longer and she fell to the steps, her dress tearing, nylon covered limbs spilling out. Nobody moved.

"You know this is wrong," the voice hissed. She'd heard it before somewhere, some part registered amidst her discomfort and she blinked above sticky eyes. "You know what you are, and you'd forsake it for something as fleeting as love."

She couldn't answer even if she wanted to, movement hadn't escaped her, but her limbs felt heavy, like gravity had been cranked to maximum and it was drawing her into the ground without reprieve. Hard to think, hard to focus. Her head felt like it was being squeezed, the pressure incredible against her skull. Any more and she'd hear a crack. Any defence she might have formed against that power felt painfully inadequate. Weak. Pathetic.

"I'm looking for you. I will find you. You cannot flee from me forever." It lacked emotion, just matter of fact words, cold hard statements. "You will be needed." She didn't doubt the truth behind them. What wasn't about to change was the fact that no matter how much she might be needed, she wasn't going to oblige. "If you pursue this path you currently walk, it will be your end," the voice said and slowly the spectre formed into a dark-skinned man, a hungered look to him like he'd been ill, his eyes wild and despite all attempts at personal maintenance, a little unkempt. "You have been warned. You must walk back into the light, Ascendant."

Ascendant... A title she hadn't born for a long time. She'd almost forgotten about it. Almost. The man grinned at her, teeth visible through the scruffy beard framing his mouth and chin. They were yellow, and she could feel his breath on her, hot and smelly. "We will see each other soon."

She tried to choke out sounds of defiance but all she succeeded in doing was biting down on her own tongue, fresh pain firing through her, unceasing, unending, uncaring...

She awoke with a start, face covered in sweat, Nick still asleep next to her. She glanced at him and sighed. Heavy sleeper and all that. He could stay snoring through anything, even though she was sure she'd been screaming at one point. Wow...

That had been different. And what did it mean? That was the problem, she had to admit. She knew first hand that dreams could be powerful things, portents of things yet to come and one should not blindly dismiss them because they may be ridiculous. Yet at the same time, you couldn't overrule the thought imagination was a powerful thing.

She hadn't had a prophetic dream for years now, hadn't experienced anything in her sleep that had come to pass for a long time and why it should change now, she didn't know. She hoped it wouldn't. As visions went, it had been a particularly unpleasant one. Maybe it was doubt. Cold feet. She didn't want to admit it, but she was growing more worried about the upcoming nuptials every day. It took a lot of work, time was growing short and sometimes she felt she couldn't face it.

She could. Of course, she could, it was all about working up the courage to do so. These things didn't happen overnight. They had all the time in the world. She couldn't forget the dream though. She wouldn't. Nor the words that had been uttered to her within. They'd been considerably vivid. She'd been warned what would happen if she carried on. But that man was dead, wasn't he? Dead and powerless, she'd been told. Sharon wanted so badly to believe he was her doubts given a physical form, their way of telling her not to ignore them.

She wasn't ignoring them. But neither was she listening blindly. She knew what she was doing was the right thing.

The sixteenth day of Summerpeak.

If he was honest, Pete truly couldn't believe the tournament was carrying on considering what had happened the previous day. Terrorists take over a hospital not a few miles away from the stadium and yet they were about to keep on going despite it. It was lunacy. What was Ritellia doing? He'd already been criticised in the media for saying they would not cancel the tournament because of a few disenfranchised. Fresh criticism had come his way suggesting maybe he didn't quite know what that word meant. Either way he'd proved before he had the thick skin of an armoured rhino and if it was getting to him, it wasn't showing.

Still it was what it was. And privately, although he'd never admit it aloud, he was glad it was continuing, he wanted to win after all. He didn't think there was any shame in admitting that. Now he'd gotten this far, he had a chance. Shame he had such an impressive obstacle in his path in the shape of Katherine Sommer. He didn't know her personally, yet he knew of her. She had a reputation as a juggernaut, someone implacable, someone unstoppable but that couldn't be true. Everyone and everything had a weak spot, proved the previous day when Sharon had faced that Theobald kid and despite everything, been nudged out. It had largely been downplayed in the media thanks to other events, but it hadn't entirely escaped notice. He'd never known that kid was that good. The worrying thing was it hadn't looked like Sharon was having an off day either. He'd seen her at her best and her worst and she hadn't been bad. Maybe he'd just been hungrier.

Except now wasn't the time to think about Sharon, with his own bout ahead. He took a deep breath and stepped into the sunlight, hands in the pockets of his shorts. Pete could feel every set of eyes bearing down on him, he was alone on the field, Kitti Sommer hadn't arrived yet, he decided to milk the applause, raising his hands above his head in enthusiastic greeting. He'd probably look a prat when it was played back but for the time being, he couldn't care. If this was what it'd be like for a third-round tie, imagine it for the quarter or the semi or even think ahead to the final. He grinned in glee. This would be spectacular.

"Ladies and gentlemen," he heard the commentator say above the cheers and applause. "I give you contestant number one… Peter Jacobs!" If anything, the adoration intensified, and he felt a warm contented feeling in the pit of his stomach. Scott was probably among the crowd. Probably Sharon. Maybe Mia. He even wondered about Jess, if she was watching or not. Would she be rooting for him? He didn't want to speculate on that part. He could see pockets of support holding placards bearing his name and he appreciated that. Look, ma! I got supporters.

Then silence fell over the crowd and he turned his head towards the other contestant tunnel. He somehow knew she was coming. Leave it to her to be fashionably late. A dramatic entrance never hurt anyone, and he saw her ascending the steps, not walking but riding a majestic stag, head bowed low, so the antlers wouldn't catch the roof. He shook his head in disbelief, the crowd went wild, even more for her than for him.

"And the opponent, contestant number two arriving in style there… Katherine Sommer! What an entrance, she knows how to play to the crowd!" Well, it already looked like the commentators knew who they wanted to win, Pete noted with a grimace. He'd have to upset them. Oh well. If everyone in the stadium was crying because she'd lost, he'd take that.

That stag though was a majestic beast, he dwarfed Basil in size with dappled white and chocolate covered fur across his back, cream coloured down across his chest. The antlers shone in the sunlight, they looked sharp and he didn't want to think about what they might do in combat. The hooves were the size of dinner plates, he could hear them clattering against the rock on the battlefield and he gulped down a big breath of air, staring past the stag and at the caller.

Kitti Sommer had often been compared to his sister and he could sort of see why though they didn't look like each other. Sharon was taller, statuesque and blond, Kitti was shorter, curvy and her hair was cut in a short blue-black bob. Black rimmed her eyes and her lips, she wore a red and black cut vest revealing tattooed arms and a pair of tight blue shorts that showed off her legs, a sight Pete could appreciate even from across the field. The true comparison of course came with their abilities on the battlefield, they both had reputations for exceptional efficiency when it came to dispatching opponents without mercy. He thought Scott might have fought her in the past, he'd meant to ask, but never had the chance. Funny the sort of things you remembered when it was just too late.

The stag trotted onto the battlefield, clearly her first choice as the video referee relayed down the instructions and already Pete found himself contemplating strategies. There had to be an easy way to do this.

The match was on in the background but neither Arnholt, Okocha or Brendan were truly paying attention to it. They had too much on their minds. The mission the previous day had gone off without a hitch, there hadn't been any collateral damage, but some disturbing signs had been found in the post situation analysis. Such as one hostile being unaccounted for, they'd spied fourteen men entering the building across security footage, only twelve bodies and one prisoner found after the fact. Okocha wanted so very much to believe that they'd made a mistake. Arnholt wasn't having it. Then there was the second detail they weren't quite ready to release yet. Those who had been gunned down in the administrator's office, those who held the hostages had had their weapons examined by Noorland and Leclerc in the aftermath. None had been packed with live energy cells meaning they couldn't have been fired even if they'd wanted to.

Okocha had been stunned when he'd heard, Arnholt more so. If it got out that they'd executed a bunch of people who couldn't really fight back, it wouldn't look great. It'd tarnish what they'd thought a great victory. Some had possessed live weapons, that was something that couldn't be disputed. In the corridors, the attack teams had run into them but beyond that, nothing. Okocha had been against concealing the information for the time being. Whoever had organised the attack knew and all it took was one rogue communication to make it look like Unisco was concealing things.

"Something about this whole thing stinks," Brendan said. "We still don't have a motive. Despite what Wade thinks…"

Okocha had read that as well. It was perhaps the most worrying piece of the whole thing. Wade, when Aldiss and Harper had found him, had claimed they'd come to his room and opened fire on his bed. They'd intended to kill him after killing Mallinson. Okocha didn't know the man. Obviously, it was a tragedy a Unisco agent had been killed in the line of duty, but he couldn't feel too sorry for someone whom everyone considered a massive prick. It was his family he pitied, but by all accounts, they couldn't stand the man either so how much pity they wanted was up for debate.

How and why they'd made the choice to kill Wade, he couldn't say, and it frustrated him. He possessed one of the finest analytical minds in the company, even if he did say so himself, and it was eluding him. He couldn't have given an answer if he'd wanted to and that stung a lot. The only possible solution was that someone had worked out who he really worked for. But that was supposed to be extremely difficult, if not impossible. Had someone said something? Let something slip? Surely not. All options sounded just as ridiculous as the last, but he was worried. If Wade had been compromised, then everyone needed to be worried. With that in mind, Wade had made the decision to vanish, rest and recuperate in peace following his quitting of the tournament. He promised to be back before it finished but Leclerc had flown him out personally. Nobody knew where outside the two of them.

"I wouldn't discount everything that Wade has said," Arnholt said. Although many people truly didn't know he was the director of Unisco, it wasn't as closely guarded a secret as most other identities in the agency. Okocha recalled the conversation with Phillipe Mazoud Crumley and Arnholt had engaged in. Mazoud was one of the biggest scumbags in Vazara and he could do a lot of damage with that information. Privately Okocha still believed that business with his daughter's kidnapping wasn't entirely unrelated from his role in the organisation. He'd just been lucky that Wade had... Could that have a link with it? Rocastle was unaccounted for. Rocastle who'd tangled with Wade prior to his capture. They'd found the remains of Wolfmeyer's squadron in the ocean, four HAX's settled on the floor but no trace of the prisoner transport nor the two missing pilots. Was it so unfeasible that Rocastle could have tried for some retribution towards Wade. "I trust him implicitly."

"He's also half blind and doped up on painkillers," Brendan said. "His mind went wild..."

"He was still competent enough to defend himself," Okocha pointed out. "Director, Chief, this is just the latest in a line of incidents on this island we can't explain. So much has happened and despite everything we're still in the dark. We're all fumbling blind, not just

Wade. We're trying to grasp something without knowing what we're looking for. It's not good."

"I spoke to Ritellia this morning," Arnholt said, a look of intense disdain on his face. "Tried to get him to cancel the tournament. Told him about the bodies down below."

"Let me guess," Okocha said, glancing over to the viewing screen. "He didn't like the idea?"

"Told me to get out of his office and stop scaremongering," Arnholt said in a quietly outraged tone. "I'm lodging a complaint with the Senate first available opportunity about his behaviour. Anything else happens here, I'm lobbying to them to step in. It's about all I can do now. Ritellia..." He sighed in resignation. "I really do dislike that man. How he got to be president of anything is a mystery to me. No, I think we've started the job now and we're not going to stop them through other means. We need to see this through to the end."

Brendan sighed. "I hate to voice this, Director. But maybe we're just trying to make too much into this. Maybe it just really was a bad place to hold the tournament. These might be Vazaran things. You know what they can be like around here."

Okocha felt a stab of annoyance at the way Brendan had just dug at his heritage. He shoved it down. Starting an argument now wouldn't help things. "Yeah, I really do," he said dryly. "I got some results back I wanted to run by you both, if you'll allow me?"

Arnholt nodded at him. "Go ahead, Will."

"Well, that tentacle Wilsin and Roper recovered from Operation Monsoon..." Their unsanctioned shootout had been tagged that due to the nature of the events leading to the whole thing, a quick action on Arnholt's part to make the whole thing look legitimate should major action ever need to be taken. "I got the results back from our lab. Inconclusive. They think it's from some breed of giant squid, it matches the body shape..."

"I've seen giant squid," Brendan said. "Never one that big. It'd have to be bigger than this cabin to have part of a tentacle that size."

"Plus, it has a strange genetic makeup they haven't ever seen before," Okocha added. "I mean it. There's stuff in its DNA that makes literally no sense to them. Talliver's exact words to me." If that was what Dean Talliver, a colleague and expert in natural biology had to say, then Okocha backed him. "It doesn't look like any normal squid."

Arnholt sighed. "Terrific. It's infuriating for Talliver of course but I can't see that information affecting us too much in the long term. The door is closed."

"And yet doors can be opened again," Brendan said. "At the very least, we should consider some sort of deterrent against whatever it was. I'll talk to Talliver in the morning. It's late where he is."

"And just an update of my examination into Reims," Okocha said. "Remember you asked me to do it?"

Arnholt gave him a smile. "I do. Please, speak."

"Okay, CEO is named Claudia Coppinger, one of the richest women in the five kingdoms, parents both dead, one daughter, father's identity unknown. Daughter is a spirit dancer..." It was on the tip of his tongue to add maybe Arnholt's daughter knew her, but he kept it professional. Arnholt doubtless already had thought that. "But the company itself is thriving. Reims is the parent company; their primary focus originally was software, but they've gone into a lot of other business since then. Reims makes a stunning amount of credits every year."

He grinned nervously. "Believe me, I've never seen so many zeroes. It's enough to make you envious. Some of the subsidiary businesses though, they're in different markets. Auction houses. Antique dealerships. Ship builders. Architects. Biochemistry. Medicine. Real estate. Spirit calling equipment. There's even rumours they moved into weapons design, but I couldn't confirm or deny it. It's staggering. I'm surprised the whole place hasn't collapsed under its own weight. All of this is before you consider what they did on this very island."

"Sort of enemy you don't want to have," Brendan said dryly. "I'm glad we didn't declare war on them."

"There's more though," Okocha said. "And it's weird. You've heard of Harval-Pek? Premier ship design and construction?"

"They designed the HAX," Arnholt said absentmindedly.

"Owned by Reims. They're one of the premier ship constructors in the five kingdoms. Biggest. Best. Busiest. They have at least six workshops in every kingdom. At least. They churn out more than a thousand ships per workshop a year. Even with their workforce, they should be making huge profits. Everyone wants to use them. So why are they running at a massive loss?"

He saw Arnholt's eyebrows narrow. "Excuse me?"

"It doesn't make any sense. I had a bit of a poke around, it seems that there's been some massive orders been placed but there's yet to be any payment. It's like they've been built and left to gather dust."

"It's unusual," Brendan said. "But one year of massive losses for a successful manufacturer doesn't mean there's any criminal activity. That sounds more like incompetence than insinuation."

"It's not one year," Okocha said. "Reims acquired Harval-Pek six years ago. These orders have been going in ever since then. And they've been running at a loss ever since. It's not just HP either? Reims itself as a company are reporting mass profits. Everything tied to them as a subsidiary isn't. It's suspicious."

"But it's also nothing to do with us," Arnholt said gently. "At the most it sounds like a tax matter."

"You or I have never run a business like that," Brendan said. "The Reims CEO obviously has. She must know what she's doing."

Arnholt leaned back in his chair and brought his fingers together in a pyramid thoughtfully. Brendan said nothing.

"Maybe," Okocha said. "That was all I was able to ascertain in a small amount of time. I didn't want to hack into their database further without reasonable cause. I wouldn't have minded finding out what these huge orders were." He looked at Arnholt. "Do you want me to dig deeper?"

"I'm not here to be underestimated. I'm here to get as far as I can, maybe even go and win the whole thing. Wouldn't that be something?"
Weronika Saarth before her bout with Scott Taylor.

The seventeenth day of Summerpeak.

WHAT WENT WRONG?
Five dead in hospital shooting in Quin-C adds to Carcaradis chaos

Exclusive by Kate Kinsella.

The Competitive Centenary Calling Challenge Cup was once more thrown into chaos two days ago as gunfire was exchanged in the halls of a Carcaradis Island hospital between terrorists and Unisco agents in a senseless attack leaving five civilians dead and several more injured in the latest of several incidents fully exposing the folly behind the politics at the ICCC.
Yes, Unisco can be praised for swift and decisive action in snuffing out a threat before it could turn into a tragedy. But what hasn't been mentioned as much is the way it was handed over to them without so much as a protest by a vastly understaffed Carcaradis Island constabulary with neither the personnel or the equipment or the training to undertake such a rescue attempt. Nor has it been mentioned that such an action should not have needed to happen. Nor has it been mentioned this is just the latest mishap to mar this year's tournament and we aren't even at the quarter finals yet.
What makes this whole thing even more astonishing is that following the attack, Ronald Ritellia, 78, President of the International Competitive Calling Committee and self-proclaimed most important man in the five kingdoms refused to call the tournament off following such a brutal attack citing it as 'unrelated to the incident at hand' and how 'it would be a travesty to deny the public what they so desperately want to see.' Once again, Ritellia appears to not be living in the same world as the rest of us, rather occupying his own world filled by his impressive sense of self-importance, more credits than can ever be spent and questionable bedroom liaisons with shady women.
Yes, you read that right, the woman seen on married Ritellia's arm throughout recent weeks of this tournament is none other than Reims executive and mother of one, Alana Fuller, 37. Reims, you might

remember being the company that moved kingdom and sky to ensure the tournament ended up in a quite frankly unsuitable location which has already seen natural disasters, murders, attempted kidnapping and domestic terrorism (Which this correspondent might add are just the off-field issues plaguing the tournament). Indeed, Ritellia was not quite so casual when the ICCC building was nearly destroyed by an unknown figure, his exact words at the time being 'if there was any justice, then the bastards would be strung up and their families made to pay for it.'

It is often easy to be dispassionate when it doesn't concern you and nobody exemplifies this more than the gargantuan figure in the sporting world, but what he doesn't seem to realise is that given his efforts to bring the tournament here, any sort of controversy DOES concern him. Any person who dies on this island while the tournament is ongoing SHOULD be laid at his feet. And this is something he MUST realise rather than spouting off his own philosophy of greed. When Maxwell Brudel, 26, and Darren Maddley, 20, and even renowned Unisco investigator Stelwyn Mallinson, 44, do not come home to their families because of incidents beyond their control, it is time to question whether the right decision was made.

And what about the tournament itself so far? For the first time in its history, it has been held in Vazara and has it been a success so far? From a competitive point of view, it has sometimes flattered to deceive, often feeling like there has yet to be a standout competitor on show, someone truly deserving to win. Of course, it is still early days, but with both Wade Wallerington and Sharon Arventino tipped as early favourites, both have gone out earlier than expected, Wallerington, 33 retiring due to injuries suffered in the terrorist attack on the ICCC building and Arventino, 28 falling two days ago to exciting newcomer Theobald Jameson, 22 in a performance that looked like she had her mind more on her upcoming wedding than the bout at hand. Arventino was involved in controversy earlier on in the tournament when it was claimed she had deliberately thrown a bout with her brother to enable him to reclaim a point. Both she and half-brother Peter Jacobs, 20 insisted the rumour was false.

At the time, retired ICCC official Boudwjin Kacar, 71, called for an inquiry into Ms Arventino, an action never followed up on. Because after all, the ICCC aren't amiss to having a pretty face front and centre of the action. A shame the controversy arose in this bout because it is largely believed by the public on the ground at Carcaradis Island it was one of the best bouts of the tournament so far.

Of course, you never completely flee the past and if Jacobs was involved in any sort of fix earlier on in the tournament it has not *benefitted him in the end, following his defeat to Katherine Sommer yesterday in a defeat where she showed the difference in class between the two of them. Ms Sommer, 26, said after the bout that 'she was happy to make it through to the next round and she wished her opponent luck in the future,' thanking him for a good bout. With the future Mr Sharon Arventino, Nicholas Roper, 29 still in the tournament and promoted to favourite ahead of his bout in three days' time versus Blake Reinhardt, 36, it might be questioned whether Sommer can win the whole thing, but one thing is certain, we all await finding out.*

Today, relative unknowns Scott Taylor, 22 and Weronika Saarth, 24 will walk out to take one step closer on the road to making their name a part of history. Given the way the tournament has unfolded so far (and I use that word in every sense of the term), one can only hope that it is not a history permanently scarred by controversy and the stubbornness of a man who should long since have left office.

Our hearts go out to the families of all those who will never come back from this island. If they were to be asked if it were worth the tournament continuing, I'm sure they would reply in the negative. It is to those people President Ritellia needs to open both his ears and his heart to. Not the money men. Not his advisors who at times appear to be little more than sycophantic yes men, lackeys of the highest order or, even worse at the other end of the scale, men and women actively working against him to further their own ambitions, nor even the empty space where his own shrivelled conscience should be. But the people. Nothing is more important than the people and to proclaim otherwise is to set yourself on the first steps of a stony path that will break your feet.

Should Ritellia wind up crippled by his own actions, it is unlikely many in the spirit calling world would shed a tear for him. Gross megalomania and alleged corruption charges can harm even the most stubborn of individuals and the man who sailed into office on the crest of a wave looks ever closer to leaving it in disgrace. Only time will tell. But this correspondent for one, thinks it can't come quickly enough.

We can all but hope his successor will be a better man.

"I'm glad I'm not Ritellia this morning," Sharon said, lifting her eyes from the article. "She goes to town a bit on him, doesn't she? I don't think you can blame everything bad that happened here on him. Tempting as some people might find that."

Pete said nothing, just took a gulp of his juice and swilled the contents slowly around his mouth, letting it dribble down his throat without really tasting it.

"You're still upset I can see."

Still he said nothing. He hadn't since they'd gotten to the Verdant Café for breakfast, quality brother-sister time she'd called it and she gotten the impression he'd been moping since the end of the bout. At least that's all he needs to worry about. Least he's not having dreams of his own death...

And she wasn't either. Not really. She wasn't letting that dream get to her. She couldn't. After all she'd long since learned not to take dreams at face value. Sure, there might be instances where they were mildly prophetic. It wasn't uncommon. There was a ton of lore on it, she'd spent an hour the previous day going through some of what she could remember and a great deal of time it wasn't so much about what was on the surface, rather about the subtext. Just because she'd suffered and been told she was going to die didn't mean it was going to happen. It might just have been nerves telling her that her life was going to change. Death was a pretty over-the-top way of emphasising the point, but it did the job. To move on and become a new person, the old you would have to die. Bleak but there you go. Either way, it wasn't important, despite the way she was dwelling on it. It didn't change what she would do. It just meant she'd take a little more care with things.

"That's a spooky ability you got, sis," Pete said grumpily. "You see me grinding my teeth here, bit quiet and you can tell I'm upset."

"There's always next time," Sharon said. "There's no shame in losing to someone better. It's not like it's the first time you've lost at this tournament, is it?"

"No but I've gone out now," Pete said. "And I didn't just lose, I bombed."

"I think that's a bit harsh. I thought you did well," Sharon said. "Different people develop their abilities at different ages. Some are better younger..."

"Like you?!" It came out as a challenge and she blew out a hard breath.

"I was well trained. See you never had that. I had a lot of experience on you by the time I was your age."

"Yeah, we can't all get trained by Ruud Baxter," Pete said dryly. She raised an eyebrow in surprise at the sudden comment. That, she hadn't been expecting.

"I wasn't aware I'd ever told you about that." Baxter had showed her some spirit calling techniques, sure, but most of what she'd learned from him had been about as far away from the sport as you could get.

"It's in the public domain, Sharon. There's pictures of you two looking all cosy at tournaments."

"Either way, it's irrelevant," she said, her voice going hard. She liked the effect. He sat up a little, like he was at least taking notice which was good. Maybe she could shock him out of his funk "I've not seen him for ages. I've become my own woman since then. I've built on the foundations he helped lay and become someone new. It's not where you start, it's where you finish. Pete, you're still young and there's no limit to the number of these things you can enter while you're alive. If you keep on qualifying, you keep giving yourself a chance to win."

She paused to take a sip of her steaming drink, the bitter taste flooding her mouth. It tasted good, although the way her brother was going on, perhaps there was enough bitterness present already. "My point was, before you interrupted me, some are better younger but it's very hard to keep up youthful potential. Look at what happened to me. There's always someone out there who'll want to knock you off your perch. When you get to the top, you never stay there as long as you think. That's when the hard work really begins. It's better to start off slow and get better with age. Learn from your defeats, make your mistakes early."

She sighed, leaning down to look him in the eyes. "I don't know why I thought of him, but Luke Maddley did it the right way. Took some beatings, won some, got to the top, lost it all, died." It came off callous, but she didn't care. "That's the natural order of things."

"I've never heard you talk about him before," Pete said. His funk looked to have faded now, what with her mention of Maddley. It was good to see she was getting through. Maddley was always a good example for making people realise things could be worse. Her brother was no different in that regard. "Thought it was a touchy subject. Do you ever think about him?"

"Sometimes."

"You ever regret that he killed himself?"

"No."

"Why?" He sounded surprised, if anything that annoyed her. They might share blood, but it didn't mean he knew her. Far from it. Maybe if their ages had been closer together then they'd be closer as siblings. If they'd shared the same parents… Then he might be dead. She didn't want to think about what might have happened if Canderous Arventino were his father.

"I didn't make him kill himself," she said. "I didn't hand him the pills or the rope. He was an adult and he did it of his own accord. He did not kill himself because I beat him in a bout. That might have been the start of it all, but a lot of time passed between then and the end. He was a sick man and he took the only way out of it he thought he could. I'm not saying he was right but that was his choice and I had nothing to do with it. If I felt guilt for what he did, it'd be like feeling guilty that people died in that hospital shooting because they came to the island to watch a tournament I was competing in. It's sad but that's life."

"Huh." He genuinely looked like he'd never considered it that way before and shrugged. "Fair enough."

"What, you thought your sister was a killer all this time?" she said, mock-hurt. "Thanks, bro. I appreciate that."

"Nah, nah, I didn't," Pete said. He was quiet for a moment. "Sorry."

"You don't have to be sorry."

Silence for a few moments and then he grinned at her. "Being fair though, Sommer was pretty good, wasn't she?"

"Outstanding," Sharon admitted. "She's a talented girl. I wouldn't like to face her the form she's in." She shrugged her shoulders. "I mean I would, but I'd be worried."

"Hey, you got beat by some no-mark," Pete scoffed. "At least I went out to someone decent."

"You going to the bout today?" Sharon asked. "Scott's?"

Pete nodded. "Yeah, I'll go support him for the rest of the tournament. He's done it for me. Even if he is getting a bit obsessive lately."

Sharon gave him a quizzical look. "Obsessive? With the tournament? Some people do chase winning like it's a drug."

"Strangely enough no," Pete said. "It's not the tournament. It's a ghost."

"What?"

"He's chasing a ghost. He even got Alvin Noorland to build him a particle barrier. Says it appeared to him, spoke to him, kicked the crap out of him and now…"

"Spoke to him?!" Sharon exclaimed. "Are you sure?"

"Well I didn't see it," Pete admitted. "Or hear it. I'm going solely on his word of mouth. But he claims he had a fight with this ghost, it spoke to him and ran off. He says he can feel it on the island. Seriously!"

Sharon said nothing for a moment, not quite able to believe it. "He does know that's impossible, right?"

"I should hope so."

"Does he have a history of delusion?"

"Unless you count most of his relationships? Not that I know of." Pete smirked as he said it, she noticed and felt relief. If he got out of his funk, that'd be good for all of them. Nobody said defeat was easy. But there was a right way and a wrong way.

"Maybe he imagined it."

"He did look pretty messed up after the whole thing," Pete said. "I mean it was after he beat Steven Silver."

That caught Sharon's attention. She'd seen that bout after all. Who hadn't? She'd seen it more than once, bemused by it all. Down to the wire and apparently against insurmountable odds, Scott Taylor should not have been able to win. But he had. And he'd done it in such a way that suggested there was something strange involved. It wasn't normal the way he'd reacted like that, bordering on supernatural. If he fought like that every time he took to the field, he'd win ninety-eight percent of his bouts.

So, why didn't he? She had a strange suspicion, one she had no way of proving. In conjunction with being able to sense this apparent ghost from far away... It all became apparent Scott Taylor was not a normal man by any stretch of the imagination. She found that interesting.

"You know what," she said. "I think I might come to his bout later. Should be worth seeing, I think."

And I want to see if he does it again, she added silently. It was entirely possible his previous round bout had been a fluke, in which case she would have nothing to worry about. If it was, he'd be found out sooner or later.

Weronika Saarth was a slender girl with flaming red hair tied back against her head in a series of knots, a shade of colour not unlike Jesseka Blake's but perhaps more pronouncedly ginger, a pretty face beneath the hair. Her eyes were covered by a pair of heart shaped glasses and she smiled at Scott from across the field as the two stared each other down. When she moved her head, the afternoon sun caught against the piercings hung from her ears. There were no unnecessary additions to the battlefield this time, just flat duraturf between them, he'd tested it with his foot to find it spongy. Her stare felt uncomfortable, but he didn't tear his eyes away. This was part of the psychological process. If he looked away now, he'd be less effective come the actual bout.

Across from them, the video referee was going through the rules of the bout, three spirits each and no time limit... He didn't know why they stated that. He'd never seen a bout yet at this tournament that involved a time limit... and the victor would be declared when one caller had three spirits unable to keep on fighting. In the event of a tie, sudden death would be enabled. He'd heard it all before. It lost its effect after a while. Instead he thought about his choices of spirits. He'd be onto the quarter final before long. Ha, see you in my dust, Pete.

He didn't know why he sounded so jubilant at that thought. He doubted he'd do much better against Katherine Sommer should it happen. She'd swept Pete aside the previous day and he'd felt gutted for his friend. Still what were the chances he'd have to face her next round?

Getting smaller every time he won, was the simple answer.

"Good luck, Scott." He looked up, jerked out of his thoughts by the soft musical voice of his opponent.

"You too," he said, before grinning. "But obviously not too much of it, yeah?"

She laughed at that. "Of course."

That was when she unleashed her first spirit, it took him a moment to realise what exactly it was. Four feet tall on four legs with a thick bushy crimson mane distinctive against its glossy caramel coloured pelt and a heavy tail dragging across the ground behind it, the face had a distinctly fox-like feel to it. The eyes were piercing black and surrounded by patches of cream-coloured fur shaped like flames.

"Kirofax!" he couldn't help but exclaim. The realisation hit him, he hadn't seen one for a while. Few people knew where to find them these days, they'd been hunted almost to extinction and while he wasn't one of those who did know where to find them, Saarth obviously did.

"You got it, baby," Saarth chuckled. Her laugh was just as lilting as her voice. He ignored the possible insult and made his own choice, throwing out Seasel who landed on the duraturf with a sound probably passing as a roar for the sea weasel. To anyone else, it sounded like a constipated squeak.

"Rare doesn't mean tough," Scott said, still aware Seasel was baring his fangs at the kirofax, claws digging into the turf as if ready to get going. He wasn't the only one, the crowd's buzz of anticipation had lowered but he could feel the tensions rippling through them as they awaited the signal to get the bout underway. He gave Seasel the mental command spliced in with the order to wait, silently urging the weasel not to go just yet… Wait for it, wait for it… Now!

With the roar of the buzzer signalling the start, Seasel opened his mouth and the gout of water erupted from within him, tearing towards the kirofax who nimbly leapt out of the way. Scott wasn't fooled for a moment, he'd been expecting some sort of dodge, they were supposed to be nimble after all and he urged Seasel to keep trying to trace it out with the blast, water striking empty air as the rake followed it into the air. He saw Saarth's look of surprise as it caught the kirofax square in the face and threw it back several feet, almost bouncing it off the shields protecting the crowd. It hit the ground, Scott grinned. Maybe that'd be it. He doubted it, but maybe.

Very quickly he was proved right as it jumped to its feet, shook water and dust from its fur, a mad look in its eyes as it lunged forward towards Seasel, fangs bared and glowing shiny white.

Again?!

It came out half a question, half an order as Seasel forced another burst of water towards the onrushing kirofax. Once again, the creature dodged this time careening to the left to evade and before Seasel could adjust his aim, it sprang over the moving blast of water, suddenly in close. Now Seasel was on the defensive, trying to evade the fangs on Scott's command, the weasel ducking and diving out the way as the kirofax tried to get a grip on slippery fur. He could hear the clack of fangs biting empty air, could see the frustration on the kirofax's face as it tried to bite down again and succeeded only in grazing Seasel's back, drawing a silver of crimson blood across the fur.

He felt a backlash of discomfort ripple through him, gave Seasel a command and the weasel swung to smash his skull straight into the kirofax's side. The fox-like creature let out a woofing sound of pain, he thought he heard snapping bone, maybe he'd hit a rib and suddenly they were fighting in close, tooth and claw going at each other.

If there was any thought of using their special attacks, neither of them was going for it. The other wouldn't give them the chance. No space, no time, if Seasel stopped to unleash a water blast, Scott could honestly foresee the kirofax ripping his head off. No, this was something more primal, like a scene from the wild as both bled from a dozen cuts, movement slowly becoming laboured and heavy. The kirofax let out a squeal as one of Seasel's paws swiped its face, grabbed a leg with its and swung, suddenly sending the sea weasel airborne and that was when Scott seized his chance, giving the order for another aquatic attack.

This'd be it, he felt a surge of confidence rush through him. The blast of water homed in on the kirofax and Scott rubbed his forehead, his hand coming away with a fine sheen of sweat. He hadn't been aware how hot it had gotten in the stadium. Before it could land, he heard a hiss, saw the steam and the attack never landed. His eyes widened. Sweat ran down his face. Saarth looked unperturbed. He was closer to the action, everything had exclusively been in his half of the field so far. Seasel came to a land, shrieked in discomfort as he already saw blisters forming across the he glossy coat.

So many pieces fell together simultaneously, and he could have kicked himself. The little flames around the kirofax's eyes... Fire abilities... The sudden rise in temperature... The way the attack had fizzled out before landing... Evaporation...

Fuck!

Little bastard was superheating the air around it as protection. If Seasel went in close, he'd get badly burned by the searing temperature. If he attacked from distance, it'd just evaporate out before it came close to doing critical damage.

Clever, very clever, Ms Saarth. But I'm smarter. I might not know how to get around this right at this moment, but I will work it out.

Next the kirofax opened its mouth and spat out a barrage of supersized embers towards Seasel, the weasel barely dodging at his command. Powerful legs tensed, and he rose up into the air, evading neatly.

Stutter hits!

He wouldn't win by doing the same thing repeatedly and hoping for different results. That way lay insanity. He had to try different things. Seasel spat his own barrage of water blasts out, three, four, five, six narrow streams lancing out towards the kirofax in rapid succession, each of them sizzling out as they hit the invisible orb of heat swaddling the furred body.

"Good, Scorch, good," Saarth cooed, her voice filled with pride. Okay, so that hadn't worked. Scott idly wondered how long Scorch could hold up the barrier of heat and how effective it would remain long term. An attack was only as useful as the ability to maintain it. Looking at it logically, he couldn't see it failing anytime soon. It was already a hot day and intensifying that heat would use up less energy than creating it from scratch.

He might have to just go for it, send Seasel straight into the fray and hope that his spirit could down the opponent before succumbing to the horrific heat. It was starting to make him feel uncomfortable so who knew how Seasel was feeling on the field. More attacks came from Scorch and Seasel had to lunge out the way, Scott not even giving the order to counter attack. It was useless now, he needed an opening...

Somehow, he doubted he was going to get one. Sometimes you had to make sacrifices. It was with a heavy heart he gave the command and Seasel shot in close to the kirofax as if fired from a blaster, claws outstretched and raking across the body. Scorch hadn't expected it, let out a howl as keratin bit through flesh, blood sizzling as it met the oppressive heat outside.

He saw Scorch rise onto its hind legs and he gave the command. Seasel lunged up and with razor sharp teeth, had the throat out in one slick violent twist. It plopped down onto the ground as the weasel spat it out and let out a shrieking sound of triumph. The heat faded but it had done its damage. The blisters were even more pronounced, the fur blackening in places, the burns affecting Seasel's ability to move freely.

Saarth said nothing, just brought back her fallen kirofax and smiled at him as announcer and video referee declared him to be winning. He ignored her, just folded his arms. One to me, bitch.

Her next choice gave him a little more cause for worry, a giant silver ape with very pronounced fangs that immediately rose onto its hind legs and powerfully beat its chest with both hands. The hands that were bigger than Scott's head. It dwarfed him too, it could have bent him in half with very minimal effort. He looked at Seasel in his stricken state and gulped. Not a chance this was going to be a winning victory for the weasel. It wasn't defeatist, it was realism.

Still it didn't mean they couldn't get a few good blows in. The command to get underway was given and it was punctuated by Seasel's water blast. If nothing else, it'd be a good way to gauge its strength. The heat had died down; the attacks should be working again. They were, he saw the blast hit the gorilla in the stomach and he'd hoped it'd double over in pain. No such luck, it rubbed the area with the back of a clawed hand and bellowed angrily. Well, they'd made it angry. That was a good start.

Saarth cocked her head to the side and the ape charged towards Seasel, bringing one of those huge fists back with the very clear intent of smashing him into the ground. Even wounded, Seasel was quick enough to evade the cumbersome blow, darting out the way. Scott could feel his discomfort through their link and he winced. Seasel genuinely was hurting out there. The heat had done a number on him.

Come on, come on, just a little more.

The teeth flashed in the sunlight again and Seasel bit down on the back of the gorilla's leg, about the only part of it he could reach from the ground, holding on there for several long moments. The ape turned its head, glanced down at the weasel, a puzzled look on its face as if to say 'really?' They'd been aiming for the hamstring, hoping to lame it but he got the impression it hadn't been the best idea in hindsight.

As the other leg came stamping down with intent of crushing Seasel beneath its weight, the weasel got away but barely. Until the other giant fat foot came down on his tail and the weasel howled in utter agony, the sound of breaking bone filling the stadium and silencing the crowd. It wouldn't be a fatal wound, but it'd hurt like a son of a bitch and Scott couldn't bear to hear that sound ever again.

Genuinely speaking, it didn't do for a spirit caller to be squeamish. But you'd have to have a heart of stone not to be touched by that sound. Saarth looked sick, her mouth turning down in disgust. But not for long, he saw as her spirit reached down and scooped the shuddering Seasel up in both hands. Scott knew it was over, didn't close his eyes as he saw the ape take a half of the weasel in each hand and twist. Shutting his eyes wouldn't have cut out the sound Seasel's spine made as it was shattered. He stiffened though, held his breath and exhaled sharply.

Fuck!

He wasn't having that. Not a chance. Seasel had done a good job, he murmured that to the crystal as he selected his next option. Wasn't his fault he got beat, he'd just run into an opponent in which he'd been physically outmatched while gravely injured following the previous bout. This shit happened sometimes. Next choice was Herc, the giant stagbug coming in to fight. This'd be a much more even contest. With that thick armour making up his carapace and prodigious strength, Herc'd win this one no sweat no doubt.

"Good job, Sarge," Saarth said, rubbing her hands together. She'd painted her nails a different colour on each finger. "Now let's do more."

Scott grinned coldly. "I couldn't have put it better myself. Herc. Put it down."

He didn't hear the buzz so much as feel it and Herc and Sarge went at each other the moment permission came, limbs dealing savage blows and Scott kept up the instructions. The horn was where Herc's true strength lay, a blow with that could overturn a speeder but at the same time, he guessed Saarth might know that he knew that. As an opening gambit, he couldn't stomach it. The limbs could deal heavy blows themselves, she probably wouldn't expect him to turn it into a scrap.

Herc reached the surang ape first, moved his head as if to swing his horn and Scott spotted the movements in Sarge's body, commanded Herc to feint and punch. He heard the blow hit hard stomach muscle and he winced. He was quite glad his overgrown bug didn't have any bones. Sarge's nostrils flared and the ape flung out a huge fist straight into Herc's midsection. Another crack, Scott's eyes began to twitch at the echoing force of the blow, almost felt like the stadium was shaking. He didn't want to see what might have come of that. Herc's carapace was thick. He'd modified it to be thick. But he didn't want to know how strong that damn ape might be up close.

Change of plan. We're not going toe to toe here now. Up into the air.

Translucent wings snapped out from the rear of Herc's shell, fluttered too fast for the eye to see and he hovered up out the way of the next blow, not moving as easily as he might have before.

It felt cold in the stadium suddenly, he wrapped his arms around himself and shivered. That wasn't right, surely. The sun was blazing down still. Was the big ape doing something? Could be. He didn't know. If it was, then he needed to take it out as soon as he could. This was distracting. Technically there were rules about targeting the caller, but only if you could prove intent. Raise the temperature, lower it, it'd affect the caller of the enemy spirit, but it could be argued that it wasn't the intention of the opponent. The best way to deal with it was to knock the spirit causing the problem out as fast as possible.

He tried to move his attention back to the fight, ordered Herc to swoop in and deal vicious thrusts into Sarge's face with his forelegs. There was something here that didn't feel right. If Saarth's spirit was lowering the temperature, then surely Herc would be affected. But that wasn't the case. Blow injury aside, everything looked normal, both combatants moving at the same speed. He heard Sarge bellow in pained anger as clawed forelegs dug into the squashed face, blood ran down the silver fur and a big meaty forearm swung out blindly, hoping to catch Herc.

It wasn't a wild miss but a miss all the same. He breathed a sigh of relief. Still in it for now.

Chapter Nineteen. Caged Rage.

"The important thing is not knowing when to strike. It is knowing when not to strike. No cage will ever hold you. No mortal man will ever break you, ever be able to tame you. You both are heirs of the legacy of the Cavanda. I promise you that. You are better than everyone else!"

Blade Amalfus to Kyra Sinclair and Gideon Cobb, long ago.

The seventeenth day of Summerdawn.

The cage wasn't the best situation, she had to admit but it could have been worse. They'd fed and watered her, kept her comfortable. So far, she was waiting for the other foot to fall. To what end did it benefit them keeping her like this? Maybe they planned to take it all away to make her talk. An interesting theory and perhaps it would work on someone not trained the way she'd been. From everything to nothing. An interesting interrogation technique to be sure. She didn't doubt it was probably their intention. To make her spill whatever secrets they thought she had. Good. If they thought that she was valuable she could continue to play this charade.

That she could escape at any upcoming time she desired did not even come into her thinking. She'd been captured and that stung, but she intended to turn this around on them. Being caged didn't make her a captive. Far from it. If anything, that cage just kept them safe from her a little while longer. It had been the first thing she'd done upon awaking from her slumber, her body sore and complaining from the stun blasts but she'd checked out all avenues of exit. The Kjarn guided her, told her the bars to her cage could be overcome given the right amount of effort. Time was hard to fathom but she'd spent enough of it weakening the structure to the point minimal effort on her part would see them collapse.

More than that, she had to leave with something if only for her own peace of mind. The way she'd fallen in battle grated and she needed to avenge it. Falling was fine if it served a purpose, only a fool fought gravity. If she destroyed an enemy out of being captured, then it would not seem weak on her part. Cobb might buy that. The master probably wouldn't. But should it gain results, he wouldn't care. Besides it wasn't like he was around to approve or disapprove of her actions either way.

Her thoughts went to him, to the kickback she'd felt in the Kjarn when she'd killed those men, when she'd let loose with all the force she could muster and hammered them to death. He'd always warned her and Cobb. Kill with the Kjarn and it will hurt more than you can imagine. The first few times anyway, Master Amalfus was someone she'd seen do it with such abandon she'd thought it wouldn't be that bad. How wrong had she been? The kjarnblade was the loophole for it. Despite the weapon utilising the energy as a power source for its potent blade, using it hurt no more than it would using a blaster to snuff them out.

Maybe when she'd killed two of them simultaneously, the cumulative effect had just overwritten her ability to cope. She'd felt it, she knew that much, knew there wasn't any other likely reason, just as if they hadn't been using stun blasts, she'd be dead. Kyra wondered where her kjarnblade was, hoped they hadn't left it in that cave. Retrieving it or fashioning a new one would be a hassle she could do without.

As time went by, she'd spent it in meditation, honing, refining, forging anew her connections to the Kjarn. In teasing out her time, renewing her acquaintances, she found things she'd failed to grasp before were slowly becoming clearer. Maybe this time wouldn't be a complete waste. More than once though, she could have sworn she sensed another presence close by, touching the Kjarn and she wondered if she was the prisoner of the Vedo. She rejected it almost immediately. For one, they were all dead, and they wouldn't use shock troops to catch her. Besides, if she was close to Vedo, she'd surely sense more than a few sporadic bursts. Although they were getting more frequent, she thought. The boredom was starting to get to her. How much more time before she gave up on it as a bad job and walked out of here? As a torture technique, boredom was worse than deprivation.

Still some part of her held back, refused to give in and she meditated continuously, focused to the point she didn't eat or sleep. Meals went untouched. Sometimes she didn't even need to use the bathroom, her bodily functions creeping towards minimal. When she finally broke for breaks, it was often with great relief.

Then it happened. She found herself with a visitor. She'd been alone for what felt so long now, nobody but her own company, the sound of her voice startling as she took in the arrivals. Six of the same black clad masked goons flanking a fat guy with long purpling hair and a ratty acid green jacket. She caught a sense of him immediately and she didn't like it, an unpleasant aura about him in the Kjarn, foul and malignant.

She decided she didn't want to look past the fleeting glance she'd gotten. Still, there was no point revealing he'd unnerved her. More than that, there was something familiar about him she couldn't place, a face without a name. She'd seen him before somewhere. The goons were still a mystery she couldn't figure out, again not six single figures but rather an overlapping pool lacking any sort of individuality.

"Welcome, welcome," she said, rising to her feet. She'd cast her shoes aside long since and winced as she felt the circulation returning to her legs. "If I'd known you were coming here, I'd have tidied up a little. Maybe baked a cake."

He didn't reply but shot her a mean little glance, his plump pale lips folding at the corners. "You're quiet," she said, folding her arms. "Not here to talk? You're going to hurt my feelings."

Still he said nothing.

"Silent treatment? Really?" She almost scoffed out the words. "I can do that with the best of them." And yet, I'm still talking now. There's irony for you. "If you're not going to talk, I'm not going to pay you any attention."

She dropped into a sitting position and went back to meditation. At least she didn't have to dwell on this fucking fool for long. Anger at him was good. It'd keep her strong, a razorblade of emotions to balance on. The right amount would keep her strong. Too much or too little would be disastrous. Maybe she should use the Kjarn to slam him face-first into the bars of her cage, laugh as she heard his bones break.

Before she could go under, she heard the tap-tap-tap of metal on metal and opened her eyes in irritation. He'd leaned forward onto the bars of her cage, something tapping against them. She knew what it was without looking, it'd be a poor day when she failed to recognise her own weapon.

"Interesting," he said. "Very interesting weapon that you have here. How does it work?"

It was a taunt, she knew. If she reacted now, it could be fatal. What chances she could snatch it from him, cut her way free and block the first flurry of shots that came her way without being hurt? It wasn't impossible. In theory, she could do it. Of course, putting theory into practice was something entirely different.

"Same as any weapon," she said breezily. "In the right hands, it is lethal. In the wrong ones, it'll take your hand off."

He probably already knew the answer. If she'd thought it'd work, she'd tell him exactly how to impale himself. Kjarnblades had undergone a radical design change in recent decades her master had once told her. Once they had only been able to be handled by those with a connection to the Kjarn. Now however, that was no longer the case. There were always opportunists in the world. Even so, it wasn't a common weapon.

"Nice to see you still have concern for my wellbeing." His voice was sarcastic, mocking. Still he tapped the metal cylinder against the bars. "I was half expecting you to be rabid and to try and chew my face off."

Tap. Tap. Tap.

"Wouldn't get me anywhere, would it?" she asked evenly. "Where am I?"

"You're on death row," he said simply. "As far as you're concerned, this will be the last room you see. You're going to spend your last days here and they'll tick away one by one. You're going to die in the most horrible way I can think of." He smiled at her coldly, his eyes glittering with malice. "Something for you to look forward to, I think."

Tap. Tap. Tap. Tap.

Kyra wondered once more if planning and patience were overrated in this situation. Playing placid was one thing but she wouldn't have another chance like this. She needed to take what was being offered to her.

"Maybe I'll eat you." He bared his teeth at her. "You look good enough to serve up for dinner." He smacked his lips, wiggled his tongue at her, she studied him in disgust. Loathing filled her being, anger at being put in this situation.

"And you might choke," she said. "Hard to eat anything ever again with no teeth... Seriously where have I seen you before?" It was starting to bug her. "You like famous or something?"

"Famous?!" He looked offended. "Dear little bitch, dear sweet soon-to-be dead harlot, I'm infamous." He cracked his knuckles together. "I'm an artiste, my darling and the whole world is my canvas."

"Always knew there was something dodgy about all of you arty-types," she said roughly. "Like you've huffed too much of your own paint."

"Oh, don't worry. I'm more about cuttings and carvings to make my message." His grin was almost charming in a way as he continued to tap. "There's something so primitive about it. It's delicious I must say. Nothing like it. I thrive on fear. Are you scared yet?"

She found herself wondering if inviting the families for a part in her little enterprise had been a mistake. Like now, for instance. Here they were, she sat at the top of the room to leave them with no illusions as to how it was going to be, lest they forget, with Domis stood behind her along with the freshly cleaned and coiffed Wim Carson.

Carson had a renewed vigour about him these days. He'd spent a lot of time with Sinkins, filling in the gaps in the doctor's knowledge as well as considerable time alone, the purposes of which were a mystery to her. If he wanted her to know, he would tell her. He hadn't fulfilled his part of the deal yet, leading her to what she wanted but he had repeatedly assured her he would do so once able, all very apologetically. He'd insisted he wasn't about to waste her time when it was pointless. At least he didn't seem to fear her. She was unsure if that pleased her or not.

Now though, he was not the issue. Rather the man stood in the centre of the room was the focus of attention, having finished his report. John Cyris looked the most pleased about his presence for the man was known to the group as Silas and he was Cyris' second-hand man. She held Cyria in contempt but Cyris had proved he could be a canny operator when at the head of it. He wasn't someone you wanted as an enemy. He'd done a lot of good for his own profits and bad for many other people. She could respect that. And Silas had a legendary reputation for a sense of pragmatic ruthlessness rivalling even that of his boss.

Silas was the one who had been selected to coordinate the attack on the Carcaradis Island hospital. If Cyris looked delighted, the Fratelli family looked furious with the way things had turned out, Giovanni and his older brother Giacomo sat across from the Montella family. Giovanni was balding, his head partly covered in dark fuzz, his most distinguishing feature a scar across one eye she supposed looked menacing. Giacomo was the head of the family, she'd found him to be a dapper gentleman in his middle years with a polished bald head and a sorrowful demeanour which he'd assured her was only temporary after his grandson had been defeated in the Quin-C. She didn't mistake that claim for anything less than cold blooded ruthlessness.

Privately she was glad Cyris had not heard of his sorrow at what had transpired in that ridiculous tournament for it wasn't a secret his only son was still going strong in the competition. Doubtless wouldn't have hesitated to say so. That his son hated him and hadn't spoken to him since he was legally old enough to leave home and had foresworn the Cyris name, would likely not have been mentioned.

Offspring!

It almost came out as a snarl in her head, she was starting to think they were all ungrateful little bastards better off not being born. Let humanity thin its ranks. Something to consider for the future. Still she didn't let her mask of impassiveness slip as Silas continued to regale them with his tale, how accurate it was she would soon see when the Unisco operating file found its way to her desk. Her man, Subtractor, was more reliable than anything Silas could tell her.

"I left via the sewer hatches in the basement," Silas finished. "The hostages had been secured and although the secondary task was a failure, my assessment is that when organised sufficiently, the groups present here can function efficiently in tandem. I left barely seconds before Unisco arrived on the scene, entering through my exit point. It was my mission to deliver this report and here I am."

She was glad too many questions hadn't been asked about the secondary task, the death of Wade Wallerington. It had been her primary reason for the attack, despite what she'd told those in front of her. Wallerington could potentially identify her. Despite her precautions, he might have seen her face. Silencing him was something she needed done and they'd failed. If he was killed in a terrorist attack, it would look less suspicious than if by an assassin. They'd accepted that he was to be an opportunity target in a training exercise. Undoubtedly, Silas loved being the sole survivor of the mission, she could see the smug look of glee in his eyes. Thankfully few else could or there might have been trouble. Both the Fratelli's had already complained about the high number of their people killed in the attack, some of their most loyal figures who, as Giovanni had already pointed out, felt like they'd been strung out to dry. Already she knew this partnership would not survive long term. Someone would leave. Or die. She couldn't do anything about that. But those that stuck it out long term would find the rewards great.

"Thank you, Silas," she said. "You did well."

A smattering of applause accompanied him as he sat, louder in some quarters than others. Cyris was particularly rapturous, both Fratelli's looked ready to kill. She ignored their looks. Maybe she should start to favour the Montella family, the Fratelli brothers' traditional rivals for supremacy. Let them know where they stood and that their petulance would not be tolerated on any level.

"And with the announcement that together we can function as a unit, I hope that relaxes any further worries that might be held," she said. "In-fighting does not do any good. What do individual loyalties matter when all are united under the great banner Coppinger. Gentlemen and lady…"

That sole lady was Ahana Kirozama, representative of Kenzo Fojila, the infamous Burykian assassins. She'd decided that they should be involved. Nobody better to have on your side on a venture like this than highly trained professional killers. Maybe she should have sent them after Wallerington. Still could if she desired. "We are about to take the future from the masses and put it in our own hands. That is worth whatever cost we might be required to pay; would you not say? We will mourn our dead but know their sacrifice has been one of value. With their death, they will accomplish far more than they ever did in life."

Are you scared yet?

Those words echoed through her mind and something snapped inside her. He thrives on fear? Thrives? Who the fuck does he think he is? I am something so much greater than fear, I am anger and passion unrestrained. I do not fear, I inspire it.

"Not even in the slightest," she smiled. "Not of you. I've seen things that'd make you piss yourself. A lot. I've done things that'd make you weep. I do not fear the likes of you!"

The temptation was too great as she almost screamed the last word and sprang to her feet at the next series of taps on the bar, the hatred for rushing through her and Kyra didn't pull in with the Kjarn to call her blade towards her, but rather pushed outwards. All her efforts spent weakening the bars came to fruition, they couldn't hold against her as she pushed out with telekinetic force sending them exploding in all directions. The fat man suddenly looked worried as two of them clonked him in the face, her blade falling from his grasp. Even before it hit the ground, it was moving towards her hand as those guards that hadn't been staggered by the flailing bars aimed their weapons.

She ignited it, her blade sprang to life and she deflected the first two blasts. Unlike their co-workers in that cave, they were aiming to kill, and the blasts were easy to turn aside, back in the direction from whence they'd come. She saw them fall, felt their life forces fade. More came her way, her blade little more than a blur of pink and silver as she intercepted, deflecting them with ease.

Six might have been hard. Four was tricky, suddenly it was three. And two. She cut the last two down with ease, running them through with no resistance. They winked out of existence and only in death did she feel them individually. A shot rang high over her shoulder, she turned and saw the fat bastard with a weapon in hand, a snub-nosed blaster he'd yanked from somewhere. She grinned at him and took a deliberate step forward. He fired again, this time with more accuracy and she deflected it into the ground.

"Come on, I'll give you a free shot!" Kyra smiled. "Come on, you can do it!" He emptied his power pack at her, eleven shots that never even came close to her. She was playing with him, she could see he knew that and the look of worry on his face was delicious. She could sense his fear. "I'd like to kill you. But…"

She sprang forward, letting the Kjarn move her legs and suddenly she was in front of him, her kjarnblade at his throat. "I don't think I will." His eyes widened, and she saw another blaster in his hand suddenly and she didn't think, just acted. Her blade flash, and she heard him scream like a stuck pig, his weapon clattering to the ground with four cauterised fingers. She drew back her fist and thrust forwards, smashing it square into his breastbone, the power of the Kjarn behind her and she saw him crash backwards into the wall, his body going limb as he landed in an untidy heap. She spared his fingers a quick glance, saw they weren't getting reattached any time soon.

"Enjoy the rest of your days, half-hand," she said before turning to the door. "I'm checking out. Giving you four and a half stars in the book. Hospitality good, food, okay. Ease of escape, fantastic."

She didn't look back.

Silas was waiting for her as she exited the room, the last to leave bar Domis, a capricious grin on his face as she passed. "Madam Coppinger," he said with a tidy little bow she saw was more for effect than respect. Still she acknowledged him.

"Silas," she said. Or should I call you Simon Lassiter? She decided against it, she didn't want him knowing that she knew his true name just yet. "What do you want?"

His grin grew. "I just wanted to inform you that I know."

If he was expecting some great reaction from her, he was to be disappointed. Her face remained impassive. "You know? Good for you. What do you know exactly?"

"What you didn't want anyone else to," he smiled. "About the mission."

"Congratulations on getting out alive by the way," she said. "It's exactly what I'd expect from one of John Cyris' rats."

"I think survivability is a skill," he said listlessly. "And I was just following my orders. Well some of them anyway. I don't think Cyris would like it if he knew you were playing him. Just like you're playing the rest of the people in that room."

"Want me to break him in two?" Domis rumbled.

She shook her head. "That won't be necessary. You see, Silas, I think you're obviously an intelligent man. You wouldn't be making these statements to me unless you had ulterior motives. Now what do you want?"

"You wanted Wade Wallerington dead," Silas said, as if he'd not heard her. "You could have picked anyone in the hospital, you didn't even have to pick a hospital when there's hotels aplenty on that island, but you picked him. Now I can't help wondering why. And at the same time, I can't help but wonder why you wanted so badly to get rid of some Fratelli guys to the point you'd slip them defective weapons."

He was good, she had to admit that. The weapons had been defective. They'd been tampered with, shot counters fudged to look like they were loaded. The power packs had read as full when really, they had been mostly depleted. Killing hostages was not the priority. And she had known Unisco would come to kill the hostiles. Their lives would be enough. Maybe those who didn't have defective weapons would take some agents with them. Still, she didn't like the idea of needlessly throwing away the lives of hostages to be used as shields. It wasn't their fault they'd been there. Sure, they might still be harmed. But it was eliminating some of the risk. Why, she couldn't say. It wasn't in her character. She didn't care if they lived or not. But she'd gone with her gut and decided to give them more of a chance.

Besides, he was right. It had been Fratelli's people given those weapons. They were the ones she didn't trust, a precaution she wasn't unhappy to take. Nor would she shed any tears for them. "Those are some serious accusations," she said. "I hope you're prepared to back them up with something rather than just making them for the sake of batting your lips."

"You know, John Cyris and I are cut from the same cloth," he said. "Once there were three of us, now there's just me. Mara was arrested and turned traitor. Jenghis was killed by Unisco. He's devoted a lot of time to me. He can read me just as I can read him. Maybe. See I know how this will go. He'll use you and then stick you in the back the first chance he gets."

"Really?!" She sounded surprised, though she wasn't. Whether her lack of bemusement was at the apparent betrayal Cyris wished to inflict upon her or that Silas was actively perpetrating it in her direction, she couldn't say.

"He has a habit for it," Silas said. "He's a snake. He'll work you, you won't even see it coming. Just when you think you're safe…" He drew a finger across his throat theatrically.

"She'll have me," Domis growled. "And no harm will come to her while I draw breath."

Silas regarded Domis with the sort of withering glance one normally reserved for something squelchy. "That's adorable but what part of not seeing it coming do neither of you understand? Madam Coppinger, I like what you're doing here. I can see it benefitting us all. If you promise me one thing, I will deal with Cyris. Cyria has floundered for far too long and I say time for a change. And in exchange, you will have my loyalty until the day I cease to draw breath."

She considered his words. "What do you need me to do?"

"Nothing." Silas grinned at her. "Absolutely nothing. Just let it be and I'll arrange for Cyris to have an unfortunate accident. I'll inherit the organisation. His son wants nothing to do with him. Nobody will miss him. I always dreamed of working for someone like you."

She raised an eyebrow. "Someone like me?"

"Powerful, ruthless, someone worth killing for…" He paused. "Someone beautiful. Face it, you're like the ideal superior."

If it was meant to flatter, she was ashamed to admit it was working. Just a little. "I'll consider what you've said," she said. "For the time being, do what you do best."

He bowed again, this time a lot lower and decidedly more respectful. "Thank you for hearing me out, Madam Coppinger. I look forward to our next conversation."

"You know that one can't be trusted," Domis said as they watched Silas stride away purposefully. Like he owned the place. She didn't like that, something in his walk clashing with her desire to believe his sincerity.

"I don't trust anyone here," she said. "Except you. You'll never let me down, Domis. Will you?"

He looked at her and his face shifted into an uncomfortable expression approximating what she guessed to be a smile. "No! Never, Mistress."

Resistance wasn't quite as she'd anticipated but that was good as she hacked through the lock to her cell, shoved it open with the flat of her hand. She was in the corridor, weapon still ignited. Nobody. Left, or right? She bobbed her head, not sure where she was or how to leave but she couldn't stay here. She went left, ran at full pace without calling on the Kjarn to augment her speed. She might need it down the line, frequent exaggerated use left the body exhausted and the mind slow to react. She'd need to be sharp. Kyra rounded a corner, caught sight of two more of the black-clad figures, these with auras in the Kjarn and she reacted before they could, cutting into one through the stomach, almost hewing him in two before she went for the second one. He put an arm up to block and leaned back from her in one desperate motion, her blade hacked through his limb, permanently ruined his looks as she drove it through his face. He was dead before he hit the ground and she didn't spare them a look back as she moved on, no regrets about what she'd done. This was survival and they'd picked the wrong bitch to mess with here.

She continued to move deeper through the corridors, not sure where she was going but confident if she kept going, an exit would present itself. This place was huge, she didn't encounter more than token resistance, some of them not even threats but still needing to be eliminated. She couldn't leave any witnesses. She just had to keep going.

She turned another corner, hurdled a pipe and buried her blade between the shoulder blades of someone who hadn't seen her coming, felt him fall before she felt something, the sudden sensation bringing her to a halt. It was faint, regardless it tugged at the back of her senses. She couldn't have ignored it if she'd wanted to, following it down a slightly nicer corridor, all previous walls uniform grey and sterile, but here there was carpet. It felt spongy to run on, with a door up ahead. She had a good feeling about this as she ran towards it, slashing the lock into two pieces, she carried on, straight into the largest room she'd ever seen.

It was huge. Although Kyra only took in her surroundings for a moment before focusing on the people inside, she couldn't help acknowledging the depths of design that had gone into it. Three people turned, their attention on her. A middle-aged woman, a hulking man in a large hat and a dapper dark-skinned man with a neat beard and dreadlocks. She could feel them, surprise from the woman tinging above the sense of superiority, devotion from the big man…

From the Vazaran, she sensed nothing, but she saw the window towards the back of them and knew it'd be her way out. If she had to jump, so be it. The Kjarn would slow her fall. She couldn't stay here; she was outmatched as it was. She charged, weapon still lit in front of her, she'd kill anyone who stepped in her way. The big man stepped in her path, straight in front of the woman but it was the Vazaran who reacted, rising to his feet and hurling a fist at her.

Too late she sensed the surge in the Kjarn and the rush of power caught her by surprise, hurling her back the way she had come, almost back through the door and out into the corridor. Pain shot through her, though not as much as the shock. Her heart caught in her mouth, Kyra looked at him more closely as she jumped to her feet, entire body aching. He didn't appear to be carrying a weapon. Not that he needed one given he'd just hurled the fucking Kjarn at her!

This wasn't good! She remembered the presence she'd felt through her captivity and realised she might have found the source. He was old, a lot older than her but perhaps younger than her master. Raw power had hammered her, not a lot of finesse. She could work with that. Unfortunately, from what she'd felt, she could tell he was stronger than her.

"That's an interesting weapon," the Vazaran said, some of his teeth missing. He wasn't as dapper and clean-cut up close as she'd first guessed, old and tired, somehow soiled by his experiences. "Haven't seen one for a while."

251

"Allow me to give it to you," she replied. "Straight through the heart."

He wagged his finger. "Hardly a fair fight now, is it?" For a moment, she hesitated, unsure what he had meant, and it nearly proved to be a fatal as she felt the Kjarn tugging at her, warning her something was coming. She barely got the weapon up in time to block, his fingers arching out and dozens of little streams of electricity twisting from them, crimson lightning fizzling out on her blade. Dispelling it wasn't easy, but she managed it, the blade of her weapon flickering under the assault.

That made her mind up. The longer she remained here, the more chance she'd make some fatal mistake and not live to regret it. She stared at the man, obviously skilled in the arts of the Kjarn and realised she might be out of her depths. She was tired and running on empty, a long fight would be suicide right now. Past them was the window, she could make it. Nobody would expect her to run. She wouldn't have expected herself to run.

She smiled at him, thrust out a hand of her own and drove him back several paces with the full force of the Kjarn. He resisted it, just barely managed to stay on his feet but then she was past him before he could react, past the brute and the woman, kjarnblade in front of her like a spear, she could see blue sky up ahead of her, the first sight of freedom!

She hit it, the window shattered into a thousand pieces, glass blowing back against her bare skin from the onrush of incoming atmosphere and suddenly she was out into the sweet embrace of fresh air. Kyra's legs left solid ground and she was airborne. She looked down and didn't even have the time to realise how screwed she suddenly was. Rather than be above a city somewhere, just a hundred or so feet from the ground, she couldn't even see the ground for the clouds.

Shit!

Wim Carson doubled over, suddenly exhausted from the fatigue of drawing so much so quickly while still out of shape. He'd forgotten how effective the Kjarn could be in a fight when it was used in the right way. Casting the elements had once been so easy for him, he'd been a powerful Vedo Elementalist back in the day. He'd get back there soon, time was the greatest healer of them all. The girl was crazy; she'd leaped straight out into the blue beyond.

But was she dead? He wasn't entirely sure. He'd tried to lock down her presence the moment she'd entered the room and he hadn't felt her snuff out yet. Maybe he hadn't done it right. But whether she had survived or not was a question for another time. Right now, he was more concerned that she existed at all.

Here? Now?

It shouldn't have surprised him but the presence of one of them here, a possible Cavanda running around unchecked was something that worried him immensely. The Cavanda were the ancient enemy of the Vedo, everything that they were not. And if there was one, there was at least one more out there somewhere. One could not gain these skills accidentally. Not the skill needed to build a kjarnblade. Not potent telekinesis. About the best one could hope for by oneself without training was mild unwitting precognition. Maybe prophetic foresight in dreams. Even then, they were more by accident than intent, often uncontrolled and wild. Such was the limit without training. That was perhaps a relief. Being able to draw on the Kjarn and its power without the discipline of training and control was a recipe for disaster.

He needed a weapon. If the Cavanda had returned to the five kingdoms, he didn't want to have to resort solely on Kjarn abilities to defend himself. Before he could make the plans, he saw her staring at him as his attention came back to the room, a bemused look on her face. The woman who'd been his saviour.

"Want to explain what just happened?" she asked, not a hint of amusement in her voice.

"Two people meet for the first time. Don't know each other. One's a good fella, the other ain't so good. But the not so good fella, let's call him Jim, he asks the good fella, who we'll call Moe for a few credits to tide him over. And Moe, being the good fella, he gives him some. Don't trouble him none. Jim takes the credits, Moe don't get no word of thanks and then Jim vanishes. Them's the breaks. Few weeks later, same story. They meet, Jim needs credits, Moe gives him a few more than last time. No thanks. See ya. Them's the breaks. Few months later, same story. Jim asks for the credits, Moe, this time he say no, and Jim pulls a knife on him. Them's the breaks."

Cautionary tale from Premesoir about human nature, entitled Them's the Breaks. Author P. William Rashford.

The seventeenth day of Summerpeak.

Still the bug and the ape traded blows, neither willing to let up until one went down. A dozen small cuts had left Sarge bloodied, Scott could sense Herc was flagging. Bruises and breaks had left his body distorted under thunderous punches that would have broken less stubborn opponents. Herc had stayed up though, Saarth looking more frustrated now than she had through most of the bout and Scott felt relieved. If she lost her focus, he'd be able to drag her down closer to defeat. It was a good feeling, though he needed to keep his focus.

Finally, Herc brought the great horn into play, rushing Sarge and jabbing several neat hooks with his horn. All intended to put the opponent on the back foot. Just as predicted, Sarge wove back to avoid being impaled, the tip of the horn only grazing his impressive six pack... Privately Scott wished he had muscles like that... leaving a fresh trace of blood staining the silver fur.

He was to be surprised again. What he hadn't expected was Sarge to reach out and grab the horn, Herc suddenly struggling to break free as both hands clasped around the appendage, holding him in place. Despite his struggles, it was a futile effort as Sarge went hand over hand, pulling the bug closer with each tug. Herc's wings fluttered uselessly, the ape's hands bleeding from caressing the razor edges of the horn, even if neither were giving up. They had too much to lose.

The cold feeling still assaulted him, threatening to sap his focus. He didn't let it, frantically barking out mental orders to Herc to try and get out of it any way he could. There had to be one. Arms flailed out more in hope than expectation and Sarge growled as clawed arms bit at his fur, ripping it out in chunks. Patches of pale pink skin glared in the daylight sun and Scott silently urged Herc on.

It was too late, Sarge let go and wound up a big punch straight into the bugs face, Scott heard a terrific crack as the blow cracked the carapace, Herc tottering back on unsteady legs as if drunk. The second blow put him to the ground. Saarth suddenly looked hungry for the victory, Scott's heart fell as Herc hit dirt with a thud. On his front and barely moving, the giant bug looked frail and weak. Sarge let out a bellow of triumph and beat his chest for several long seconds, but Scott didn't see it, still too busy trying to reach Herc. The stagbug wasn't defeated, he'd have felt it if he'd expired but whether Sarge realised or not was open to debate.

Come on Herc… Come on! You can get up. He's not expecting it. One more hit and then you can rest. Just give me one more, please! You've got to!

He saw Herc twitch and his heart leaped from its pit of anguish. Sarge saw it as well, stopped beating his chest and raised both fists above his head like a hammer, Herc sprang from the dirt in one clumsy motion and drove his horn straight into the flexing pectoral muscle above him. It wasn't an easy penetration, Scott saw the bug reach out with his arms, pull himself even further into Sarge before the fists came down on his back. That was that, he realised as the bug was almost broken in two by the force of the blow, brown matter already flooding from the break in his back. But still the gorilla was impaled, he still needed to pull Herc off before he could do anything else.

Credit to him, he tried. He got both hands around Herc's upper body and yanked, arms trembling with the effort. The sounds of pain rippling from the ape's mouth were unlike anything Scott had ever heard before, anguished agony as fresh blood spurted out in a fountain, mingling with Herc's innards to paint the ground a mud colour. The movements became less vigorous the further the horn came out; he could see the ape weakening by the second. Herc was almost gone, he could see giant fingers digging into the stagbug's body, each movement sending reverberations through him.

They collapsed at the same time, neither of them moving. He doubted they could. It wasn't quite the clean victory he'd hoped it to be, but a knockout was a knockout. That gorilla had been a tough opponent, not something he'd have expected from someone like Saarth. Then again, he'd learned plenty of times appearances could be deceiving. Just because she looked like a flirty young woman didn't mean she lacked a ruthless streak. She wasn't a pushover to make it this far. Maybe he'd forgotten that just for a moment and he'd paid for it. It wasn't a mistake he could afford to make again.

She offered a few words he couldn't understand to her gorilla as she returned the ape to the crystal and shot Scott another smile as he took Herc back. His own thanks came, brief but poignant. He wondered what to do next. Already she had made her choice and he saw her send out a veek to decide the battle for her. At least, that was her plan. He stroked his chin. Now what would be the best thing to fight the giant cat lizard? They could be tricky bastards in a fight and if he chose wrong, it would cost him dearly. Amidst contemplating his choice, he heard the laughter and stiffened up.

"You struggle, bagmeat."

He reacted to the voice by almost jumping into the air in surprise. He turned, saw the face staring up from his shadow. Three eyes, yellow and lined with malice, huge mouth and brows. Same eerie high voice. Same damn ghost.

That explained the cold.

"How long you been stood there," he hissed out the corner of his mouth. He couldn't stand here and have a conversation. Not in the middle of a bout. And not in a live one. People would think he was going crazy talking to what looked like himself. Particularly since he wasn't sure if anyone else could see the ghost. Nobody had reacted, plus he'd face disqualification if he took too long to decide. "And how the hells can I understand you?"

No reply. The eyes blinked several times as they studied him. "Where else I go? Everything seems fun round you. Fun and violent."

"Well I'm busy," Scott hissed. "Leave me alone, we'll do this later." It probably looked weird, him with his head leaned over his shoulder and his mouth moving too quietly to hear the words. He hoped there were no lip readers in attendance watching what he said.

"Later? But I bored now. Want to do something."

He blinked. "You're not mine." He almost said it out loud. "Why are you telling me this?"

"You here bagmeat."

Scott knew somewhere at the back of his mind, he was running out of time. He'd be getting a warning very shortly if he didn't pick it up. On the field, Saarth's veek with its tawny fur and acid green scales continued to pace, razor sharp claws leaving shallow gouges in the battlefield. So much menace in such a compact package.

"What?!"

"You here. I here."

"I didn't claim you!"

"Don't know what that is. I know you."

"Don't think you know how this whole thing works." Only then did Scott realise just quite how ridiculous this was, almost laughed out loud. Would have done if it wasn't such an inconvenient time. Nothing about this felt natural.

"I don't. Just feel you. You feel I?"

He couldn't deny that at all no matter how much he might have wanted to. "Yeah. Yeah I do."

"There we go. We link. I know you bagmeat Scitt."

"Scott," he said almost as a reflex. "My name is Scott."

"Yo."

"What's yours?" It sounded stupid even as he said it, the realisation dawned the ghost probably didn't have a name. He. It was probably a male. It sounded like it was male. Then again given that spirits shouldn't be speaking at all, he could probably sound like whatever the hells he wanted. His head hurt thinking about it. The video referee beeped a warning, the stadium announcer was coming out with a list of consequences for inaction, he could hear murmurings amongst the crowd that he hadn't done anything yet.

"Want a name."

"And I'll give you one," he said. "Look…" The sense of urgency wasn't lost on him, didn't need to get kicked out of the tournament on a technicality. "… In a few. I really need to get back to this now. I'll deal with you later." It sounded callous, he couldn't help that.

"Want to fight."

"I can't fight with you now." He drew Sangare's crystal, prepped to slot it into his summoner. He'd have to do this now, just hope the ghost didn't interfere. That'd be a disaster, especially if he started telling tales on him.

"Not with you, bagmeat. With that." He stuck his head out of Scott's shadow and pointed a hand at the veek. "Want to fight that. It smells funky. Like bad meat."

That took him by surprise, cutting off the words in the small of his throat before he could let them loose. "What?! You…"

Can't. He was about to say can't, yet why couldn't he? Granted he might well regret it. It could go horribly wrong for him. Without being linked to him via a crystal, there'd be nothing to stop the ghost going walkabout and leaving him in the lurch. But he'd seen first-hand how powerful he could be, plus it'd be one hells of a trump card. If Saarth had researched him, she wouldn't see it coming. Plus, there was undoubtedly some sort of link between them. It could work. Sometimes, it just felt like you needed to take a gamble. Shuffle the cards and let them guide you on your path. He grinned.

"Okay," he said. "Do your worst."

The ghost sprang out of his shadow and landed on the field, waving confidently to a surprised crowd, even blowing kisses to the opponent. They were a mismatched pair, the veek all feline and lizard grace, deadly in its movements and the ghost, short and fat with four ears, three eyes and a mohawk. He felt the silence blanket the stadium, surprise and shock in the air. Hey, it wasn't any less unconventional an entrance than the way Kitti Sommer had rode into her battle with Pete yesterday. It was convention to use a container crystal. Not a requirement. He smiled at Saarth.

"Hey," he said out the corner of his mouth to the ghost. He turned his head back and glanced at him with a bemused expression as if to say 'what?' "Permear."

"What?!"

"I'm calling you Permear if you're sticking with me. You get me?"

"I Permear." The ghost didn't look unhappy with the name, he only shrugged. "Fair."

The buzzer went to signal the start of the round, he suddenly felt the first traces of doubt creep into him. He tried to quash them, not quite sure if he was ready to admit he'd just made a horrible mistake or not. Either way, he'd live or die by his decision. He couldn't look back, had to keep staring forward and hope for the best. As strategies went, it was a poor one but when victory came, he had no doubt it'd taste that much sweeter.

Of course, there were going to be problems. The first thing he realised was with no traditional bond between them, he couldn't issue silent commands. The second thing being he didn't know the complete capabilities of the spirit he was commanding. The third... That veek looked pissed off and ready for battle. Already it lunged for Permear and swiped with glimmering claws.

Dodge... "Dodge!" he yelled, the action bringing a surprised look from Saarth. Fourth problem. When you could issue the command mentally, it was like working with an extension of your own body. You thought, you did. Here, you thought, you spoke, you did. Split seconds might make the difference, tiny margins measured success.

He was starting to regret it more by the second, especially as the dodge was delayed, Permear lunged backwards and the claws only raked his front, scattering ectoplasm onto the ground. It faded into the dirt almost immediately, it wasn't a good sight. If the veek could hurt Permear, it might be a short fight. Part of what made ghosts such an intimidating foe was that they were hard to hurt. Techniques to trap and damage them were becoming more common, callers becoming more ingenious in their strategies, but you couldn't plan for everything.

"That hurt I," Permear groaned. He wasn't sure if Saarth could hear the ghost or not. If it was only him that could hear Permear, it might get awkward. "Let me at him."

"What can you actually do?" Scott wondered. "Got anything powerful?"

"I powerful." The ghost sounded insulted. "Want I prove it?"

"Wait, no…!" Scott almost yelled, saw the veek coming and he didn't know what Permear had in mind, but it didn't feel a good idea to let the ghost call the shots. The claws were outstretched again, ready to slash deep into the permeable membrane that was Permear's skin and then suddenly the ghost wasn't there any longer. Saarth's eyes widened, the veek crashed gracelessly into the ground and rose to all four feet, hissing angrily as Scott saw it sweeping its head back and forth in search of the opponent. It didn't see Permear burst from the ground below, swinging a shining purple fist into its face. Scott heard the thud, saw blood fly and heard the howl. As Permear ducked, hiding again, he saw the bloody mess the blow had left of the face.

His spirits leapt, he silently urged the ghost on, even if he wasn't sure he could hear him or not. The feline face lashed back and forth, half blind, searching out a possible target it couldn't find. Not until Permear swept up behind it and tugged the tail playfully. It brought a laugh out of the crowd, even a smile to Scott's face and Saarth looked furious as her veek lunged backwards, snapping crooked yellow teeth at the ghost. They passed harmlessly through his skin and the next thing Scott knew, something flashed with a malignant black energy and suddenly the veek was airborne, thrown skyward by a wave of pure force. Scott saw it crumple as it hit the ground and winced. That had looked painful.

"Damn right it painful," Permear said. One moment he was stood several feet from the fallen veek, the next he took one step and suddenly stood above it, body contorting almost acrobatically to make the movement.

"Sataris!" Saarth yelled, her façade of cool broken as Permear stood lazily above the veek as if contemplating how best to break it. It was comparable with the look of a destructive child and Scott found himself wondering if that wasn't such a bad comparison. There was something almost appalling in the state of careless innocence around the ghost.

"What you reckon? Painful or effective? Which best?" Those words emphasised the point, if anything and he recoiled slightly. They just sounded so casual, devoid entirely of compassion. "These bones break right?"

"Yeah, they break," Scott said. The words felt hollow in his mouth, as quiet as they might have been. He knew Permear would hear him, knew Saarth would see his lips move and read something into it.

"Fatal?"

"If you're going to do it, just bloody do it!" Scott almost yelled out, acutely aware of how it must look on camera. Like he was losing his cool. "Don't talk back about the best way to kill something!" He swallowed hard. This wasn't going to plan, he'd need to do something drastic to keep things under control. He could feel that victory slipping away from him.

"Oh, aye-aye, bagmeat," Permear said, moving to the veek's head. It had started to get to its feet, shaking itself woozily. It had taken a few big hits; its eyes were vacant, and Scott could tell that it didn't have much left. Then again Saarth had thought that with Herc in round two. He wasn't taking anything for granted. Sataris was quickly put back to the ground with a punch to the back of the head, bones tearing out through the muscle and the flesh of its legs as bones snapped violently under the crushing force of the blow.

For something composed entirely of smog and a void, Permear could certainly pack a punch. It'd be worth knowing for future. The ghost hadn't stopped there though, both hands forced through Sataris' skull and all three eyes furrowing in concentration. The veek's head jerked under the motions of whatever Permear was doing, eyes slowly regaining some focus, mouth snapping back and forth aimlessly. It was drooling, like it was fucked in the head.

"Hey, check out," Permear yelled. "Puppets."

He could hear some disgruntled sounds coming from the crowd and Scott had to admit he felt a little uncomfortable. People didn't know Permear wasn't under his control, they'd... Yipes... Somehow, he knew he was going to be portrayed as a seriously deranged human being come the end.

"Permear, that's enough!" he said, trying to keep some authority in his voice. "Stop it!"

"No! It fun!"

"Permear, just kill it and have done with it!" He whispered harshly. "Please!"

All three eyes swept towards him in exasperation and suddenly all movement stopped. The head hung there in the ghost's grasp for a moment and then Permear gave him a huge grin. Not a pleasant one either, he had a feeling he wasn't going to like what came next. It almost looked like the ghost was tugging on something. Somewhere he heard the crack starting to fill the air, growing in volume by the second and saw the look of determined focus flash across ghostly features, he realised too late what was going to happen.

Silence filled the stadium as something soft hit the ground at Permear's feet, he wiped his hands on the dead veek's fur. "It cool if I eat them?" he inquired of Scott who was doing his best to avoid being sick. That image really didn't help. Did the ghost even eat? Suddenly it felt like the last question he ever wanted answered.

Only the announcer could be heard amidst the stunned silence, narrating exactly what had just happened, as if people needed to be reminded. The people listening on the radio were probably in for an audio treat. Saarth looked furious. Scott didn't exactly feel pleased about it himself as the video referee signalled the end of the bout, he grabbed a container crystal out of his pocket, an empty one and tore onto the field. Permear glanced around, didn't even react as Scott jumped on him and clapped the crystal into him. There was no resistance, he didn't feel him fight the process. For better or worse, Permear had accepted him. And now he was laid in veek brains, squashed them beneath him as he'd landed.

Fantastic. This day had just gotten that little bit better.

Why didn't he feel good about his victory? He didn't know as he strode out the changing room and straight into the pack of press waiting for him, flashes forcing him to shield his eyes as images were snapped and recorders thrust into him. Suddenly he was glad Permear wasn't about, he could imagine the ghost taking ultimate exception to this sort of ambush.

Given what he'd just done, he didn't want to be the one explaining a dozen maimed corpses. There usually was some press hanging about for quotes following the end of bouts but never like this. One or two, maybe four at most but twenty?! Overkill. He had a feeling he might know what the first questions would be too.

"Guys, I just went through a tough battle," he said. "And I've got to assure some people I'm not losing the plot. Just get your questions asked and I'll answer them. Let's not make it longer than it has to be." It sounded rougher than he meant it to. Screw it. It worked for him. It felt right.

"Scott was that really the best way for you to win that bout?!"

First question and he shook his head. "Look I won, I'm happy with that and it was just the way it evolved in the flow of battle. I didn't go into the bout planning it. Next question?"

"Did you think there was excessive force employed in what you just did?"

Once more, he shook his head, tried to keep a straight face. He had a headache and a feeling this was going to get tiresome very quickly. "It could be argued anything that results in the opponent being defeated is just the right amount of force. It was a brutal finishing move but hey, it's a brutal sport."

"Did it show a lack of respect for your opponent?!"

The third question and it came from the same reporter as the first, a Serranian journalist who looked somewhat familiar, a brown-haired man whose face he couldn't place. "No, that wasn't my intention. If I'd known who Weronika Saarth was before the tournament, I'd have the highest respect for her in getting here."

He blanched inwardly at the answer. It sounded a lot more arrogant out loud than in his head. Oh well, no taking it back now. Then again, maybe arrogance was the wrong word. Condescending, yes. Arrogance, perhaps not.

"Is it true that you hadn't actually claimed that ghost until after you'd won?"

This came from someone whose name he did know; he'd read her article about how the island was a stupid place to hold the tournament earlier. Kate Kinsella. She'd slated Ritellia, he had a horrible feeling he might be next. "Well I think actions speak louder than words on this answer. You saw what I did. Draw your own conclusions."

He hadn't denied it but neither had he confirmed it and that felt like the best way to go. Scott saw a flash of something in her eyes and that confirmed it for him. Yep, he was going to get it in the media at some point in the next few days. "I mean, when I say draw your own conclusion... If I'd used a spirit I hadn't claimed, that'd be either phenomenally stupid or tremendously skilful, wouldn't you say? I mean there'd be nothing making it listen to me. I mean obviously I'd like to lean towards the latter but hey that might just be me being a bit big-headed and nobody likes that, right?"

When nobody answered, he gave one final comment on the matter. "I don't want to come off like that. But preferably not as psychotic either." So far nobody had mentioned he'd looked like he was talking to his shadow. That was a relief, a big one, if he was honest. He didn't have an answer to that. "I mean, you enter, you win or lose. Them's the breaks, right?"

"Are you worried you might be kicked out the competition?"

A Vazaran had asked the question and he laughed nervously. "No. Not even in the slightest. Nobody has ever been kicked out of this tournament for winning like that, not to my knowledge. It sets dangerous precedent. Or does the ICCC want nice clean wins with no blood now? Seems like something they'd come out with. Violence by its nature is never tame and this is a violent sport. Sometimes people forget that. Thank you, no more questions!"

He grinned at them, quickly made his way past and out into the stadium proper, a little pleased with himself given that answer. It had felt clever. He'd enjoyed it, felt like a middle finger to anyone who criticised him for the way things had gone down.

"Hey, Mr Taylor!"

One final question and he half- turned his head to the speaker, unable to help himself. Kinsella again. He had a feeling he might be about to regret answering this. She had a sweet venomous smile about her scarlet lips. Like tongue kissing poison ivy.

"What's happening with you and Mia Arnholt?"

"None of your business!" It came out brusque, he was already gone before anything else could come his way. It had been a cheap shot from her, wasn't any of her business though too late he realised he'd probably just confirmed there was something going on. If there hadn't been, he'd have said nothing and that would have been the end. Instead, he'd made a rod for his own back and chances were that it'd come swinging down sooner or later.

Especially if her dad found out... He liked Terrence Arnholt from what little knowledge of him he had, he'd gotten on with him whenever he'd talked to him, but he was a pretty imposing figure. He could be intimidating, thankfully he'd never seen him in that light, but it didn't take a lot of imagination to picture him a violent, protective father who felt vengeful when it came to guys sniffing round his daughter.

He'd worry about it when it came down to it. That was all he could do. It might not get that far. In his heart of hearts, Scott Taylor knew he could always hope for nothing. If it came up roses, it'd just be a big bonus.

Walking past the locker rooms and the media area and up into the concourse, he saw them waiting for him. There was a special area in most stadiums for nominated guests to meet the contestants after the bout, just out of sight of the public, a walled off area about a fourth the size of an average spirit calling battlefield. The one in this stadium was a pretty plain affair, cold grey flooring beneath his shoes and sparsely decorated walls with just one poster stuck on them filled with just a few words. He glanced to his left, read the words as he passed by and smiled. He'd heard it before, but it was a good one.

If you think you can, do. If you think you can't, why? – Ruud Baxter.

As quotes went, it spoke to him. He'd always seen it about never letting other people impose limits on you. You were the master of your own destiny, you made your own choices and you lived or died by them.

Pete saw him first, a smirk passing across his face as their eyes met. Scott knew how much Pete had been hurt by going out of the tournament though he hoped his friend would throw all his support behind him now. It was what he would have done for him in the same situation. Doubly so now Sharon had gone out as well for Scott might have been a leery about asking Pete to pick his friend over his sister but now he had no excuse. Matt out. Pete out. Sharon out… He wasn't doing too bad really to get to the last twelve. Matt and Mia were both there making up the trio. The three people he felt closest to on the island right now and they'd all made his guest list. Granted it was also a list Jess had once been on, but he'd struck her off it at the first available opportunity. That'd be awkward if she and Mia came face to face down here.

Smiles all around, Mia almost leaped on him with a hug, he had to steady himself to avoid toppling backwards. He felt her lips on his and grinned, returning the gesture. Suddenly he was glad this hadn't happened a dozen feet back, would have given the media an unexpected exclusive. At the same time, Matt and Pete were both wringing his hands, offering their congratulations and their compliments, even if he could hear Matt muttering about how he didn't need to see his sister doing this. If anything, that made the whole experience sweeter.

As Mia broke away, he saw the emotion in her eyes and just for a moment, felt a little guilty. She looked like she'd been through the emotional wringer watching him fight. "Hey," he said. "Someone's happy to see me."

"We're all happy to see you," Matt said. "Probably more than some people on the island anyway… You see Weronika's comments after the bout?!"

Scott groaned. It hadn't taken long for his good mood to fade, his smile vanishing. He hadn't seen what she'd said, had a feeling that he was about to find out though. And that it was linked in with what he'd been asked a few moments ago by journalists. "I didn't. Did she take the loss badly?"

"Yeah," Pete said trying to sound offhand. "She didn't sound impressed. She said you went out to humiliate her. Think the words arrogant, condescending and cheat were all mentioned… Speaking of, where the fuck did you get that ghost from?!"

"I was just wondering that," Matt said. "I've never seen you with it before. And I did my research. I wanted to be prepped in case I had to fight you. And I didn't see no ghost."

"Guys," Scott said, breaking from Mia and holding his hands up. "You're right. I didn't own the ghost before this bout. Remember how I told you about my previous encounter with him?"

"Oh, it's a him now?" Mia asked. She sounded like she was finding it a little hard to swallow. He couldn't blame her. He had no idea what was going on either.

"I thought ghosts were gender neutral," Pete mused. "Is this the same ghost that talked?"

"He does talk," Scott protested. "I had a nice chat with him before the bout. He calls me bagmeat and I think he might be completely bloody insane!"

Matt and Pete looked at each other. Mia backed away from him. That hurt the most, Scott thought as he looked the three of them up and down. "What?!"

"Scott, I..." Words failed Pete completely and he glanced at Mia and Matt. "No, you do it."

"Scott, spirits don't talk," Matt said gently. "You should know that by now."

"I'll prove it to you!" Scott almost yelled, although not quite with as much conviction as he could have. Something told him he wouldn't be able to prove it. After all, now he thought on, Saarth hadn't been able to hear what Permear had been saying during the bout. And some of what the ghost HAD said... It probably would have garnered a reaction. Still, he'd said he'd do it and now he had to at least make the effort. It was then he reached for the container crystal in which he'd trapped Permear and brought it to his summoner. As it caught the light, he blinked several times, brought it closer to his eyes for further study.

Huh? He said it in his head just as he did out loud, holding the crystal to the light, not quite believing what he was seeing. Maybe it had been a defective item. He hoped it was anyway. They were supposed to be unbreakable. Yet if that was the case, why was the thing cracking before his very eyes, a thin web of lines spreading over the surface of the object?

"That's not right," he said aloud.

The eighteenth day of Summerpeak.

Her summoner beeped with an incoming communication and, still in a huff over the way she'd been defeated, she hit answer without thinking about it. The ID wasn't present, no way of determining who it was beforehand.

"Hello?!" she demanded. "Who is this?!

The voice that came back was eerily creepy, almost dangerously velvety as it purred out an answer. "My dear, who I am is not important. What is important is what I can do for you. And believe me..." He broke into a series of senseless giggles before clearing his throat, regaining composure. "Sorry, been that kind of day. Believe me, right now I can do wonders for you."

"Oh really?" Suddenly she was interested. Only a little. "Like what?!"

"Demanding little thing, aren't you? Bossy... Oh that's the stuff. I'm sorry, these painkillers are unbelievable. Take it all away. Had a bit of an industrial accident earlier. Lost some fingers. Enough about me, not important. Anyway. You. You had some rotten luck there, did you not?"

"Shit happens." It was about all she wanted to say on the matter. "You deal with it and move on."

"You CAN do that, of course. It's up to you, my dear Weronika... Can I call you Ronnie? Or shall I stick with Ms Saarth? Your choice." Without waiting for an answer, he carried on. "Anyway. Why deal with it? Why should you have to take humiliation like that? I'm not going to lie to you, I don't like people. They're a bunch of horrible ignorant bastards who don't appreciate radiance when it strikes them in their nasty judgemental faces. But all that is going to cha-cha-change."

He descended into more giggles and she considered cutting the communication, found it hard to take him seriously. "There's going to be a reckoning in this world. A burning. And out of the ashes, a new world will rise. Can't build the new without destroying the old."

"I'll agree with you there. Still don't know what you're talking about."

"I'm not explaining this well. Probably shouldn't be explaining it at all..." Long deep breath and another laugh. "Should be resting. But I wanted to catch you before you left the island. Please. If I arrange a meeting, can we talk? It might be worth your while. Fabulous opportunity and all that."

It went all against her better judgement. For a long time, she'd thought it was a prank call and cutting it out might have been the best thing she could do. But...

Chances. You sometimes had to take them.

"Okay," she said. "I don't have anything else to do now. I'll listen."

"Lovely, lovely… You have a nice voice Ronnie, I got to say. Like a canary or something. Run along little bird, I have your number and I'll be in touch. Toodles."

It went dead as abruptly as it had come to life. Weronika Saarth tossed her summoner onto the bed and looked at herself in the mirror thoughtfully. Doors and windows. When one closes, another opens. She needed to consider this. It could be just the thing she'd been looking for.

"Container crystals, also sometimes known as capture crystals and lock glasses depending on who you talk to, are intended by their very nature to be indestructible. They're fashioned out of a synthetic substance which on the outside is low grade diamond-quality and on the inside a form of malleable glass capable of holding the spirit without damage. It used to be that there were many poor knock-offs once and spirits were getting damaged and lost before and after claiming. That's why the ICCC brought in legislation to ensure there was a standard set across the board for the crystals. Anyone not adhering to the protocols faces an automatic fine plus chance of incarceration."

Professor David Fleck to a class, on the nature of container crystals.

The seventeenth day of Summerpeak.

"That's not right," Pete said, clapping his eyes on the shattering crystal with confusion filling them. "That shouldn't happen."

"I never heard of anything like that before," Matt agreed. "Might want to…"

It gave, suddenly he had a handful of broken fragments clapped in his palm. Some of them fell away, tinkled to the floor about their feet. One bounced off his shoe. Mia, wearing sandals, gave him a rueful shake of the head as he tossed them in the nearest trashcan. What apparently had survived the shattering was Permear, the ghost shaking himself off as he floated aimlessly above the ground.

"That was cramped," he said. "You have bigger? I'm a ghost of considerable girth. And I think my word range is going up as well." He narrowed his eyes at Scott. "Think I'm getting some thoughts back from you… You're annoyed."

"Yeah, I'm annoyed!" Scott said angrily. "What the hells did you just do?"

"Sweetheart, I dead. There no hells." Permear blew on his hands loftily as he spoke before stretching his arms. "Take it from me. I know what I talk about. Trust me, I ghost."

Scott tore his attention away from his chatty spirit and glanced to his friends, an almost pleading look on his face. "Tell me you guys just heard that."

"What did he say?" Mia asked. Of them all, she looked the least like she thought he was a crazy person. Neither Matt nor Pete had backed away and made a run for the exit, but they looked like the thought had crossed their mind.

"Just said trust me I'm a ghost and there's no hells. Apparently, he knows what he's talking about."

"To be fair, he is cute," Mia said. "In a darkly malevolent sort of way. I like him."

"Aww, thanks," Permear said, hovering up to stare at her. "This your mate? She less unappealing than some of the other bagmeat here. Especially you." He raised a prominent brow at Scott and waggled it.

It came out so blunt, Scott couldn't help but react. "No, she's not my mate, floaty purple douche!"

"Not nice!" Permear protested. "I only being nice."

"Mate?" Mia asked, raising an eyebrow. "Really? That what we're calling it now?"

"I think it's a good term," Permear said to her. Her expression didn't change. "You can't understand a word I say, eh?" Still no change, she kept her gaze on Scott, almost patiently waiting for him to say something.

"Of course, she can't understand you!" Scott snapped at the ghost. "She'd have kicked your ass if she could. And she's not my mate."

"But you want her to be?" That ghostly grin grew by the second.

"I'm not answering that question!"

"You think he's insane?" Pete said in Matt's ear in a stage whisper missed by nobody.

"I think insane is a strong word," Matt said. "Scott, none of us can hear whatever you think you're hearing. And…" He looked up at Pete. "Your turn."

"Okay, maybe you've been working too hard," Pete said, unable to suppress the smile. "As much as I never thought I'd use those words about you. It's not uncommon to crack under strain…"

"Want me to crack him under strain?" Permear inquired. "I could rip his brains out, I good at that." He flexed his smoky fingers. "Pro."

"No!" Scott quickly said. He felt he needed to put his foot down quickly before it got out of hand. Permear looked like he wouldn't take kindly to being told what to do, regardless he needed to try and at least exert some authority and fast. "No more brain ripping."

"Yeah what was with that?" Matt asked. "Seemed a bit of a violent way to end the bout."

"Aww, he squeamish?" Permear asked. "Can I kill birds and throw them at him?"

"What the fuck's wrong with you?" Scott demanded, shaking his head violently. "Don't do that!"

"Okay, be like that then," Matt replied. "Only asking."

"Not you, Perme... Oh forget it. That ghost has a bit of a strong personality. He thought it was the best idea to win. I didn't tell him to do it."

"Oh yeah, blame the ghost." Permear sounded insulted. "That always works. Not. Ha, you crazy! Woo-woo crazy-crazy!" He started doing a little dance, spinning on one leg, letting out woo-ing sounds every few moments as he did.

"What the hells is he doing now?" Pete inquired, staring at the ghost with some sort of fascination that Scott found amusing if he was honest. Admittedly it was weird, but it wasn't that strange.

"Think he's dancing," Mia said. Permear nodded in agreement, winked at her. Scott saw the flush in her cheeks, the smile light up her face. "Think he likes me."

"Think I can see why you do," Permear mused, giving Scott a sideways look. "She pretty nice. Don't like those two though. They strange."

"Ah give them a break," Scott said. "They're not that bad. That's Mia, that's Pete and that's Matt. And this is Permear. My new spirit. Apparently."

"Yo," Matt said. The ghost looked at him, then shook his head dismissively, muttering dark words about the audacity of people who dare speak to him. It was unfortunate really, Scott thought, grimacing as he stared at Permear. He could hear the ghost speak, it would appear everyone else was deaf to it for now

"Hey, all conversations are best when nobody else hears them, bagmeat," Permear laughed, the comment jerking Scott up out of his thoughts.

"What?! Oh, that's not fair. You can hear my thoughts as well?"

"Well yeah. You and I connected now. I deep inside you. I be yours and you be mine."

"Oh gods... You make it sound so seedy." Trying to put his mind off it, Scott took a fresh crystal from his pocket, ran his eyes over in examination. It looked okay, better than okay. It looked like the flawless specimen that he'd have expected. He handed it to Pete. "This look okay to you?"

"What sounds seedy?" Matt inquired. "You two aren't having a private discussion about my sister, are you?" He sounded outraged. Scott ignored him, instead looking at Pete as he shook his head. Permear stared at Matt for ten seconds, eventually forcing the younger caller to look away.

"Looks fine. Can't see any problems with it. Matt?" He held the crystal up for him and Matt took it, giving it an appraising eye. His conclusion was the same as Pete's, offering the opinion the crystal was perfectly fine to be used. Mia said the same thing.

"Want me to look?" Permear offered. "Won't work you know."

"Quiet you," Scott said as he took focus and pressed the crystal against the ghost's head, using his will to draw the spirit into the crystal. "And stay still."

He gave his friends a nervous grin as he clamped his hand shut around the settled stone. "That should do it, let us talk in private. Come on, I know you're all thinking it."

He raised an eyebrow when nobody spoke up. "Come on? Nobody? Nothing about me acting like a crazy person. Believe me, I can hear him speak. He's insane. Dangerously so. Or possibly just maladjusted. I don't know."

"You know something?" Pete asked. "I think you might have wasted your time asking Al Noorland to build that particle barrier."

Scott groaned, letting his head hang. His hand burned, he tried to ignore it. "I'd forgotten about that. Maybe he'll have seen the bout and drawn the conclusion I don't need it any more. Maybe he's not spent much time on it. Maybe…"

"Look on the bright side though," Mia said. "At least the cost wasn't too high. I mean, a quick bout with him… That's cheap for me."

Matt laughed at that. "You managed to swap a bout for a working particle barrier? Good show, Scott. Nice work. That's ridiculously balanced in your favour. Those things are awesome if you're ghost hunting."

"Which I'm not anymore…" He couldn't hold it any longer, Scott let out a yelp as he put the crystal down on the ground, the steam rising off it as it sat there several moments, felt like the temperature rose a few degrees with it.

"I think I really need to get that thing checked out," he muttered, a mere few seconds before the crystal shattered under the heat and Permear rose from the broken fragments, shaking himself off.

"Who you call a thing?" he inquired. "That species-ist or something. I dunno."

"I don't think there's need for this," Permear said, giving the four of them a sad look from the chamber. Even with his incorporeal abilities, he wouldn't be able to get out of there. The SEC's were impenetrable, even to ghosts. Once you were in, you didn't get out. Spiritual Examination Chambers. There was something about the look the ghost gave them, something almost human in the expression. Scott tried to look away but couldn't. He felt a shudder of amusement ripple through him as if the ghost were saying 'you don't get off that easy boyo'. "Really don't."

"You sure you don't hear that?" Scott asked the technician, a bored looking Vazaran with oversized glasses and a lab coat just a little too small for his girth. His expression of ennui didn't change.

"Hear what, sir?"

"I thought not," Scott said. "I'm not hearing things, guys. You know that, right?"

"I know that maybe you believe you think you're hearing things," Pete said. "And that usually boils down to crazy person in my book."

"Oh, hang on for a moment," Scott said acerbically. "I just remember. I mistook you for someone whose opinion I actually give a crap about."

"You asked a question, I gave you an answer," Pete said. "Don't shoot the messenger because you don't like what the note says."

They'd found themselves in the Spirit Regulation Building, a structure just off the under-repair ICCC building that had avoided most of the fire damage following the attack a week ago. This place filled a special function, equal parts hospital, diagnostic laboratory, modification technology outlet and bazaar, the sort of place every caller needed to go some time or another. Pete and Matt had accompanied him, Mia had left with her apologies but a promise to see him again later, something he was already looking forward to.

Permear had kicked up a fuss about going into the chamber, Scott had had to use all his skill to try and coax him into the confines, still it hadn't been enough, he'd run off screaming in defiance. At least until he'd suddenly reappeared in front of Scott, much to their collective surprise. He'd tried again, this time they'd watched as he'd gotten about twenty feet away and then faded from sight, returning to the same spot.

"This is just humiliating," the ghost had grumbled, reluctantly stomping into the chamber and wearing his sorrowful face as the door slammed shut. He beat a palm against the door, letting a pained little ouch escape him. Scott rolled his eyes. "I'm going to find some way of making you regret this, you know. You're going to regret it! Regret it I say!" The one-sided conversation had continued in the same vein until the scan had finished, an aurora coloured beam shining over Permear several times from many different angles. More than once he let out a huff and a look of intense savagery Scott found more unsettling than he wanted to admit.

It wasn't uncommon to use these places to get specs on a newly acquired spirit, to assess their capabilities. The readout handed to Scott was on a par with others he'd read, same layout, same text, same dry language.

"What does it say?" Pete asked. "Anything unusual."

Scott barked out a laugh. "Get this. Subject is deceased. Categorised as ghost-slash-spectral-slash-non-corporeal. And I needed a machine to tell me that."

"Can you let me out yet?" Permear asked. "I need to be let free to spread my wings."

"You don't have wings," Scott replied absentmindedly. "Or I would."

"If I flap my arms and hoot like an owl, will you believe me?" Permear asked. "If not, it's discrimination. I get someone on you. Hoot! Hoot! I will!"

"Let him out," Scott said, glancing over to the technician. "Please. He won't shut up until you do."

He received another strange look but the tech obliged. Probably bloody should be obliging given the fee he was paying here. The ghost certainly had a spring in his step as he exited the chamber. "Some spooky good hearing you got there, buddy."

"And this guy smells of goat," Permear said, looking at the tech. "Think he eats it or just bathes in its blood? I don't know."

Scott ignored him, continued to run his eyes over the readout on the pad in front of him. Subject currently attached to Caller ID 14051991. Yeah, that was his number. Body composition, three tenths carbon monoxide, two tenths charcoal smog, half ectoplasm. Sounded about right. Ghosts used ectoplasm to keep themselves held together, make themselves visible.

The other stuff was interesting though, none of it particularly good for the lungs. He didn't have any specific knowledge about chemicals, but he knew that much. Subject displays strong gravitational fluctuations. May be able to manipulate them. He'd seen the void inside. Never been that close to a ghost before. Maybe they all were like that. Either way it was something he could use. Potential power levels unknown. That was helpful. Subject displays stronger than normal electrical synaptic ability...

"What does that mean?" he asked, glancing over at the tech. If he had a name, it wasn't revealing itself any time soon. He wore no name tag. "About the synaptic ability?"

"Synapses are in the brain, they're the bits that enable you to think, to feel, to communicate. On most spirits, they're a lot lower than human but slightly higher than you'd expect from a creature in the wild. Like part of the caller is rubbing off on them. That's the theory."

The tech shrugged. "On your ghost, it's a lot stronger, it's a lot smarter. Not quite human but... I don't know, I think there's elements missing from your ghost you'd find in a human."

"Such as?"

"Conscience. Restraint. Fear. These are all specific notions, argue about nature or nurture all you like but they each plot their own specific path through the brain. They leave their own patterns, every new experience opens new synapses, literally changes who you are. This ghost is doing the same thing. I've not seen anything like it before."

As he said it, Scott thought back to the bout, not just some of the things that he'd seen but some of what he'd heard, and he could see it, no matter how disturbing he found it. Still Permear couldn't hurt him. If they truly were bonded, then the ghost was as much part of him as he was Permear.

"And what does that mean about power levels?"

"Is this the ghost you used in your bout, Mister Taylor?"

"Yeah."

"A veek is a ferocious opponent, would you say? Tough, savage, uncompromising?"

"Sounds like a veek," Pete said. "And it did for Saarth's pretty easily. Too easy."

"Schooled it, I'd say," Matt offered, smacking his fist into his palm. "Beat its ass. She didn't see it coming." The technician nodded in agreement.

"There you have it then. It means its potential power levels are difficult to gauge. They could be exponentially many times what we've already seen."

"Wait, are you telling us he happened onto a super powerful ghost entirely by chance?" Pete sounded a little outraged by the suggestion. Never had Scott heard the words 'lucky' and 'bastard' inflexed in a voice without them being uttered. This day was already turning out to be informative in more ways than one.

"I wouldn't put it in those words." The tech considered it for a moment before shrugging his shoulders. "I'd say that everything happens for a reason. Every action has a reaction. Nothing in nature is this powerful by accident."

"Damn straight baby, I'm number one unique."

"Just like everyone else," Scott muttered out the corner of his mouth to the ghost, giving him a sardonic look. "Sorry. And why can't I keep him in the container crystal? He's broken two already."

"Same problem. His power levels might be too great to contain in a normal crystal. There's only a finite number of energies they can hold before structural integrity is compromised. It's not unheard of but I wouldn't say it's common."

"What do I do then?"

"Honest opinion? You've put yourself in a hole really. Want a shovel?"

"Gee thanks, that's helpful."

"Professional opinion," the tech continued as if Scott hadn't spoken. "About the only thing you can do for the time being is keep doing as you are. The handy thing here is that unlike a conventional spirit, say your stagbug or your weasel… Yeah I watched your bout, can I get your autograph after this is done." Scott nodded, folded his arms but managed to hide his impatience. "Anyway, the difference here is that your ghost is just that. A ghost. You throw him out into a bout, he might fall and then what? It's not like he has a physical body to be retrieved."

"Wow he manages to make it sound so callous," Permear mused. "Reckon if I toss him out the window, he be a little more sympathetic? I think he might."

"That ghost has some weird personality quirks," Scott mused. "So just keep as I am until I can find a more stable crystal? Know where I can get one?"

The tech shrugged. "Not easy to find. Or cheap. I did hear a rumour about a place in Serran that used to weaponize crystals like them. But like I said. Rumour. Depends on how badly you want to go looking. They're always available. For a price."

Scott shrugged. "You hear anything, let me know." He offered him a hand which the technician shook. "I mean I guess you come across all sorts of stuff like that, right?"

"Not as often as you might think. I'll let you know. I got your contact details. Scott. Name's Samandou N'Kong. Call me Sam, if you like. Also respond to Sammie. And S-Dog."

"Of course, he does," Permear said dryly. "Fucking weirdo."

"I'll keep that in mind," Scott said. "And there's going to be no side effects at keeping him outside a crystal?"

"Well given you kinda don't have a choice," Sam said. "It's not like there's much you can do. All I'd say is keep him well drilled. Get him good around people."

"Oh, he's doing fine. He's already not murdered like a dozen people since I got my hands on him."

"You are connected. You already saw he can't go too far from you. But like I said, just remember that he might act human sometimes, he isn't. Not even close. Permear huh? I like that name. Because he's permeable?"

"That was my thinking."

"Why couldn't I get a cool ghost name? Like MC Roast?"

You really want to be called MC Roast? Scott asked the ghost silently. Why? To Sam, he only grinned. "I was a bit pressed for time. You come up with a better name on the fly."

"Damn straight. MC Roast is an awesome name I think. It says I'm badass."

"It says you're an idiot," Scott muttered quietly. "Sorry. Get some unusual backlash from him, emotion-wise." Sam looked like he accepted that. "Anyway, autograph... I'll get that done. Got plans tonight. Need to head off for them."

"Doing anything nice?" Samandou wondered. Scott couldn't help the grin that flashed across his face.

"Got a date with that special someone." He took the pad and the stylus, scrawled his signature over it. He'd paid upfront, always a risky thing but not here. These were reputable businesses after all. Right now, it felt credits well spent.

"Sounds nice."

"He doesn't think so," Pete said, jerking a thumb towards Matt. "It's his sister."

"Matthew Arnholt?" Samandou asked. "Then your sister would be... Heh very nice, Scott. I saw that interview. You were asked about it."

"What's that?" Matt asked.

"Kate Kinsella suddenly got interested in my love life," Scott replied. "Told her it was none of her business."

"Bet that was a snappy comeback," Pete said. "You do know that's probably going to make things worse?"

"Yeah but I'm prepared for the bitch. If in doubt, remain silent. Ignore everything I get accused of. Let my silence sell my innocence, show I have nothing to dignify her responses with. She might get bored after a while and write about how Ritellia murders kittens."

"Yeah that should work," Matt said sarcastically. "You can't take the moral high ground with journalists. Nobody ever tell you that?"

"I'm not talking about Kinsella, I'm talking about Mia," Pete said urgently. "You know what women are like."

Scott didn't say anything, instead thought about his experiences with women and felt the blood draining from his face. "Oh."

"Yeah," Pete said. "You should take my advice. I know what I'm talking about. I'm an absolute monster with women."

"That doesn't sound as good as you probably mean it to," Matt offered dryly, winking at Scott. "Makes you sound a domestically abusive control freak son of a bitch."

"It's true, it does," Sam said unhelpfully. Permear nodded, chuckled. He clearly found the whole discussion amusing.

"Pete, when was the last time you had any sort of physical contact with a woman who wasn't virtual?" Scott asked.

"I'm not dignifying that with a comment. Hey, I was hoping to give Weronika Saarth some comforting later. I would destroy that. Bet she's tight as fuck. Right body on her."

Scott and Matt looked first at him, then at each other for a moment.

"You going to have to explain that to me at some point," Permear said. "Can you call me Nightmare actually?"

"No. On both counts." Scott shook his head. "Not a chance I'm doing that."

"You no fun." He was sure Permear was pouting. "And you mean. Boo!"

"I guess I'll see you some point soon," Matt said, already heading for the door. "Oh, and be a gentleman with my sister, yeah?"

As he left, Pete snickered sarcastically. "I can't see that," he said. "You hit that yet?"

"What... No!" It took a moment for him to get the double meaning. Sam went back to work and it was just the two of them alone, barring Permear, who since nobody could understand him wouldn't be repeating the conversation to anyone. He had his suspicions about that ghost, them being that he might turn out to be a little shit prone to abusing his unique abilities. "No, I haven't yet. Best I got off her was head."

"Hey, high five." Scott slapped his upheld palm, Pete looked in way too good a mood to ruin the images for him.

At least he'd not picked a Willie's for their date. There were better places on the island. As comfortingly familiar as the food at Willie's might be, it wasn't the best atmosphere to be together in.

"You know," Scott said thoughtfully as he speared a chunk of beef with his fork. He'd found himself thinking about why he was glad they hadn't gone to Willie's. The restaurant they'd chosen... Well the one he'd picked... was a Vazaran speciality place. The secret to Vazaran cooking was that if it didn't burn the skin off the top of your mouth, there wasn't enough spice in it. "I often think of opening a restaurant one day."

"Yeah?" Mia looked fantastic, her hair a new style he hadn't seen before, an array of black, blue and gold cornrows that she must literally have spent every waking second on prepping ever since his bout earlier. It was taking all his self-control not to talk to her breasts, barely contained in the scarlet slashes of velvet making up her dress.

When he'd first seen her, words had failed him, and she'd seemed pleased with the effect she'd created. He couldn't explain it but as they'd taken the short journey from her hotel to Makabubu's, it was like he'd felt every set of eyes they'd passed fall on her. Not just the guys but women as well. Even the owner had glanced for a moment, a jolly overweight woman with dark skin, long darker hair and clothes so brightly coloured they hurt his eyes.

It was an unusual feeling, simultaneous pride and jealousy. For all he'd experienced with her, he'd never had that feeling with Jesseka. Then again, he found it hard to compare. Jess was fire, angry and passionate until burnt out, Mia was ice, cool and steadfastly determined but with hidden depths beneath the surface.

"Yeah. Thought about calling it Peace and Quiet and charging two hundred credits minimum for a kiddie meal." He gave her a grin. "Seem a solid idea?"

"I don't know... Are we being serious or..."

"No, it was a joke. Forget it. Are you enjoying your meal?"

"I don't think I've heard you crack too many jokes before," she said. She'd picked a fiery lamb wakashoon, chilli spices mixed with muscardo mushrooms and toro peppers and she was genuinely looking like it didn't bother her. She hadn't touched her water. His teeth felt like they were burning and apparently it was only half as spicy as hers. "Stick with the day job, flyboy."

"Ha. Least I can say I'm good at that," he replied before quickly shooting her an apologetic look. "Not that you're not good at yours. You're like the best spirit dancer I've met recently."

Given that the other was a psychopath, he added silently. Bringing that up didn't feel a good idea. "I'm really glad you came here to support your brother... You know what, scratch that. I'm glad your brother was good enough to get here. Because if he wasn't, you might not have come out here and I'd have never met you and..."

"You'd still be stuck in a relationship with Blake?" She said the name without a hint of emotion. In a way, he found that troubling.

"Well that's a bit of a sore subject," he said. "I mean don't get me wrong, I'm glad to be out of it, but..."

"Can I ask you an honest question?"

"Only if I ask you one in return about something else," he said. "And you don't hold it against me for talking about my ex on our second date."

"Well, I did ask. And well, given that we never finished our first one…"

"Yeah… I'm trying not to think about that," he said. "I'd apologise for that but…"

"Wasn't your fault. Okay, so you really didn't like her. You were tired of being with her, yeah?"

"Yeah." It didn't sound like a betrayal. It was in the past now. Ancient history where he was concerned.

"Why did you stick with her? Why not just end it?" She held both hands up defensively as if expecting a retort, putting them down when none came her way. "I'm just curious."

He put his fork down, took a long draw from his water glass as he considered the question. Of all the things he might have been asked on this date, this wasn't one of them. The respite for his mouth was welcome. He looked at her for a moment and then sighed.

"I don't know, okay? I must have had the discussion with Pete more than once. That's how serious it was. We're guys, okay? We only talk about that stuff when it is bad. Otherwise we just crack wise and skirt around it."

"Yeah I have noticed that." The grin on her face was palpable.

"I suppose I did love her. Yeah, she was my first love. We'd been together for a while. Stuff doesn't last. Time has its ways of burning holes in things you thought would last forever." That sounded pretentious even as he said it, he tried to mask it with a shrug. "I saw that written down somewhere. Thought it sounded good. But it applies. I guess I remembered the good times a little more fondly than the bad."

"Yes, but every relationship has good and bad in it. You should take it as it comes. Too much of one thing isn't good for anyone," Mia said. "You need balance."

"I'm not disputing that. I remembered the good times, I thought that they'd come again. We'd somehow work through it. And you know what else? I didn't want to hurt her. I know, I know, she doesn't seem like the hurting type. I think it'd be easier for her to hurt me than the other way, but you never know. If I'd broken up with her and she'd cried, I don't think I could have dealt with my final memory of her being that."

He picked his fork back up and took another bite of his stupid hot cow meat. Next time, he wasn't going to pick a place just solely because it'd make him look masculine eating something mouth burning. "Does that make sense?"

She reached across the table, putting her hand on his. "Yeah, I think it does. And it puts you in a good light. It shows you care, makes me glad I'm here with you. Hope it was true." She winked at him, he almost laughed. "So, what do you want to ask me?"

Scott studied her for a moment, considered what she'd said and then smiled. "Okay. One question to ask you and you answer truthfully. When we first met, I got the impression you were really into me."

"Yeah. I was. Okay, question answered, let's…" She tailed off, still smiling. "Okay, carry on."

"I got the impression you were really into me. Why?"

He saw her exhale thoughtfully. She'd finished her meal, still barely breaking sweat under the intense heat of her food. He let her think while he managed another several mouthfuls of his own until his plate was clear of all bar a few sparse lentils and rice grains.

"Well physically, you're not bad looking." She shot him an impish grin. "That didn't hurt your chances none."

"Oh thanks!" he said sarcastically. "Nice to know."

"Well you did ask. But it's more than that. It's a bit of a weird story. And you need to go back a few months for that. I hadn't even seen Matt for a few months before. Hadn't seen any of the family, I'd been going solo. And I was in Canterage. Belderhampton, I think it was. There's a large traveller population there…"

"Yeah I know. It's a nice city that. They still have that carnival?"

"Yes!" she said pointedly. "If you'll let me tell the story, I'll tell you that that was where I was. I was there at the carnival with a few others, Harvey, Andy, Selena, just enjoying the sights and the experience. It's quite a flurry of activity, so many lives just pulling together at the same time to create a tapestry you need to be a part of, I remember Harvey was thrilled," she said before seeing the look in Scott's eyes. "He wasn't always bad. He used to be okay. I don't know what happened to make him snap. Anyway, it's not about him. We were wandering. And there was a fortune teller there."

"Is the gist of your story about to be that some old fraud told you that you were destined to meet a dark handsome man at the Quin-C?" Scott asked. Mia rolled her eyes and sighed.

"Well obviously not a fraud," she said. "Because I did meet someone dark and handsome at the Quin-C. She said my brother would qualify. She said I'd meet him here and it'd be a good reunion for a broken family. And that my brother'd guide me to someone special who I'd need to work hard to attain. Matt was the one who told me who you were. You were pretty much unobtainable at the time. I did have to work. I had to be patient." She said it with a smile. "And aren't you glad that I did? Whether you believe that Lady Ancuta was a fraud or not, it worked out for the best, wouldn't you say? She didn't foresee the bomb attack later that night, but hey, it worked out for me."

"You know what?" Scott said, smiling at her across the table. "I really, really would say that. I'm glad you listened to her. Because where would we be if you hadn't?" One of the waiters came to take their plates. "Desert?"

"I'm not hungry," she replied.

"Me neither." His grin only grew as he looked at the waiter. "Just the bill then, please."

The eighteenth day of Summerpeak.

Neither of them went to the draw for the last twelve. It was the first time he'd seen Mia's hotel room, chose to curl up in bed with her while it was being broadcast, Ronald Ritellia and Tommy Jerome being seen together for the first time since the tournament had started. Neither of them looked happy to be there. Right now, Scott didn't care as the two of them lay intertwined, her skin soft and slowly gaining a tan. He'd never known she had a tattoo on her thigh, a rose, or some butterfly wings on her lower back, the Burykian letters on her arm being the only ones he'd been aware of.

The night had been good, they'd come back merry from the restaurant and although she'd been coyly resistant at first, he'd been surprised when she'd almost violently relented and jumped him with enthusiasm bordering on manic. The passion was something he'd missed, they'd torn each other's clothes off and explored each other's bodies. He felt like he knew more about her now than ever had when she'd finally crawled off him, panting in frenzied ecstasy. They'd slept where they'd lain, her body warm and welcoming. During the night, he'd awoken to find her still asleep and with a grin on his face, had ducked his head beneath the covers. He'd felt her jolt awake, almost wrap her legs around his face until she was satisfied he was finished and her juices stained his lips and chin. Only then did she let him go, playfully wiping his mouth with the back of her hand, the motion delicately tender.

Now unfortunately, it'd be soon back to business. Moments like this couldn't last forever. He saw the list of the last twelve competitors, saw his name on the list along with Theobald Jameson, Katherine Sommer, Nicholas Roper, Harry Devine, Yvette Martial, David Wilsin, Nwando Eliki, Reginald Tendolini, Lucy Tate, Rei Renderson and Kayleigh Chambers. Some big names there, and he'd found himself in their company.

He'd found himself in the arms of a loving woman and just a few matches from winning the biggest tournament in the five kingdoms. Things felt pretty good right now.

Chapter Twenty-Two. Press Release.

"You know, I'm in complete disagreement with that statement. Traditions became tradition for a reason, they seemed like a good idea at the time, enough to keep repeating them. In this day, if they didn't work, we'd be rid of them. Yes, we still do the photo ceremony, it's a vital part of the tournament. As much as the bouts and the stadia and everything else that makes this what it is. We've been asked whether it's worth carrying on with it before. And I can say unequivocally, yes, it is. That's the way it has been and that is the way it will continue to be. President Ritellia believes that and I do too."

Raul de Blanco, ICCC Master of Ceremonies, on whether the photo ceremony is relevant anymore.

The eighteenth day of Summerpeak.

"And that is the last of the bouts to be drawn here on the Billy Noddle and Trevor Carson show live from Carcaradis Island. So just to recap, the last twelve of the Competitive Centenary Calling Challenge Cup have just been drawn for their bouts. We have some interesting ties to come, wouldn't you say Trevor?"

"Absolutely Billy. Personally, I'm looking forward to seeing Katherine Sommer facing Harry Devine. It's the favourite versus the plucky underdog and I think young Devine might have a chance here. He might be able to do what nobody else has so far and knock the lovely Ms Sommer off her perch."

"Though, David Wilsin versus Nicholas Roper seems like it might be a top bout as well. That's the one I'm looking forward to."

"Yeah I'd say that's the other plum tie. I mean don't get me wrong, everyone here is pretty good. You don't reach this point unless you have something about you, I know it's a cliché but it's true. You can't coast on luck alone. Don't get me wrong, Bill, sometimes it feels like you need a bit of luck, sometimes something goes your way you didn't expect but you also need skill and you need talent. There's no duffers here that's for sure."

"Trevor, who do you expect to go through here to the quarter final because there's some pretty hard to pick bouts here."

"Like I said, I think Devine has a chance against Sommer. Not saying he will beat her. But I think he has a chance. Perhaps better than Peter Jacobs did in the last round. Jacobs tried to take her at her own game and he failed miserably. Devine, I think is cannier than that. If he heeds what's gone before and doesn't play to his opponent's strengths while at the same time, imposing his own strategy on her, it could pay dividends. Roper versus Wilsin, yeah I'd say this is a lot less clear cut."

"Roper has experience and power. What does David Wilsin bring to the tournament? What sets him apart from those who've fallen before now?"

"Wilsin is an excellent tactician, Billy. He sees paths to victory, assesses them and then takes the most efficient. I think he might be the ablest tactician left in the tournament. I think Wade Wallerington could do it well but maybe not quite as well as this guy. Roper against him is much more of a reactionary. He doesn't think as much about what his opponent might do as react to them. He has fantastic reflexes, he has an ability to plan on the fly and it's gotten him far. But I think there's a point where that just might not be enough. This is the one I genuinely do not want to call. It could go either way, I think. They're as good as each other, I can't pick them, everyone makes Roper the favourite slightly, but their records aren't as vastly different as you might think."

"On Roper, let's move to the third bout. Theobald Jameson, conqueror of Roper's fiancé, Sharon Arventino, lest we not forget the fireworks that took place in that bout. He's facing the last Vazaran competitor in Nwando Eliki. Eliki has become a bit of the darling of the kingdom because of his performances, wouldn't you say?"

"You know what, Billy? I think I would; I don't like you putting words in my mouth, but he has surpassed expectations. Every Quin-C we get a dark horse, someone who wouldn't have had a prayer before the start, and they do better than expected. This tournament, I'd say we've had quite a few to be fair. Jameson himself, Devine, Scott Taylor, they're also all first timers and they've done well getting this far. It makes things interesting."

"Trevor, do you think it detracts from the tournament that some bigger names have gone out, the likes of Arventino and Wallerington and even say, Steven Silver, they've gone out but instead we've got Devine, Jameson and Taylor?"

"Well yesterday's champions ultimately become just that. Yesterday. I don't want to say that their achievements have been diminished but just because they're notorious doesn't mean they have a Divines-given right to walk into the latter stages of this competition. You earn what you get here, if they haven't made it, then it's because there was someone better and there's no shame in that, I've always thought. You show up, think it's going to be easy and don't give your best, that's something to be ashamed of. But these new callers have something that maybe the older, experienced callers don't, Billy."

"What's that?"

"A lack of fear. Burning desire to prove themselves. Youthful exuberance. We all remember what it's like to be that age, can't we? You think you know it all and you want to show the world you do. Well fortunately for these young men and women, they can do that. Far from these newcomers getting here, I'd say the likes of Kayleigh Chambers and Reginald Tendolini being here is more surprising, despite their odds. I can't see them winning it. They've already beaten their previous best performances at this tournament, they'll probably never get to this point again. Younger callers are getting better and better."

"We've gone a little off subject here, back to Jameson versus Eliki. Who do you think will win this one, Trevor?"

"Eliki carries the hopes of Vazara on his shoulders. He wants so badly to win for them, but I think that's weight nobody should have to bear. Being the last pure Vazaran in the competition, for want of a better term, he's the favourite of the crowds on the mainland. Very top Vazaran callers are becoming rarer and rarer, nobody knows why, it seems that the best ones are usually half Vazaran, half some other kingdom and they don't like that."

"Yes, that is curious, well, look at Scott Taylor. Only half-Vazaran by birth, never set foot in the kingdom before."

"Exactly! Back to the question, for the third attempt, Eliki has done well to get to this part. It's not his first tournament, it's his first time at this point though and let's not detract from his achievements for he has done well. But I think that he will run out of steam here. Jameson is only going to get better. He's changed his style as the tournament has progressed, he started off all power and intensity and he stormed out of the group stage that way. He's done well to make it this far, I think he will make it through this round and into the quarter final, I'm not sure he'll be able to go much further though. Depends who he gets in the next round, should he make it. A good draw, he could hit the semi-finals."

"And that would be an achievement for a young caller."

"Oh, absolutely. Plus, he's been training with Anne Sullivan and that'll only help him. It's a radical new idea, so many callers insist on doing it on their own without asking for help. The idea of asking for help from a more experienced caller is not something done often but I think you can see signs of temperance in his fights now. He couldn't keep going like he did in the group stage at that intensity, somebody would have figured him out eventually and he'd have burnt out. Now, he's a much more rounded fighter. I'll say it again, there are going to be Vazarans throwing things at their radios, but I can't see Eliki winning. But wouldn't that be exactly the sort of twist we've seen in this tournament. Jameson beats one of the favourites, someone you wouldn't expect him to beat and then does exactly the opposite. It's a funny old game sometimes."

"Trevor, rest your vocal cords a moment, we'll have a quick break and then we'll talk about the last three bouts. Kayleigh Chambers versus Lucy Tait, Rei Renderson versus Reginald Tendolini and Yvette Martial versus Scott Taylor."

"Those were our sponsors and we're back, I'm Billy Noddle, he's Trevor Carson and we're dissecting the draw for the next round of the Quin-C. Talk to me about Chambers versus Tait. What can we expect from this bout, do you think?"

"Well it's two fighters from Premesoir facing each other, so there's local rivalry, as much as you can call an entire kingdom local. Tait, I like, I'm going to be honest, there's something about her. She has good decision-making skills under fire and you can't have enough of that here. Chambers, I'd say probably has more raw power, but I think this one might be slightly harder to call than the others. I mean, none of them are going to be easy to call, I'd say five out of the six bouts could go either way."

"Who's the sixth, Trevor?"

"I wouldn't like to say. This sport has a horrible way of rebounding on you when you least expect it. I think Tait to win this one between her and Chambers. Narrowly. Won't be pretty. But she SHOULD do it."

"Okay, how about Rei Renderson and Reginald Tendolini? Who's going to be the winner of this one? You've already spoken about Tendolini, saying you're surprised he's made it this far in the tournament."

"Well Billy, that's no indictment against the man, he has made it this far, but I think there's better callers gone out because of the draw. Then again, shocks are the fruit of competition and He's made it this far so therefore he has a chance. I'd say there are better callers still competing, so it's a small chance but even a slight chance is better than none. He needs four good bouts and he's into the final. Four good performances and he's done it. And I think he has a chance against Rei Renderson. Like Eliki with Vazara, she's holding the hopes of Burykia on her shoulders, but I think she might go out here. That pressure can crack even a tough caller. I wouldn't describe Renderson as a top competitor even on her best day, she's been fortunate to get this far. I'm willing to be proved wrong on this, but I honestly can't see either of these two troubling some of the other competitors in the tournament. This could go either way, I think Tendolini. Just. Whoever gets through would want the winner of this bout in the quarter final, I know that much."

"Okay so one last bout to preview, talk to me of Martial versus Taylor, Trevor."

"Billy, Billy, Billy. Every tournament has someone who comes out of nowhere and takes it by storm. Someone who wins the hearts and minds of the public. Scott Taylor was selected at random, via wild card. Before this tournament, he hadn't competed in a bout for nearly two months, he'd taken some time out. He's never won a major tournament and so far, he's competed admirably at the biggest of them all. His victory over Steven Silver, particularly that final round was perhaps the most comprehensively in-control performance I've ever seen on the battlefield. In that bout, he didn't just react, he pro-acted. You watch it in slow motion, he's acting before the attack even comes, showing great anticipation skills. Those are a double-edged sword; I do have to say. You can't keep that up. Its good when it comes off, disastrous when it fails. Because you can't predict every attack every time and sooner or later it'll cost you dearly. He didn't do it versus Weronika Saarth in the last round, he didn't need to. There might have been a few sticky moments, but he looked in control for the whole bout, barring that long moment when he did nothing, confusing everyone."

"Can Martial beat him?"

"She can. But I think she'll have to perform way past what we've seen from her so far. I think she has a tough tie here; I mean there are no easy bouts at this level, but she's experienced enough to know the rawness from a caller like Taylor can be as much help as hindrance. That lack of fear can carry you through. Don't get me wrong, I like Yvette Martial as a caller a lot, she has a lot of redeeming qualities, decent tactically, no slouch in the strength department and good judgement skills. She'll need all of them. Before the tournament, if you'd said this would be a bout in the last twelve, then you'd have made her the favourite. Here and now, it's too close to call. If they both fight at their best, which is what we'd all hope to see, I can't split them."

"What are Scott Taylor's strengths?"

"Well, I've studied him in a couple of bouts this tournament and the best I can say about him is he's stubborn. He doesn't seem to know when to give up. You wouldn't look at his spirits, except maybe his dragon and his leaf lizard and say that there's anything extraordinary there. I think that's part of his strategy. He tries to get opponents to underestimate him and the further he goes in this tournament, the less likely it is to work."

"What about that ghost?"

"I think the thing we need to point about that, Billy, is he broke no rules. It might be interfering with the spirit of the sport, but I like what he did. Using something he hadn't even bent entirely to his will, it could have gone so wrong for him, but it came off. He backed himself and he kicked Saarth out of the tournament. Even if he does go out, I think he has a bright future in the sport. To be fair, a lot of the first timers to this tournament can say the same. In five years, what chance Taylor, Jameson and Devine will be in this situation again? All three of them are probably going to get better and better for this experience."

"Who do you fancy for the tournament, Trevor?"

"What, the whole thing?"

"Yeah."

"Erm... Wow. Very tough to call. Very. I don't know. It's the hardest three words to say in punditry but there's so many variables, it could go so many ways, I can't say for sure. I have a good feeling about Katherine Sommer if she gets past Devine. I think she could lift the trophy. Lots of people say Roper, but he looks as if he has a lot on his mind lately, affecting his performances, I wouldn't make him favourite against David Wilsin."

"And today we have that oldest of time honoured traditions. The Photo Ceremony."

"Yeah, it's an event for the bigwigs, isn't it? I'm sure there's other things the callers would rather be doing today, I know I was back in the day but sometimes you have to suck it up and take the rough with the smooth."

This was something, Nick had to admit to himself, which was turning into farce now. There wasn't any need for it, it felt like it became more outdated and unnecessary every time they did it. He'd been alive for five Quin-C tournaments, four of which he was old enough to remember and it had felt like it was something special when he was younger. Now, being embroiled in the middle of it, he could see the magic was greatly exaggerated.

Every time, they did it. They got the last twelve competitors left in the tournament and put them together in a room with the head of the ICCC and the head of state, got them to have a big commemorative picture together. Being this close to Ronald Ritellia was starting to grate, the porcine president holding court in one corner of the big room with his entourage. Interestingly, the Falcon was nowhere to be seen, Tommy Jerome conspicuous by his absence. He found himself close to David Wilsin, both taking in the room. First time he'd seen him for a while and he looked different, unsettled about some unknown problem. He'd seen that look before, on his own face, nothing conscious about it but it managed to sneak in and ingratiate itself to your expression without realising. The product of a troubled soul.

"Want to talk about it?" he asked. "You seem troubled."

"It's classified," Wilsin said automatically. "It's that sort of troubling."

Nick nodded. "An internal issue?" He was still on leave, but he knew enough of what was going on to be interested. Okocha had sent him a mission report of the whole hospital-under-siege operation on the sly, and he'd read through. It made for troubling reading, might explain his friend's mood. Especially since Wilsin had been involved in putting it down.

"A confusing one. Look, maybe I'll talk later. I don't know how much you know. It's a whole mess."

He shut up as Lucy Tait wandered over, a slender blond caller in her mid-twenties clad in a red dress. Instead he turned his attention to her and smiled.

"Ms Tait. Or might I call you Lucy."

She shrugged. "Most people do, Mister Wilsin. Mister Roper."

"You ready for your bout?" Nick asked. He didn't feel much like any sort of small talk beyond polite necessity.

Lucy nodded. "I think I can beat her. I'm going all the way."

"Well good luck with that," Wilsin said. "Long as you don't come against me, I won't have to disillusion you of that notion." He grinned at her. "But even if I do, it's nothing personal. Only business."

"That's funny. You two are facing each other and yet you're still being pally. How come? Shouldn't you be like trying to secretly stab the other in the back."

"I wouldn't stab him in the back," Nick said absentmindedly. "He'd get it across the throat." He winked first at Tait, then to Wilsin he made a throat-slitting gesture. Tait looked a little taken aback, he hid the smirk. "Joking, of course."

"It's all fun until someone loses an eye," Wilsin said. "Or their skin. Look, it's serious but we're not going to worry about it until the day. Then it's every man for himself. Until then, I'm just going to keep an eye on my food and drink in case he slips something in it."

"And I'm just going to hang around until he gives me more ideas like that," Nick said, glancing around the room at the other competitors. Kitti Sommer was chatting to Nwando Eliki and Yvette Martial, Scott Taylor and Harry Devine exchanging words with Kayleigh Chambers, Rei Renderson and Reginald Tendolini. Only Theobald Jameson stood alone, back to the wall at the rear of the room, a little moody. "It's quite remarkable really, isn't it? First there were two hundred and now there's twelve. It's brutal when you think about it."

"Feeling philosophical?"

"No, I'd say lucky," he replied. "Very lucky. We all are to be here. A little more luck and some will go further."

"Do you believe in luck?" Lucy Tait asked. She sounded surprised. "Seems like you wouldn't. I didn't think you'd hold so much on it."

"You remember Cryan Brough?" Nick asked her. "He was a spirit caller about twenty years ago, a good one. He once came out with this famous quote about luck."

"He'd rather be extraordinarily lucky than exceptionally skilled," Wilsin said. "And to be fair to him, he did have a pretty good turn of fortune sometimes when he needed it. But what nobody remembers about him is that he was pretty good to start with. And a lot of the time, he made his own luck."

"That's what I believe in," Nick said. "Sometimes stuff falls for you. But you got to be able to make sure it doesn't fall on you. Luck is a pretty cruel mistress; it can favour your opponent just as much as you. I wouldn't go into a bout with it as your sole strategy. That's just moronic. But sometimes it works as a tipping point."

Across the room, Ritellia must have said something supposedly funny for most of his entourage broke out into laughter. Nick and Wilsin looked at each other and rolled their eyes.

"Wish I could make people laugh like that," Wilsin said dryly. Some of the sounds really did give the impression of being forced. Nobody in their right mind could buy it as sincere but apparently Ritellia did. The mirth lingered for several seconds until Vazaran Premier Leonard Nwakili strode in, on his own unlike the array of cronies Ritellia had surrounded himself with. His bodyguard, a tall Vazaran woman in an expensively tailored suit the same colour as her skin, followed behind. He moved like a man without a care in the world. It was the first time that Nick had seen him up close and he was even more impressive in the flesh. He was widely regarded as one of the best callers ever produced by Vazara, a fighter and a gentleman and a rampant womaniser in his youth although that had soon calmed down after he'd married, settling for nothing less than one of the most desirable women ever to emerge from the kingdom.

"Morning all," Nwakili said, grinning his opalescent grin to the entire room. It was a smile anyone who'd been on the Vazaran mainland in the last ten years would have seen at least once. The Nwakili grin. That 'everything's going to go fine' look that was so disarming and threatening simultaneously. "Nice to be back here.

Everyone having a good time? I'm sure you are." Ritellia's entourage broke aside to reveal him stood in the middle of them all.

Just for a moment, neither of them reacted and Nick wasn't surprised. Nwakili was the most important man in Vazara but that didn't matter to someone with Ritellia's ego. He doubted the president of the ICCC would go to him, not without some sort of concession to his authority. He was pretty sure it was in the job description for being president, come lead us and think the sun shines out of your own arse, make yourself out to be the most important man in the five kingdoms when most wouldn't trust you to run a corner shop…

"Mr President," Nwakili said. "A pleasure to see you again." It was embarrassing, the height difference between the two of them, Nwakili towered over the much shorter Ritellia. He didn't move. Nick wondered which of them would give first. A question answered when the doors opened again, and two men entered, one carrying a picture box and the other wearing a suit with an elaborate purple stole. In the presence of the picture box, the part of Ritellia that was a slimy little reptile intent on his own survival came into play and he strode to Nwakili and shook his hand vigorously.

"Premier," he said graciously. Of course, his type of grace sounded extraordinarily like condescension. Nick saw Nwakili's grip tighten around Ritellia's hand and he hid a smirk at the wince. "Indeed, it is. Welcome to the ceremony, we're happy to have you."

Nwakili said nothing, just smiled in a fashion resembling a hungry panther. Ritellia backed away, Nick saw the discomfort in his eyes. "And to the president's men and women." Nwakili nodded at the entourage, moving around shaking hands. "Very nice to see you all as well. My thanks on putting on a superb tournament so far. Everyone does their part."

That was the difference between them, Nick supposed as he watched them. Ritellia gave the impression he was playing at being politician. Nwakili was a politician. Finally, the premier moved over to the two new arrivals and embraced them both.

"A thousand welcomes," he said. "Ladies and gentlemen, Grayson Fox, photographer, documenter and historian." Fox was a dapper man with cropped close silvering hair and incongruously, an earring. The fingers clutching the picture box were delicate-looking, but he moved with an assured grace. His clothes were casual but not cheap-looking. Far from it. "And, last but by no means the least important man here, Raul de Blanco, the ICCC master of ceremonies…"

"Reckon that means he's corrupt or incompetent then?" Nick muttered out the corner of his mouth into Wilsin's ear. "Or both." de

Blanco looked very much of the Ronald Ritellia school of politics. Move your mouth to the trough and shove everyone else out the way as quickly as possible. The only hair he had on his head grew in unkempt tufts around his ears, his eyes sunken in a face almost eighty percent jowl. Perhaps one of the strangest looking human beings Nick had ever seen.

"I think both," Wilsin agreed. "Something about him screams soul sucker."

"Soul sucker?"

"You know? He'll draw your soul out through your body and then bill you for the act. Services rendered and all that stuff. Probably eats babies too."

"Dave, nobody eats babies."

"What about that Chicaran Baby Eater?"

"Nope. That's a Premesoiran myth incorporated by immigrants perpetuating bad things will happen to those who try oppressing them." Nick's voice remained deadpan.

It felt like the whole thing was descending into farce as Fox tried to line them up for the photograph. Of course, Ritellia insisted on sitting slap-bang in the middle of the seating arrangement, one hand on the legs of Katherine Sommer and Yvette Martial sat to either side of him. Lucy Tait and Rei Renderson on the left and right of Sommer and Martial respectively. Nwakili stood behind Ritellia, looming high above him. A couple of times, Nick saw the Premier's fingers flexing as if with desire to strangle the man in front of him. Kayleigh Chambers and Harry Devine stood at the ends, beyond Tait and Renderson, with Tendolini and Eliki inside the two of them, Nick and Wilsin next to them, only removed from Ritellia by the presence of Theobald Jameson and Scott Taylor. Fourteen people crammed into a small space, fourteen people who would probably never be so close together again.

"Lovely," Fox said. "Big smiles, guys and gals and… Boom!" The snap of the picture box echoed, followed by the flash and Nick did his best to keep the smile plastered across his face. He couldn't be doing with this. Of course, Fox wasn't done. They all had to hold their smiles for another few minutes as he took several more shots of them. "Just fantastic, people. Okay, you're done. And relax."

Nick felt something in the small of his back, something nudging him. He kept his face straight, reached around and felt a slip of rough paper being jabbed there. He took it, didn't react at all as he slipped it to his front and unfolded it. Fox continued to speak, Ritellia got to his feet and sounded like he was about to break into speech. He didn't hear any of it, just glanced down at the message. It just consisted of five words in elaborate scripture.

Wait Behind. Both of You.

That sent alarm bells ringing, he glanced around. There weren't too many who could have passed it, either Taylor or Tendolini. Or Nwakili. None of them seemed the type to set a trap. Still he'd play their game. On his own rules, of course.

It didn't take long for dispersal at the conclusion, Theobald Jameson straight out the door after a quick word with Premier Nwakili, he blanked Ritellia completely. That made Nick smirk, despite his earlier antipathy with the Jameson kid, he'd proved to be a talented fighter. He wasn't entirely sure a rematch would go in his favour. Either that, or he needed to find out what Anne Sullivan was telling him. The look on Ritellia's face as Jameson strode past him without a word was priceless.

The distraction was enough to tell Wilsin to wait with him. They were needed. Some were more diplomatic with their exits. Sommer and Tait both had hugs for the ICCC president, Kayleigh Chambers kissed him although all three had looked a lot more enthused when offering the same gesture to Leonard Nwakili. Taylor and Tendolini and Devine left together, all thanking both President and Premier. Nwakili and Eliki had a moment together, exchanging words in their native Vazaran tongue, Nwakili all but putting an arm around his shoulder. Nick didn't speak it, he saw Wilsin cocking his ear sideways as if listening.

Finally, it was just him and Wilsin, Ritellia, Nwakili, Nwakili's bodyguard, Fox and de Blanco in the room, the attention turning to them. "Good luck, the pair of you," Ritellia said, offering them both handshakes before he strode out with de Blanco in tow. Fox bowed briefly, inclining his head before shaking Nwakili's hand and exchanging the gesture to both Nick and Wilsin as well.

"Same, guys. If either of you win, look me up. I'll do you a great commemorative picture. Maybe release some sort of merchandise. It's all about cashing in while you can. Just keep it in mind." He looked at Nick even more pointedly. "If you need a wedding photographer too…"

"That is Mr Fox for you," Nwakili said. "His reputation precedes him even further than mine, it would seem. A man dedicated to his craft…"

"You're making me blush, your premiership," Fox said, a red tinge coming to his cheeks almost on cue.

"One who can sniff out a credit in a sandstorm," Nwakili said. "I can think of worse people out there. This man photographed me for my inauguration. He's worked countless times for me."

"You just pay so well," Fox grinned. "Anyway, I'm going to be off. Pleasant days to the three of you."

As he left, Nwakili exhaled sharply and turned to them both. "I think we're alone now, wouldn't you say?"

"Premier," Nick said. "With the greatest of respect, what do you want? I'm not sure what either of us can do for you, your grace." He inclined his head respectfully. Maybe he could have worded that better.

"It's amazing, you know," Nwakili said, looking at him and Wilsin. "I've been out of Unisco nearly two decades and they still operate the same procedure... Hells, they even still teach you to stand the same way. Like a pair of doormen sizing up a situation. Made you both as I walked in. Only the old academy at Torlis taught people that."

"Good memories," Wilsin said dryly, no doubt thinking of the time that he'd spent in Unisco training, which if Nick's memory of the experience was anything to go by, was probably only matched in pleasantness by juggling scorpions. "Really good memories."

"Take solace. It was probably worse back in my day," Nwakili said. "I need you to pass on a message to Director Arnholt for me."

"Best talk to him then," Nick said, jabbing his thumb at Wilsin. "I'm currently on leave."

"You can both pass it on," Nwakili said in his imperious tone, a voice that left no interpretation for argument. "It might be good for you to hear this."

"Premier, why do you need us to pass this on?" Wilsin asked. "Can't you contact him yourself?"

Nwakili shook his head. "This information is sensitive. I do not wish for it to be overheard by unfriendly parties. You know my palace is bugged? I know it is, some have been planted by my allies as well as my enemies. You know perhaps who my greatest enemy in Vazara is at this moment in time?"

"Who's that guy who wants to displace you?" Wilsin asked. Nwakili's expression didn't change. "Come on, there's always someone who wants to knock the top man off his perch."

"Mazoud?" Nick asked. "By any chance."

Nwakili exhaled. "You're right. It is Philippe Mazoud. There's something going on there. My spies have been unable to ascertain exactly what, but I think it can't be anything good. Mazoud was a good man once, but some of his decisions lately have become worrying. He and I were in Unisco once, we mustered out at the same time. I went into politics, I wanted to make my kingdom a better place. Mazoud on the other hand, he made different choices. He used what he knew to muscle his way to the top of the Suns. To be fair to him, he is better than previous leaders, not that that says much. I worked with him. I saw no choice. For all their flaws, the Suns do have their uses. I reached an agreement with him. The Suns were too powerful then to contain. But I spoke. I made it clear I would risk everything to topple him. I think I compared him to cancer. It was an impassioned speech."

He grinned lightly. "The oratory has always come easily to me. I told him that he could continue to do what he needed to. But if he stepped out of line, I'd squash him like a bug. The Suns did not always do their part for keeping the peace. Now they do. Things are better. But lately, Mazoud seems troubled. Conflicted. There was an incident in which he directed an attack on Unisco Wolf Squadron…"

"That was the Suns?!" Wilsin exclaimed. "I heard about that. Didn't know it was them."

"My home and office are not the only ones bugged. I saw Arnholt's conversation with Mazoud myself. It was not pleasant viewing."

"I can imagine," Nick said. "What is it that you want us to pass on to the director?"

Nwakili smiled. Before, it had been light. Now it sucked all emotion from the room, a serious expression and he tightened his lips before speaking. "I wish to turn over all my files and footage I have of Mazoud's contacts and conversations over the last several months. That was when he started to act weird. You understand I can't openly declare war on him. The Suns are a lot more powerful and unfortunately, better organised than anything I can put together quickly. But that doesn't mean I can't act as a concerned citizen. If he is up to something a lot more untoward than usual, then who better than Unisco investigate the matter. If I know Terrence, and I don't believe he has changed, then he'll want an excuse to investigate the man. He wanted to know who paid for the assault on Wolf Squadron. Well this might be his chance to find out."

He held out a memory pack and Wilsin took it. "Thank you, Premier."

"Premier Nwakili," Nick said. "This might answer a lot of questions." And if we do get something on Mazoud, you get a Unisco hit team to take him out. Saves you a lot of trouble and effort. He didn't bother to hide his smile. Every time he found out more about how the political world worked, he found he wished he hadn't. "We'll put it to good use. We'll head straight over and see he gets his hands on it."

"Excellent. Well, I have places to be. Good luck in your bout, the pair of you. Although there can only be one winner, never forget what is important." He shook their hands and then swept out, his bodyguard behind him.

"So that's what become if we make it to retirement then," Wilsin said sarcastically. "Something to look forward to."

"I've always believed the key to conquering is not how to win the battles, rather ensuring you keep hold of everything afterwards. Moving troops around? That's easy. Balancing everything else… That's the tricky part. You've got to have a plan."

General Arkadeus Tomorov, former head of the SUAF (Serran United Armed Forces) and later of the Allied Kingdoms Army.

The twentieth day of Summerpeak.

This, Wim Carson had to admit, would not be the perfect weapon. It would be flawed for he did not have to hand the proper equipment to build one perfect. Yet as with so much in his life of late, he'd made the best he could with what he had, scavenging from maintenance, the armoury, from general supplies and it had not been easy for always there would be those set on thwarting his path.

Still, again he had to admit to himself there was a certain tranquillity to be had in putting together these items to create of something so much more. Always remember, the sum of the parts is not equal to the whole. Boil it down to its composite pieces and it loses the mystique. When he looked at the various items on the workbench in front of him, he saw them as they would become, not as they were. He'd worked day and night now, ever since the attack from that girl. The Cavanda. It wasn't so much the girl herself that worrying him, more everything she represented. Greed. Selfishness. Cruelty. Danger. All those and more, she had the Kjarn to back her up, wielding it with more lethality than any other weapon. She wasn't the finished article. Somebody had to have trained her. The Cavanda were a ruthless organisation, they prized power and ambition above all else. More than that, he wasn't convinced that she'd died.

He'd been lucky when she'd barged into the office. He'd been unarmed, she'd been more interested in fleeing. Had she wanted to kill him, it wouldn't have been impossible. Her master, whoever he may be, wouldn't have made that mistake. The circumstances had been perfect for her, for his strength with the Kjarn was only now returning to him, mind aching as he sought to rebuild atrophied muscles. He would get back to where he was. It was just a matter of time. Even if Madam Coppinger sought to hurry him along, he would not move to her timetable. Some things all the credits in the five kingdoms couldn't speed up.

His thoughts moved to her as he toyed with the steel casing, connecting the crystal to the section housing the emitter muzzle, soldering the circuits. He could have done with a specialist crystal for the job but for now, a charged container crystal would have to do. It wouldn't last long, he knew as he held it in his hand and squeezed, let the energies from his own body transfer into the small gem. When he felt the humming resonance of the Kjarn bubbling from it, he halted. These things could be delicate when overwhelmed. They were supposed to be unbreakable.

He disagreed. Nothing was so strong that under the right circumstances it couldn't be shattered. Delicately he slipped the crystal into the cushioned housing, telekinetically shifting it until he was satisfied it was locked. He'd need to keep a track on this until he could acquire a more permanent solution. If it exploded while in the weapon, he'd lose his hand at the very least.

Somehow, he doubted he'd be as fortunate to get the same quality medical treatment from his hosts under a second affliction. He knew what they were. That Rocastle fellow was like cancer, malignantly looming in the Kjarn like something unspeakable, a spectre of hate and rage while Domis' had no presence beyond a trace, barely comparable with his hulking presence in life. Doctor Hota who'd made him whole again had been a shade wracked with guilt, a man who'd once wanted to help people twisted into doing work he wasn't entirely satisfied with. Wim had looked deeper and seen the remnants of his dreams, found it sad.

And Madam Coppinger was another matter entirely. Considering her psyche had been an interesting experience. No doubt. No regret. No questions. Just iron conviction she was going about the right course of action. She genuinely sought to make the five kingdoms a better place. Her meetings with all those criminals spoke volumes about her ambitions. To take the lowest of society, those who thrived on the suffering of others and turn them to the cause of making everything better was an interesting idea, one he didn't know if it was genius or lunacy. Maybe they were two sides of the same credit where she was concerned. He could remember their first discussion, the first true one they'd shared since he'd awoken in that hospital bed.

They'd given him clothes, smartly casual but no robes. Still it had been better than the rags his old clothes had become on the streets. In a way, he didn't resent that time. It had given him focus. Time to think about what needed to be do. He knew only death was permanent and the Kjarn wills as the Kjarn does. In time, opportunity would arise for him to retain what had been lost. He'd never forgotten, only waited in knowledge his time would come again.

The first thing he'd noticed about Madam Coppinger as he'd followed her through the corridors was she didn't feel evil. Of course, evil was a very subjective term. It was probably the wrong thing to think but seeking what she wanted were not the actions of a benevolent person. Or even someone in their right mind. Nobody would think what she had planned could end anything but badly. She wasn't just playing with fire; she was sinning against nature. A thought that had gestated the more she'd shown to him as they'd moved through what she'd affectionately described as her Eye.

He hadn't gotten the comment at the time, at least not until they'd arrived at the top deck, her office. Domis waiting for them, silently imposing in the background but constantly on the balls of his feet as if expecting attack. Beyond the windows, he could see the sky and the clouds, level with them. She moved to her desk and sat down.

"Mister Carson…" He fought the urge to correct her with the Master title. He wasn't worthy right now. The time would come again, but it was some ways away yet. "We are here because I have chosen to trust you. I have made an investment in you, I expect you to honour our arrangement. If you don't, I'll be most upset. You're an interesting figure to have around and I do not wish that to change."

"Our arrangement will be honoured," Wim said. Privately he was amused. There was no need for the threat. He drummed his fingers on the desk, felt the rush of static burst through them and she withdrew her hands as if stung. A harsh curse slipped her lips and he might have heard a yelp, Domis reacting immediately, grabbing Wim up by his throat in one swift hand. "I do not intend for that to… change!" He managed to gasp through the great paw threatening to crush his larynx. He didn't react. Now, it was only that. A threat. She nodded her head and Domis put him down. "If I wanted to get out of it, I could kill you and he wouldn't be able to stop me in time. Just consider that." He grinned at the great figure still looming above him.

"You wouldn't survive it."

"Madam," he said with a great deal of patience in his voice. "Do not assume to tell me what I would or wouldn't survive. I believe the reality may surprise you. I do not wish to be your enemy. You want to rearrange everything about this world that makes it what it is. I want to retire to a small corner of it, my own choosing, with several individuals with whom I might recreate what once was. You want what I can give you. You believe it will validate what you try to do…"

"No," she interrupted. "Far from it. I don't care about validation. When enough force brings a boot to the neck, you don't care whether the person standing on you is right or not. I want the power."

"Then you're a fool," he said. "Because power is a fire that consumes, a thirst that cannot be quenched. Power for the sake of power is like playing with a bomb. It does not care who is caught up in its explosion."

"I do not wish to debate philosophy with you. I have my reasons."

"And I would cling to those reasons if I were you. I will help you regardless, just don't expect me to be stood anywhere near you when it backfires. Think about why you want the power. What you intend to do with it. And think about all the people who are going to be affected by what you wreak on the five kingdoms."

Wim studied her impassive face, not sure if he was getting through. "Because this is bigger than you or me. It is going to have serious ramifications on everyone. Once you start on this path, it will consume you. You can't truly prepare for it; you can only hope there is still a part of you left after it."

"You sound like you're trying to get out of the deal." Her expression didn't change, and he felt a stab of annoyance.

"Did I not just say I wouldn't? I just feel the need to inform you of what you're getting into. A duty of care, if you would. It'd be reckless of me not to." He sighed. "But if you've got your heart set on it, then consider what I've said. I do know quite a bit about this stuff, you know. You should at least acknowledge that."

"I already know what I'm getting into," she said simply. Wim Carson knew then his words had been wasted and he felt sorrow for the time he'd spent bringing them to voice. "I know what is going to happen, I am prepared. This change is going to happen with or without your help." She pushed a button on her desk, he felt her wince with pain as she did it with her burned fingers. The desktop slid back to reveal a portable projector, Wim folded his arms and stared as it came to life. Domis had retreated to a safe distance, apparently satisfied that the threat to his Mistress was no longer present.

In front of him, the orb materialised, intricately detailed and present with dozens of technical details, only some of which he could understand. More details flashed into existence, a pair of U-Shaped extensions connected to the orb on either side. Some of the technical details, he understood. Dragon grade armour plating. Quantum-based shields. Two thousand solar panels covering the orb. Five hundred-plus on-board air defence hyper lasers. Hangars, laboratories, medical facilities… His mind raced at what this might mean if it was made an actuality. This was, for all intents and purposes, a war machine.

"This is where we currently stand," she said, and his heart did a somersault. "The Cloud Conqueror. The Eye of Claudia. It has many names but for those who would oppose me, it needs only one. Death. Come, walk with me and then doubt that I have prepared for this."

The labs were the first place they'd gone, sterile white rooms with dozens of masked men and women working away across many different positions, all with the intent of focusing on a great number of transparent tanks towards the back of the room, each filled with liquid.

"My Divines!" Wim exclaimed. "Fury of the Kjarn!" He didn't use that expression lightly as he took a closer look at the figures in the tanks. She followed him, he could feel the smug satisfaction radiating from her. Some of the figures were at different stages, some little more than infants. Some were entering puberty, both male and female, while some were just about approaching adulthood, various nodes attached to their bodies through intravenous drips. Each wore strange helmets on their heads that covered everything above their eyes. Each chamber had a readout, he paid no attention to it and instead stared into them, not with his eyes but with the Kjarn. They didn't register any sort of individual reading, rather a great overlapping sense like a bubble. Not one individual but many identical figures, an echo reverberating through the Kjarn.

"Impressed, no?"

"This is an abomination," he said. He couldn't hide his disgust. "Clones?"

"Yes. It's hard to put together an army loyal to you. They're bred for one purpose. To die for me. The criminals have their uses; they will be loyal to a point but I'm not stupid enough to think they'd betray their own should the need arise. Each has their own designate. Each for a sole purpose. Quick to breed, there's a training program, that's what the helmets are. They've already been tested, I sent some down to the Quin-C a few weeks ago to assist with Doctor Blut. Unfortunately, they were killed in action. There have been too many wiped out already between Unisco and that little bitch we had down below. She managed to slay twenty-two of them on her own across two encounters."

"Yes well," Wim said. He didn't want to be reminded of the girl. "You should have informed me about her. If you had, she might still be in custody."

"I was only vaguely aware of it myself," she said. "I blame Rocastle for that. And he lost his fingers as punishment."

"A bit draconian from you," Wim said. He didn't have to turn to know a smile had flit across her face.

"Unfortunately, he engaged the girl and she crippled him in exchange for keeping her captivity. I like that sort of malevolence. Shame she died. We might have been able to make use of her."

He didn't bother to correct her with the assumption she might not be dead nor the lunatic idea of trying to recruit her. If he had the right reading of her, she wouldn't be interested in supposition or theories she couldn't possibly understand. There was a lot of things she didn't understand, a child playing with a loaded blaster.

"I'm trying to win a war, Mister Carson. I can't afford to be ethical," she said. "I suppose you don't like this. But it's necessary. Is it not better that a thousand clones die rather than actual people?"

"And at what point do the clones not become natural people?" Wim asked quietly. "Are they not alive?"

"There's nothing natural about them," she said.

"Well I think we'll agree on that," he said, glancing towards a different chamber over the far side of the lab. "And what's that?"

"Just a different experiment," she said nonchalantly. "An experiment to create a different kind of warrior to the clones. One who isn't expendable, if you like."

He had to go and look, wouldn't have forgiven himself if he hadn't. He'd managed to get himself involved in something here which, had he known the details beforehand, wouldn't have been his choice to. Yet for better or worse, he'd made a deal. Nobody could ever say he didn't honour his promises. He had that. It was about all he had left of his old life, it felt sometimes.

A woman lay in the chamber, motionless, eyes closed and barely breathing. She was naked, and he got the impression she had once been quite lovely before the prominent black scarring marking most of her skin. He'd never seen a more wretched woman in all his life, he sensed naught but pain from her.

"She should heal sooner or later," Madam Coppinger said, following him over to the tube. The unconscious woman wore a device across her upper body, it looked lightweight and metallic, but it was strapped around her neck, under her arms and around her stomach, all leading into a metal plate grafted across her left breast. "And then things will get truly interesting."

"Who was she?"

"A spirit dancer. Now she's irrelevant. She no longer has a name. Just the urge to obey." He didn't like the smile he saw on his new associate's face. It lacked humanity, he fought the urge to turn and walk out. "I don't think they're looking for her any longer. When we're sure, we'll set her loose on our enemies. A day they will rue." She let out a small chuckle as she said it.

Beyond the lab there was what could only be described as some sort of obstacle course, many of the clones running it, training, testing themselves. He could hear and smell blaster fire, realised there had to be a range nearby, even if he couldn't see it. The two of them stood high above it all, surveying her twisted kingdom. He wondered idly if her ego had ensured the design had been deliberate, to make them look like ants far below them. It wouldn't surprise him.

"Of course, the knowing how to do it is useful but I've always found practice makes things that bit better," she said nonchalantly. "Every clone has a purpose; I don't intend to waste them. We have facilities here; we have more throughout the five kingdoms. Soldiers, spies, saboteurs, pilots, scientists all of them come out of these machines, all armed with the knowledge they'll need to complete their mission."

"Scientists… You have clones creating more clones? At what point does that become perverse?" She ignored him, instead continuing to stare at the obstacle course. When Wim Carson had been a boy, he'd been to a zoo and seen the monkeys in their enclosure. All this reminded him of that on a grander scale.

"I'm trying to win a war," she said. "And I'm trying to do it as bloodlessly as possible, Mister Carson. I have waited years for this. It's almost upon us. I just need what you promised to get me."

It was his turn to say nothing. He felt her eyes bore into him and he ignored it, resting his elbows on the railing. Far below, one of the ropes lifted lazily as if caught in a breeze. He didn't consider it a casual waste of his power. Rather an extension of his mission to reclaim what he had lost. It hovered listlessly in the air for moments and then dropped again, his interest lost. He was certain he'd need something bigger than a rope to test his limits. Something for later, perhaps. Wim stood and turned to face her.

"And I will," he said. "When the time is right. Stop trying to force the issue on this for it grows tiresome not just for me but I can't imagine you enjoy hearing the same thing repeatedly."

"My patience does have its limits; I warn you on that."

"Then I suggest you don't strain them unnecessarily." They stared at each other like two feral cats daring the other to make the first move. He wasn't intimidated. She seemed to be under the illusion he was. His expression didn't change, just kept a dead eyed stare at her that would have done a lizard proud. Eventually she gave, and he felt a faint tickle of satisfaction flood him.

"Come," she said, any hint of warmth in her voice lost.

The next room they went was even bigger, the size of an aircraft hangar filled with cages from wall to wall, he ran a quick count and appraised that maybe there were twenty, each huge and heavily reinforced. He could see the energy fields generated around them. Whatever was in there, they didn't want them getting out.

"This is something I'm exceptionally pleased with, if I'm honest," she said. Wim continued to look around, saw signs of damage to one of the walls, like it had been hastily repaired and not aesthetically completed "You know what the people of these kingdoms are like? They admire the strong. They admire their spirit callers and they appreciate their Divines. So, I thought why not combine the two."

A chill danced through his spine and Wim squeezed his eyes shut. He didn't want to think about what might come next. He didn't want to know.

"You look like you've had some trouble," he said, inclining his head towards the damaged wall. Reaching into the Kjarn, he could smell the past of the room and it wasn't pleasant. Fire, lightning, death and destruction, all one big blend. Briefly, he saw the spectral remains of a man thrown against the wall, neck bent sideways, and limbs shattered.

"Well some did escape," she said. "But we recovered them. Mostly. There's still one unaccounted for. No great loss, it was flawed really. And we still have some that remain works in progress. But I think we have the start of something truly special here."

Wim strode past her and onto the hanger floor, only then truly catching the smell of the area. It took him back to memories of that zoo, he moved to some of the cages and peered inside curiously. Some of them were empty. Others weren't. Amongst the creatures inside, he saw a huge six-eyed snake with golden coloured scales, a snow-white bear with a mane of fine blue-grey fur around its neck, a pure black leopard with thick bristly fur. That one bared its teeth at him and through the Kjarn he caught a sense of its malevolence, not just that but of the thousands of tiny microbes in its breath. He held his, involuntarily. They weren't getting through the energy field but at the same time it felt a futile gesture. Even from here, he could tell they were toxic.

He stared at the amber eyes and felt pity for the creature. It hadn't asked to be created. Quickly he moved on to a red scaled komodo dragon with black markings across the crimson, saw claws suitable only for digging. He passed a great yellow bird with a beak the size of a sword, who rose as it saw him and sent sparks of lightning crashing off the force shield that cast its cage into a bubble. He recoiled involuntarily, took a few seconds to regain composure.

"That one made it as far as Canterage," she said, by his side suddenly. "It took a lot to bring it back. The nekeriti. Of course, it wasn't the most troublesome escapee."

"No?"

"You want to meet that one? It's funny really. This one hid in a cave atop a mountain in Serran. We had to use full strength ion blasts to bring him down. Funny coincidence as it happens, it was also where we acquired that girl."

"The one unconscious upstairs?"

She shook her head. "The dead one. The one who jumped."

Again, he didn't bother to impress upon her his theory, just followed her. She stood as if not particularly impressed by what sat inside. Wim on the other hand felt a great surge of pity as he saw the creature, a bipedal feline covered with thin tawny covered fur cut so short it almost looked shorn. In places, black whorls had been cut into the skin, giving it a mutilated look. It looked, he thought, pitiful.

I do not require your pity.

The voice took him by surprise he had to admit as the eyes rose and met his. The feline face with its stubby ears and saucer sized eyes took upon a sinister look. He heard her laugh as she saw his reaction. The words weren't words as such, more like a booming echo of thought forcing its way through his head. It demanded attention, almost impossible to ignore.

"The trewma does that. Psychic ability is not easy to create in a living being. And the results are often unstable. We need to keep them at manageable levels to avoid him... Yes, I think of him as a him... overcoming this entire facility. Drugs, the cage is laced with dampening fields, all come into play. He wasn't anywhere near as eloquent until after he came back."

"Well I do have to say you seem to have done a good job at sinning against nature," Wim said without emotion in his voice. "In a really twisted way, I admire what you've done here you know. You've seen what you had to work with and you thought fuck that. Well done. Not many people would take it this far. On another level, it fills me with sorrow. I fear that there will be no corner of this kingdom with which you can safely flee when all this is over. It's going to end very badly for someone. That advice, I freely."

"You forget," she said, her voice almost a hiss. "It isn't going to be me. When the reckoning comes, I will be the new Divine-Queen of not just the five kingdoms but the entire world. I'm not as insular as most of these people here, I want it all. I will carve it up how I see fit and none who deserve it will escape my wrath. That includes you should you continue to make flippant remarks!"

More and more, he was starting to consider reconsidering his decision to help her. He'd never consider himself in over his head, but it felt like the water had reached his shoulders, one more step and he'd be approaching trouble.

He does not trust you.

"Shut up you," Wim said to the trewma. "This is between me and her."

She does not trust you either.

Believe it or not, he already knew that. There was very little she could hide from him emotionally with the Kjarn at his side. The depths of her deranged secrets he'd rather not know, but here they were being forced down his throat. "That's the sign of a mutually beneficial relationship. Knowing that the other isn't to be trusted." He gave the thing a grin.

You are like the other one, aren't you? The Kyra Sinclair?

That name meant nothing to him. He shrugged. "You tell me."

She isn't dead.

He shrugged again. "If she is or she isn't, not my issue. Nothing could have survived that fall."

Unless she didn't fall far enough to die.

That thought had occurred to him, Divines knew he'd tried to push it to the Mistress enough. This thing seemed to know him way too well, he shook his head at it, trying to dismiss the unease gnawing at him.

I liked her. She was entertaining.

"Wish I could say the same for you," she sneered, taking Wim's arm and moving him along past the cage. "He's not altogether there, that one. Probably a mistake creating him. He's not a weapon. He's a bomb. Best we can do is wheel him into a location and hope he doesn't cause too much collateral damage." She sighed. "I wish we'd been able to recapture the last one though. Nobody knows where that ghost went."

"You created a ghost?"

"That is correct. Good one too. Powerful. Unstable though, had too much personality. We didn't get the chance to break it."

She did nothing but take credit.

The thing's voice took on just enough of a snide tone to make him smirk. He folded his arms and looked at it. Or a him, as his host insisted on referring. He could feel the presence in the cage, like a hurricane kept barely in check by gossamer threads. If it got free, he dreaded what might happen to the kingdoms.

"I'm not like her," he said, almost surprising himself with the words. "She's different."

She is broken inside.

"Honestly, I think everyone here might be," Wim said softly. You, me, especially her… The last part he added silently. If the trewma was as telepathic as she made out, he'd hear it.

Absolutely.

He was sure the thing almost grinned at him as the words formed in his head, an eerily human look that made him want to scratch an insatiable itch on his body, his skin crawling. It had to be the room. Nothing existing in here was right, nothing natural, small wonder he felt sickened by it all.

In the next room, he saw hangars full of warships all ready to be launched, more than he could count but hundreds of people buzzed around below working to get them ready. Some truly were people, some were clones, for he could feel the intermingling of their Kjarn auras. And beyond that, he saw a classroom, Harvey Rocastle stood at the front, arm in a sling and his lips moving.

"What's happening there?" he asked curiously. "And shouldn't Rocastle be resting up? He took a grievous wound."

"He'll be missing his fingers permanently," she said. "They can't grow them back. Not quickly. And I need him. It was his own fault that he lost half his hand and guards died. It will be his fault if he falls behind on his task because of his own ineptitude. These are his Angels. Before the start of the Quin-C I despatched him to the island to have a look for the disenfranchised callers among the bunch, those who might be angry and desperate enough to strike back at a cruel world. Nothing like a bit of sport to get the blood fired up. And once they're in, they're ours."

Beyond the glass, a slender red-haired girl with heart shaped glasses was at the front of the class, not a stitch on her, not in uniform like the rest of the students. Her cheeks were flushed, and it looked like the others were laughing. Possibly at her expense if the embarrassment Wim got through the Kjarn was anything to go by. Poor girl, he tried to avoid studying her naked form, especially as Rocastle's good hand flashed up, her body arching, mouth opening in silent screams as birch bit milky skin leaving a welt under its kiss.

"He wants them to be every bit as sneaky and sadistic as him. Of course, there's some indoctrination, just a little something to keep them leaning towards our point of view, can't have them suddenly growing a conscience and giving the game away. In a way, it's doing them a favour you say. That would be unfortunate if they had a change of heart and a horrible accident befell them. Because this is such a dangerous place."

"Why them?"

"Well with spirits like those in there," she said, inclining her head back towards the way they'd come. "They're going to need a strong practiced hand to guide them. A spirit that can't be controlled is no good to anyone."

And who keeps you in check? He had a strange feeling he knew the answer. Nobody. She'd burn across the five kingdoms like wildfire given the chance, unchecked and implacable, hungry for death and destruction.

"I see."

"You're not impressed, I see." She sounded a little disappointed. That surprised him, like she'd been eager for his approval.

"It's not that I'm not impressed. I'm more worried. It seems you've thought about everything here, you've stockpiled resources beyond most. How the hells did you even manage to put all this together without someone working it out?"

"Oh that?" She waved a hand dismissively. "That was easier than you'd think. Classic misdirection, you see. What did my company do all those years ago? All the materials were dug out of the Vazaran sands, we sucked half the country dry of metal and mineral. Of course, transporting it was going to be a problem." She narrowed an eyebrow at him, his reaction apparently still not what she'd been expecting. "Unless…" He still didn't bite and she tsked her tongue against her teeth. "Unless they're already expecting you to be building something in Vazara. Something requiring a lot of material and transportation and manpower. You know, like a hotel resort to provide a tournament for example."

Her laughter brought a scrape to his nerves, he involuntarily winced. For laughter, there was nothing worse than it being devoid of joy. It was cruel, plain and simple, a relishing of her own genius. Worse, he'd examined it from all angles and realised the truth. She had plenty to be pleased about.

That had been then, and this was now. Wim Carson had thought more about it in the days since and he'd found himself not only convinced that she could pull it off but that she would. The woman had a sense of sheer bloody minded will which meant she wasn't going to let go of something until it was pried from her cold dead hand. Soon. He'd have to help her soon. Then he could return to his life, the one torn from him before his time and things could go back to normal. They could hide away in the Fangs and nobody would be any the wiser to his presence. They… He would need to rebuild. He needed to find Vedo. Not actual Vedo, they were mostly dead, but those with the potential he could shape. Mould in his own image, take the flaws of what had gone before and make them better. Learn from mistakes. There were possibly some of the old ones left, they'd be welcomed in if they submit to him. And by a happy coincidence, he knew where to find one. He'd seen her at that tournament not too long since. That was to be his next task. A trip back to the mainland.

He looked at the cylinder in his hand and sighed. The moment of truth, it would appear. If it failed to work, perhaps it was an omen the path he was walking was the wrong one. He still hadn't ruled out failing to help her. If he chose not to, it was very unlikely she could force him to. He hit the activation button, strangely unafraid it might blow up in his hand and take it away from him like that Sinclair girl had done to Rocastle. It was a little slow, maybe a fraction of a second off but the blade erupted into life, a blue blade with sickly yellow flecks through the centre of it.

He was due to carry on then. He took several experimental swipes with it and felt old confidences returning to him. A neat downward swipe bisected the workbench down the middle with very little resistance. Both halves fell to the ground with a crash and he felt a small satisfaction he hadn't experienced for a long time. All other distractions be damned, Wim Carson felt like things were looking up.

Deep in the Eye of Claudia, something stirred, something broken and exhausted. Lost in the recesses of a Kjarn-induced healing trance, she didn't know just how defenceless she would be if found. It was unlikely, but even a slim chance wouldn't be any good if it went against her. Lacerations and cuts trailed up her arms and hands, her shoulder slowly knitting back into place where she'd hit one of the arches. As she'd fallen through the hole she'd managed to cut into the hull, she'd torn her leg on a jagged edge of metal, the floor beneath her slick with her own blood.

Deep in her trance, Kyra Sinclair didn't care. Couldn't care. As far as those above were concerned, she was dead, and the time would yet come when her resurrection would truly prove them wrong.

The End.

For Now.

To Be Continued in Revolution's Fire.

Coming Soon.

A Note from the Author.

Thank you for the time spent reading this book, taking the time to spend your days in this world I created. I hope that you enjoyed reading it just as much as I did when I wrote it. Just a quick note, if you did, please, please, please leave a review on Amazon for me. Even if it's just two words, it can make a lot of difference for an independent author like me.

Eternal thanks in advance. If you enjoyed this one, why not check out other books I've written available at Amazon.

If you wish to be notified about upcoming works, and even get a free short story from the Spirit Callers Saga, sign up to my mailing list at http://eepurl.com/dDQEDn

Thanks again. Without readers, writers are nothing. You guys are incredible.

OJ.

Special thanks to Ethan DeJonge for beta-ing purposes

Also, by the Author.

The Spirit Callers Saga.

Wild Card. – Out Now
Outlaw Complex. – Coming Soon
Revolution's Fire. – Coming Soon
Innocence Lost. – Coming Soon
Divine Born. – Coming Soon

Tales of the Spirit Callers Saga.

Appropriate Force.
Kjarn Plague. – Coming 2018

The Novisarium.

God of Lions – Coming 2018
Blessed Bullets – Coming soon

About the Author.

Born in 1990 in Wakefield, OJ Lowe always knew that one day he'd want to become a writer. He tried lots of other things, including being a student, being unemployed, being a salesman and working in the fashion industry. None of them really replaced that urge in his heart, so a writer he became and after several false starts, The Great Game was published although it has recently been re-released as three smaller books, Wild Card, Outlaw Complex and Revolution's Fire, now officially the first three books in the Spirit Callers Saga, a planned epic of some sixteen books. He remains to be found typing away at a laptop in Yorkshire, moving closer every day to making childhood dreams a reality.

He can be found on Twitter at @OJLowe_Author.

Printed in Poland
by Amazon Fulfillment
Poland Sp. z o.o., Wrocław